HAPPINESS
& Other Diseases

SUMIKO SAULSON

Iconoclast Productions
SAN FRANCISCO * OAKLAND * VALLEJO

The Somnalia Series by Sumiko Saulson

Happiness and Other Diseases
Somnalia
Insatiable

Other Series by Sumiko Saulson

The Moon Cried Blood Series
Legend of the Luna
Bloodlines
Dreams of the Departed
Death Omen
Shadows and Substance

Other Fiction by Sumiko Saulson

Solitude
Warmth
Disillusionment
Things That Go Bump In My Head

Non-Fiction by Sumiko Saulson

60 Black Women in Horror Fiction

HAPPINESS
& Other Diseases

SUMIKO SAULSON

To Crystal — Enjoy the story

Iconoclast Productions

SAN FRANCISCO * OAKLAND * VALLEJO

Sumiko Saulson

Copyright Notice

Happiness and Other Diseases
Book One: Somnalia Series
By Sumiko Saulson
Copyright 2014 Sumiko Saulson
First Edition 2014

    This book contains material protected under International and Federal Copyright Laws and Treaties. Any unauthorized reprint or use of this material is prohibited. No part of this book may be reproduced or transmitted in any form or by any means, electronic or mechanical, including photocopying, recording, or by any information storage and retrieval system without express written permission from the author.
    This is a work of fiction. Names, characters, places and incidents either are products of the author's imagination or are used fictitiously. Any resemblance to actual events or locales or persons, living, dead, or undead is entirely coincidental.

www.SumikoSaulson.com
www.IconoclastProductions.com

Overview: Flynn Keahi has had a rough year. His nightmares are starting to manifest in reality, but no one believes him. Terrifying creatures are trying to cross out of dreams into the physical realm. Only Flynn can stop them – but doing so might cost him his life. Complicating matters further, one of these creatures cannot help wanting him -- in every forbidden way. Will she be able to save him from his fate? Can she even protect him from herself?

Genres: Dark Fantasy, Dark Romance, and Horror

Acknowledgements:

Editor: Michael Minch

Proofreaders and Beta Readers: Amy Bellino, David Watson, Turner Morgan, Buffie Peterson, and Kateryna Fury.

A special acknowledgement to Amy Bellino, who was so kind as to read this book while I was in the process of writing it. Some people say that you should write a book for only one person. I wrote this book for two people.

I wrote it for myself because it was the story I wanted to tell.

I also wrote it for Amy Bellino, the one individual who was reading it and asking me what was going to come next.

"Sanity and happiness are an impossible combination."

— Mark Twain

VIII

Introduction by Rain Graves

I first met Sumiko Saulson at Blow Salon in Berkeley, during a Sunday Streets reading. Fellow poet, author, and musician Serena Toxicat had introduced us; I had been invited to read at the event. Sumiko was a bright personality with good energy and green hair. I liked her instantly, and we became colleagues and friends.

You can never have too many of those in the Bay Area, navigating the often over-saturated literary events and offerings in a scene of largely mainstream fictionists. Sumiko was very dialed in to the larger community on all positive levels. It was the icing on the cake that she wrote horror, and that her work was well worth reading. She often made horror the delicacy on the menu for these events, rather than the fruitcake no one wants to eat.

If you have never read Sumiko Saulson's work, this book is a good place to start, but by no means should it be the end. Her cleverness is also well-achieved in her series, *The Moon Cried Blood*, as well as *Solitude* and *Warmth*. She has moved beyond being an honored poet and the editor of the compilation, *60 Black Women in Horror*, a not-to-be-missed and much needed reference collection of interviews and biographies for the genre. Her work improves and gains more depth with each book. Which brings me to where we are now:

Sumiko has a succulent style and voice that invites you to play with the intelligence of her layers and meanings. *Happiness and Other Diseases* is along those lines; a dreamscape of layers meant to be unraveled like the sweater on a man that smells good, or the sweet threads of a skirt worn by an experienced, happily mysterious maiden.

You might stop and go as you read her *Happiness and Other Diseases*, taking in some parts like tracing the curve of a woman's breast or investigating the ripples of a six-pack on a well-groomed man. Make no mistake: This is not a romance. It is horror that lends itself, at moments, to dark fantasy in a modern setting with snippets of a demonic, fantastical world. The best plot parts lead you to believe at first that they are ambiguous in nature, but do not disappoint in their twists and revelation.

The mark of any good writer is how well she writes and develops her characters. Sumiko does this well. Here you will meet Flynn, an unwilling but not unlikely victim of a Succubus-like Dream Daemon, haunted from another plane into to reality. It's hard to write a succubus without redundancy; Sumiko does this well. You will meet Gods and Monsters, playing with humans in new and interesting ways, filling in the grey areas between the black and white of Good vs. Evil. You will warm up to an unlikely heroine in Charlotte. You will be left, each chapter, wanting more.

I give you warning, however. This novel might make you hungry. Maybe it's bacon; maybe it's *Solyent Green*. Maybe it's the dream…Maybe it's ice cream, power, or just sex. Whatever it is, be sure to take only what you need, and do not anger your Gods in the doing so. Keep your friends close, and your enemies closer. Just sayin'.

Rain Graves
San Francisco, September 2014

Rain Graves is a two-time Bram Stoker Award Winning Poet (2002, 2013), whom Publisher's Weekly hailed as "Bukowski meets Lovecraft," for her work in BARFODDER: Poetry Written in Dark Bars and Questionable Cafes in 2009. She lives and writes in San Francisco.

Prelude

Her skin was black as pitch, and her obsidian hair unfurled into the sky in waves of endlessly flowing darkness. It swirled and danced like ink spilled into water. Curling tendrils waved, as they were set adrift, threatening to engulf the sky where she reclined. As she settled in for the evening, her ebony skin erupted with the bright, pinpoint lights of twinkling stars. They were her birthmarks, separated by space and time. Her name was Nyx, and she was the Night.

She opened her alabaster white eye, gazed down upon the Earth, and was troubled. Something was amiss. Reluctantly descending from her resting place in the sky, she retired to one of her many palaces. This particular abode was a mountain on the surface of Venus. She chose it because a human had named it in her honor, which pleased her immensely. Once she settled in, she summoned her twin sons, Somnus and Thanatos, who were Sleep and Death.

"Somnus. Thanatos. Sit, we have much to speak of," she bade them, gesturing towards the two seats at her table. Thanatos gave Somnus a sideways glance. Both of the boys knew they were in trouble.

"Thanatos," Nyx began, "I have noticed a disturbing trend lately. More and more of the humans are dying in their sleep, and I can't help but think you or your brother are up to no good."

Act I: The Arrival of Happiness

Nightmares

It was the same dream he'd had every night for the past year, but every time it haunted him, little details changed. Minor changes in setting and action were not the only differences in his bedtime story. Each time he had the dream, things went a little bit further than the last.

The last couple of dreams had taken place in a powder gray office chair behind the plain white Formica-coated IKEA computer desk in his cubicle at work. He was tired of staring at the navy blue cubicle tiles. Four mismatched pushpins secured a print out of the company's phone directory. He was more than a little relieved for the change of scenery.

This time he was sitting on a barstool at Murphy's Tavern. A half dozen co-workers from the call center were seated around the bar, sucking down shots of tequila and pint glasses of domestic beer poured out in abundance from the various ten-dollar pitchers purchased for the party. Richard and Cindy from accounting were on stage, belting out their drunken rendition of *Summer Lovin'* from the musical *Grease*. Richard hammed it up with gratuitous hip gyrations, winking and serenading the secretaries seated in the front row. By contrast, Cindy failed to make eye contact with anyone, keeping her doe-eyed gaze fixed firmly on the karaoke monitor.

Flynn remembered that part of the dream from last October. It was a going-away party for someone from the constantly rotating administrative pool temporary staff. He couldn't remember the girl's name, but he remembered her suits. She was in her late twenties or early thirties, yet she wore these tailored pink and powder blue designer suits that put him in mind of Nancy Reagan, of all things. They seemed very incongruous for a woman of her age and economics. He had always wondered if they were hand-me-downs from a formerly fashionable maiden aunt.

Richard and Cindy finished their song right after he finished his beer. Four drunken, obnoxious dudes from the IT department were half way through their voluminous and off-key rendition of Queen's *Bohemian Rhapsody* when that thing finally showed up.

Just like in every previous nightmare, it materialized suddenly, out of thin air. One moment he was looking at his own dog-tired mug in the mirror on the bar back, the next he was staring into the gaping maw of whatever it was that terrorized his dreams. It rarely took the same form twice. This time, it was shadowy and semi-translucent. It had withered legs and arms resembling the gnarled branches of a lightning-struck tree. They were almost humanoid, yet woefully emaciated. The creature was straddling his lap, facing him, with its talons resting on either side of his shoulders.

Flynn gasped as he felt its claws sliding effortlessly into the flesh of his right shoulder. He felt a hot gush of blood flow out of his wounds and then slowly trickle down the back of his white t-shirt. He would have screamed, but he knew from experience no one in the bar would hear him. His breath came in ragged, gasping pants as he struggled to maintain his composure. That creature knew it was hurting him, but Flynn didn't want it to see him sweat.

"So," he hissed under his breath, "The last time you showed up as a foxy-looking redhead. You aren't bothering with pretenses this time I see?"

"This isn't my true form, either," the thing cooed back, leaning over and licking the side of his face with its wide, green tongue. In the mirror Flynn could see a thick trail of snail-like goo on his face where its saliva touched him. Its breath was mossy and tepid, but not entirely unpleasant. It smelled like the inside of a cave on a camping trip he remembered from childhood. Without wanting to, he found himself relaxing into the short leather back of the barstool. He felt warm and a little dizzy, but he knew it wasn't the alcohol.

"I thought I would see if you like it rough this time," the creature whispered in his ear.

Flynn turned away and lifted a hand in front of his face.

"Don't, please don't," he begged knowing before the words left his lips that all of his pleas would be in vain. A slender tendril of quivering flesh extended from a spot in its forehead, above and between where its eyes would have been. Instead of eyes it had a row of five vacant dimples, each a shallow, empty socket lined with a membranous gel that breathed in and out like the gills on a fish.

The appendage was as thick around as a large earthworm and lengthened rapidly, engorged until the throbbing tip touched his skin. He could feel it writhing its way up his cheek. Although he knew what to expect by now, his body convulsed involuntarily. He felt the tendril wind its way up to his nose. It thrust itself into his nostril, sliding in deeper until it penetrated his brain.

In this incarnation, the creature's mouth was as wide as his own head. Behind the series of fleshy polyps that jiggled, dangling from its moist lips, its hideous jaws were lined with sharp, jagged teeth. Its voice was wet and sucking, the sound a puddle of hot shit in a clogged up bar toilet would probably make if it started to speak. Flynn hated its voice.

"I can do whatever I want to you," it cruelly purred. "I can even make you like it."

A mucilaginous blue fluid pulsated through the fleshy appendage, and Flynn watched helplessly as the drug traveled through the tendril and entered his bloodstream, headed directly for his brain. Wave after wave of chemical stimulation hit his nervous system and as he succumbed to the intoxicant, his fear gradually gave way to intense, almost painful arousal.

The air molecules surrounding the creature's form trembled slightly, in a way only Flynn could see. He watched as its form slowly shifted, reverting to the familiar freckle-faced buxom bar girl with the rust-colored hair. Over her shoulder, he could see his face in the bar-back mirror. He could feel something foreign invading his flesh, throbbing under his skin in perfect counterpoint to his heartbeat. As each fresh wave of euphoria hit him, he observed a strange, orange glow pulsating in the veins that were pounding out a rhythm in his temples.

When the girl bent over and bit his neck, he whimpered.

"I don't know what you're doing to me," he mumbled, "but I don't really want you to stop."

It laughed at him.

"But you should want me to stop," the woman told him. "I am a parasite and I'm feeding off you. I will gradually drain the life out of you, and leave you a dead and empty husk. And you would like that, wouldn't you?"

"Yes," Flynn muttered compliantly. "Yes, you should eat all of me until there is nothing left." His reflection stared back at him, slack jawed and vacant. The whites of his eyes were clouded by bubbling peach-colored swirls of viscous alien matter, like tiny ocular lava lamps. There was even a slightly pink tinge to the tear that was sliding down his cheek.

Cindy and Richard were standing on either side of him now, watching the scene unfold in eager anticipation. Four drunkards from the information technologies department joined the telemarketing team. The whole group was riveted by the theatrics. The secretarial pool held him in its hungry gaze as the temp with the pastel Bill Blass suit pulled out a pair of orange-handled office scissors and slit open the front of his t-shirt.

"I love playing with my food!" the monster shrilly announced to its admiring sycophants.

The crowd oohed and aahed appreciatively as she used her razor sharp fingernails to shred the rest of his t-shirt before removing it from his body. It was white cotton, the perfect medium for absorbing the blood that had been expressed from the many little abrasions she'd clumsily left on his torso while removing the garment.

When the creature bent down to bite his nipple, Flynn threw his arms around its neck and arched his back to make it easier for the thing to completely devour him. His labored breathing gave way to moaning and trembling with anticipation as he resolved to give himself over to this monster completely.

Then he woke up.

"Fuck you, bitch!" he screamed at no one in the room. "I want to live!"

"Fuck you, too!" his neighbor screamed back from the apartment above, punctuating the exclamation with a stomp on the floor. A stream of further expletives followed. They were laced with creative suggestions for what kinds of objects Flynn, and the whore the old man upstairs imagined he must have been banging last night, could unceremoniously shove up their collective ass.

Flynn jumped up from the soiled beige frameless futon mattress he called a bed, and ran into the cramped little closet-like bathroom of his tiny apartment. He barely reached the toilet in time to grasp the sides of it and lean his head forward in order to evacuate his meager stomach contents into the bowl.

Waves of unrelenting nausea caused him to vomit repeatedly until his stomach was empty. After all of the food was gone, he sat on the floor for another half an hour feeling his throat burn as he dry heaved and spat up stomach acid.

He was sick like this a lot lately.

Flynn stood up and turned to face the sink. There was no walking necessary… it was about two feet away from the toilet. The room was so small he could extend his arm and touch the plastic curtain of the claustrophobic, coffin-sized shower.

He looked into the mirror on the medicine cabinet. It was about three feet high and two feet wide, bordered with a thin strip of discolored chrome, covered in a film of soap scum, and occasionally dotted with random drops of toothpaste and dried dirty bathwater.

He didn't look so hot.

Under his eyes were bags deep enough for a weekend shopping spree. His solemn brown eyes were bloodshot and red-rimmed. His once golden skin was now sallow and jaundiced. His cheeks were the gaunt, his eyes were sunken.

He decided he looked like a junkie.

"This shit is killing me," he told his reflection.

He could still feel pain in his shoulder blade where the witch had impaled his flesh with her claws in the dream. His body hurt in other places, but that was the worst. He lifted his hand and touched the side of his neck. When he pulled away his fingers, they were covered in blood.

He stood back from the mirror and observed a dozen tiny lines on his chest, miniscule scabs where she barely grazed the skin, and the blood had already dried. His nipple was still bleeding a little bit, and it was sore when he touched it.

Flynn sharply sucked in his breath.

He was very shaken up. He was afraid he was going to burst into tears.

Pulling himself together, he stumbled into the nearby shower and stripped off his boxer briefs. He tossed them out past the slightly moldy plastic shower curtain with the gaudy tropical fish and seahorses painted on it. They landed inside out, and he shook his head a little when he noticed the stain from last night's involuntary emission.

He turned on the shower and enjoyed the hot water coursing down over his aching flesh. He was exhausted, but he knew he had a doctor's appointment that morning. He didn't want to walk into Dr. Lester's office smelling like jizz, sweat and shame.

He tried not to think about his night terrors, but the harder he tried to forget about them, the more persistently they prodded at his waking mind. Soon, he found himself with a raging boner. It was hard to deny that he did like it rough.

Still… that was not something he wanted that nightmare succubus to know and he most certainly had no desire to be eaten alive.

Of course, there was a very good chance this succubus creature did not exist.

Flynn had begun to doubt his sanity sometime last summer, about a month after the dreams began. His therapist had assured him this monster did not, could not, actually exist. He must be hurting himself somehow in his sleep. The exhaustion must be a sign of his depression. Lots of depressed people felt tired. He would feel better soon, when the medications started working.

Dr. Lester had an explanation for everything.

She even told him he should not be ashamed of his fantasies, no matter how perverse he might deem them to be. They were only fantasies, and everyone has fantasies. In fact, his fantasies weren't even all that uncommon.

There was no need to be embarrassed by them.

With that in mind, he decided it would be very therapeutic to beat off in the shower.

COMMENTARY

Nyx was impatiently waiting for an answer.

"Plot and scheme?" her son Thanatos, the god of death protested. "We would never."

"Settle down, brother," Somnus interrupted. "Mother, it is not his fault. I know what you speak of. It is the work of my son, Brash, and his children. They've grown unusually bloodthirsty as of late. I apologize for their behavior."

"Aaahhh," his mother said. "I am aware of what you speak of and I appreciate your honesty in this matter. It seems Brash and several of his children have been dissatisfied with their rightful place in the underworld in the Demos Oneiroi and have instead decided to enter the mortal realm and inflict themselves upon the living like some plague or disease."

"I will speak with them," Somnus reassured her.

"It has gone beyond that," Nyx warned. "They threaten to disrupt the natural order of things and to cause war between myself and those of greater power than even myself. I have decided they must be tested, and punished if necessary."

"How will you test them?" Somnus asked.

Nyx lifted a burdensome scroll to the table and partially unfurled it, revealing a spot in the middle. It was a map of the Demos Oneiroi, the Greco-Roman mythological realm of dreams. She pointed to a tiny spot on the map with the very tip of her slim, tapered finger.

"Do you see that young man there?" she asked, tapping the spot twice. "Look closely, and you will see him. He is the one begging your granddaughter Mercy for his life."

"I see him," Somnus responded.

"The fate of the entire line of Brash lies with him." she said. "Let's say that mortal is able to persevere. Let's say he is able to survive for the short span these fragile creatures are intended to live. Perhaps he will become the progenitor of a bloodline, for offspring are the closest any mortal being comes to immortality. If he is able to thrive, then they shall as well. If not…"

"If not?" Thanatos asked a little too eagerly. Being the god of death, he had a pleasant feeling about where this might be going.

"If not, then as they so envy the mortals, let them be mortal. Let their endless lives, with which they have become so bored and tired, come to an end," Nyx ordered. "Let them die, like all the rest."

"He is my son," Somnus protested. "Surely, you will at least allow me to call forth a champion, to protect this mortal upon whose fragile shoulders you place such a heavy burden?"

"Very well," Nyx relented, after a moment of silent consideration. "You may, but you must call forth a champion from your own line. More specifically, this champion should be one of Brash's progeny. To the best of my knowledge they are cruel, brutal and irredeemable, but if you have one with whom you might trust such a charge, name him."

"Her," Somnus corrected. "Happiness. I name her. She will protect him."

Nyx furrowed her brow. "I have not heard this name before. Who is she?"

"She is a demigoddess," Somnus explained. "She is the offspring of the most recent dalliance between Brash and a mortal mistress."

Nyx laughed. "You mean a demisomnali? To be a demigoddess, she would need to be the child of a god, and surely we are not elevating your wayward son Brash to the same status as you or your brother?"

"Very well," Somnus conceded, not wishing to offend his mother. Certain among his thousand sons the Oneiroi were considered gods. Morpheus was the god of dreams, and Phobetor the god of nightmares, for example. Brash would have been the god of erotic nightmares, but he was obscure and had no worshippers. "A demisomnali, as you say. I name her."

"For their sakes, I hope she's a great deal gentler than her sisters," Thanatos remarked. "They've sent many a mortal my way."

THERAPY

Flynn wished all things therapeutic could be as relaxing and comfortable as morning shower masturbation. After a year of listening to his bizarre nightmares, Dr. Madeline Lester continued to seem unimpressed. She didn't believe him when he said the dreams were real. She was an older, professional woman who was not easily shocked by anything he had to say.

What he described as nightmares, she claimed were merely fantasies. She insinuated that he secretly wanted to be some monster's juice box. He wanted the creature to plunge a straw into him and suck him dry. He shifted uneasily in the office chair while he relayed the latest of his strange dreams.

Dr. Lester took notes.

"Okay," she said when he was done, "so, do you think this dream was different from your other dreams?"

"Well, yes," he said, gesturing nervously with his hands. "Usually, it dopes me up first, but this time, it wanted to hurt me."

"Did you want to be hurt?" the doctor asked.

"Well, no, I didn't want that monster to hurt me," he lied. "Look, I don't want to talk about this."

"That's fine," she said. "I respect that. So, let's talk about something else."

"Okay," he said, breathing a sigh of relief.

"Earlier, you told me you hurt yourself this morning…" she began.

"No!" he protested. "I never said I hurt myself! I said the creature in my dreams hurt me. It scratched the shit out of me. I mean, look at my back. It still hurts, and so do these holes in my neck." He neglected to mention several scrapes and bruises on more private parts of his anatomy.

"Can you see how that sounds? We both agree it's not real," she reminded him. "It could not have hurt you. Therefore, we must conclude you have hurt yourself, mustn't we?"

"This is so fucked up!" he shouted. "You're setting me up. If I say yes, you're going to say this is self-harm, if I say no, you're going to say I'm psychotic, or suffering from delusions. It's like no matter what I say, you're going to… you know, you're trying to get me 5150ed"

"Do you think you need to be committed and placed on a three day psychiatric hold for evaluation?" Dr. Lester asked.

"No," he snapped back, "No, no of course not. I'm fine."

"You don't look fine," Dr. Lester responded calmly. "You look like you haven't been sleeping, or eating, and you seem rather agitated."

"I've been eating," he claimed. "It's like I told you, I keep throwing up. Haven't you found anything on the blood tests?"

"You are a little anemic," the doctor explained patiently, "but otherwise, all of your blood work is fine. So, how are you sleeping?"

"Not very well," he admitted. "I'm afraid to sleep."

"So, you're afraid you'll hurt yourself?" she asked.

"No, I'm afraid that thing is going to hurt me," he repeated. "I'm afraid it's going to kill me. It keeps saying it's going to kill me, so of course I'm not sleeping well. I'm terrified."

As soon as the words left his mouth, Flynn realized his error. Dr. Lester didn't believe there was any creature. She would interpret what he just said as meaning that he was afraid he would kill himself. There weren't any mirrors in her office, but he could remember how haggard he looked in the bathroom mirror this morning. He didn't imagine he could look any better right now.

He searched in vain for a hint of his own reflection in the shiny surface of the plastic Zoloft advertisement on her desk. Then he spotted her toy with the metal balls that dangled from chains and clicked against each other, bouncing back and forth when you knocked the first one into the second. He spotted his eye in the nearest steel ball. It looked like a lunar eclipse or that creepy black circle people saw just before they died in the movie *The Ring*. Whatever his eye looked like, it did not look good. It looked like a deep, dark pit of despair.

"Look," he said quickly, "that didn't sound the way I meant it to say. I can see why you might be concerned, though." He was doing his best to sound as sane and reasonable as possible.

"Well," Dr. Lester said carefully, "if you are sure you won't be hurting yourself…"

"I already told you!" he shrieked. "I didn't hurt myself, the monster hurt me!" He had forgotten all about his plan to stay calm and out of the hospital. Suddenly, he remembered. "I mean… look, I won't hurt myself, okay? I'm sorry if I sound agitated. I am just really tired."

"It's clear you are not sleeping well," she said, leaning her swivel chair back against her desk and picking up the pen like a little conductor's wand. Flynn could not take his eyes off the pen.

"I think your medications aren't working properly and they need to be adjusted," she continued. "I think a voluntary stay of just a few days, at the most a week, would be in your best interest. I'm not trying to put you on a 5150 psychiatric hold. I just think you and I can both agree that you have been having some issues with your self-care. You could use better tools to manage your condition. You need to get some rest and we need to get you on the right medication."

"But I don't want to miss work," he insisted. "I could lose my job."

"You know they can't fire you for that," she said reassuringly. "It would be discrimination. You can't fire someone for being out sick."

Flynn sighed in exasperation and shook his head.

"If I thought you were a danger to yourself," Dr. Lester reminded him, "I would be forced to put you on an involuntary hold. We don't want that. Don't you think it's better if we can agree to get you the help you need, before it comes down to that?"

He threw his hands up in the air.

"Fine," he mumbled in resignation.

Hospitalization

Everything went fine at first. It was around lunch when they admitted him to the hospital. He surrendered his shoelaces. He slipped on the hospital gown and pants that he'd reconciled himself to wearing until they'd had time to go through the clothes he'd bought along with him. They had to make sure there was nothing in there that he could potentially hang or cut himself with.

He had no desire to strangle himself with dirty white tennis shoelaces, but he was still obligated to walk around without any. The tongue dangled listlessly from the front of his black high top Converse All Stars. The blue and white patterned hospital gown fastened in the back with a couple of plastic snaps because ties had been adjudged too dangerous for mental patients. The gown was loose on his emaciated frame. The uppermost snap near his neck would not stay shut and the cloth flapped down, leaving the fresh wounds on his shoulder to peek out accusingly for everyone to see.

Flynn felt like a prisoner. The orderlies escorted him to the lunchroom, where the other inmates were already seated, eating from their trays. They walked him over to an empty seat at a round table with four short benches welded into each side. It resembled the fiberglass outdoor seating at a fast food restaurant. He sat directly across from a large, uncommunicative man in his thirties who gazed out the window between forks full of Chicken Parmigiana. On one side of him was a black woman in her early fifties, and on the other one a Latino girl who appeared to be in her late teens. It seemed as though the crazies afflicted people of every age, race, and gender. The woman was chipping away at what was supposed to be Beef Wellington, while the girl picked at a rice pilaf dish that he supposed was the vegetarian option. He guessed there was a fish choice as well.

"Do you have any special dietary needs?" asked a cafeteria lady who had approached with the nub of a pencil and two paper menus. "You can select your meal choices for tomorrow, and for dinner tonight," she explained, placing the menus beside him, "but I am afraid we can only offer you the chicken or vegetarian plates for lunch. You arrived so close to the end of lunch that those are all we have left."

"The chicken would be lovely, mademoiselle," he said with a grin.

"Oh, so we have a comedian at the table," the older woman at the table said with a grumpy affection. "Glad to see you haven't lost your sense of humor yet."

He nodded appreciatively. "Thank you."

"You will," she assured him. "You can only watch Wheel of Fortune in the day room so many days in a row before you go catatonic like Gary here." She gestured towards the big man.

He liked her sense of humor, dry and dark. The young girl at their table seemed more alert than poor Gary, who was either very psychiatric or overmedicated, or possibly, both. She didn't exhibit any interest in talking to either of them, however. She vacillated between staring at the crumbling remains of her pink nail polish and a boy her age with a shaggy bowl cut two tables over.

"My name is Flynn," he said, holding his hand out to his most amusing tablemate.

"My name is Lorena," she said with a nod, ignoring the hand. "I'm not going to touch your hand, young man. I'm married, and I've been here enough times to know how those little institutional romances get started."

Flynn laughed. He was twenty-six years old. She was old enough to be his mother. In fact, as he was the result of a teenage pregnancy, his own mother was almost certainly younger than Lorena. Lorena was a handsome woman, though. He did not doubt that she had her fair share of suitors among the inpatients. In fact, judging by the dirty look Gary was giving her, she probably had one at this very table.

"I'm not hitting on you, Lorena," he reassured her. "I'm no home wrecker. You're a married woman." Gary narrowed his eyes.

"Thank you very much," she replied. "Thirty two years now. But I've been in here a few times lately. It's hard when you get to a certain age, and your parents start having health problems. That's how I ended up in here the first time, three years ago. My dad died. There's nothing wrong with getting some help now, so don't feel ashamed of whatever you're going through. I'm going through menopause, that'll make you crazy right there." She winked.

He laughed a little. "Yea, I remember when my mom went through it."

"I'm not that old," Lorena said huffily. "I mean your mom? My kids are still in high school. You look like you're pushing thirty. And don't you dare call me ma'am."

"No ma'a... erm... no sir, I mean. I won't." Flynn decided to quit while he was ahead. He stuffed his face full of chicken before he could alienate his one and only friend in this place. He'd been in the hospital two or three times before, and he never seemed to make friends very easily here or anywhere for that matter. She made him laugh and that was very good.

Flynn began to feel self-conscious about the bags under his eyes. He'd slept less than five hours in the past three days. Did he really look like he was thirty?

The chicken was expectedly bland, but unexpectedly delicious.

He hadn't realized it until that very moment, but he was starving.

TELEVISION

After lunch, they dispensed the noon medications. He didn't get any because Dr. Lester was weaning him off the ones he was on now so she could transition him on to some new ones. He was informed that he would still get his night meds. While the others were in line for their medicine, a nurse escorted him to his room, showed him which bed he would be sleeping in, and handed him a hospital bag with a few approved items of clothing.

He slipped off the gown, and pulled on his old Final Fantasy XII t-shirt. It smelled like fabric softener and innocence. Putting it on gave him pleasure. It reminded him of happier days, before the nightmares. He wished he were still in college, going to conventions with his friend Danny who moved out of town to take a job with some start-up in Palo Alto five years ago. Those were carefree days, before he started having problems and dropped out of school.

Admitting he had any kind of mental problems before the nightmares began troubled him, and Flynn quickly put it out of his mind. He still wore the hospital pants, baggy and comfortable. He decided to kick off the Converse and put on the hospital slipper socks. He wasn't going outside, why bother wearing shoes?

He didn't want to be alone with his thoughts anymore. Flynn padded down the hall to the television room, and sat down in one of the big, green easy chairs.

It wasn't as comfortable as the overstuffed brown plaid chair his dad used to have in the living room. Dad's chair was plush, and soft, like a sofa cushion. This chair was made of cold plastic that would stick to the backs of your legs if you had shorts on, the kind of material that was easy to sponge down if one of the patients had an accident.

Flynn tried not to think about how many people might have defecated or urinated on themselves in this very chair over the years.

He leaned back to kick his feet up in the air, and was a little disappointed by how low the footrest remained at its highest point. He wasn't worried about that for very long. After a little while, he became drowsy. He was in a room full of people. Some were drawing or coloring with the art supplies, and a few were playing the board games Scrabble and Monopoly. Most of the people were watching an old rerun of Two and a Half Men, from back when Charlie Sheen was on it. He felt very safe here.

He was almost asleep when a woman's voice disrupted the flow of his growing reverie.

"You like games?" she chirped. "I like playing games." She was leaning right over his head.

Flynn bolted upright in his chair. The footrest snapped down, and this goth chick stepped back a little to avoid being hit by his face when the back of the chair straightened up.

He looked at her. "Whoa! Damn, girl. You scared me."

"I'm sorry about that. I'm Charlotte," she said, extending her hand.

Flynn reached out to shake it, completely forgetting Lorena's warning about hospital romances. Charlotte took his hand and kissed it, the way knights and debonair European cats kissed women's hands in movies.

"I think guys are supposed to do that," he blurted out, stunned. He quickly pulled his hand back and cradled it in his other one as though she'd mortally wounded it.

"Who cares about supposed to?" she asked.

Not understanding the rhetorical nature of the question, Flynn opened his mouth to answer it, but Charlotte cut him off before he could get a word in edgewise.

"So Final Fantasy," she said. "I liked that game. I've played X through XIII-2"

"XII was the best one," Flynn said, relieved for a change of topic.

"I like other games too," she said suggestively.

He swallowed nervously, and began looking around the room for some kind of reprieve. Shades of the dream began to creep in to the periphery of his conscious mind. For a moment he thought that people were looking at him, like the coworkers in the dream.

But no one was looking. Everyone was staring at the TV, or whatever else they were busy with, or they were just staring out at nothing. Some people were talking to each other. Gary was still staring at Lorena, and the girl from his table was still staring at that boy. And Charlotte... she was staring at him, waiting for him to say something.

She was a pretty girl, with a wicked smile and little dots in her ears and nose and under her lip where piercings would have been if she weren't standing in the middle of a psych ward. He imagined that they forced her to take them out. He suddenly registered the fact that none of the other women were wearing earrings, or necklaces. He wondered if any of her piercings would close while she was in here. He noticed that her hair was dyed purple. She was in her early twenties and old enough to go in a nightclub, twenty-two or three was his guess.

"Like what kinds of games?" he asked. "Do you like first person shooters, or do you only like RPGs?"

"I do like first person shooters," she said. "I also like role playing games, all kinds of role playing games. The ones I like the most are not played on a game system or a computer."

"You mean like board games?" he asked, feigning innocence. He knew what she was talking about. He began to feel a little warm.

She stood behind his chair, leaned over him again and whispered. "I saw those marks on your back when you first came in here, and I just wanted to let you know you don't have to hurt yourself. I could do it for you. Would you like that?"

He felt every hair on his arm begin to rise as he turned his head to look up at her.

"Stop that, girl," Lorena interrupted. "You're about to embarrass that boy publicly." She looked right at Charlotte and winked at her. Charlotte smirked. The two seemed to know one another.

Flynn hastily sat up and arranged his hands on his lap in such a way as to conceal the source of this public embarrassment. He wasn't able to do so before Charlotte took notice, though.

Satisfied, she turned around and walked away.

"See?" Lorena said. "Now you've got a hospital girlfriend, don't say I didn't warn you. Have fun with that."

"Do you know her?" he asked.

Lorena laughed. "I know her mother a whole lot better than I know that child. But that girl is a grown woman, so whatever is trying to happen between you two is none of my business."

"I need to get some rest," he said quickly, trying to change the subject. He really was tired, though. He hadn't been sleeping much lately, but suddenly he was totally exhausted.

"Best not to do that in the recreation room," Lorena told him. "It's filled with crazy people. You don't need a bunch of wingnuts watching you sleep. Some of them may get the wrong idea."

"Okay," he agreed. "I'll go to my room. I'm allowed to do that, right?"

"Until group," she said. "That's at three, so you have an hour. If you don't want that girl following you in there, you better close the door."

He nodded and got up to leave.

Lorena smiled knowingly. He was half way down the hall by the time she'd returned her attention to the sitcom at hand.

GROUP

Flynn closed the door behind him, and fell asleep the instant his head hit the pillow. His sleep was sound, and blessedly dreamless. It was the best sleep he'd had in months, but it wasn't nearly enough. He slept through the announcement, so a nurse came in the room and woke him up for group at three.

"My name is Pam," she said as she stood in the doorway. "You look like you need the rest, so I'm sorry I had to wake you, but it's the self-harm group and that one is required for you."

He stood up and wrapped his arms around himself.

"I feel horrible," he complained. "I'm going, I mean I have to, but I think I might have a fever. Also, my back hurts."

"I can get you a thermometer," Pam said. "And I can get you some ibuprofen for your pain, that's in your chart, you know, for your injuries. I can also give you a bandage if you think you need it, but the intake nurse didn't think it was necessary. But you can't skip group. You need to go there. I'll come get you out of group when I get the thermometer, okay?"

"And the Band-Aid?" he asked. He didn't think he needed one, either, but if it would keep him out of group longer, it would be worth it.

"Bandage," she corrected. "It's kind of too big for a Band-Aid."

He smiled, and obediently followed her up to the community room for the group. He noticed other groups were meeting in other rooms as they walked down the hall. There was a group for substance abuse and another one for domestic violence survivors. He vaguely wondered what would happen if someone happened to be a domestic violence survivor with substance abuse issues and was also a cutter?

He was not surprised to see Charlotte in his group. If he was self-conscious about discussing his nightmares before, he was even more so now. Knowing she'd be in the room, he feared her hanging on to his every word with voyeuristic glee. It did not help that he couldn't stop considering her offer. Every time she spoke, his skin tingled with anticipation. He couldn't even look at her.

"You can sit over there," the facilitator said, pointing to an empty chair on the opposite side of the room from Charlotte. Either someone on staff had witnessed their exchange in the recreation room, or their body language was broadcasting messages that were easy for the psychologist to read. Flynn looked down at his feet and nervously rubbed the side of his neck with the palm of his hand. He knew everyone could see the wounds where the monster bit him.

They went around the room, and everyone introduced himself or herself. Too self-conscious to pay attention to anything except his own body, Flynn carefully regulated his breathing in order to calm himself. He was slightly relieved to note that his thoughts were occupied with a real live person rather than a terrifying formless monster that lived in his nightmares.

He was hoping to get out of speaking, but apparently the nurse had warned the facilitator that he might have to leave early.

"Are you awake there, Flynn?" the facilitator asked cheerfully. He was a prematurely balding man in his early thirties with a mustache. Flynn had noticed some time ago that balding men often enjoyed sporting facial hair. He frequently thought of it as compensatory hair.

A pin on his white lab coat said the facilitator's name was Dr. J.D. Smith. His first name was actually Jaydee. Dr. Smith had determined back in med school that the abbreviation looked more substantial on a resume. When forced to divulge a first name, he generally misreported it as James.

"I'm awake," Flynn mumbled, staring dolefully at Dr. Smith's mustache. The mustache was much safer than making eye contact. A mustache was something he believed would be a significant ward against Charlotte's sultry voice and any erections it might cause. He mostly associated facial hair with his mom's hairy ex-boyfriend Karl, who was a sloppy eater and went around with stale crusted food clotting his beard and mustache. Sometimes when Flynn was sitting beside him at the dinner table, Karl's mustache smelled like sour milk. Flynn carefully invoked the memory of Karl and his stinking beard.

"Hello Flynn. What would you like to tell us about yourself today?" Dr. Smith asked cheerfully. "You don't have to say anything you're uncomfortable with, but you're safe here."

"Well," Flynn said carefully, "I don't remember hurting myself. I have these bad dreams, and when I wake up, sometimes I have cuts and bruises. My doctor says I'm doing this to myself, but I can't remember. It's hard for me to believe I could be injuring myself in this way. In my dream, it's a monster that is doing these things to me. Sometimes it doesn't hurt me, but it just kind of sucks all my energy away. I'm tired all the time. My doctor said that's because I'm depressed."

He stopped there, hoping for a quick reprieve from the nurse.

"That's good, Flynn," Dr. Smith said. "So you've heard a couple of people talk before you, but you came in late, so I'm not sure if you know how this works, but now the other people in the group who may have had similar experiences themselves are going to share their experiences or any advice they might have for you. Is that okay with you?"

"Yes, that's fine." Flynn said amiably.

"I think my dreams are telling me something," Charlotte said immediately. "I believe in dream interpretation, and I try to listen to my dreams, you know? Find out what's going on in my life that they relate to, you know? You know?"

Flynn had this sense she was just waiting for him to say something so she could pounce on it, like a ravenous hyena on a decaying gazelle carcass. He did not know how he felt about her, and didn't want to think about it right now, so he started checking to see if there was any food in Dr. Smith's beard. He barely suppressed the urge to giggle at his own rambling thoughts about beards and lice and roaches.

Once, he thought he saw a roach leap out of Karl's beard. Another time, Karl had to shave his beard off, because Flynn caught head lice in preschool. He couldn't stop snickering at the unfamiliar, beardless Karl. Karl had a big, round face, like the clown on the Jack in the Box logo. He probably grew a beard to disguise his chinless condition. These thoughts amused Flynn, but there was nothing interesting in Dr. Smith's beard.

His nurse, Pam, showed up to rescue him from having to deal with Charlotte, his own fucked up sexual desires, his nightmares, and the thought they might somehow be an expression of aforementioned twisted desires.

She took him back to the first aid station, and had him take off his Final Fantasy XII t-shirt and put on the white hospital gown with the little blue florets. He sat backward with his arms folded on the back of a chair while she cleaned his wound with saline solution and taped a square of gauze over it. Flynn just wanted to stay there, and be cared for, like a baby. He was upset to see bloodstains on the shoulder of his beloved t-shirt.

"You can put your shirt back on," Pam said when she was done.

He started to take his gown off without waiting for her to give him privacy, as she'd done the first time.

"Oh, wait. I have something for you," she said. She fished something out of her breast pocket and handed it to him.

Flynn dropped the hospital gown back over his chest and reached out to take the object from her hand. It was a children's bandage with cartoons of Sponge Bob on it.

"I work in pediatrics," she explained. "It's for the hickey or whatever that is on your neck."

She laughed and turned around for a minute so he could put his t-shirt on.

Naptime

All he wanted to do was to sleep and not dream. He felt like he could sleep for two weeks straight. There wouldn't be any more groups until tomorrow. Visiting hours were four to nine, and he didn't have any visitors, so he was free to sleep until dinner at six.

This time, his sleep was not dreamless.

He was back in college, sitting alone at a table in a coffee shop on campus, wearing the same t-shirt he fell asleep in. An old familiar song was playing on the radio, something about a girl named Delilah. He could feel the warmth radiating from the green ceramic mug in his hand, and he closed his eyes and inhaled the bracing aroma of the Sumatra coffee he always used to order there. It was all so solid, so real, but somehow, he knew he was asleep.

When he opened his eyes, Danny was coming through the door. Flynn smiled and waved.

Then he saw the woman standing directly behind Danny, and froze.

"Hey, Flynn," Danny said convivially, "I want you to meet this new girl in my class. Her name is Charlotte."

Charlotte pulled up a chair and sat down next to Flynn. She offered him her hand.

This time, he took her hand and kissed it.

"How charming," she said with a wink. "Do I taste good?"

"I think she likes you," Danny said, pulling up another chair on the opposite side of him.

A wave of distortion drifted across Danny's face, like the picture on an old television set going out of tune, or on an old tube monitor when something with a magnet is near it.

"She's a monster," Flynn said, pulling his hand back and eying her warily.

"Something's been eating you," she joked, "but I swear, it's not me."

"Flynn should be so lucky," Danny said with a wink.

Charlotte pulled a shot glass out of her pocket and set it on the table. She fished a vial filled with tangerine colored liquid out of her purse and poured it into the little glass.

"Drink this," she said, lifting the glass and offering it to him. "It will help you go to sleep."

"What is it?" he asked, recognizing the texture and color of the fluid. "I've seen it before, in my dreams. It was given to me."

She frowned. "You mean you've been forcibly overdosed with it. I bet you've been waking up puking your guts out the next morning. You don't have to lie to me, and we don't have to beat around the bush about this. I already know about Mercy."

"Mercy?" he asked.

"Yes, that's the name of the somnali who has been using you as her personal fast food restaurant for the past eleven months," Charlotte said. "She calls herself that, because it's usually what she leaves her victims begging for – mercy."

Flynn pursed his lips. "I see."

"It's hard to explain to a human," she shrugged.

"I think you should try," he suggested.

"Well, you know how bacon is delicious? And you know how there are people who keep potbellied pigs for pets, because they're adorable?" She continued before he could interrupt her awkward analogy. "You, my dear, are both delicious and adorable."

Flynn blushed and looked away. He started to rub the top of one foot with the other under the table. It was a nervous habit of his. "Uhm, thanks? I think?"

She laughed. "You're welcome. Now a human might eat bacon, and a person might have a pet pig. Although they are domesticated for slaughter, they're intelligent, affectionate creatures and they make great pets, you know? But you would never kill someone's pet pig and eat it just because you love bacon. And if you had a pet, you couldn't just amputate its leg one day so you could eat a ham hock. That would be amoral, you know, cruelty to animals. Only a real sick son of a bitch would do something like that. Those kinds of people really shouldn't be allowed to have pets."

He gave her a look of incredulity and shook his head. "That there is some majorly fucked up shit. Did you really just compare me to a plate of bacon?"

"Yeah, that wasn't good," she admitted. "I'm totally fucking this up. Look, I really am a monster, but just know, I'm not trying to hurt you. I'm trying to protect you. You should drink this. It's a pheromone we secrete. If I gave you a lot, you would do anything I wanted you to do, but this is just enough to relax you, so you can sleep and not dream up any more weird shit."

"So, you're drugging me?" he asked.

"I'm doing more than just drugging you," she said nervously. "I'm marking you. Not the way Mercy did, but more like the way you'd electronically tag your dog or your cat. That way you'd be my human. It won't actually stop her, but it would discourage her. There'd be penalties, because you'd be mine."

"So you want me to be your pet?" he asked.

"Yes," she admitted. "Pretty much. Look, just drink it, and get some rest. There's no commitment in just drinking some. We can discuss the rest of this later."

Flynn shrugged. "Whatever you are, thank you for not just sticking some tentacles up my nose and mainlining whatever this is into my brain. Of course I don't trust you. Not at all. But fine."

He shrugged again. Then he picked up the shot glass.

"I guess its medication time." He drank all of the fluid.

He didn't dream again, at least not that he remembered. When he woke up, it was dinnertime.

CREEPY-CRAWLIES

Being denied her intended prey left Mercy more than a little bit frustrated. Fortunately, she had other playthings with which to occupy her time. Distance in the physical world was not an issue for her, because time and space were both very fluid in the dark realms. She could appear in any human's dream at any time in a matter of seconds if that person had entered R.E.M sleep.

She might have selected someone across the country, or even across the world from Flynn, if she hadn't had a vested interest in attempting to further traumatize the man who was now, at least temporarily, out of her reach. She might not be able to harm him directly, but she could definitely upset him and all of the other wards of this institution if she could push another patient over the edge.

She'd previously haunted the nightmares of Howard Lowe, a patient who had a particularly close proximity to Flynn in the physical realm as one of the three roommates sandwiched into his four-bed hospital room. Howard had extreme entomophobia, or an irrational fear of insects.

Unfortunately, Howard was still awake. That situation could be anticipated to change with the administration of his nightly medications. In the meantime he was sufficiently sedated such as to allow her to insinuate an unpleasant creeping sensation under his skin, one that would suggest to the unfortunate Mr. Lowe that his epidermis was infested with hordes of breeding fly larvae.

Howard began to scratch at himself nervously, and his eye developed a distinct nervous twitch.

Mercy decided not to overplay her hand. If he started screaming and running down the hall, the orderlies might remove him from the general ward and isolate him in a solitary lockdown padded room. She had to time everything just right, to ensure that Flynn was there to witness the upcoming implosion.

My, but this was a fun game to play.

AWAKENING

Flynn got up and wandered over to the bathroom before heading back to the lunchroom. There were public restrooms in the hall, men's and women's. The men's room had three stalls and two urinals. There was a dividing wall between the places where one might relieve himself and a corridor with four sinks, two lining each wall. There was a mirror over each sink with a little ledge below it on which one might place a tiny tube of toothpaste, a toothbrush, and a bar of soap.

Each of these items had been provided to him upon his admission. They were in neat little packages that suggested a hotel stay, but this was no hotel. If he wanted to take a bath, or to shave, he had to ask a nurse or any orderly to attend him. They would keep an eye on him and make sure he didn't drown himself or try to break open a safety razor and cut his own wrist. Afterwards, the razor would be locked away in a place that was safe and inaccessible to the patients. No doubt it was the same place where all of their lighters and shoelaces were hidden.

Flynn peed first. Afterward, he came back out to the sink and swished some water around in his mouth to rinse away the stickiness in his mouth and the sour aroma of morning breath. Dry mouth was a common med side effect. He recalled what the girl said about the medicinal properties of the concoction she had given him. Then he took a good look at himself in the mirror.

The black circles were disappearing from below his eyes, and the color was beginning to return to his skin. He looked less like a drug addict and more like someone who was recovering from the flu. The whites of his eyes were no longer bloodshot, and they were also a great deal less yellow. His irises, so dark brown that in a poorly lit room, it was impossible to distinguish them from his pupils, were clear and bright. He looked a lot healthier after resting. He was relieved.

He didn't know what this new monster Charlotte was planning to do to him, but so far, she did not seem to be doing him any harm. In fact, she seemed to be doing him some good.

DINNER

He took one last look in the mirror and winked at himself. He joked to his reflection, "Flynn. It's what's for dinner."

Heading out for the dining room, he felt strangely euphoric. If he admitted these feelings to his therapist or in a group they might adjust his medications to balance him out. Once he took his meds this feeling might go away. He wasn't sure, though. He thought that maybe he might just be happy.

He was cautiously hopeful.

By the time he reached the dining area, his tray was the only untouched meal in the room, and so it was easy to spot his seat. A lid was over the main course to keep his meal warm. Lorena and Gary were sitting on either side of his tray, but the teenage girl was no longer there. It seemed she'd finally gathered the courage to go to the other table and sit next to the boy she'd been staring at.

Another familiar face sat in the spot across from him. It was Charlotte.

"Hi there," she said sweetly.

Flynn smiled at his strange new friend. The thought of the things she might want to do to him made his skin flush. He started drinking the little cafeteria lunch sized carton of apple juice that came with his dinner, and call upon the image of Karl's crumb-infested beard to help him regain his composure.

"I'm busting out of this joint tomorrow," Lorena wisecracked. "I'm sure old Gary here will be heartbroken. I'm glad you have a new friend, Flynn. You kids play nice together."

"Uhm, yeah," Flynn mumbled, quickly changing the subject. "So, yea, I got the baked chicken and rice. How is the Salisbury Steak?"

"Bland, like everything in here," Lorena groused, scooping up another spoonful of mashed potatoes. "Look at this beige water they like to call gravy. Are they joking? I guess they must have everyone on the heart healthy diet, because it doesn't taste like they put any salt into anything."

Flynn was tearing into his food with such gusto that Lorena did a double take. She said, "Maybe I should have ordered what you're having."

"I'm sorry," he managed between forks of green beans. "It all tastes great to me. This is the first time I've been able to keep anything down in months."

"In months?" she asked, "Seems to me like you need a medical doctor, not just the head shrinking kind."

"Heh." He coughed. "I uh, I've been suffering from some kind of parasite."

Lorena shook her head. "Well I hope it's not contagious."

"I'm happy to see you looking better," Charlotte said, casting him an admiring glance. She thought he had beautiful eyes, almond shaped, and nearly black with long, dark lashes. His skin was also pretty, smooth and the color of honey. She wondered again, what it would be like to taste him. She wondered if he was considering allowing her to, but she didn't want to say anything.

"Thanks," he said shyly. "I feel a lot better, too. I didn't want to be here, but maybe it's good for me to be in here."

She nodded. "Listen, if I'd met you somewhere else, I might ask you to coffee, or dinner. I suppose we're already having dinner together, aren't we? I was thinking that after they give us our meds, if you'd like, we could sit in the recreation room and play a game of Scrabble."

"I'd like that," he said. He thought for a moment and then asked her, "Do you actually like video games, too? Or were you just, you know…"

"Yes, and yes," she said. "Yes, I like video games, and yes, I was flirting with you. It's entirely possible to do both things at once. Yes, I like RPGs, I like Elder Scrolls, especially Skyrim, and I like Dragon Age, and I'm not totally in to first person shooters but I like Mass Effect, so there you go."

"I have an Xbox," he said stupidly.

"Right and I have a PlayStation," she retorted. "So, it will probably never work out. Do you use Windows or something? Because I have a Mac, and Microsoft makes Xbox. You know, these things are really important. They are crucial things to base a relationship on. I'm starting to think we're incompatible."

Flynn's jaw dropped. "You're just fucking with me right now, aren't you?"

"Yes, I'm just fucking with you," she said. "I so totally don't give a shit what gaming system you use."

"You kids need to stop swearing and keep your voices down," Lorena warned. "That orderly there is watching. They might decide you need a time out if you keep acting so animated. Dose you up real good like Gary over there."

Flynn laughed.

He felt happy now.

He decided it couldn't last.

GAMES

Neither of them had any visitors, so Charlotte and Flynn grabbed the Scrabble board after dinner and took a small, round table off to one side. It was furthest from the door, and close to a window, so it afforded them the most privacy, but what privacy they could have was limited.

About fifteen minutes into the game, they were called to get in line and pick up their medications. There was another two hours before they would be sent off to their rooms to get ready for bed at nine pm, but he knew from experience that the medications he took would make it almost impossible for him to stay awake thirty to forty minutes from now.

Charlotte went first, and put the word "dreamer" on the board.

"Wow, seven letter bonus on the first word," Flynn whistled. "You're already kicking my ass."

"I'm pretty good at this game," she confessed.

Flynn looked at his letters for a couple of minutes before putting down "retail"

"Six letters isn't bad," Charlotte said.

"There's no bonus for almost," Flynn responded. "So... I wanted to ask you something."

"Go ahead," she replied, looking up from her tiles. "I imagine you have a lot of questions." Without her piercing jewelry, the little holes in her ears and her face looked like tiny bug bites or something. For an instant, he remembered how they looked in the dream.

Things in real life were different. Impressions were no longer fuzzy. Everything had more detail, and he could see all of the little flaws that weren't there in the dream world. Here, her complexion was uneven and she had pimples. Her fingers were still long and graceful, but the knuckles were red, and one of her long nails was broken.

"I saw you in my dream," he said.

"That's not a question," she stated. "I was in your dream. I remember."

"What is or are somnali?" he asked.

"We're monsters," she said. "You know, we invade your dreams."

"Like Freddy Krueger?" he asked.

"No, not really," she replied. "People have compared us to baku, succubi, ghouls, vampires, and various other creatures that enjoy the taste of human. We are something else entirely, something very ancient and hungry. Once we get in your head, we devour your flesh, your lust, your emotions, your dreams, or your energy. There are so many delicious meals to be made from a human. Sometimes it's hard to pick just one of the many ways in which we can consume you.

We originate in the dark dimensions you refer to as the dream world. We live there, whereas humans are merely tourists in the realm of sleep. If we want to invade your physical world, then we gorge ourselves until we have enough energy to have corporeal form. Some of us are more able to maintain corporeal form than others. Somnali procreate with humans to create half-breed creatures who can easily traverse the bridge between your world and the darker realms. I am one those talented creatures. We are called demisomnali. It's like dual citizenship, I guess. But a pure somnali like my father can only remain in the physical universe for a short time. They have to offer sacrifices and binge on human emotion in order to do it.

And look! I think I've said too much. Here comes Nurse Betty."

Charlotte smiled and waved at the med nurse, who was standing in the doorway, looking around the room   No words needed to be exchanged for both of them to know that it was no good having any kind of conversation that might be interpreted as psychotic when overheard by the staff.

Sure enough, she walked right over to them. Her name wasn't actually Betty, it was Mavis.

"So nice to see the board games being used," Mavis said lightheartedly. She spoke in a cheerfully condescending singsong voice generally used to speak to young children, baby animals, the developmentally disabled, and the insane. "Whatever are you two talking about?"

"Oh, she was just telling me about this new video game," Flynn lied. "It's about monsters that enter your dreams and drain you while you're sleeping."

"I see," Mavis said. "And, Flynn, don't you have nightmares about monsters that attack you when you're sleeping?"

"I do," he admitted. "That's why I was curious about this game. Do you think that's unhealthy?"

"If you're talking about what's bothering you, I think that's probably a good thing," Mavis reassured him. "But just be mindful of the other patients around you. You have to be careful not to say things that might upset people when you're not in a safe place, like a therapy session."

"That's fine with me," Charlotte lied. "Why don't I go get a yogurt from the lunch room while you two, you know, talk about this private stuff. Hey, Flynn, do you want a yogurt?"

"Sure," he said to her back, as she was already up and walking out the door. "Uhm, strawberry please?"

"I didn't realize that you consider these nightmares that you have to be a private matter," Mavis said by way of apology. "If you aren't ready to talk about them in public, I respect your wishes. Enjoy your game."

By the time Charlotte returned, Mavis was gone. Flynn realized the young woman was more than a little bit manipulative.

He didn't mind.

She knelt down on the floor beside him and pushed one of the yogurts in front of him. There was a little plastic spoon on top. She put her hand on the back of his chair, and as she stood up she bent over a little and whispered in his ear.

"I want to taste your pain."

He shivered. She walked over to her chair and sat down across from him.

"Why that?" he asked. "Why not something positive, like happiness?"

"Well if I eat your happiness, you won't have any left," she said irritably. "How would that be? Mercy used to do that. I've been keeping her out. Can't you feel the difference?"

"I have been happy," he said softly. "I like it."

"So, yea, I don't want to take that from you," she reiterated. "But pain… you have a complicated relationship to it, an interesting one, for me. And you know there is so much of it in the world that if I taste some, there will still be plenty left."

"I guess I see the logic in that," he agreed.

"Are you getting sleepy?" she asked.

"I am," he admitted. "It's the meds."

"You need your sleep," she said. "You haven't been getting enough. Go ahead and get some rest, I'll talk to you later."

He wanted to give her a hug, but he knew this was neither the time nor the place, so he got an orderly to help him take a bath, slipped into some clean hospital clothes, and climbed into bed.

SHAME

He fell into an immediate and sound sleep that was not interrupted by dreams or anything else until about four in the morning. The sun wouldn't rise for a couple of hours. They were not allowed to leave the room or wander around. He rested on his belly face down with his arms folded over his pillow. He was trying to go back to sleep and avoid making any sound that might awaken any of the three other men who shared the room. There were four low beds, one in each corner with no curtains or dividers, like a hostel. Each bed had a short nightstand with two drawers in it for personal belongings.

He had been in that position for about twenty minutes when he felt a hand on the small of his back. He turned his head to one side and saw the girl sitting there.

"Don't say anything," Charlotte whispered. "No one else can see or hear me right now, so you'd seem pretty crazy."

She unfastened the lowest snap on his nightgown and put her bare palm on his back. She ran her hand up and down his spine, caressing the curve of his lower back. He was beginning to feel drowsy again. He started to wonder if he was being sedated, but he didn't have long to ponder the thought before he was deep in the throes of sleep again.

Once again, his dreams were laced with the trappings of old memories. He found himself curled up with his face buried in a creepy powder pink My Melody comforter that he recognized as belonging to his high school sweetheart, Tamara. Without getting up, he turned his head to look around. The wall of boy band posters and shelves loaded with stuffed animals stared back at him accusingly, just like they used to back in the day. They weren't allowed to be alone in the room with the door closed, but Tamara didn't actually appear to be in the room.

Flynn sat up. He was wearing skintight black jeans and a Resident Evil t-shirt.

He spotted the envelope slipped between the paws of her stuffed Bad Badtz Maru and suddenly registered what day this must be. He leaned over to pick it up; already knowing what would be inside.

"Happy Birthday, Flynn! XOXOX" was written on the outside of the envelope in big, girlish cursive. She had used a heart to dot the i in Birthday, and left a big messy red lipstick kiss below the Xs and Os. He remembered the deceptively innocent looking card, what was in it, and the intention behind it.

It was his eighteenth birthday, the summer before he went off to college. The envelope had already been torn open. He pulled out the greeting card. It was a dog on a motorcycle wearing a leather jacket, inscribed with the words *Bad to the Bone*. It was a musical card, and actually played the old George Thorogood tune when opened up. He opened it, and a gift card fell out.

It was for a local shop that offered tattoos and other body modifications such as piercings. When this had actually happened, when she had given him the card he didn't realize what he would come to understand later. Tamara was afraid of him leaving for college, afraid of the ways in which time and distance would inevitably pull their relationship apart. She wanted to mark him in some way that was permanent and unforgettable. She wanted him to think of her whenever he looked in the mirror. She believed that somehow, this would keep him from straying when they were apart. She thought that he would be chastened if he undressed in front of any other woman, and saw the place where she left her mark.

She was his first love, and she did leave a mark. Just not in the way she had intended.

When he originally received the gift, he naively interpreted it as an acknowledgment of his newly gained adulthood and the rights and privileges that were allowed to him now that he was legally of age. His mother would have never allowed him to get a tattoo or a piercing.

He was hit with the unmistakable stirrings of anticipation and arousal as he thought about reliving that day. His skin tingled. He'd gone over this day in his mind many times over. It was the source of a number of deeply secret, shameful urges and masturbatory fantasies for years afterward. It was absolutely defining, and not just because it was the day he lost his virginity.

Tamara burst into the room with her big lipstick smile and oversized see-through plastic handbag. She was wearing khaki cargo shorts that had been hemmed up to the shortest possible length that could not be considered vulgar. They ended just below the curve of her ass. Her striped Old Navy tank top was low cut and fitted, and she wore frilly ankle socks under her strappy high heel shoes.

"Are you ready?" she asked.

"I am," he said, standing and carefully pulling his shirt down to conceal the start of an erection. Her intentionally showcased cleavage and near-perfect figure were not the only reason he was getting excited. He was looking forward to the appointment.

"Are you sure about the piercings?" she asked. "I heard they hurt."

"I'm sure," he said, looking away. "I don't mind the pain. Will you hold my hand?"

"Of course!" she agreed.

It was an understatement. He craved the experience. He'd spent the last hour lying face down on her bed because every time he thought about what it would feel like, he got really hard. The thought of his girlfriend holding his hand, or touching him in any way while it was happening made him even more excited. He wondered if he would still be sore afterward, and how that would feel when they made love for the first time, as she had promised they would, for his birthday. She already had a hotel room.

He was too ashamed to share his line of thinking with her. He thought he was probably perverted, or dirty, or wrong. He liked to hurt himself when he was masturbating, but he wouldn't tell anyone about that. He was so excited by the idea that someone else would be doing it this time. He ran his hand over his shirt and felt the nipples brushing against the cloth. He wondered if they would be more sensitive once they were pierced.

He also wished that Tamara could just slide the needle into his welcoming flesh; penetrate him with cold, hard steel instead of tenderly holding his hand while a trained professional did it. He wondered if he was the only one who ever felt that way. He no longer remembered that he was dreaming.

It was the way of dreams that time had no real meaning. In an instant, he was no longer in her bedroom. He was sitting on the edge of a metal table at the tattoo shop, pulling his shirt off. He tossed it on the table next to him, and put on a brave face. Tamara was sitting next to him, holding his right hand in both of hers.

He expected to see the same apron-wearing tattooed man who did it the first time, but when he looked up, Charlotte was standing there, putting plastic gloves on her hands.

"I hope you don't mind," she said with a grin." After all, I might be opening up some old wounds here."

Flynn swallowed. He didn't say anything.

Charlotte grabbed a package containing a long, silver needle from off of a steel tray. "So, this won't take long," she said in a friendly but clinical tone. "Let me tell you what I'm doing here. I'm going to pinch your nipple between these forceps and pull on it a little so I can get it in the right position to jab this giant needle through it. And you're going to have to sit very still, which will be difficult for you, because you're already practically squirming in your seat. You're such a dirty boy."

He blushed, but didn't say anything. Tamara patted his hand reassuringly. She smiled at him and said, "Don't worry baby. Everything will be okay. Charlotte loves the fact that you're a fucking pervert."

"Don't interrupt," Charlotte ordered. "As I was saying, this needle is sterile. I will put the barbells in instead of the rings, because it's easier for them to heal. You can put the rings in after they heal if you like. But it will take longer for them to heal, because we all know you are going to be touching them and playing with yourself every chance you get."

Flynn was thoroughly chagrined and a little bit humiliated by her amusing rant, which he supposed was the point. Charlotte enjoyed his emotions, and he had already noticed that she was rather manipulative. He didn't think she was beyond provoking said emotions if it gave her pleasure to do so. He was more than a little conflicted and embarrassed by his closeted masochism.

She stooped over a little and leveled her gaze so she could look directly into his eyes. He looked back at her.

"So, are you ready?" she asked him.

He smiled softly before responding with a breathy "Yes."

Charlotte nodded. "Very well, then. Pay attention, Flynn. You'll want to watch this. Tamara, you should watch, too. That way we can fulfill his little repressed exhibitionist fantasy. Don't forget to hold his hand."

He looked down at her gloved hands and carefully observed what she was doing. His nipple was already hard and it looked like a plump little brown raisin. He gasped a little as she pinched his tender flesh with the forceps and clamped them shut. He gave Tamara's hand a squeeze and paid rapt attention as Charlotte tugged on his nipple and stretched the skin. He felt a sharp pain as the needle penetrated, but it was over soon, replaced by a dull, throbbing ache as she removed the forceps and screwed the second ball on the end of the post. She surprised him by bending down and kissing it.

"There. I kissed it to make it better. I'm afraid that wasn't sterile," she apologized afterwards.

Flynn was smiling and slowly melting into the table. This was the best dream he'd had in forever.

"So, what do you think?" Charlotte asked. She was looking at his chest as if it were a wall upon which she'd recently mounted some artwork. "Aesthetically, I think it's very pleasing. Should we do the same thing to the other one, or are we good? Some people like the look of asymmetry."

Flynn blinked. Was she joking?

"Don't stop," he begged.

"Are you sure you know what you're doing?" Tamara asked, placing his hand on her lap. "I think you trust her too much. She's not human. She wants something from you, and you don't even fight back – you just give it to her."

Charlotte narrowed her eyes. "It's true. I do want something from you, Flynn. You absolutely delight me, with your overblown sense of guilt and shame about your relatively benign and fairly common little fantasies about being spanked and scratched and bitten. You keep it all bottled up, and I want to uncork your vintage bottle of delicious sexual repression and drink it all up. I just want to know one thing. Are you going to let me?"

He chewed on his lower lip for a moment and avoided eye contact with either one of them, looking down at the floor.

"She's going to hurt you!" Tamara exclaimed in exasperation.

Finally, he looked up at Charlotte. She was eying him as if he were a juicy ripe plum she was waiting to pluck and eat. She wanted him, and he wanted to be had by her. He made his choice.

"You can," he told her. "You can taste me. You can hurt me."

Charlotte didn't need to be told twice. She presented him with a wicked grin and rammed the needle into his other nipple with unnatural speed and force. It began to bleed all over her hand.

"It's not supposed to do that," Tamara complained.

Charlotte shoved him back down on the cold metal table, and climbed up on top of him. Straddling him, with her face on his chest, she ran her tongue over the blood that trickled from his wound. When it was gone, she started licking off the blood that had spilled onto her hand off her fingers.

"You taste so good," she cooed, looking down at him. "I don't think it's enough, though. I want more."

She started biting and sucking on his nipple, piercing the tender flesh with her teeth and bringing forth fresh rivulets of hot, salty fluid that spilled into her parted lips, all over her tongue and her mouth. Flynn tossed his arms around her shoulders while she did this and began whimpering like a little puppy dog. He was a little afraid she would become so carried away with her extremely enthusiastic feeding frenzy that it led to his accidental exsanguination.

Nonetheless, he was beyond all self-control by now. He gave himself to her in an act of complete, unfettered trust. He had to rely on her to keep her promise not to hurt him because he was simply too aroused to resist her. This was not magic beyond the ordinary human sexual kind. He was in the throes of an orgasm. He trembled in her arms and came in his pants.

As soon as this happened she stopped. She looked up at him and smiled. There wasn't a drop of blood on her face. She'd swallowed everything. She patted him on the stomach in an affectionate gesture.

"That's enough," she said. "Thank you for feeding me."

Flynn woke up alone in his hospital bed. The sun was peeking in through the vertical venetian blinds, and his roommates were already up and shuffling towards the bathroom or the recreation room. It was 5:35 A.M. according to the clock on the wall. They were allowed to sleep until 6:00 A.M. and breakfast was served at 6:30.

He would have gone back to sleep for another twenty-five minutes if he hadn't woken up in the middle of a wet spot on the bed. Alarmed, he looked at his hospital gown and the white sheets below him to see if the mysterious fluid was blood. A brief investigation revealed that while his top was mostly dry, there was a damp stain in the lap of his blue cotton hospital pants.

He'd just had a wet dream.

Embarrassed, he stood up and began to gather his blankets and sheets into a ball to cover up the mess he'd made. He remembered there being a laundry basket in the hall, He wondered how he would get to it without letting anyone see the spot on his pants.

He was in the middle of constructing an elaborate scheme for the disposal of his messy sheets and garments when Pam walked in.

"6:15, it is morning med time," she said. "You take yours before breakfast." Then she spotted the pile of blankets and did a double take. "What's going on here? Is something wrong?"

"I had a... I had an accident," Flynn stuttered. "I was just trying to clean up my bed. Uhm and, I need to change clothes."

"Leave it there," she ordered. "Just change your clothes and get your medication. You have street clothes, right? If not I can get you a hospital gown. Oh wait a minute. You probably need a bath. Do you need a bath?"

"I think so," he said, looking down at the moisture on his lap.

"Wow," she said a little nervously, "I need to make a note in your chart. Your doctor needs to make sure your kidneys are alright, some meds can harm your kidneys."

"It wasn't that kind of an accident," he admitted. "I had a dream. Look, I really don't want to talk about this."

Pam nodded. "I'll send Bill in here with your meds and the key to the shower. Don't worry about the covers, okay? We'll have the staff take care of that while you eat your breakfast. Do you need a change of clothes?"

"No, I have clothes," he said, going through his drawer.

"Okay, good," Pam said, leaving the room without further comment.

CLEAN

"I'll be back in ten minutes," the orderly said, turning off the bathwater. He handed Flynn a clean towel, a washcloth, and a baggie containing a little bar of soap still wrapped in paper and a tiny bottle of combination shampoo and conditioner. Flynn set it on the table next to the tub, and Bill walked out and locked the door behind him. Flynn understood that he was locked in the room. He was relieved that everyone else was locked out.

There was steam coming off the surface of the bathwater, which was crystal clear and unpolluted by any kind of soap. He put three of his fingers into the water, and checked the temperature. It was pleasingly on the hot side of warm. He didn't have much time. Quickly undressing, he climbed into the tub and slid down the side, closing his eyes as he went down under the water.

Being immersed gave him a feeling of distance from the world around him and his persistent pile of personal problems. He couldn't hear anything except the gentle slosh of the displaced water and his own pulse throbbing in his temples. He couldn't see anything but the fuzzy red halo the overhead florescent lights created behind his closed eyelids. He wondered if the light caused the reddish tint, or the eyelids themselves? He held his breath as long as he could, afloat in warm liquid, unconcerned, and unashamed.

When he finally sat up and caught his breath, his worries came rushing in.

How could he have allowed what had happened to him? The dream Tamara was right. He had trusted that creature – Charlotte, if it actually was her – far too easily. He didn't know what it actually was, if it was real, or a figment of his tortured imagination. He didn't really know if it was any different than the monster that he had been fighting off in his dreams for more than a year now. After a year of doing battle, why suddenly cave in?

What was wrong with him? Why was he plagued by these troubling visions? He was in the hospital to recover, not to go further down the rabbit hole. Why would he endanger that by engaging in such risky behavior?

How could anyone care about him if he didn't care about himself?

Soaping up his skin as best as he could with the pitiful silver of soap, he carefully inspected its surface to see if he'd awakened with any kinds of injuries. To his relief, all of the scratches and scrapes were old ones, already healing. Even the bite on his neck was closed. It was now little more than a penny-sized bruise.

Then he ran a hand over his chest.

"Ow!" he yelped. There wasn't any visible bruising, but he was sore. The sensation bought back last night's dream with absolute clarity. Now that he was alone with his thoughts, it was easy for him to remember everything that happened, the things Charlotte did to him and how much he enjoyed them. There was something pleasing about all the little ways in which ways his body continued to ache.

He smiled. Then his happy memory was interrupted by the recollection of what came next.

Last night's experiences had been amazing, right up until the horrifying moment when he woke up in the middle of a puddle of seminal fluid with a wet spot on his crotch. He remembered the anxiety that he felt as he became aware of the fact that he was standing in a semi-public room where anyone could come in at any moment. He remembered the fear of humiliation, chest tight, breath shallow, worrying that others in the room – his roommates, the nurses, orderlies, maids, whoever came in to clean the bed, random passersby in the hallways – all knew about his wet dream.

It was that last unwanted bit of public humiliation that spoiled everything.

He let out his breath with a whistle. Well, if they did know, he would try to find a way to live with it, but he decided that except for Pam, people probably didn't know about it.

Flynn decided to stop fucking around and get his head on straight. He didn't know whether or not what went on between him and that girl Charlotte was real, or a particularly vivid fantasy, and he wasn't losing his mind over it. Maybe he had been hallucinating the whole time. If not, then telling a girl he didn't know very well that she could hurt him and devour his flesh might be considered risky behavior. He remembered some psychiatric jargon or the other about risk-taking behavior.

He got out of the tub, dried himself off with the infuriatingly inadequate towel. It was slightly larger than a pillowcase, and by the time he finished drying his legs and patting his ass a few times it was too wet to use to dry his hair. In the process of attempting to sponge the water off of his chest with the soggy white hospital towel, he noticed something new about his body.

He stopped wearing the nipple rings about two weeks after Tamara dumped him, because they reminded him of her, and having a constant memorial to a failed relationship buried in his flesh was fairly depressing. The day he took them out and tossed them in a trashcan, he remembered thinking how lucky he was that he didn't get the tattoo like she wanted him to because a tattoo would be much harder to get rid of.

That was five and a half years ago, and the holes that the piercing jewelry fit in had healed in such a way that it wasn't really possible to tell they'd been there in the first place. That was why he was surprised to notice that they were back again, like he just took his nipple rings out an hour ago, or perhaps as if the events of last night actually occurred.

He didn't really have time to hang around the bathroom playing with his self before breakfast, but he remembered an old trick from back in college, from the first time he was locked up. It was before the bad break up with Tamara. He didn't want the piercings to close while he was locked up, so he broke two of the teeth off his plastic comb and used them in place of the jewelry.

He quickly tossed his soiled clothing into a big plastic bag with handles on it that said PATIENT on it and had his name written below that word with a marker pen. He fished a smaller plastic baggie out of it, which had a brush, a comb, a toothbrush and some toothpaste. He broke two teeth off the comb and tossed it back into the bag.

He didn't know why, but the idea that Charlotte had marked his body didn't frighten him. It excited him. It wasn't what she could or would do to him that he feared. What he was afraid of was his own response to it. Would he be able to deny her anything she asked?

He began dressing himself.

By the time the orderly returned Flynn was dressed and ready to go to breakfast.

SKIN

The thing about self-consciousness is that the person who is worried about what others are thinking of him is often completely unaware of the fact that those others have concerns of their own, and he may be the last thing on their minds.

Howard Lowe was neither aware of Flynn's embarrassment nor his nocturnal emission. Howard Lowe had problems of his own. He was having terrible, terrible nightmares.

Howard's dream began pleasantly enough. He was down at the beach in Santa Cruz, relaxing in the sand on an oversized blue beach towel with the image of a dolphin leaping over a single, yellow starfish in the middle of it. He was alone on a crowded beach, which was to say that there were hundreds of people on the beach, but no one was sitting beside him. There was a band nearby playing golden oldies. The afternoon sun cast its light on his cheeks and warmed the tip of his nose. He had a love-hate relationship with the sun. Howard's mahogany skin had a lesser need for sunscreen than some others. Howard was paranoid about skin cancer, so he wore sunblock. His middle-aged brown eyes needed protection from the cataracts, which affected his brown-eyed parents later in life. He already wore dark sunglasses. He had pulled his touristy blue baseball cap down over his face and was preparing to engage in some hardcore relaxation.

That's when the first bite came.

Howard sat up, and slapped his forearm, squashing the bug against it. A splat of red blood encircled the flattened corpse of a fat brown bed bug. Howard had been terrified of them ever since the bed bug outbreak had infested the Bay Area, attacking the poorest first. He remembered lying on a filthy mattress in a Tenderloin hotel that was speckled in pea-sized bloodstains and insect husks about twice the size of a flea. He didn't think that they had bed bugs on the beach.

How did they get there?

He looked down in horror at the towel he bought with him to sunbathe. It was infested! The whole damned thing was crawling with them, and they were pouring out from between his legs in droves, spreading all over the beach like tiny, hungry sand crabs that hungered for human flesh.

He jumped up and started knocking them off his skin, screaming.

When he screamed, everyone else on the beach picked up the scream the way dogs barked in response to a single neighborhood dog barking, and soon the shrill sounds of many types of voices were merging into a high pitched, insect-like whine. It sounded like the screams of a million dying crickets. The dark cloud of tiny bloodsucking creatures launched itself at the other sunbathers, and he was horrified as they began to strip the flesh and bone off a pregnant woman and her shovel-holding toddler about five feet away.

He was overcome by guilt as he began to feel relief that the hungry bugs were after everyone else at the beach, but not him. They weren't leaving him alone so much as they were leaving him, exiting from his immediate area as if he were a hive, a mere conduit through which they might access other flesh.

This mixed emotion didn't last very long. Looking down at his arms, he noticed something disturbing about the texture of the flesh. The freckles on his skin were not flat any longer. They were bumps, raised above the flesh. These lumps started moving.

The bugs were under his skin!

Howard woke up with scratches all over his arms from where he'd tried to claw the bugs out from under his skin in his sleep. Before Flynn woke up, before the staff arrived, Howard carefully covered them. Over the upcoming week, this pattern would repeat itself. Howard woke up every morning with the meat scraped from his arms, legs, and torso; the flesh lodged under his fingernails. He spent every day hiding the carnage from the nurses and his fellow inmates.

BREAKFAST

Flynn was late for breakfast, and half of the patients were done eating and in the TV room by the time he arrived. He looked for Lorena, briefly, before remembering that she said she was going to be discharged. He would probably never see her again in this lifetime. Now that he had been there for a couple of meals, the menu he filled out had been prepared for him – a selection of hot wheat cereal, toast, bacon, eggs, and half a grapefruit.

Morning was also the only meal that was served with coffee, although he suspected it was actually decaf. He was on his way over to the cart that held their meals to look for his name, when Charlotte waved him over.

She already had his plate.

It was sitting on the table in front of the seat Flynn always sat at. Gary was still patiently grazing on one side, eyes focused out in the distance, and Charlotte on the other. Who had been sitting in the fourth spot, where Lorena used to be, he wondered? What kind of thinking convinced Charlotte it was a good idea to put his tray there? Did she consider him a friend now? Was she feeling possessive? Those were questions he had, but none of them as urgent as his need to know if she remembered if she knew about the dream. Just because she claimed to have been in the first one that did not mean he hadn't simply imagined last night.

It occurred to him that he might have imagined both nights. Maybe she was just playing along.

"What's wrong?" she asked, the minute he sat down. He decided he must not have a very good poker face.

"Nothing," he deflected. "I just had a bad dream last night, that's all. I didn't sleep very well."

"Oh, I see." Charlotte said irritably. "I'm sorry to hear that you have been having these terrible nightmares. I hope that won't happen ever again now that they've got you on a new medication." She paused for a moment, and then added, "I hope you weren't dreaming about me again."

He didn't really know how to respond. He wasn't sure if he imagined her irritation. He couldn't really trust his own mind, not after all he'd been through. He started to worry that she really had been in his dream. Maybe he had insulted her terribly. He wasn't sure that he should care how she felt if she was doing something that might be dangerous or bad for him.

He shook his head. "No, of course not," he lied. "It wasn't anything like that."

"Well that's a relief," she remarked in that same bristly tone.

Flynn nodded and went back to quietly eating his meal, hoping that he wouldn't be forced to engage in any further conversation. He was upset and confused and had no desire to discuss last night's adventures with anyone right now.

Charlotte was almost done with her food when he got there, and he kept hoping that she would finish it, leaving him to eat in peace. That didn't happen, and after a short time he picked up on the fact that she was intentionally eating as slowly as possible so she could stay there.

Eventually, Gary got up and walked out into the TV room.

The minute they were alone, Charlotte said very quietly, "Look, I'm sorry. Okay? I thought you wanted to."

Flynn swallowed. "Let me stop you right there."

"But I don't understand," Charlotte protested, "I thought you liked me. I thought you wanted me to do it."

He sighed. "Look, it's not that I don't like you, because I *do* like you. That's not the problem. That's *really* not the problem. I'm not in a good place right now. I can't tell what is real, and not real. I'm not even sure what you're trying to tell me right now, so this is all a lot to process for me."

"It was real," she insisted. "You know it was."

"No, I do not know any such thing," he said calmly. "You barely know me at all. I don't know you. I don't know who you are. Hell, I don't know what you are. But I'm not rejecting you, I'm just asking you... no, begging you, to slow your roll. This is way too fast for me, and I feel... I feel like I'm losing my fucking mind here, okay? I mean, weird shit's happening to me, and I'm in a mental hospital. Can you understand why any of this might be disturbing to me?"

Charlotte nodded. She got up and quickly walked away. She was done eating anyhow.

THERAPY

Aside from Charlotte, Flynn was without any friends now that Lorena was gone, unless Gary could be counted, a prospect he considered rather doubtful. He was now uncertain whether or not Charlotte could be considered a friend, and not just because she professed to have supernatural powers. Her notions regarding the somnali and their food sources were probably just as delusional as his beliefs about ongoing physical attacks in his dream life. Even if that was the case, she looked pretty pissed off, and he wasn't sure she would want to speak to him again.

He needn't have worried about that. Once again, they had morning group together.

Today, the morning group he was shuffled into was for people who suffered from psychosis. Lots of psychiatric conditions had psychotic features, and he personally had been diagnosed with bipolar disorder during his freshman year of college. Psychosis was defined as having a break with reality of some sort. Suffering from delusions and seeing or hearing things that weren't there were both forms of psychosis. So was experiencing hallucinatory tactile sensations, a problem he personally found extremely disturbing. Many times, he had been touched or even held down by hands that weren't there.

What if the doctors were wrong? What if these things were actually real? He shuddered.

Despite their disagreement that morning Charlotte had saved him a seat, something that had not gone unnoticed by the staff. Pam and Mavis were both helping to escort patients into the room, and exchanged a meaningful look when Flynn casually plopped down on the chair.

He tried not to look at her, but Charlotte put her hand on his shoulder to get his attention. He turned around and smiled.

"Hello, Charlotte. Why, fancy seeing you here," he joked nervously.

He turned around and did his best to focus his attention on the doctor standing in front of a dry erase board at one end of the half circle of chairs. He was glad Charlotte was sitting next to him, glad that they were still on friendly terms, but he was also anxious about it. She just made him so messy. He remembered how humiliating it was to be caught with spunk all over his pants and he kind of shriveled up inside. He was very aware of her. She was to his right, and although he wasn't looking that entire side of his body felt warm.

Dr. Stephens, a tall fellow nearing retirement age who wore steel-rimmed glasses, facilitated this group. The whites of his eyes were cloudy, his skin mottled with gray liver spots, and he sported thinning snow-white hair. His nametag sat over a pocket protector in his breast pocket, which was filled with ink pens in blue, red and black. Flynn had only ever seen a pocket protector in the movies, where they were stereotypically associated with nerds, although none of Flynn's nerdy friends would be caught dead with one. He decided that Dr. Stephens confirmed his theory that pocket protectors were in fact, the revenant of some previous generation.

Before he spoke, he gestured for Mavis and Pam to come to the front of the room.

"There is a new three o'clock group on codependency," Pam announced. "Codependency is an issue that faces a lot of people with psychiatric disorders in dealing with family members, partners, and other interpersonal relationships. We started this group at the request of several patients, most of whom are not here currently, who wanted this kind of help in navigating relationships. This is especially helpful for people who have hereditary conditions and may be dealing with parents or children who also have it, or for people whose partners have psychiatric disabilities."

She said the last five words a bit more slowly, and looked right at Charlotte and Flynn while she was saying them. Charlotte glared at Pam defiantly, while Flynn swallowed and looked down at his feet.

"I'll pass the sheet around," Mavis added, "if any of you are interested, you can sign up. We'll pick it up after this group." She handed a clipboard with a pen tied to it to the patient seated nearest to her, and started passing it around.

"Just a reminder," Pam continued, "we are aware that sometimes people strike up friendships, or even start relationships in the hospital. We do not condone non-platonic involvement between the patients. That's not what this group is for: don't get the wrong idea. This is to help you when you get out of the hospital. The group will give you tools to deal with your relationships outside of an institutional setting."

Mavis coughed. "Right," she interrupted, "but the group is open to everyone. Often these problems follow people from relationship to relationship, so you would be talking about a pattern of behavior."

Flynn realized that neither of them thought the stain on his sheet was the result of a wet dream and nothing more. They both believed Charlotte and Flynn were creeping around having sex in the hospital. That was against the rules, since it was a distraction from the central purpose of seeking treatment.

The two nurses glanced sideways at each other. Both seemed to agree to quit lecturing while they were ahead. The subtext of their announcement was loud and clear: Flynn and Charlotte were breaking the rules. Pam and Mavis both wanted to make sure the couple understood that the staff knew about their infractions. The two nurses were of conflicting opinions about whether or not these patients should seek professional help to navigate their forbidden relationship.

Pam thought that the patients needed to focus on getting better, and not mess around with each other. Mavis thought that if they were going to mess around anyway, they would be better off getting some therapy to help them deal with any fallout from their little affair. Flynn agreed with Mavis. When the clipboard came around, he signed his name up for the group. "Thanks, ladies," Dr. Stephens said, nodding and waiting for them to get out the door. When they left, he turned to the group.

"So, today we will talk about experiences all of you face in one way or another, symptoms like voices you may hear and things you may see that aren't there, called hallucinations. Others of you may experience psychosis in the form of delusions, which can be accompanied by unpleasant feelings or paranoia. This group will touch upon some of the technical reasons we believe this may happen, such as chemical imbalances in the brain. But that is not our focus. Our focus in this group is to talk about what you've been experiencing. We will discuss some of the constructive techniques you have come up with for dealing with it that you might like to share with your fellow group members."

THE GIRL

Charlotte was a pretty girl, twenty-two years of age who still had the scars of an eight-year long battle with acne. When she was younger and her complexion at the height of its spottiness, she had a notion that acquiring some facial piercings might deflect attention from her blemishes. As a result, she had several.

She had three lip rings, an eyebrow piercing, a nose ring, three earrings and a plug on one side and five earrings on the other. Some of her fellow inmates at the hospital speculated as to whether or not she had other piercings somewhere below her neck.

She had been a chubby teenager, but she went through a growth spurt in the tenth grade. The hundred and sixty pounds that used to reside on a five-foot frame were redistributed over an additional five inches of height. She lost another thirty pounds before high school was over. These days she was moderately buxom with womanly hips and a shapely behind, and Flynn wasn't the only guy who thought she was hot.

She was intelligent, witty, and fun to be around, and socially sophisticated, but she was emotionally immature. She was moderately manipulative, but she preferred the truth to a lie. She was also almost cruelly pragmatic in her knowledge that the truth wasn't always the best course of action.

Although her driver's license listed her eye color as brown, they were a reddish hue between brown and amber. They were as close as human eyes could be to the orange eye color seen in the eyes of felines and other nocturnal creatures. If she trusted someone enough, she'd tell him or her she'd inherited her eye color from her father, who wasn't human.

TOUCH

Charlotte had chosen to interpret Flynn's earlier complaints as a request that she refrain from insinuating herself into his dreams. She told herself that it must have been disorienting for him, owing to the fact that he was entirely human.

She was only half human, so navigating the dark realms was not a real issue for her. Her mother was human, but her father was some sort of dream spirit. Humans weren't like somnali. They couldn't subsist on emotion and ectoplasm. She remembered reading that they required physical contact. Human babies would sicken and sometimes die if no one held them or touched them.

She also remembered that he was being told that he had a sickness that was a sort of detachment from reality. Human reality was the physical world. They'd just been in a group, talking about psychosis and the doctor had defined a psychotic break as a break from reality. She understood what Flynn was saying: being interacted with on the purely psychic plane was confusing and unsettling for him.

She decided that she had been a little selfish in neglecting his needs.

She spent the rest of the day trying to touch him in little ways that would not attract negative attention from the staff. She tapped him on the shoulder during group, and at lunch, she touched the top of his hand with her own when she asked him if he wanted an extra juice from the fridge. She paid careful attention to him, studying his reactions.

He decided that he enjoyed being touched by her. When she came back with the fruit punch juice box, he reached up to take it from her hand. She could feel his fingers grazing her wrist and the side of her palm when they exchanged the carton.

They were miniscule displays of affection, the kind that would be relatively safe and unlikely to be easily noticed by staff or other patients. They sat at the lunch table and waited for everyone else to get up and go, and when they were alone except for the golem-like Gary, Flynn leaned over and put his hand on her knee.

When he bent over the table, his shirt rode up in the back. Charlotte reached over to touch the small of his back where the skin was exposed, and Flynn inhaled sharply, remembering the night before when he was visited by an apparition that bore a striking resemblance to her, one that sat at his bedside and caressed him in that very spot until he fell asleep.

Although Gary's bulky frame partially shielded the fledgling couple from prying eyes, they were playing a dangerous game, touching publicly. Flynn sat up quickly, and pulled his shirt down. He was bashful and flustered, but smiling appreciatively.

Charlotte decided she'd made the right move.

She was glad for it, but she was also a little frustrated. The human way of going about courtship seemed so incredibly complicated and terribly slow.

VISITATION

Charlotte was surprised to receive a visitor just after lunch. Flynn was equally surprised to learn that Charlotte was not her first name.

"Happiness Metaxas?" the new nurse shouted into the recreation room, checking to see who answered since she didn't recognize all of the patients the way Pam, Bill, or Mavis would have.

Charlotte looked up immediately and glowered in her general direction. "No one calls me that," she responded. "I go by my middle name, Charlotte. Look at the chart."

"I see," the new nurse said. Her nametag declared that she was Sarah G, probably in deference to another Sarah that worked somewhere on the ward. "Well, you have a visitor, Miss Metaxas."

She was surprised. She hadn't had a visitor in the close to two weeks she'd been hospitalized, and although it hadn't been confirmed yet, she suspected she would be released when her fourteen-day hold expired tomorrow. She had a pretty good idea who the visitor would be, though. Only one person knew where she was or would bother to come, and that was her mother.

Sarah G. escorted Maribelle Metaxas into the now-empty lunchroom. There, Maribelle's daughter Happiness Charlotte Metaxas joined her at one of the round tables. They would share some juice, cups of flavored gelatin, and conversation.

"It's too late for decaf," Charlotte said pointedly, before the nurse left. "I can offer you apple juice, orange juice, or milk."

"We can get some coffee for your mother if you like," Sarah said helpfully.

"That would be wonderful," Maribelle answered. "And some for my daughter, if you don't mind."

"She's not allowed to have any after 10:00 A.M," Sarah countered.

"Well fine, then," Charlotte's mother said, deciding that she would just give her coffee to the girl when the nurses weren't looking. She smiled and waited for the woman to leave.

The moment they were alone, she jabbed Charlotte in the shoulder and chided her. "Charlie, what is going on with you? The staff expressed some concerns about whatever you think you're doing with that boy in the other room."

Charlotte rolled her eyes. Only her mom and her old high school friends still called her by her childhood nickname Charlie. She feigned ignorance about Flynn. "I don't know what you're talking about. What boy?"

"The guy who was staring at you with those sad puppy dog eyes when I was by the door, waiting for Nurse Sarah there to go fetch you out. He's a skinny kid, Asian or Eurasian, maybe Pacific Islander. He's wearing a Wolverine t-shirt that's two sizes too small, and he has emo hair."

"Mom! He does not have emo hair," Charlotte countered.

"Yea okay so you do know what guy I am talking about," her mom confirmed, snapping her fingers. "You suck at lying."

"I like a guy," Charlotte sighed, "So that's not Earth-shattering news or anything. What's the big deal?"

Her mother smiled broadly. "Wow. And he's human, isn't he?"

"Yes," Charlotte replied, holding her face in her hands. "He is very human."

"That's great!" Maribelle said hopefully. "I mean... I didn't think you liked human boys. But uhm... well yes, they don't want you to date in here so maybe you should give him your number, or email, or whatever young people are doing these days."

The women looked up just in time to see Sarah G. approaching with the coffee.

"Sorry it took so long," Sarah said cheerfully. "I had to get it from the employee's lounge; I guess that there is no coffee at all around here this time of day. It was getting a little cold, so I put it in the microwave."

"You are so kind," Maribelle said convivially. "I was just wondering if it would be okay for me to go in the T.V. room with my daughter and play a little Scrabble."

Maribelle had very little interest in playing Scrabble, but she was quite interested in meeting this young man. Up until now, Charlotte had only been romantically tied to somnali, shunning her human heritage and everything associated with it. A human suitor opened up new possibilities. If this worked out, one day Maribelle might have a grandchild. Here, on the physical plane. Not some dream child she would never be able to see, or hold, or take to the park.

She was forty-nine years old and with no other children and menopause right around the corner, this idea held a strong appeal for Maribelle. The thought that there might be a human grandchild, or at any rate a mostly human one. Such a grandchild would be even more human than Charlotte. Charlotte was capable of tenderness and concern for others in a way her somnali brethren were not, even if it wasn't her default setting. If they had a child, it would be even more human. That made Maribelle very happy. She definitely wanted to meet this young man, and do whatever she could do to be supportive of the budding relationship.

"That would be fine," Sarah said. "She has group at three, but you can stay until then. There is another visiting period for three hours after dinner, six to nine. You can get something to eat while she's in group and then come back for the second round of visits."

SCRABBLE

Scrabble can be a four-player game, but in the recreation room, it was most often played with two. Charlotte invited a woman named Nancy from today's group to join them, so it would be less obvious that this was a set-up for her mom to come check out Flynn.

Flynn understood this, and despite his doubts about Charlotte, he was on his best behavior. He liked her and enjoyed her company, and beyond that, he was a desperately lonely person. He'd had few friends and fewer romances since his breakdown in college. Danny had been his only friend after his freshman year, everyone else distancing from him after he spun out of control in public. The sickness took its toll on his studies as well. It took him four years to earn a two-year degree, and their differences in academic progress, above anything, eventually separated the two best friends.

Nancy joining in on the game pleased the staff to no end, not just because it made "inappropriate" contact between Flynn and Charlotte less likely, but also because Nancy was new and had no one to socialize with. They were also happy to see Nancy making some new friends. They wanted the patients to be friendly with each other; they just didn't want them dating one another.

Charlotte sat directly across from Nancy, a pleasant woman in her late thirties with an extreme interest in cats. Nancy was wearing an oversized t-shirt with an enormous tabby's face on it. The way the cat's eyes stared out from over her breasts was slightly off-putting. Nancy was a big girl with a big chest, and although the bagginess of the shirt helped a bit, the kitten on the shirt looked kind of bulgy-eyed.

They each pulled a tile from the pile in the middle, and turned it over to see who would go first.

"Mom wins," Charlotte said, casually placing her hand on Flynn's knee when no one was looking. Flynn put his hand over the top of her hand and squeezed it, which she found very reassuring. Maybe this could work. She just had to be careful.

Maribelle caught the exchange, although Nancy, deep in the throes of a tale she was telling about her new kittens, and what a big surprise they were, was completely oblivious.

"That's great!" Nancy said. "So, yea, back to what I was saying… she was a feral living in my yard, only six months old, so when I trapped and rescued her, it didn't occur to me that she was already pregnant. I was on my way to the clinic to get her spayed when she started popping out kittens in the cat carrier right there in the back of my car. Of course, I didn't know she was in labor, I figured she was howling like that because she hated being cooped up in a cage or maybe that she was upset by the motion of the car. Can you imagine my surprise when I opened the carrier and three kittens crawled out?"

"I love cats, too," Maribelle said kindly. She wasn't lying. She had two geriatric Siamese at home who were of an age where they were increasingly in need of medical care. She didn't have any cat health insurance – if there was such a thing – and over the past two years, the girls had cost her as much money as purchasing an economy car. Fortunately, she could afford it.

She loved cats, but her mind was elsewhere. She was reminded of her own bad experiences with Charlotte's father, and worrying that her child might have picked up too many of her sire's non-human tendencies. Like Brash, Charlotte could be abrasive and cruel. Maribelle noticed that Charlie was plying the boy with affectionate gestures in a way that reminded her of a high school boy trying to get into his virgin girlfriend's panties. In either of these cases, it was not definitive evidence of a lack of affection. Someone could care about someone and be unfortunately greedy and self-serving at the same time, especially if that someone was emotionally immature.

And how could Charlotte possibly be emotionally mature? Half of her genetic material came from a creature that did not experience emotions as humans did, but instead fed off the emotions of others. Maribelle counted herself lucky that her daughter wasn't an utter psychopath. Her father, Brash, certainly was. She tried to forgive herself for her own foolishness in agreeing to the pairing. It was her youthful indiscretion and ill-advised interest in the bad boy types that took her down that path.

"PATH," she spelled out on the board.

Conversely, Maribelle thought, what if things got serious? What if Charlotte was too tenderhearted to complete the Ritual of Binding? Could she bear to subject the boy to all of the suffering he must willingly endure?

Brash was cruel, but at least he was able to protect Maribelle from certain parasites hailing from the darker realms that she and others like herself tended to attract. Even now, he protected her for the sake of their daughter, his only corporeal child.

Nancy was up next. She added four tiles to the letter "A" to spell out her ominous five-letter word, "BRASH." Maribelle frowned. The somnali rarely interfered with objects and actions on the physical plane when doing so involved people who were wide awake. Most of their control over the physical bodies of others occurred during sleep, often involving sleepwalking.

As far as she could tell, Nancy seemed alert but she and the other patients were on medications with sedative side effects that would make them more vulnerable to somnali. Maribelle had already been touched by the somnali, and Charlotte contained somnali genetic material. If Charlie found this boy attractive, them other dream entities probably would as well. Maribelle might be paranoid, but she could not rule out the possibility Nancy's actions were being controlled and that they were being spied on.

Flynn was next. "Woo! Seven letter bonus!" he shouted.

Charlotte and Maribelle were both taken aback when they saw the five-letter word he constructed from the B in BRASH, "BINDING." Flynn himself was not aware of its significance.

Charlotte shook her head, and looked at Flynn, and then looked at her mother. Charlie hadn't told her mother that she'd already started the Ritual of Binding. She had also taken great liberties with Flynn by being deceptively, unethically vague when informing Flynn of what they were doing. She told him that it would protect him from Mercy, which was a half-truth. The protection was only temporary if the ritual remained incomplete.

Charlotte also told him that it would make him her pet, which was a gross oversimplification. He was still blissfully innocent of knowing what the implications of the Ritual were, and what would be demanded from him in order to complete it.

It seemed, however, that Charlotte's father knew, and he was either warning her, or snitching to her mother, or both.

"I should... uh, call dad," Charlotte told Maribelle. "Let him know how I've been doing, what I've been up to. It's been a while since we've spoken."

"Indeed," Maribelle agreed. "Although we are divorced, you know your father and I both care about you very deeply. In fact, your father has been trying to call me lately, but I've been refusing to take his calls. Maybe I should speak to him. He's probably just worried about you."

Charlie sighed deeply. The last thing she wanted or needed was a parental intervention. She noted the tiles she had and the hand she could play. It wasn't the worst possibility. Working back from the H in PATH, she spelled the word HAPPY.

That was Charlotte, a fucking glowing ball of happiness.

"Oh, I meant to tell you something." Maribelle said. "Your doctor told me he thinks you're going to be released tomorrow. He asked if I could pick you up."

"You're leaving?" Flynn nearly shouted. He looked very alarmed.

Nancy took no notice of the outburst. She was calmly adding four letters to the "Y" at the end of HAPPY to spell out "MERCY." "Hah!" she yelped. "Flynn might be ahead now, but I'll beat him. I'm in it to win it! Check me out! Triple word score!"

Maribelle furrowed her brow. Apparently, the young man had already attracted negative attention from among the somnali, and Mercy was a somnali of a brutal and capricious nature. Worse, she was one of Brash's dozens of children with other somnali, and when it came to her flesh and blood sibling Charlotte, the child of nightmares had a raging case of sibling rivalry.

Flynn looked like he had been slapped in the face.

"Hey, don't look so glum," Nancy consoled. "It's only a game."

"He's bummed out because I'm leaving tomorrow," Charlotte explained. "Hold up, I'll give you my number." She reached over to the art supplies and wrote her information down on a piece of white drawing paper with a big crayon.

Maribelle fished something out of the breast pocket of her natty little pantsuit. "Here's my card, young man. You can also reach my daughter through me, if you need to."

"Wow, it's nice you're friends," Nancy said dolefully.

"I'm sure we'll all be friends, Nancy," Charlotte said, patting the cat lady's hand. "Give her a card, why don't you mom? We can hang out sometime when we are all out."

Maribelle smiled indulgently. "You should add me on Facebook," she told Nancy. "I'm a member of several cat fancy groups, and you can never have too many cute kitten pictures on your wall, am I right?"

"Yeah, totally!" Nancy agreed, taking the card.

Charlie and Nancy never did become friends. Nancy had much more in common with Maribelle. The friendship initially budded over the Internet, but it still managed to develop real substance. Three weeks from now, the two women would be playing Scrabble online on a regular basis. The online friendship wouldn't be one sided, either. Nancy would be very supportive when Maribelle's geezer meezers, sweet girls named Emily and Anne, started to experience declining health in their final months. The cats were only four years younger than her daughter, and she was very attached to them.

Charlotte, Emily and Anne were all named after the Bronte sisters. Charlotte was also named after the book *Charlotte's Web* and the Cure song *Charlotte Sometimes*. Maribelle was a great fan of the name. She would have given Charlie the first name Charlotte, but the unfortunate title Happiness was the chosen by her father, who insisted on naming her for some sort of emotional characteristic, and already had daughters named Mercy and Sympathy.

Two months from now, when Emily and Anne passed on within two months of each other, Nancy would come and attend their feline funerals. Afterward, Nancy would invite Maribelle to adopt a cat from the rescue she volunteered for. Processing the grief from her loss, Maribelle would throw herself into the cat rescue's affairs, providing them with much-needed expertise for their advertising campaign. Cats were the reason a forty-nine year old well-to-do advertising executive would become friends with a thirty-eight year old military veteran. Her time in active service left Nancy diagnosed with an anxiety disorder. She used her V.A. mortgage loan to buy a house, currently full of cats. She rented a room to her college bound niece. She held down a part time job as a mall security guard.

But this story is not about Nancy or kittens. It is about a battered ragdoll named Flynn and a contagious condition called Happiness.

FIRST INTERMISSION

Somnus was beginning to grow desperate. He was not allowed to inform Happiness of her role in the scheme of things. He could not let her know that the survival of her father and all of her sisters depended upon her choices. Further, he was beginning to be glad that she did not know. The relationship between Happiness and Mercy was so strained that he wondered if Happy would just suicide the whole mission to wipe out her sister. She wasn't any closer to her other siblings, and her relationship with Brash, her overbearing father, was strained.

If the relationship she had with her family couldn't motivate her, then Somnus would have to hedge his bets another way.

That is why he had called upon an old friend for a favor. Perhaps more than a friend, for some might say he was an uncle, or a brother.

Eros was his Greek name, but the Romans knew him as Cupid. He was the god of love. He had the unique condition of having been born twice. The first time he was born was not long after Nyx was spat out of the primordial void that was Chaos. Nyx herself laid the egg that the first incarnation of Eros was born from.

His second birth was necessitated by the shift from asexual to sexual production. It was a shift he bought about himself when he established this way of mating in pairs. He was later reborn through to Aphrodite in this very way, sexual reproduction. There were doubts about who was his father.

In this way, Eros was and yet was not Somnus' brother. Some rumors held that Eros was even older than Nyx herself, but Eros denied them. In fact, his desire to conceal his true origins and cloak himself in humbler ones is what led to Somnus' favor. In a haze of sleep and hypnosis, Somnus convinced all of creation that there were three gods named Eros – the three Erotes.

In this way, Eros was freed from the heavy burden of propriety that forced all of the primordial gods to be as dignified as Nyx herself. He was allowed to become the playful, mischievous imp that would one day be known the world over as Cupid.

"Eros," he said to his old friend, "do you think it is possible? Do you think that you can make her love this boy?"

"Oh, that I can do quite easily," he said, leaning back in Somnus' black cloud easy chair. "What I cannot do is to give her the good sense to protect that love. Do you know how foolish young lovers can be? Haven't you read Romeo and Juliet? Don't you remember Orpheus? What makes you think that love will save him?"

"I can't be sure," Somnus glumly admitted. "But it's the only chance I've got. Clearly, she cares something for the boy. She saved him from Mercy."

"At your suggestion," Eros reminded him pointedly. "You gave it your best shot, old chum, but let's face it. You would never be able to do my job. You are the king of hypnosis, though, aren't you? But I suppose you are afraid your little spell will wear off and she'll join her sisters in feasting upon his bones."

Somnus wailed. "Please, you must make her love him. You must."

"Fine," Eros agreed, "but if this all goes somehow terribly wrong, don't blame me. It's your funeral."

Then Eros left, and Somnus returned to quietly observing the activities of his children and grandchildren. Somnus had a thousand sons. If the line of Brash were extinguished, his many other progeny would continue on.

Brash and his kids, they never called. They never wrote. It was a surprise that Somnus even cared about them, but like any grandparent, he was proud. Now that his company was gone, he waved his hand over his cave walls and over a dozen monitors popped up showing the activities of Brash and his children.

Act II: The Quality of Mercy

Daddy Issues

  Charlotte had only been out of the hospital for two days when her father dropped by for a visit. She was quite relieved that he did not arrive in his physical form. It took a great deal of blood and human suffering for Brash or any of his pure somnali children to cross over into the material world, even for a short time because his line was cursed. This difficulty at traversing planes of existence was the reason only one of Brash's thirteen living children was born in the flesh. Most of his children were girls, but he had two sons.

  All of his sons and daughters were born in the dream realm, either to somnali women, or to human women with whom the relationship had been consummated in dreams, the so-called "dream children."

  Human men spawned dream children on a regular basis, having erotic dreams and then going on with their lives as though nothing happened. For human woman, the experience was a bit more disturbing, as they would have repeated dreams of pregnancy, and then afterward gave birth to a child they would never see or know. Sometimes the mothers of dream children had phantom pregnancies in the material world, other times they were nearly as unaffected by the experience as men.

  Dream children such as Mercy lived forever unless they were either intentionally destroyed or starved to death. Charlotte's big sister was more than three hundred fifty years old.

  But the somnali were not content to remain in the world of dreams. They sought to enter and dominate the fleshly realm occupied by mortals. In order to do so, they required demisomnali such as Charlotte.

It was very difficult for a cursed somnali to spill human life in the physical world. For the most part, they could only drain and exhaust people, or interfere with their mental wellbeing. Tormented thoroughly enough, a human might take his or her own life. This was not the case with demisomnali who could traverse the veil with ease. They could, and often did, sacrifice large numbers of humans in order to create a temporary portal into the human world for creatures like Brash.

Because their bodies were made of flesh and bone, they could live in the human world and influence its politics, sometimes on a global scale. The more ambitious among them started large and bloody wars. Those who were equally motivated but less strategically gifted became serial killers or mass murderers. The resulting slaughter allowed even more cursed somnali to enter the earthly world and impregnate its women.

The demisomnali were told that a high body count would assure them an afterlife in the Demos Oneiroi. Charlotte thought it was just a clever myth designed to turn the half-breeds into suicide bombers.

There was always a fly in the ointment. Some of the demisomnali were infected with human emotions, like Happiness. They could not be relied upon to willingly assume their roles because they were burdened by sympathies, affections, and something called a conscience.

Brash wasn't happy about his daughter's infirmities, but Happiness – or Charlotte, as she liked to be called – was his only living flesh-and-blood child. Her conception was difficult, and she could not easily be replaced. On the day that Charlotte was conceived, he performed a great blood ritual called The Sacrifice of the Innocents.

On that day he caused seventeen women within a five-mile radius to miscarry. It took careful planning. For one thing, he spent two years poisoning the mind of a single obstetrics nurse, an Angel of Mercy killer. Once tipped over the edge, this already disturbed man was easily manipulated. He murdered three pregnant women in the same hospital ward, killing their babies with them. He caused two other mothers to miscarry during failed attempts on their lives.

The other twelve women were each dispatched individually. One of them was hit by a car driven by a man who fell asleep at the wheel after Mercy deprived him of sleep for the brunt of six months. Another woman attempted suicide after four months of terrifying, unending nightmares.

Brash was not going to let all that hard work go to waste, so he never bothered to have Charlotte killed, or to punish her in any way. His leniency was the reason why Mercy, formerly his favorite, hated the girl so much.

If he were mortal, those two would be the death of him.

He was speaking with his youngest child in a phantom zone assembled in the back of her mind that she liked to call "The Recreation Room". Charlotte had set it up to look like the television room at the psych ward, the one where Brash had controlled Nancy during a game of Scrabble.

"I don't know why you think it is fun to have me visit you in a virtual psych ward," Brash complained.

"If you were any kind of father," Charlotte countered, "you'd come visit me when I was locked up in the psych ward. I only have to go there because of you, and the horrible dreams you gave me all through adolescence when you kept trying to convince me to go on a killing spree at my high school."

"You can't blame a father for trying," Brash said. "Well, that never happened, but I hear you might redeem yourself, make me a grandfather. You're young and healthy. You could spawn a number of mortal grandchildren for me to help justify your existence and my patience with you thus far."

"So that's why you finally visited me in the hospital," Charlotte surmised. "You're looking forward to some meat grandkids. Nice."

"They could be easier to manipulate than you are," Brash admitted. "Should there be more than one child, even better. The chance that at least one will be either pure evil or just very gullible will go up. No matter what they do, by their very existence, my hold on the mortal world is strengthened. They'll be easier to possess than other mortals if I need a vessel… you know, like that Nancy, a very distant relation to your long dead brother."

"What was that trick with Nancy all about?" Charlotte asked.

"I wanted to warn you to beware of Mercy," Brash explained. "I told her to give you the boy. Do you like your little present?"

"Present?" Charlotte inquired.

"I thought you might like him, that's all. In fact, my father Somnus suggested it. He knows that I want earthly grandchildren," Brash shrugged. "The human boy seemed like your type. He's such a tender morsel. I told Mercy to give you a gift. But your sister claims that you're just playing at the ritual. She says you will never have a child with him. She says you merely marked the boy because you believed you were stealing him away from her. She's rather possessive. She said if you don't follow through, she wants her toy back."

"He's not hers," Charlotte argued, "he's mine now. I fed him and consumed him as required for the Ritual of Marking, and I will complete the Ritual of Binding as required."

"But the ritual must be completed within a year," Brash warned. "Not just the Ritual of Binding, one of the ritual for procreation. Either the Slaughter of the Innocents, or the Feast of Tears, it's up to you. Otherwise, you may lose your consort. You enjoy him, don't you?"

"Really, father?" Charlotte protested. "Consort? Isn't that a woman?"

"No not necessarily," Brash said, "and anyway, I'm over five thousand years old. I'm not going to change my language just to suit you. You're the first child of the flesh I've had in four hundred years, and you're just as much a pain in the ass as the last. You will perform the ritual. You will use the boy the way he was intended to be used, or else there will be consequences."

"What consequences?" Charlotte challenged, not believing for a moment that her father would hurt her.

"Of course I would never kill you," Brash admitted. "You are precious to me, a valuable commodity not to be so easily squandered. Mercy insists that I punish you in some way. In fact, she asked that I force you to watch as she repeatedly skins your mother alive in the dark realms until Maribelle is so consumed with pain and fear that she kills herself upon waking."

"Mother!" Charlotte screamed. She was horrified. She loved her mother. "But I thought you were supposed to protect her. How could you?"

Her father sighed. "I could not," he said pointedly. "She is bound to me, and even though I don't have feelings for her, or feelings at all, for that matter, I am obligated to keep my promise. I must protect her for the rest of her natural life, and unnatural, I suppose, if such a thing becomes possible which, with this newfangled human science, you never know."

"Very funny, Dad," Charlotte replied. It wasn't all that funny, but at least he wasn't discussing torturing and murdering her mother.

"So I told her that if you don't complete the ritual as required, she can have the boy back, and I will make you watch as Mercy systematically destroys him in the most horrible ways she can cook up with her substantial imagination. She might also try to get a few of your near and dear mentally unstable friends to commit suicide in especially painful and gruesome manners."

"That's fucked up," Charlotte said. "Get the fuck out of my head, Dad."

She snapped her fingers, and he was gone. Charlotte possessed control over the bridge between dreams and the waking world that her father and those like him would never possess. She was fully awake now, sitting up on the couch in her mother's living room. One of mom's cats, Emily, was carefully kneading a spot on the blanket just below her knees.

She smiled and stroked the cat between the ears.

Charlotte had her own tiny, seedy apartment not five miles away. Maribelle had not one, but two guest rooms now that her only child was living on her own. Charlie slept on the couch not out of economic necessity, but because it felt safer than anywhere else. She didn't want to be home by herself with everything that was going on. She didn't even want to be locked away in some guest room. She just wanted to plop down in front of the television with her mother's two ancient felines.

The Dream

Charlotte was reluctant to visit Flynn on the ethereal plane after he'd expressly requested that she refrain from doing so. However, her options for contacting him in any other way were severely limited. The hospital rules stated that former patients could not return for visits, call or write to other patients within a thirty-day period of being released.

Of course, there was no rule against Charlotte's mother writing to Flynn, and so Maribelle Metaxas took on the role of intermediary, letting him know how Charlotte was doing, and asking after his wellbeing for her daughter's benefit, behavior that was not disallowed. It was during one of these exchanges that she mentioned that Charlotte was looking forward to seeing him and speaking to him again, and he wrote back that he was looking forward to seeing her, too, as soon as it was possible. He said that he didn't think he would get out for another week and a half, and he wished that he might be able to see or speak to her sooner than that. She decided to take a chance and hope that he was giving her permission to visit him while he was sleeping.

Entering a dream he was already in the process of having was a little different than creating a dream from scratch. She would not be able to determine the setting for this dream, or at what point in the dreaming she might enter it.

Flynn was dreaming about college again, his glory days, back before he had a nervous breakdown and his whole world fell apart. Charlotte simply materialized, standing at the edge of a track that encircled the interior of a college football stadium. She was beginning to notice the theme here, these dreams he had of returning to a time before his symptoms became noticeable and his family and friends grew increasingly distant.

These were the happier times before his dreams were crushed, and he was left broken and unstable. He was relegated to a series of temporary clerical, sales, and administrative jobs for staffing agencies. He would probably be laid off from the job he had now while he was here in the hospital. It was easy to get rid of a temp because the jobs, by their very nature, were not meant to last. Firing him for being hospitalized would have violated the Americans with Disabilities Act. The firm he worked for could get around it by eliminating his position instead.

In college, he had been studying multimedia design hoping to work in the field of game development. He was never much of a programmer but he was a talented artist and he hoped to spend the rest of his life creating backgrounds for games. He loved the landscapes, depictions of battlegrounds where historical conflicts had taken place, or complete fictionalized environments for science fiction or fantasy games. He even got jobs in game testing, starting with an internship when he was only sixteen. He got paying gigs later, which he took during summer when he didn't have classes.

His future seemed bright at the age of nineteen but by the time he was twenty-two he would be counting himself lucky to complete a more generalized Liberal Arts AA without transfer. It would take him four years to get that two-year degree. He wouldn't get any decent work after he graduation. Still, his college days – even the ones that were marred by occasional hospitalizations – were the best in his life.

In the dream, he was jogging on the track that encircled the football field at his college. It was the last spring semester he there before transferring to university. It was a glorious time when Flynn had just made his awkward debut on the nightclub scene at the age of twenty-one. His best friend Danny had been going to clubs for five years, thanks to his fake ID. He laughed at Flynn's inexperience and his skinny body. Flynn started trying to get in shape, hoping to pick up girls more easily.

This was the scene Charlotte walked into.

The moment he recognized her, he snapped out of his reverie.

"Charlotte!" he shouted out. "Wow… you're here! I'm so glad to see you. I missed you so much."

He raced across the field and did not slow down until he was standing two feet in front of her. He threw his arms around her shoulders and crushed her body against his. He wore a tank top. His skin was hot and sticky. He smelled of grass and sweat and some heinous body spray that was supposed to attract women like flies. Charlotte personally found it repugnant.

His enthusiasm was contagious. She held him tightly, despite the potent cologne.

"You smell like a boy's locker room," she complained, rubbing her face against his chest. The affectionate gesture made him giddy. He hadn't had a girl touch him that way in years. He pulled her even tighter against him.

"Wow," he grinned. "You must really like me, then. You're totally ignoring my B.O, and man perfume stench. The commercials said it would cause girls to flock around me, but in reality it mostly seemed to attract mosquitoes and horseflies."

"So you know you're dreaming," Charlotte surmised.

"I do," he nodded.

She took his hand and led him off the field. "Let's go sit in the bleachers. We need to talk."

"Just talk?" he teased. "That will be different. It's because of the body spray, isn't it?"

"Hah! If only things were that simple." She laughed. Then she leaned into him and wrapped her left arm around his waist as they were walking. He looked down at her, pleasantly surprised.

"Everything feels so real," Flynn said.

"I know," Charlotte confessed. "It's because we've already started the Rite of Binding."

"We started the rite of what?" Flynn asked. He looked confused. Charlotte shook her head and kept walking. It was weird for him, traveling in real time in a dream. He kept expecting them to just be there.

Finally, they arrived. Charlotte sat down and patted the bench next to her, gesturing for him to do the same. He gave her an inquisitive look.

"Trust me, you're going to want to sit down for this," she said. She took one of his hands in both of hers. Flynn found the gesture disturbing. His uncle was a marine who had died in the Persian Gulf. That was the way his relatives patted his aunt's hand at the funeral.

This couldn't be anything good.

"So, I haven't been entirely honest with you," Charlotte began.

Flynn sucked his breath in. It made a whistling noise between his teeth. He felt like he was bracing himself for a punch in the gut or a slap in the face. He remembered the dream where Tamara told him he trusted too easily, and how worried he was the next day.

"Remember how I told you that drinking that stuff in the cup would let me protect you," she continued. "You know, from people like me. Not people, but dream spirits. I'm half human, so I mean creatures like the ones on my father's side of the family."

"Did you lie?" he asked pointedly.

"No, I didn't lie exactly. That was true. I just might have left some crucial information out, that's all," she rambled. "Like yeah, remember how I said you'd be something like a pet?"

"That was charming," he said sarcastically.

"Wasn't it, though?" she groaned. "And that liquid was my ectoplasm which is my essence. I suppose you would consider to be a bodily fluid."

"Okay," he said. "So you fed me your bodily fluids. Well, I guess that wouldn't be the first time I swallowed a woman's bodily fluids and to be honest I hope won't be the last. Are you trying to tell me that I caught some kind of disease?"

"Do you think I'm a disease?" she asked.

"No," he said.

"Then, no," she continued. "And then, the next time, you recall, I asked to taste you, and you let me, so I drank your blood?"

"I'll never forget it," he said. He felt himself blush a little.

"So, that was your essence on this plane," she explained. "You don't have ectoplasm like I do because you're a living human being. I understand that you will have it after you die, but I've never met a dead human spirit that I know of. But I digress. Sorry, I'm nervous. That was the second part of the ritual, for me to consume your essence."

"Okay, fine," he said. "What is this ritual for, and what does it mean to us?"

"Weeeeellll..." she said hesitantly, "the closest I could come up with in human terms is a courtship ritual. Maybe like a dowry tradition, except for instead of exchanging money and cattle, we exchange emotions, experiences, and bodily fluids."

Flynn jerked back and pulled his hand away from hers.

"Whoa, wait a minute," he stammered. "So you're trying to tell me that, like, you're trying to marry me? I... wow, damn. I think that this is rather sudden. I mean this is way too fast. I just met you last week, we barely know each other, so what the fuck? Fuck. Fuck."

Charlotte sighed. "It's not like that. Well, not exactly."

"What do you mean not exactly?" he asked. He looked very alarmed. "Shit... what do you mean?"

"I wanted to keep Mercy's hands off you so I had to formally declare my intentions towards you," she defended. "People like you attract these dream spirits. Nowadays they call it psychosis, but in the past they might have said you were psychically sensitive, or some kind of shaman. Regardless of what you choose to call it, you attract spirits just like my mother did. The only way a somnali can protect a mortal from other somnali is to declare an intention to court exclusively for a year."

"For a year," he repeated slowly. "Okay... so not marriage, or anything. Just a year, and then we can see if we want to stay together or whatever?"

"Up to a year," she explained. "The ritual protects you for up to a year, as long as we complete the steps in the ritual. After that... well, after that, the courtship has to end one way or the other."

"One way meaning we break up," he guessed. "And what is the other?"

"You can pledge yourself to me as my consort," she said. "But can I explain to you what that means and what the implications are at another time?"

"Sure," he said. "I'm starting to get a headache."

"Great," she responded, shaking her head. "You think about what I've said, and I'll talk to you later, okay?"

"Okay," he said. "In person, when I get out, alright?"

"It's a date," she said.

He laughed. "Ha! Yes, a date. I haven't heard that word in a while. It almost sounds kind of old fashioned. But I guess that's what it is."

Charlotte turned to go.

"Wait," Flynn said quickly. "I wanted to give you something before you go."

He took her in his arms and kissed her passionately. They wouldn't see each other again for a week and he wanted to remember everything. How she smelled, the way her skin felt against his, and how she tasted. More importantly, he wanted to make sure that she knew how he felt about her.

"I can't wait to do that in person," he said, touching her hair. She smiled.

He watched her as she turned and walked away.

SISTERS

Denizens of the dark realms had no need for human form or architecture, but eons of interacting with humans and weaving in and out of the dreams of men had influenced the culture of the somnali. Mercy's home did not have stairs or elevators, and was not entered using doors. It drifted with no perceivable pattern through the dark space, and so it had no address. Although it had the illusion of dimension, it had no permanent location, and could properly be viewed as a vehicle. One might say she had a mobile home.

The outside of her traveling castle didn't have any entryways. The interior contained more doors and staircases that led to nowhere than the Winchester Mystery House. It was a maze of sorts, designed to keep visitors from the mortal realm from escaping.

Today, she received a visitor who was just as immortal as she was.

"Hello, Sympathy," she said. Mercy did not turn around to look at her, because there was no need to. She could see, but she didn't actually have eyes. She had the illusion of eyes. She could actually see Sympathy with any part of her expansive being.

As it happened Mercy was in a human form at the moment as a red haired girl with whom Flynn had been acquainted. She was sitting in front of a table, staring into a hamster cage that was placed in the middle of the square structure.

"Did our sister enjoy your gift?" Sympathy asked.

"Hah!" Mercy answered. "She enjoyed it, alright. In fact, she can't seem to keep her hands off it. She doesn't know it was a gift. She thinks she stole one of her big sister's playthings. She's just so excited about it, having wrested it away from me. She thinks she got away with something. She doesn't realize that my little toy was used up, broken. I didn't want it anymore anyway."

"That's not what father says," Sympathy countered. "He says that you've been raising hell over it, demanding that the pretty little thing be returned to you immediately."

"Would Happiness even want it if she did not believe it was valuable, and highly prized by someone else?" Mercy asked. "Has she ever shown interest in a human before?"

"Charlotte does not like being called Happiness," Sympathy observed. Then suddenly, she noticed the hamster cage in the middle of Mercy's table. "What do you have in there?" she asked, leaning over it. There were two tiny figures curled up in the woodchips at the bottom of the cage. Sympathy leaned back and squeezed her tentacles together, chortling with delight.

"They are tiny clay golems!" she squealed. "Oh ooh look at them! They are just adorable." The figures in the cage were like little dolls, perfect replicas of Flynn and Charlotte, each wearing a diminutive hospital gown. The creatures were about six inches tall, but they were to scale so the Charlotte model was shorter. They appeared to be statuettes until the one that resembled Flynn raised its head and put both hands over its ears in response to Sympathy's shrieks of delight.

"They are not made of only clay, Mercy explained. "They are also made of hair, dust, blood, tears, and refracted emotion. I stole some of each of their essences to create these scale models. The little creatures aren't alive in the same way as a human being is, but are simple reflections, mirrors if you will. I use these effigies for intelligence, to help me divine the extent of the emotional connection between the two little lovebirds in real life."

"Ew, they are just lying there in the place they poop and pee in," Sympathy squalled. She was a silly and juvenile creature, despite her nine hundred and fifty two years of existence.

"How adolescent of you," Mercy countered, shaking her head. "They are mere simulations, like the plastic dolls that human children play with. As such, they have no need to consume food or water, so they do not urinate or defecate. I had no need for them to be anatomically correct, so they aren't. But let me assuage your clear curiosity."

When she opened the door in the side of the cage and fished out the little replica of Flynn, the female golem stood up and ran to the side of the cage, where it stood, pressing its palms against the plastic, searching for its partner. Mercy sat the male doll in the palm of her hand and held it up close to Sympathy's face, which presently consisted of a deep pit of a mouth lined with multiple rows of razor-sharp teeth surrounded by a series of eight bulbous, gelatinous eyes.

"Ooh," Sympathy cooed appreciatively. "Thank you."

The little man tried to pull away as a series of microscopic, hair like tentacles extended from along the edges of Sympathy's mouth, where lips would have been if she had any. Mercy laughed when her sister used some of the appendages to hold him down, while pulling his clothes off with others.

Once she removed its pants, she could see that the golem was without any genitalia, possessing a featureless mound of mannequin-like crotch instead. Its hairless body had no bellybutton or nipples, and when Sympathy held it close enough to look at its fingers, she noticed it didn't have fingernails, either – just indentations to suggest where nails might have been.

"Well, that's no fun!" Sympathy complained. "Why couldn't you have given him a little pecker and a tiny belly button? He doesn't even have a proper butt crack, just a little line. It looks really creepy naked."

The tiny creature did not seem offended. It sat on the edge of Mercy's hand kicking its feet in the air. Mercy grasped it by the waist, using the index finger and thumb of her opposing hand to set it gently back inside its the cage. She picked up its torn pajamas afterward. All of the buttons were missing and the pants had a tear in the back.

"Well, these are ruined now." Mercy said, shaking her illusionary red locks. "And I doubt they want to see you naked, either, Symp."

Sympathy was back to observing the two caged creatures, leaning over the cage to get a better look at them. The suckers on her bulbous face were attaching to the plastic, leaving slimy snail trails in their wake, and one of her bulging eye bumps stretched out as it slid against the wall.

There were many shapes either of them could assume, none of them being their true form, which was amorphous to other dream denizens and unknowable to human beings. Sympathy had been on a tentacle kick since the days of H.P. Lovecraft. She delighted in them, and wore them the way fashion conscious humans might develop a taste for whatever happened to be in season – shoulder pads in the eighties or polka dots in the fifties. The alien creature flicks of the fifties and repositories of tentacle monster hentai reinforced her idea that multiple slimy appendages were the way to go.

Usually, Mercy was spared the nauseating spectacle of watching her sister consume or play with her food, but she remembered a few lavish parties back during World War II, when the sheer volume of human trauma, death, and destruction created a decadent atmosphere for all somnali. Sympathy frequently left the humans covered in raised, red welts caused by the puckered little suction cups all over her many writhing arms. Once, Mercy saw her slap a tentacle down the back of a woman and yank it away, taking a strip of flesh off of her back and buttocks along with it. Her saccharine, mincing ways aptly disguised the fact that she, just like Mercy, was truly a monster.

Right now, Sympathy was hungrily eying the two little figures in the cage, which had returned to snuggling in the debris under the hamster wheel. Mercy had sealed the front door, but she removed a metal grate from the top of the cage and reached in to grab the female figure. She pulled it up by the hair and dumped it into a little square room at the top of one of the turrets extending up from the cage. The little beast immediately began crawling back down to its mate, who was likewise, crawling up towards its partner.

"Look at how they cling to each other," Mercy marveled. "Whenever I separate them, they just run back to each other. It really is fascinating. I enjoy watching them."

"The dolls?" Sympathy asked. "Or did you mean Charlotte and Flynn?"

"The dolls and the real versions both," Mercy admitted. "Have you ever noticed how different it is being in our sister's dreams than in any other human's?"

"Of course," Sympathy answered. "It's why people like father continue to create those half-breed abominations. When you are closely related to one of them, you can feel what they feel. It's a novel experience for us, because we don't feel in the way they feel."

"That's not all," Mercy revealed. "Because of her, I've been able to penetrate the physical realm. It hasn't been all that much, really… tiny injuries, miniscule amounts of blood spilled. I know it's not encouraged, but it is not expressly forbidden for me to use her essence as fuel. I have. It's like none other."

"And your point is?" Sympathy asked.

"If it is like that with her, then it might be the same with her children," Mercy said excitedly. "Once father told me he had a brother, a meat brother. They were close. His sibling voluntarily fed him, and he grew powerful, so powerful that he was able to perform the Ritual of Binding for the first time and create a human hybrid. Father gained energies from his brother, and from his brother's children, as well as his own child. While they lived, he maintained a window into the human world. The thing is, later generations grew to resent their father and to refuse to allow him to feed. Eventually, they went as far as to refuse to procreate, just to shut him out."

"So you are hoping that if you manipulate things enough, Charlotte and this guy you've put in her path will perform the Ritual of Binding?" Sympathy asked.

"Maybe," Mercy shrugged. "I hope they do. It would please father, put me in his good graces. The boy was to be my blood sacrifice, if I could gain enough power to destroy him in his world, or convince him to destroy himself from ours. I think, though, he would serve me much better by becoming my sister's consort. And I wouldn't mind having meat nieces and nephews, would you?"

"No, not at all," Sympathy trilled. "I think they'd be absolutely delicious. But what will you do if your plan doesn't work?"

Mercy gave her sister an evil smile. She reached back into the cage again and dragged the male golem out by the hair. The creatures couldn't speak, but they both saw his struggling and silent screams. Mercy knocked him over on his back and forcefully pressed the metal lid from the cage down on him with both hands.

It took a while for it to be over. Mercy shoved all her weight down onto it, as strings of flesh and clay poured out of the holes in it like cheese through a grater. A puddle of orange and green goo leaked out of the creature onto the table. After several minutes of squirming, the manikin's movements ceased altogether.

"If he doesn't comply," Mercy said coldly, "I'll squish him like a bug."

The female golem stood there, sobbing in silence, its tormented face pressed against the transparent wall of the cage. Sympathy smiled at it as she picked up the cage lid and used the side of it as a utensil to shovel the still-warm chunks of the male golem down her gaping maw.

"Stop crying," Mercy told the little woman in the cage. "I'll make you a new one, even better than before."

BOUNDARIES

Unaware of the otherworldly goings on involving Mercy and Sympathy, the real Flynn sat nervously on the edge of a hard wooden chair in group therapy. He had been in the hospital for eight days. Charlotte had been released six days ago. He had received the letter from Maribelle three days later. Charlotte visited him in his sleep just last night, and he was anxious and restless and filled with thoughts of her. He had mixed feelings about sending her away for a week, but he felt in many ways that his sanity depended on it.

Nancy, who was still in the hospital and would remain until a couple days before Flynn left, was speaking about her cats.

"And Tess said that I belonged on Animal Hoarders," Nancy said, wiping a tear from her eye. "My own niece was comparing me to those filthy animal abusers on that show. I don't hurt my cats, and I only have six of them. They're all fixed. I don't just let them breed. I always clean their litter boxes. I have three set up and I'm just so worried about them now that I'm in here. There is no one to change their litter box except Tess, and she's so lazy."

"We can't control the behavior of others," the facilitator reminded. "We are here to talk about how we can modify our reactions to them. What do you think you could do that might help you and Tess to get along?"

Tess was Nancy's nineteen-year-old niece, who had rented a room from her and was going to a local college. Tess could have rented a room for a bit more from someone unrelated, and Nancy could have rented her room to a college student unrelated and charged more, but the two chose to stay together.

"I could move the litter box out of the bathroom that is by her room," Nancy sighed. "I could change the litter box every day instead of every other day. I could… I guess I could feed them dry food, it's less stinky."

"I'm not asking you to be a doormat," Dr. Lee said. "This group is about boundaries, and I think you should set some with Tess. Does Tess have to live with you?"

"No, but… " Nancy started.

"You don't have a landlord. Are there any neighbors or health inspectors complaining about you having six cats in your house?" Dr. Lee asked.

"No. I guess not," Nancy admitted. "I guess she chooses to stay with me, to save a hundred dollars a month on her rent. I guess that I let her eat whatever she wants to out of my kitchen, and she saves money on groceries, too. I guess I'm doing her a favor, and if she doesn't like it, she can move."

"Exactly," said Mike, a new guy who had been in the hospital for two days now. Mike had been sitting at the table with Flynn, Nancy, and a girl named Hannah.

Nancy was finished. It was Flynn's turn now.

He wasn't ready, but he supposed he never would be, and now was as good a time as any other. He relaxed his death grip on the edge of his seat and slid back in the chair.

"So, I've been seeing this girl lately," he started. "I guess you could say we're dating, that's what she calls it. It's not super serious yet. But the thing is that I have a hard time saying no to her. She has said some things that make me think she wants to get really serious, really fast. I think it is too quick, and I'm kind of trying to slow things down. But I'm afraid every time I say no, or wait, that I'm going to lose her. So I guess I can't blame her for everything because I don't think she's said or done anything to make me as afraid to stand up to her as I am."

"Well, that's good." Dr. Lee said. "It sounds like you've thought about this and you're doing a good job of seeing how you can control your own reactions and decisions. Trying to understand yourself and change yourself to change the situation is a lot more effective than trying to change your girlfriend."

Flynn shifted in his chair a little and felt his hands grow warm and damp when he heard the word "girlfriend." Was Charlotte his girlfriend? He wasn't so sure. He hadn't had a girlfriend in four years, since shortly after he left college.

"So do you think I'm doing the right thing by asking her to wait?" Flynn asked Dr. Lee

"I think that depends on how you feel, and no one can decide that for you. But maybe someone else has some advice. Let's see what the group thinks," Dr. Lee said.

Mike shook his head. "When you say going too fast I hope you don't mean sex, because there's no such thing as too fast. I mean, what's up with waiting? Isn't that for girls?"

Flynn laughed. "That's mean, bro."

Gary gave him a really weird look. He was moving all funny and jerky-like for a minute, like a sock puppet with someone's hand crammed up its ass. After a brief pause his body movements and hand gestures started to stabilize, and Flynn decided that it was probably just some kind of weird medication side effect, one of those tics they were always warning you about on the side effects list on the label.

"Charlotte's a swell girl. Watch what you say about her," Gary said, sporting an eerily sardonic grin that closely resembled the open-mouthed, slack-jawed gape of a half-rotting Jack-O-Lantern. As he spoke, his head bobbed up and down like a dashboard Elvis.

Nancy's jaw dropped. "Shit! What the fuck?" Mike screamed, startled and scooting his chair away from Gary so hard and fast that he nearly fell into the lap of the next guy over.

Gary hadn't said a word since being admitted, and it was hard to tell who or what was speaking now. He moved like heavily medicated meat-puppet, channeling God only knows what through his beefy, flaccid jaws. The heavy dosage of antipsychotic medications he was on, his poorly managed schizophrenia, and a childhood head injury that complicated the other two factors combined to make him easily prone to a sleep-like state.

Brash had come by for a visit.

Gary's clumsy possessed body patted Flynn on the hand, then slumped back down the chair. Gary resumed staring at a vacant spot somewhere over Dr. Lee's head. The incident was over.

Pam shook her head and narrowed her eyes. Mavis started scrawling something on her notepad. As a result of Gary's sudden outburst, the team would begin monitoring those letters Flynn had been getting from Maribelle Metaxas. Flynn wouldn't be given any new incoming letters until the day he left, because he staff thought they might impair his recovery. They didn't stop Flynn from sending his letters out to Maribelle, though.

Parental Advisory

Maribelle corned Charlotte in the kitchen that morning before work.

"Sit down and have a cup of coffee with me, Charlie. We need to talk," she said, setting two cups of coffee down at the kitchen table. She nervously fussed with the sugar and milk until her daughter sat down.

Charlotte rolled her eyes, but took a seat.

"It's about your young man," Maribelle started.

"What is it?" Charlotte asked, smiling. She wasn't sure Flynn was *hers* but the idea made her feel all warm and fuzzy inside, not to mention a little hot and moist. She wanted him to be hers. She was surprised. She didn't think she was the possessive type.

"You need to be careful," Maribelle started. "Your father has taken an unhealthy interest in what is going on between you two. He's visited that boy in the hospital twice that I know of. Once when we were there with that poor sweet Nancy channeling him with the Scrabble tiles like the damned thing was an Ouija board. Then a letter just arrived from Flynn describing the outright possession of that silent giant Gary. I can't know for sure it was Brash, but it certainly sounds like him."

"That is disturbing," Charlotte admitted. "Why?"

"I am not sure," Maribelle said. "I can only guess. When you were born, it strengthened his connection to the physical plane. I don't think he could have done the sleepwalker stunt he pulled with Gary if he didn't have an earthly child. The promise of earthly grandchildren means a lot to me admittedly, but it would seem that to him it means even more."

"And so he's spying on me," Charlotte complained. "Me and my... whatever Flynn is to me. I don't like it."

Maribelle raised an eyebrow. "I don't know what you've been telling him, but Flynn thinks you're his girlfriend."

"He does?" Charlotte was surprised. He was the one who was always trying to slow things down.

"Of course he does," Maribelle retorted. "He's written me a letter every single day. In every single one of the letters he asks about you and talks about how much he wants to see you. He isn't writing me because of my scintillating conversational skill. He's writing to me because he isn't allowed to communicate with you directly."

"Okay, that's good to know," Charlie admitted. "But even if he is my boyfriend, I don't think that gives my father any excuse to spy on him. Maybe my dad thinks he's looking out for my best interests, but I still don't like it."

"You shouldn't," Maribelle said with a heavy sigh. "I've been where Flynn is now when your father approached me. Things were a lot worse for me than they will be for him. You still need to be careful with him. He's human. He needs to stay grounded in this world. Now there is more to it than that. It will be much harder for your father and your sisters to observe or meddle with your interactions here in the material world. I am afraid Flynn is right: you should limit the amount of time you spend together in dreams."

"But the Rite of Binding," Charlotte countered. "Some of it has to occur in dreams. It would kill him otherwise."

"I know," Maribelle said. "I know all too well. Still, the more you are able to engage in the required tasks in the earthly realm, the better. It will reduce the ability of your father and siblings to interfere with your relationship. You have to protect yourselves. And you're going to need this."

Maribelle lifted a large leather-bound book off the seat next to her and dropped it on the table in front of her daughter. On the cover in elegant raised script were the words, "Rites of Undoing."

"It is a book of counter rituals and counter spells," Maribelle explained. "These rituals weaken the power your father and siblings can exert over you or Flynn. They'll also protect any child that might be produced from your union. It is my gift to you."

"I hope father doesn't find out," Charlotte remarked. "He would be very unhappy."

"He didn't find out when I used them," Maribelle countered. "I used them when I was pregnant with you. It's why you are able to be so independent and free-spirited. And isn't that what you would want for your child? Freedom?"

Charlie nodded. "Indeed. If there ever are children, that is. Flynn says I am moving too fast. I'm not sure he will want to complete the rituals. I guess I'll have to wait and see when he gets out. He is uncomfortable with being visited in his dreams."

"Some of the rituals are difficult to complete even if you *want* to do them," Maribelle pointed out. "If he is unmotivated, it is definitely not going to happen."

"I don't think he is entirely unmotivated," Charlotte said. "He still wants to see me. He just wants to wait until he can do it in person. When we performed the second rite, he seemed happy, but then later, something went wrong. I don't know what, but he kind of pulled back. I think he wants to make sure I'll respect him in the morning or something, I don't really know, exactly. I guess it takes time to get to know someone. I'm just not used to waiting, and I am not sure I have the patience. Somnali men never want to wait. They don't play these little games."

"And they don't care about you, either," Maribelle said with a shrug. "Your father cared about what I could give him, you. For him, it was like a political arrangement with someone you like or respect. He could never love me. The way he cares for you is the closest he ever can come to love, and a part of that is merely reflected and refracted emotions. When he is with you, he feels what you feel. He borrows your emotions. Without you, he feels nothing. Because of you he feels something towards me, a desire to protect the mother of his child. He can be very cruel. Before you were born he was crueler still."

"You're right, Mom," Charlotte acknowledged. "I do like Flynn because he is a sweet creature. He's very different than what I'm used to. Whimsy and Sorrow were both a lot of fun, but I can't see any future being with a guy like that. Whimsy was nice to me, but brutal to other human beings. He couldn't see how I, being half human, might identify with them, or be offended. Sorrow was just mean to everyone, me included."

Maribelle nodded. "Whimsy was a lot like your father, so you can imagine what that was like for me. He always acted protectively towards me, not in a loving way, but in the same way as a man might protect his expensive sports car or a prize pony. With other people, even those I cared for, he was without pity."

Charlotte hugged her mother. "I'm so sorry for what you've been through," she said softly. "I wish that I could have prevented it. I wish that you didn't go through so many terrible things because of me."

"Don't worry about that," Maribelle reassured her. "As you know, I was in an automobile accident when I was about your age. What I may not have told you is that, due to my injuries, it was thought that I would never be able to have children. Your dad had something to offer me that he knew I wanted. I suppose he'd observed me long enough to know I would probably agree to his terms. Haven't you observed Flynn?"

"I did," Charlotte admitted.

"So you know what he will and won't do," Maribelle suggested.

"I know what he likes and what he doesn't like," Charlotte agreed.

"Whatever he may like," Maribelle said carefully, "he's human. He may be a lot pickier about who he sleeps with than Whimsy or Sorrow. He cares about who you are, and he needs you to be clear about what your relationship with him is. Maybe he doesn't want to sleep with someone he doesn't know well or trust. He has feelings matter to him. I think you should be patient about it."

"Great, fine," Charlotte huffed "I get the picture, so you can stop lecturing me now. But I'm glad that you like Flynn and want to look out for him and everything."

She drank the rest of her coffee in a single gulp, scooted her chair back and stood up to go.

"I think you should go home," Maribelle said, shaking her head a little. "I get it, he's dragging his feet about sex and you're frustrated. You have a good reason to be. You want to keep Mercy and your father off his back. You know that you will need to consummate your relationship soon if you want them to respect your claim that he is your consort. You're nervous about that. It's understandable. But if he has hang-ups about having sex with you in a dream, then I seriously doubt he is the kind of guy who is going to want to do it on your mother's couch. He's probably too proper to do it in my guest room. He will want some privacy. You need to stop sleeping in my living room. You need to take him home. To your apartment, where your bed is."

Charlotte's eyes widened. "Okay now so let me get this right, my mom is telling me I should just take this guy home and fuck him."

Maribelle looked kind of pissed off, but retained her composure. "Why do you have to be so crude? Was that really necessary? If you don't want him then forget about it. But if you intend to complete the Ritual of Binding you will have to sleep with him. In a dream or in your bed, it's required to finish the ritual. You are just as aware of this as I am."

"Fine," Charlotte said. "I'll go home. Love you too, mom."

Maribelle smiled. "You know I love you, Charlie."

"Did you find his friend Danny yet?" Charlotte asked, suddenly needing to change the subject.

"Yes," Maribelle nodded. "I did. I spoke with him. He lives fifty miles from here. He's in Cupertino these days. But he said he would call Flynn and write, that would be good, don't you think? He's going to need a support system."

Charlotte nodded. "Okay, I gotta go now, mom. I've got classes."

ISSUES

As his expected release date grew closer, Flynn found himself increasingly inclined to worry over the problems he'd left behind on the day he was hospitalized. He was laid off from the call center three days after he was locked up in the psych ward, and he wouldn't be able to go down and apply for Unemployment or State Disability until he got out of the hospital. He was thinking that maybe Dr. Lester would sign off on the State Disability form, given that she'd said she believed that he'd stabbed himself in the neck with a BBQ fork or something the day she admitted him.

Whether he applied for Disability or Unemployment, he wouldn't get his first check until three weeks after the date he applied, and he had to apply in person, something he couldn't do from the hospital.

In the meantime, he was sure that the last check from his job was at home, in his mailbox, but rent had been due three days ago, and he would be in the hospital another four days. He would be lucky if he came home to find a Three-Day Notice to Pay or Quit posted on his door. If he were unlucky, he'd come home to changed door locks and a Notice of Abandonment. He'd sent his landlord a letter with a post-dated check that the management company was under no obligation to accept.

His life was falling apart here.

None of his personal concerns changed the fact that he was where he was. He was locked up with people with mental disabilities like himself who were recovering. This convalescence seemed to involve repeated invocations of the relaxations that were television, small talk and Scrabble. Some of the patients also enjoyed creating artwork.

Not secondary to these simple pleasures were the joys of eating and gossip. With Gary's bizarre revelation regarding Charlotte, gossip was the dessert du jour at Flynn's dinner table. Hannah also enjoyed a small slice of pumpkin pie and a generous helping of double entendres.

"She should be the one who is asking you to slow down, bro," Mike bellowed, greedily inhaling his plate of spaghetti and meatballs. Mike was a slightly overweight virgin whose hobbies included collecting comic books and performing mediocre skateboard tricks. Recently, he'd become deeply invested in reading books on how to pick up women.

"I mean, you're the man," Mike barked between slurps of marinara sauce. "You know, alpha dog, alpha male. You can't let these girls push you around, bro."

"I know Charlotte Metaxas," Hannah chuckled, toying with her pie. "We haven't been hanging out that much over the last couple of years, but we were close friends in high school. People don't change that much. If she's into him I don't think he's an alpha dog. She likes her men like I like my pie, spicy and sweet with lots of whipping… cream."

"You women all think you know so much," Mike complained. "I'm sure he's not p-whipped, or whatever you're suggesting. He's probably just afraid of being tied down." He was so dismayed he actually stopped sucking food down for a full five minutes.

"He looks pretty whipped to me. What do you say?" Hannah asked Flynn. "Are you afraid of Charlotte tying you down? You look like the kind of guy who might enjoy that kind of thing."

Flynn laughed. Hannah was a wiry, heavily tattooed twenty-two year old with retro cat-eye shaped glasses. Today, she sported baggy parachute pants. If she had not been locked up in a place where belts and shoestrings were forbidden, she'd probably be wearing bondage pants. Her mohawk was its natural brown color and partially grown out. Flynn didn't have any problem imagining her hanging out with Charlotte in high school. Hannah had a cute girlfriend named Shelby who visited her in the hospital on the regular. Flynn sometimes wished that Charlotte could just walk in the door and visit like that, but it was against the rules.

"You kids," Nancy said, shaking her head. She still sat at Flynn's table out of habit, and because she enjoyed discussing their mutual acquaintance with Maribelle Metaxas. However, she grew increasingly annoyed with the youthful shenanigans of Mike and Hannah. When they were hanging out together, Flynn acted just as childish as they did, although he was older. Mike was only nineteen. Like many people his age, he already knew everything.

"I'm sorry," Hannah said. "I was just trying to cheer Flynn up. He looks worried a lot lately."

Flynn sighed. "I am. I have a lot of problems waiting for me at home."

"I can relate to that," Nancy said, shaking her head. "I know I have a pile of bills to deal with when I get out of here. I love Tess, bless her heart, but she's not really responsible enough for me to trust with my banking information, if you know what I mean."

"Yeah," Flynn commiserated. "It's hard to relax when you know you're going to be tossed back out with the sharks the minute they let you out of here. It's like all the same old issues, only worse."

"But at least you aren't alone," Nancy suggested. "At least you have someone."

"Charlotte is hot," Hannah said. "Not for nothing, but I had a big crush on her in high school. Not that I was ever her type. But Flynn… yeah, you know she likes that shit right there. She probably likes to tear that shit up real good."

"Hannah!" Nancy said, shocked. Flynn blushed and looked down at his plate.

"I'm so disappointed," Mike said. "I can't believe you're letting her do you like that, man. You just let that girl Hannah walk all over you, the same way Charlotte does."

"Nah, she probably does it with high heels on," Hannah quipped.

"Stop it, Hannah! You're going to make me choke on my broccoli." Flynn burst out laughing, not just at Hannah's steady stream of bawdy BDSM laced innuendo, but at the way it all kept flying over Mike's head. Nancy was less oblivious, and more disturbed.

"I think I'll go to the television room now," Nancy said stiffly, picking up her tray.

"Don't leave," Hannah mock-pled with her. "I'll be good, I promise."

"You shouldn't leave," Mike confirmed. "Here comes her girl. Hannah will be getting up and leaving soon enough."

"We'll talk later," Hannah told Flynn with a wink. "I better get off my ass and go get my girl before she comes over and gives me a spanking."

Conversation

Another two days went by before Hannah followed up on her promise to talk to Flynn later. They were in the television room after dinner, watching some terrible reality show that involved random contestants performing even more random acts of alleged talent. A preteen in a fedora was on stage tap dancing now. Flynn couldn't tell whether the skinny nine or ten year old was a boy or a girl.

Mike had been transferred to a boarding care home. Nancy had also been released that morning, and was at home happily posting photos of her six cats and accepting Maribelle's friend request on Facebook. Gary was still sitting in the same easy chair he always sat in, staring blankly through the television. Shelby and Hannah were playing checkers in the corner, and Flynn was writing a letter to Danny.

"Hah hah! I win, again," Shelby cackled gleefully, shoving Hannah's last piece off the board. Hannah winked at her. Checkers was more of an excuse for them to sit at the tiny card table with their knees touching than it was a serious competition. Hannah let Shelby win every single time.

Shelby was a leggy brunette with a caramel complexion. She wore her thick, black hair in a twist on one side of her head, where it hung at least a foot past her shoulder. She didn't need any make up to make her smoky brown eyes look sultry. If Hannah had a crush on Charlotte back in the day, Flynn decided she must be long over it. She looked at Shelby as if she were the only woman in the world.

Flynn was a little surprised when Shelby called him over.

"My lady wants to show you something," gesturing with a single long index finger tipped in glittery electric blue nail polish. Hannah nodded and smiled. Flynn walked over and pulled up a chair. Without asking, Shelby began clearing the checkers away and bought over a box of Uno cards. No words needed to be exchanged because all three of them knew that they should have a game that could accommodate more than two players on the table when the monitoring staff came by.

"See this?" Hannah asked, showing him a brand on the inside of her left arm that was shaped like a three leaf clover. "Your girlfriend gave this to me, when we were in the tenth grade."

Flynn's eyes widened as he took a closer look at her extended arm. "She did that? You wanted her to do that, right?"

"Charlotte doesn't do anything to anyone that they don't want her to do," Hannah said. "Keep that in mind. I heard you in group, and I know you worry about that, but you shouldn't. If you don't want to do something, just tell her no. If you want her to stop, just say stop. You know, communicate."

"Don't you think they need a safe word or something?" Shelby asked Hannah while cutting and shuffling the cards.

"That's up to them, babe," Hannah said, patting Shelby's hand. "They're two consenting adults, I'm sure they can work it out."

"What my girlfriend is trying to say is that she doesn't want you to feel ashamed," Shelby said in a too-soothing tone. "Your feelings are natural, and you're not alone."

Hannah laughed. "You sound like a public service announcement directed at fragile adolescents, baby. Seriously, it's not necessary. He's two years older than you are."

"I don't mind," Flynn said gently. "She's right. I've been pretty confused and conflicted about all of this. I need someone safe to talk to about how I feel. I don't have many friends."

"You're a squishy one," Hannah teased. "No wonder she likes you."

"You can talk to us," Shelby reassured him. "We know all about these things, and are unlikely to be shocked. We won't judge you."

"Yeah, totally," Hannah agreed. "We know a lot about these kinds of things. I also know about some other, less terrestrial concerns you might have if you know what I mean."

Flynn looked a little nervous. "What kind of things?"

"Things called somnali," Hannah said, holding her arm up. "This isn't just a brand, its protection against otherworldly spirits, the kind that attack you and channel through you when you're out of it and overmedicated. Charlotte told me she gave me this to protect me from being possessed."

Gary, who had been passing out, moaned loudly in the corner and suddenly sat upright.

"You have got to fucking kidding me," Shelby said. "It's a damned three leaf clover. What is it supposed to be warding off, evil leprechauns?"

Hannah shook her head and rolled her eyes a little. She looked at Flynn and said, "Right, I forgot to mention the fact that Shelby thinks I'm nucking futz every time I try to tell her about this. But I'm not crazy, or at least not that crazy. The somnali are real."

Then she dropped his gaze and turned back to her girlfriend. "I already told you, Shelby, this isn't a clover, it's a fleur-de-lis, the lily among thorns, symbol of the Blessed Virgin, the Madonna, and of all that is good and pure among women."

"Superstitious madness," Shelby argued. "First of all, it's a flower, so it's got to have a pagan symbolism that predates your personal understanding. Secondly, it's all madness, this idea you have that you can seal yourself off against dream demons by scarring yourself with an emblem that represents female purity, something you don't possess and haven't had for years. It's absurd."

Hannah threw her hands up in the air. "You just don't get it!"

Shelby and Hannah were so wrapped up in their animated conversation that they didn't notice Gary leap out of his chair and sprint across the room toward their table. Gary was a four hundred pound man, but in that moment he moved with the grace and speed of a ravenous leopard closing in on a wounded gazelle.

Flynn was the first one to spot the massive man barreling down on the table. He snatched Hannah by the arm and tried to get her out of harm's way, the whole time shouting, "Move! Get out of the way!"

Shelby looked up to see what the screaming was about. She spotted Gary just in time to duck down with her head in her lap seconds before Gary swooped down and tried to snatch her up by the hair. Shelby dropped the chair down on its side and rolled her body under the table like a kid in a cold war era duck and cover A-bomb drill, kicking the overturned chair out behind her.

Hannah wasn't quite so lucky. Gary managed to get both hands around her throat and commence strangulation before Flynn could pull her out of the way. He had to drop her arm when Gary picked her by the neck and held her dangling three feet in the air. Gary kicked the table, still going after Shelby while his arms were around Hannah's neck. The madman sure could multitask. He gave it another rough kick and the table tumbled over and struck Flynn squarely in the chest, knocking him over.

This all happened in a matter of seconds.

By now, the staff had been alerted, and three burly orderlies ran into the room. Two of the men tackled him and tried to knock him to the ground, while the third jabbed a needle into his hip and depressed the plunger.

Hannah turned her arm around so that the brand was facing Gary and began to smack him repeatedly in the face with it. Her voice was a thin hiss, but Flynn could distinguish the words. "Get out of him! Get out! Get out!"

Moments later, a drugged and hexed Gary fell backwards, striking his head on the recreation room television. The two orderlies pinned him down to the ground while the third called for reinforcements. Hannah's neck fell out of his now-limp hands as both Gary and the television set tumbled to the floor.

Most of the patients ran out of the room when Gary turned to violence, but a pair of particularly doped up denizens had remained, staring mindlessly at the spot where the now-fallen television used to be. Hannah eyed them warily, aware of their vulnerability to the somnali.

A young woman rolled a gurney into the room. Four orderlies were required to lift Gary's unconscious body on to it and strap it down. Two of them quietly escorted the other two semi-unconscious patients out to the lunchroom, because they were partially obstructing the path to the door, and Gary's bulk was wider than an empty gurney. One of the others rolled Gary out into the hallway, while the fourth man went over to Hannah to assess the extent of her injuries, if any. There was some bruising around her neck, but otherwise she was okay.

Pam and Mavis came in the room last.

"I'm sorry you had to see this," Mavis told Shelby. "I'm also afraid that Hannah can't have a visitor now. We are about to send all the visitors home until things settle down here."

"Do you believe me now?" Hannah asked Shelby, who nodded in wide-eyed agreement as she was being hauled out of the door.

BUGGING OUT

Mavis was busy escorting Shelby to safety and Bill the orderly was half way out the door taking Hannah to the nursing station to tend to her wounds when the second ticking time bomb went off.

Howard Lowe was one of the semi-comatose patients who had not left the room during Gary's rampage. Almost as if suddenly sensing that the staff was otherwise occupied, the tattered remains of what used to be Howard leapt suddenly from its reclining chair and began to howl.

"Bed bugs! Bed bugs! The damned place is filled with bugs! Bug bug bug bug bug bug bug" he screamed, ripping off his imaginarily bug infested hospital shirt. He tossed it aside to reveal a chest that resembled raw, red hamburger meat. The man had systematically scraped almost all of his outermost epidermis and some of it was already scabbing and infected.

"What the actual fuck?" Flynn asked incredulously, ducking back behind the still-overturned table Shelby was hiding behind not ten minutes earlier. He felt queasy and he definitely didn't want to get a closer look. The way things were going; being in the hospital was turning out to be more traumatic than being outside.

Pam was reaching over to press the alert and the intercom to call the orderlies back in when Howard, out of other skin to scratch, began scraping his face off. Flynn suddenly realized that Pam was the only staff member in the room, and stood back up again just in time to witness Howard attempting to gouge out his own eyes.

"Do you need some help?" Flynn asked a beleaguered Pam, who was loading up a needle full of something to try and knock Howard out.

"Get out of here!" she shouted at Flynn, "It's not safe! Go get someone! Get! Go get Bill!"

Bill was the closest orderly, having just dropped Hannah off at the nursing station. He barreled back into the room seconds later, and pinned Howard's arms behind his back to prevent further self-injury. Pam was injecting Howard with a sedative by the time two more orderlies showed up.

The crisis was over.

Flynn slumped down to the floor and started chanting, "Fuck. Fuck fuck fuck. Fuck."

Pam turned and looked at him, so Flynn stopped himself from speaking. He was not okay. He was totally freaked out. But he couldn't be caught acting crazy. He had to get out of this place.

SAFETY NET

On the day he got out of the hospital, the first thing Flynn did after retrieving everything they took from him and stored when he checked in two weeks prior was to start adding new telephone numbers to his cell phone. He sat at the table with a stack of papers that included letters he'd written and handwritten notes with telephone numbers and email addresses.

Lorena Young. Charlotte Metaxas. Maribelle Metaxas. Nancy Allen. Hannah Cohen. Shelby Baptista. Michael Shaw. That was all of them, all of the new friends he made in the hospital all of the people he thought could potentially become part of the shiny new social life that he'd promised he'd try to develop while he had been in therapy.

Lorena had invited him to go to her church, Hannah and Shelby said they wanted to take him out to play pool and have drinks at their local sports bar. Nancy and Michael just wanted to add him on social media and talk shit about cats or comic books, respectively. Maybe one day, he might manage to make it to a convention with Michael, one never knew. They were a part of that support system he said that he'd work on. That way he would have people to lean. He needed a better social life than Dr. Lester, the emergency psychiatric system, and a family that lived more than two thousand miles away could provide.

Flynn grew up in San Mateo, California, but his mother was from Kaneohe, Hawaii so he had been born in Honolulu. He was up at UC Davis, failing what would be the first and last semester he would spend in a non-community college during the spring of his mother's twentieth high school reunion. While she was off in Hawaii, his mom reignited a romance with some old flame. He was not Flynn's unidentified father.

No one knew who Flynn's dad was, except for his mother, who refused to tell. One of the consequences of getting pregnant and having a baby at the age of fifteen was that Samantha Keahi wasn't allowed to date, or go to prom. She couldn't do anything except go to school, study, and change Flynn Keahi's shitty diapers for the next two and a half years. Another consequence was that Flynn grew up with no father and a mother who resented him.

Samantha Keahi was Samantha Flynn now, in some sickening cosmic joke. It turned out that Flynn was named after the guy Sammie had had a crush on, Joey Flynn, and not whoever donated a sperm sample to assist in Flynn's creation. It wasn't Joseph Flynn, that's for sure. Joey Flynn was a fair skinned, fair-haired, freckled haole of entirely Irish heritage. Flynn Keahi's daddy was reportedly either "Chinese or something," or "Chinese and something," depending on how drunk and pissed off his mom was when she was ranting about him.

His mom called him one day, not long after to explain to him that she was only thirty-eight, and had her whole life ahead of her. She was young, but her childbearing years wouldn't last much longer. She'd already sacrificed the best years of her life to raise him, she claimed. She deserved this. So Sammie K. became Sammie F. and sold her home in San Mateo. Flynn continued his downward spiral and spent most of his twenty-third year homeless and in and out of mental institutions.

His mother was now married, with a new family, and Flynn had a sixteen-month old half-sister named Tabitha whom he had never met. His mom spoke to him on the phone once a month and texted him with photos of Tabby or posted them on Instagram. He and his mother weren't what you'd call 'close'.

But he had one friend after his mother left, and that was Danny. It was the last number he added to his cell phone, Daniel Santiago. That was it. This was his support system. That was all of them. He scrolled through his phone and was not surprised to see that the only other phone numbers in it were his old job, his mother, and his therapist.

Flynn breathed a sigh of relief. He was finally getting out of here, and he wouldn't be alone. He had some friends, and he probably had a girlfriend now, and anyway, Danny would be there... not forever, but this weekend.

Danny was driving up from San Jose to pick him up from the hospital.

HOMECOMING

Danny pulled up in a shiny blue, late-model Lexus bumping the local hip-hop station KMEL 106 FM on the radio with so much bass that the air within a three-foot radius of his vehicle quaked in time to the reverberation. He didn't even bother parking, just pulled up in the patient pick-up / drop off zone next to the Emergency Room, rolled down the window. He waved for Flynn to jump in the car. Flynn ran over, dragging two white plastic PATIENT bags full of clothing.

"I'm kind of jealous," Flynn admitted, tossing his bags into the back as he clambered into the passenger seat. Once the doors were closed, the distinct and pungent aroma of high quality marijuana smoke assailed his nose.

"Put your seat belt on," Danny warned. "I mean I have my medicinal marijuana card and all my paperwork for the car is in order, but I'm still not trying to be pulled over." He wore a sharp gray suit over a pristine maroon silk shirt. His darker gray tie was undone and hanging loose around the sides of his neck like a scarf. Flynn remembered how much Danny hated ties. Apparently, he now had a job that required them.

"How are you?" Flynn asked, looking a little dazed.

"Better than you, apparently," Danny said bluntly. "Your girlfriend's mom is the one who told me where you are and gave me the number to the hospital. You know, I kind of know her, but not very well. She works for the advertising firm my company uses. I've seen her at office parties, but we never really spoke until she called me on the phone asking if I knew you. It was spooky. I mean, I was thinking about you like a week before she called."

"Maribelle?" Flynn asked. "Are you saying Maribelle called you?"

"Yea Maribelle," Danny said curiously. "What's up? You got more than one girlfriend? Pimp."

"Uhm, no," Flynn chuckled. "No, nothing like that. I was just surprised she would go through that much trouble for me. That's really sweet. Did you know that I haven't been seeing Charlotte very long?"

"I know," Danny said. "She told me. She said she was so relieved that her crazy daughter had a boyfriend she didn't know what to do. But she didn't say it like that. I'm paraphrasing. Anyway you're both fucked up. Maribelle acts like you're her daughter's best hope of not becoming a cat lady. What's up, is she hideous? I would be surprised, because her mom is kind of hot, but you never know. She might look like her dad or something, or maybe a grandparent… sometimes ugly skips a generation."

"No," Flynn protested. "She's a very pretty girl."

"Well I guess I'll find out, right?" Danny teased. "I mean, her mom invited us all out for dinner at that new overpriced California Cuisine joint, the one with the organic pumpkin and asparagus curry that my boss keeps raving about. Maribelle Metaxas is loaded, but even so, I don't think that she would be throwing money around like that if she weren't trying to impress you. You sure there is nothing wrong with her daughter? Does she have a tiny head growing out of her shoulder that used to be part of her unformed twin before she absorbed it in the womb?"

Flynn laughed. "Nothing is wrong with her that isn't wrong with me."

"Okay now," Danny prodded, "Juicy details. What's she like? Is she cool, funny, what kinds of things is she in to? Does she have a nice rack? Is she freaky between the sheets?"

"Yes," Flynn said. "Yes. She likes a lot of the same things I do. Yes. And I don't know for sure yet, but I'm pretty sure she is."

"Oh," Danny nodded. "So you didn't hit it, but you have a girlfriend. Okay. I think you need to work on that."

"Fuck you, dude," Flynn answered.

"I'm just messing with you," Danny told him.

"I know, man," Flynn replied. "Just like old times."

Flynn clicked his seatbelt and Danny sped off towards the onramp to I-80 W, headed for the 680 interchange. Soon, they were high above the place where Suisun Lake emptied out into the Carquinez Strait, crossing the Benicia-Martinez Bridge. The height made Flynn nervous, and he dug his fingers into the tops of his knees as he desperately attempted to avoid looking over the edge. His heart pounded in time with the Tech N9ne blaring out of Danny's car stereo. His stomach bounced up and down in synch with the paper skull-and-crossbones air freshener dangling from Danny's rearview mirror.

Flynn thought about how much Danny seemed to have his shit together. He felt that his own life was comparatively embarrassing. He cringed as his friend drove him down to the crappy one bedroom apartment he kept near the railroad tracks on the back end of Vallejo's Historic District. His neighborhood wasn't bad, but it was a little square of residential mediocrity sandwiched between the crime-ridden area behind the transit depot on Lemon Street, the less dangerous but trashier stretch near Tennessee Street where people kept old couches and derelict automobiles on their front yards.

Its primary redeeming value was being located up the hill and about a half a mile away from the resurgent art scene in downtown Vallejo. Flynn would go down there once in a while to check out the galleries or grab a cup of coffee. Sometimes he had bought fresh vegetables at the Farmers Market, or stopped to watch a live band in the summer. On those days, he almost felt like he lived in a city he could be proud of. There were things he liked about Vallejo, but he felt very isolated there. Most of the time, he had to drive over to Benicia to buy video games or comic books, and when he did, he was surrounded by teenagers. He wished he could live in Berkeley like Charlotte did. He might fit in better.

It bothered him that Danny knew and worked with Maribelle. When Maribelle wrote to him, she told him about her swanky three-bedroom home in the hills over U.C. Berkeley. He envisioned the path Charlotte must have taken out of Concord ten days ago, Maribelle Metaxas dropping her daughter off at her cute little Berkeley studio apartment before speeding off to her million-dollar home. Why would she want her daughter going out with a guy who was unemployed and practically homeless?

Neither Danny nor Maribelle qualified as wealthy, no matter what Danny said. Flynn knew that they were just the last tattered remains of the middle class. Danny worked in tech, and Maribelle was in advertising. Danny bragged that he earned over 100k a year. Maribelle was a prominent executive and reportedly earned more than twice that much. Unfortunately, the cost of living in the Bay Area was very high. One of the things Maribelle mailed him in the hospital was an old picture of her hugging a teenage Charlotte in front of her two-story home in hills over the University of California in Berkeley. A house like that would easily be worth about 1.5 million. She could have had the same house and the same lifestyle on a quarter of her income in Middle America.

He wondered what his life would be like if he hadn't been so broken down, so needy and so desperately lonely. Maybe if he had more options, he wouldn't be so fucking happy that this girl wanted to pay some attention to him. Maybe he'd be more concerned about all of the weird, possibly supernatural, possibly insane hallucinatory occurrences that seemed to surround her.

DINING AND DANCING

It was a Friday night, and dinner soon segued into drinking and dancing at a Berkeley bar and grill with a live band that was a little too hipster trendy for Danny. He wasn't into seeing unknown local bands in tiny venues in college towns. His idea of live music was tickets to Coachella. That didn't stop him from happily allowing Maribelle Metaxas, his gracious hostess to instruct him on the finer points of swing dance while his friend got close and comfortable with her tipsy daughter across the room.

Danny wouldn't be caught dead hitting on his friend's girlfriend's mother. He was a popular guy who was used to receiving a good deal of female attention, and he really wasn't that thirsty. He did like Maribelle, though. She was bubbly and enthusiastic and fun to be around. He treated her the same way he would have treated a coworker at one of the numerous office parties he was obligated to attend in order to blend in with his company's corporate culture. She was pretty cool, though. He didn't have to pretend to laugh at her jokes. They were actually funny.

Besides, he thought Flynn and his girl needed as much privacy as possible in order to conduct the socially awkward courtship they had going on over there in a dark corner of the dance floor. Danny was slightly embarrassed for them.

Flynn either could not dance, or was too caught up in his emotions and hormones to pay any attention whatsoever to the beat of the music. He was holding Charlotte against him, dying inside every time she turned her head and her hair brushed the side of his cheek. When he kissed her, her mouth tasted like hot pilsner and desire. The sweat on the back of her neck smelled like the antidote to whatever psych drug had been medicating his libido out of existence for the past three years. When she bit his ear, he couldn't think anymore. He was kind of losing it. He was seriously hoping that sooner rather than later, the two of them would end up somewhere a lot more private.

The next day was Saturday, and although the rest of them had the weekend off, Maribelle had to be at a conference in Sacramento the next morning. She was a guest speaker on some kind of panel or other. Danny, who saw all socializing as a potential networking opportunity, managed to get invited along. His company had a booth there, but he didn't have her kind of clout. She had an extra guest pass, one that her daughter didn't really want, and taking Danny seemed like a win-win situation. She wouldn't have to drag Charlotte along.

Maribelle took off around 11:00 PM and Danny excused himself half an hour later. He was going to meet Ms. Metaxas in Sacramento, and he could just head out around 10:00 AM since his hotel was in Fairfield, way closer to Sacramento than Berkeley was. Flynn was going to take off with his friend when Charlotte mentioned that she lived half a block away and invited him to come stay the night. All of these things came together just so, and through a combination of happy coincidence and parental plotting, Flynn ended up stumbling into Charlotte's apartment just after closing time.

BODIES

Fifteen minutes went by and some clumsy disrobing occurred before Flynn found himself on his back in his underwear in the middle of Charlotte's double bed. She was stark naked, straddling his chest, and giggling. He threw his arms up in front of his face just before she hit him with her pillow.

"Stop it!" Flynn yelled. He was laughing as he half-heartedly attempted to roll over on his side. He was six feet tall and weighed about a hundred and sixty pounds. She was five foot five and weighed about one thirty. He could have gotten out from under her if he wanted to, but he didn't. She grabbed him by the wrists and pressed down with her full body weight. Then she bit him on the neck.

"Ah.... Oh wow, what are you doing?" he moaned, turning his head away from her to allow her easier access.

"You know what I'm doing," she teased, quickly nipping at his ear and then biting him on the shoulder. He began to writhe and make little whimpering noises.

"You like that, don't you?" she asked. Before he could verbalize a response, she relaxed her seated pose and slid her hips down his torso until his stiffening cock was pressing up against her belly through his tented black underpants.

"Yes, you do like it," she repeated, biting him on the chest.

He could feel the weight of her breasts against his belly as she snaked further down his torso. They were full, plump little breasts the size of ripe peaches, and he was sure that if he could get her to slow down long enough to let him get his mouth on one of them, it would taste just the same. He reached down to touch her and caught his fingers in her thick, wavy hair. Those fingers tightened when she pulled down one side of his boxer briefs and sunk her teeth into the skin just above his hip. He clinched his hand into a fist, pulled her hair, and began to scream.

"We can't have you doing that," she said, digging her nails into the side of his torso and dragging them down over his hipbone towards his ass. Flynn yelped.

"See what you've done?" Charlotte chided. "Now I've broken the skin. Maybe I should tie you down so you won't be tempted to do anything like that again."

Flynn panted, and then he made a little hissing noise. "Give me a minute," he said.

Charlotte nodded. "It's up to you," she told him.

"Yes," he begged. "Please. Yes, please."

He held out his wrists to her. He tried to regulate his breathing, to slow it down, and calm himself. He hoped this would give him a little time to catch his breath, and avoid cumming in his pants again. It would be even more embarrassing now, since this wasn't a dream.

He also had a really good idea about why his psychiatric medication wasn't currently preventing him from getting an erection. She wasn't judging him. He remembered all of the times he awkwardly attempted to broach the subject with Tamara, the only girl he'd been with for longer than a couple of weeks. The only one he knew well or trusted enough to ask. Tamara was afraid of this. He had to beg her. He didn't have to beg Charlotte. He didn't even have to ask. She was just as into this as he was.

"These have to come off first," she said, yanking his underwear down with both hands. They were down past his knees and on the floor before she finished the sentence.

A moment later she was leaning over his crotch inspecting his goodies.

"Wow," she said, taking his dick in her hand, "you're uncircumcised."

"Yea," he said hesitantly. "I hope that's not a problem. I mean, when it's all the way hard you won't even know the difference." This little turn in the conversation was making his partial erection disappear.

"No, it's not a problem," she said. "Hopefully, you're Wiccan or something, because I've always wanted to fuck an uncircumcised heathen."

She stopped talking and put his dick in her mouth. He found the gesture entirely more effective than words. She started by licking a drop of pre-seminal fluid off the side of it like melted ice cream off a cone while her hand was wrapped around the base of it. A little while later, she had her mouth all over him and she dropped her hand.

The minute his dick was hard, she stopped sucking it.

"There we go," she said. "See? You have a very lovely penis." She climbed back on top of him and threw her arms around his neck. He didn't really mind the fact that her mouth had just been all over his dick when she started to kiss him. He put his arms around her hips and tasted himself all over her. He was glad that she kissed him. It was comforting to know that she liked his dick and she liked him, too. He and his dick were both pretty average, and he was glad she was able to enjoy them.

"Are you going to tie me up?" he asked her. "I would like to offer myself to you. If you want to have me, you should have me. If you don't want me to be able to resist, I don't think that I should be allowed to struggle. I think you have me naked and bound, and you should take me and do whatever you want to do to me." He closed his eyes, and on his face was an expression of absolute longing. He wanted so much to be taken.

She laughed.

"It would be very dangerous for me to just do whatever I wanted to you without regard for what you wanted, liked, or cared about," she said carefully. Charlotte liked Flynn a lot. She cared about him, but she thought of him as someone very insecure and vulnerable with a really hot body. When she thought about what kinds of inhuman things the non-human members of her family would require her to do to him if he allowed her, it made her sad. The only thing that protected him was his right to say no. She couldn't let him give that away.

"If you don't like something," she said gently, "you tell me to stop, or say no, okay? I won't do anything to you that you don't want."

"Okay," he said softly, "but I trust you."

"What if we aren't always together?" she asked him. "Whatever I teach you now, you might take that into a situation with someone else, someone you can't trust. You don't even know me that well, Flynn."

"Are we together?" he asked.

"If you want that, then yes," she said, touching his cheek with the back of her fingers.

"I do," he said, "but I also want you to tie me up."

Charlotte got some cotton rope she used for moving furniture, the sort that they used to use for clothesline back in the day, when people still hung out their clothes out to dry. She used it to bind Flynn by the wrists and ankles to her four-poster bed.

THE LOVERS

The first time they had sex, it was simultaneously the most wonderful thing imaginable and the most fucked up thing under the sun. Charlotte untied him afterward, threw the condom in the trashcan and tossed a clean towel over the wet spot. Flynn apologized for his premature ejaculation, and Charlotte calmly explained that there was no need to worry. It was a common thing, and anyway, that's what cunnilingus was invented for.

Afterward they took a bath, soaking in the luxury only a tub could provide. Flynn only had a shower at his place, and it really wasn't the same. He loved the way her skin felt, warm and wet against his own. He loved the way she touched all of his scratches and bruises, washed them with her soapy washcloth, and caressed them with damp fingertips. He loved the way she wouldn't stop kissing him. He loved everything about her.

Love was dangerous, and could lead to deeper wounds like heartbreak and shattered trust. Love was risky, and there was never any guarantee that it would be returned.

Charlotte sat in his lap, and he washed her hair. They cuddled in the tub until the bath water got cold and they both began to shiver. They wrapped one another in big, fluffy towels that smelled of fabric softener and innocence. They tumbled into her sex-stained bed and talked for hours.

Flynn looked at her and asked, "Am I yours?"

Charlotte kissed him and said, "You are mine."

Flynn looked at her and asked, "Are you mine?"

Charlotte kissed him and said, "I am yours."

What she told him was true, but she felt guilty anyway. There were so many things that he didn't know. Things she'd kept hidden from him to protect him, or because they might upset him, or because they were too hard to believe.

She hadn't told him that Mercy was her sister. She hadn't warned him about the Feast of Tears. She had some power in both the dream realm and physical one. She still wasn't able to protect him from all of the bad things that could happen to someone as mortal and delicate as he was.

But at least she could claim him now that they had consummated their relationship. He was hers, although that would cost them both. At least now, she was in the position to protect him. According to somnali tradition she now had certain rights and privileges where he was concerned. She also had certain responsibilities and obligations.

The sun was rising now. Neither of them had slept all night.

He was on his belly now, naked under a pile of blankets and watching the television. She was beside him, also on her stomach, but she shifted a little closer. She ran her hand over his back and his ass, stroking his skin, making him drowsy. It was a trick, really… a kind of hormonal magic she knew very well. In a short while, he was snoring.

She was relieved. He was going to need to sleep.

Soon, the nightmares would begin,

ONEIROI

Power among the somnali was dynastic. Whatever standing Mercy and her siblings possessed was based upon their father's impressive lineage. His influence in the world of men had declined over the years, but in the dream realms, Brash remained a force to be reckoned with. He had authority over his multitudes of offspring and the generations they, in turn, produced.

Like many an aging former powerbroker, Brash clung in his vanity to the trappings of his faded glory. Brash was one of the lesser Oneiroi, one of the thousands of sons of the Greek god Hypnos, known to the Romans as Somnus. It was Somnus for whom the somnali were named. The somnali were all grandchildren of Somnus. They were the offspring of the Oneiroi. Many men had been mistaken about the lineage of the Oneiroi, believing they were the children of Nyx. Only the poet Ovid got it right. Hypnos was the son of Nyx and the father of the Oneiroi. Of course, they had other names in other cultures, but this interpretation of their origins was the one that best suited Brash.

Brash was not as popular as his brothers, Morpheus, Phobetor and Phantasos, all three of whom had been made legendary by the poet Ovid. In his youth, dalliances between human women and Greek gods were as commonplace as those occurring between modern day politicians and their interns. To seduce mortals, Brash frequently namedropped. If they had not heard of him, they might know of one of his famous brothers.

Like many of the old gods most of the Oneiroi were formed through parthenogenesis, or asexual reproduction by a single parent. Brash was a rare exception. He was the son of Somnus with his wife and consort Pasithea. Somnali offspring such as Mercy could be produced sexually or asexually, but demigods and demisomnali could only be produced by sexual contact. It was Brash's promiscuity that led to a curse on his line. Zeus cursed Brash and all of his progeny after Brash was caught having a fling with one of Zeus' many human lovers. For Brash's cursed line of somnali, earthly reproduction involved entering the human world long enough to consummate. This required blood sacrifice. The price was high, but so were the rewards.

Some Oneiroi such as Morpheus were considered gods. What Brash understood, although the humans did not, was that this kind of legendary status among the meat men was established by seeding one's own progeny among the men. These children would be possessed with the urge to promote their immortal forebears to all of mankind. That invited worshippers, and the worshippers made them gods.

Even Charlotte was infected with this desire. She was no Ovid, but she maintained a web comic chronicling the epic adventures of Brash. In the weekly episodes, Brash resided in Demos Oneiroi, the land of dreams, and was obsessed with entering the world of men. People considered her work dark fantasy, and one or two fans might recognize her work when she was peddling it at the local underground comic conventions.

For the rest of Oneiroi, who were not as popular as Morpheus, being considered daemons or djinn, severely hampered their courtship of human women. Producing a demisomnali – or worse, demidaemon or demidjinn – did not sound nearly as glamorous as being the mother to a demigod.

The possibility of human grandchildren excited him. They would join Charlotte in spreading his name among mortals. They would solidify his ability to enter and leave the physical world; their belief would be more powerful than the traditional blood rites. That would spell a whole new world for Brash.

MERCILESS

    Knowing the importance of such a union, the day after Charlotte consummated her relationship with Flynn, Mercy decided to visit her father in his otherworldly palace and officially demand the position of Second.

    The role of the Second was in many ways similar to the original job description for Best Man. That had been assisting the groom with kidnapping the future bride, and defending the wedding party from relatives of the bride seeking her forcible return. In the world of the somnali, a Second would make sure that any barriers to a human and somnali union were removed. In the case of a demisomnali, this was especially important. The Second would invariably be a pure somnali who would be called upon to complete any rituals connected with the Rite of Binding that the half-human might be too queasy or emotional to perform.

    Being very traditional, Brash lived in a palatial estate carved into the walls of a deep, dark cavern. A river ran through the bottom of a deep ravine that cut through the center of the floor. Over it was a series of arched bridges. Along the furthest wall, on an elevated platform that jutted out over the river and could be mounted by one of three steep spiral staircases, was his throne, molded from solid magma once drawn from the blackened stone it sat upon. It was all very theatrical.

    Brash sat on his throne now. He wore thigh-high black leather boots with dozens of sharp protrusions bursting forth from them at disparate angles like thorns or brambles. He was clad in a long, multiple-belted skirt that resembled an elaborate Utilikilt. It left his well-formed chest uncovered. Brash was apparently allergic to shirts and tunics as he never wore one. His refusal to cover his upper body made it much easier for him to display his large, black wings, which moved gently to and fro as he was currently in the process of using them to generate a mild breeze. All of the Oneiroi had them. His were nothing special. Maribelle used to love them, until she developed feelings of extreme loathing towards the baby killer who possessed them.

    He was leaning to one side right now, resting his elbow on the armrest with his chin in his hand as he listened to his daughter's complaint.

"You've seen how they are," Mercy bitched to her father. "She's very tender with him. She'll never do it." In an attempt at ingratiation, she'd showed up wearing her own set of dark wings, for although the somnali were not born with them, they inherited the Oneiroi's ability to assume whatever shape they desired. She was dressed as the red-haired girl Flynn once found becoming. She wore a backless ruby-colored dress of modern design.

"She'll do it," Brash insisted. "Many half-humans have completed the Feast of Tears, I'm sure she'll be no different. Besides, she doesn't have to do it. She could just perform the Sacrifice of the Innocents instead, that's what I did with her mother."

"You must be joking," she said. "How did that work out for you?"

"It took ten years for Maribelle to find out what happened," Brash noted.

"And then she started calling you 'the baby killer' and studying spells and warding symbols to keep you away," Mercy reminded him. "Symbols and spells she taught her daughter, who used them to territorially piss all over her high school buddies. Charlotte is Maribelle's daughter. If you think she is going to slaughter seventeen unborn children, you don't know her at all."

"Why not?" Brash asked, scratching his head. His long black hair was crowned with curved animal horns and cascaded down to his shoulders. "My demisomnali brother did it before my nephew was born."

"Your brother was already in the habit of killing prostitutes for kicks," Mercy countered. "Choosing seventeen pregnant ones in order to fulfill his quota wasn't a big stretch for Jolly… or as the newspapers liked to call him, Jack the Ripper. Surely, you don't expect that kind of ruthlessness out of my sister Happiness? She was vegan for two years. She'd be hard pressed to kill seventeen fetal chickens."

"Oh she could kill chickens," Brash countered. "I saw her kill several of the roaches in her apartment with that box filled with the special glue. They literally tore themselves to pieces trying to escape, tearing off legs and antennae. No one who could use a Roach Motel would be adverse to killing chickens."

"I don't think you 'get' humans," Mercy said, shaking her head. "They don't consider roaches to be as deserving of life as birds, let alone other mammals. The humans are very hierarchical in their views on the value of various kinds of mortal life."

"I man not know much about how mortals view these kinds of things, but I have every confidence in your sister. I think she'll do it," Brash insisted. "Have you read her comic? She's so talented. Her last issue had over a thousand hits. And she wants to give me a human grandchild. She's a very dutiful daughter, I think. Because of her, my line will continue on beyond one generation in the meat world. I'm excited, aren't you? Can't you be happy for me?"

"I can never be *Happy*," Mercy said drolly, hoping her father would hear the capital letter in her rather awful pun. "But I too, would like to see Happy bring our line to life in the flesh."

"She likes being called Charlotte, though," Brash chided, his nostrils flaring in annoyance.

"But she's human," Mercy repeated. "She has feelings for this boy, feelings you can't possibly understand. She may be going through the motions, doing what she needs to in order to appear to be following the traditions, but I don't think she will be able to follow through."

"Well I think she's doing great," Brash said proudly. His chest seemed to visibly swell, and he took a few cocky strides across the royal platform as he lectured and bragged to Mercy. He began to list all of Charlotte's accomplishments one by one, counting them off on his nicely manicured fingers. "One, she consummated the relationship. Two, she kept him bound during the consummation just as she was supposed to. Third, she tasted his blood and other required fluids. Fourth, she consumed his flesh, which I am told she tore from him with her own fingernails. Don't you think she's doing what is required?"

"Those little love bites she's been giving him are just a game they play," Mercy warned. "She only inflicts such pain as he finds sexually arousing. The ritual will require her to cause him unbearable agony." She sighed. No matter how ridiculous it seemed to her, her father was nauseatingly proud of her mortal half-sister. For someone who was not supposed to have human emotions, Brash was amazingly caught up in the role of the world's most unnatural helicopter parent.

The Feast of Tears was not life threatening, but it was particularly brutal and painful for the human involved. During the Rite of Binding, the dreams between the human consort and its somnali master were particularly vivid. This heightened realism made it possible for demisomnali, who already occupied the physical realm, to replace the blood rituals required in courtship between pure somnali and their human consorts with dream rites. The dream rites were essentially various types of symbolic sacrifices that resulted in a death in the dream world but did not translate into any harm in the physical world.

The Feast of Tears was the least demanding of the procreative rituals.

"She gave him some hickeys," Mercy continued. "That doesn't mean that she's ready to devour his flesh and drink his tears as prescribed in the ritual Feast of Tears."

"Of course they'll do it," Brash repeated. "For them, it's just a dream. Sure, it'll hurt, but it's not like he will actually be dead. He'll wake up unharmed in their little human world. They can hug and pat one another on the back, telling each other how wonderful it is that they saved seventeen innocent fetuses, or fetii, or whatever they are called. Isn't that what humans do?"

"Just in case," Mercy persisted. "Just in case she can't or won't do what is required, don't you think you should have a back-up plan?"

Brash waved his hand as if clearing the air of a particularly disagreeable stench. He was tired of Mercy's nagging. He knew humans well enough to understand how Mercy stepping in might make Charlotte and her shiny new consort feel betrayed and violated. But Mercy had worn him down. His nerves were shot, and he was ready to say anything to make his loud-mouthed daughter go away.

"Fine," he said. "If she doesn't do it, then you can step in and do it for her, but not yet. It's too soon. Give them some time. If they haven't completed the ritual in nine months, come back and see me and we can proceed from there."

"Thank you, father," Mercy said. As tradition dictated, she bowed to her father and waited for his formal dismissal before she turned to go.

Brash nodded and waved her off.

Mercy disappeared without another world

WAKING

When Flynn woke up, he was naked in bed with Charlotte. He was on his side with her spooned up against the front of his body. The heat of her skin against his was intoxicating. Her backside was nestled against his groin. The backs of her legs were cradled by the front of his. Her breasts were resting against top of his right arm, which was draped over her torso. His face was buried in her hair, which smelled like aloe vera and cocoa butter. That didn't change the fact that no matter how toasty she was keeping the front of his body his bare ass was freezing. All of the blankets had been kicked off during the night and were in a pile on the floor.

He got up and scooped the blankets up off the floor.

"Hey, what are you doing?" Charlotte mumbled.

"My butt is cold," he explained. She didn't hear him. She was already half asleep. Flynn spread the covers out over her and then crawled under them and back into bed. She sought his warmth and pressed against him. Soon, she was unconscious.

But Flynn was awake now and couldn't sleep. Troubled thoughts raced through his mind.

It was great being with her, but he was still totally jobless and practically homeless. His landlord had attempted to cash that post-dated check early, and it had bounced. When he got home, there had been a note on the door demanding he pay a $65 bounced check fee and a $125 late fee on top of his usual rent. He couldn't afford it, so he'd gone to the rental office and offered them a money order for the $800 a month he paid in rent. They accepted it, but did not look happy. This was going to come up again soon. It was looming over his head.

He had spent the rest of that day applying for state disability.

He wished that he could just forget about these problems and enjoy Charlotte's company, but it was difficult. His state disability check would barely be enough for him to cover his rent and utilities, much less to pay this extra $190 his landlord was asking for. He would have to start getting his food from one of Vallejo's numerous community pantries if he wanted to eat that month. He was very fortunate to live in a town that had plenty of pantries, places that gave out free groceries. He might have some trouble scraping up enough money to pay for gas to get to them, though.

His life was a mess.

He decided he was lying to himself in the hospital when he told Charlotte that things between them were messy. It wasn't her. It wasn't even them as a couple. He was messy all by himself. His whole life was fucked up. He wasn't sure how he could pull it back together again.

Charlotte rolled over so that she was facing him and started kissing his chest.

"What's up with the jailbird piercing jewelry?" she asked, flicking the little piece of plastic comb tooth with her finger. "I realize Vallejo is kind of country, but that's tacky as hell. I'm starting to worry about you. Is there a car engine sitting on your lawn? Do you like, need some nipple rings? I mean we're in Berkeley. You can buy that kind of thing here. We have the technology."

"Ow!" he said, grabbing her hand. "I just woke up. You can torture me later." He smiled.

Then he wrapped his arms around her head and felt grateful for the timely distraction from his personal pity party. He was sure they did have a head shop in Vallejo where one might buy piercing jewelry, but her assessment of his living situation was kind of amusing. He really needed to be amused right now.

She kissed his belly button.

"I would kiss you on the mouth," she mumbled from under the covers, "but I just woke up and I probably taste like dog food."

"Lovely," he said. She was funny. He wished that he were as easy going as she was.

"Would you like to get some coffee?" she offered. "I have some Folgers here, or we could go to Peet's if you want to. I mean they have great coffee. I bet you don't have a Peet's in Vallejo."

"Uhm... we have a Starbucks?" he joked.

She laughed. "I see. So, Peet's it is."

Before he'd been admitted into the hospital, Flynn had been having so much trouble sleeping, eating, and keeping down food that he'd been losing weight at a somewhat alarming rate. In the hospital, there was nothing to do except eat and try to relax. He gained seventeen pounds during his two-week stay in the hospital. Charlotte liked the way it looked on him. She patted him on the bottom.

"You have a nice ass," she told him. "I want to bite it."

"Okay," he said, "But not right now. It's first thing in the morning."

She laughed.

She thought it was nice that they were going get up and go do things together. They could walk around and hold hands and do the things human men and women do when their relationships are new and they are just learning how to love one another. They could pretend that were going to be okay and everything was going to be fine.

He could try to convince himself he wasn't broken. She could try to convince herself Pinocchio was a real girl, not a dizzy little devil doll trying desperately to convince herself that her feelings were just as real, just as deep as anyone else's. She wondered if she could ever love him the way a human being deserved to be loved.

But people didn't get what they deserved, they got what they got, and sometimes it was better than nothing.

It could be much better.

They sat on the edge of the bed just holding one another, each of them hoping in different ways that their budding relationship could be wonderful, or maybe just safe, even a little boring. They were hoping it wouldn't somehow end up sad and terribly tragic.

But the time for worrying was over now. The time for coffee had arrived. Coffee fixes everything.

A Little Buggy

Mercy was glad that her father mentioned Charlotte's gratuitous violence towards the insect population. Sure, it was everyday business for most human beings, the slaughter of the cockroaches, the squashing of the flies. It wasn't any type of intentional blood ritual like the Slaughter of the Innocents, but given that Charlotte was demisomnali, and that Mercy was her sister, it would do.

It was a lot less dignified than what her father Brash did in the hospital, spying on Flynn in a human suit. If she'd had other options for entering the physical plane, she probably would have taken one of them but beggars can't be choosers. It was the denizens of the Roach Motel or the buzzing fly-by-night guests on the sticky flypaper strip. Mercy decided she preferred the vehicle with wings.

That was how she literally became a fly on the wall in her sister's bedroom.

Mercy whisked her hairy little front legs together in anticipation. They weren't the prettiest appendages, but she thought they were at least as fetching as Sympathy's tentacles. She was *Musca domestica Linnaeus*, the common housefly. It was a tidy little creature whose job was to feast upon the foul remains of corpses and garbage and excrement left behind by the perpetually filthy humankind.

The tiny dorm-hovel her sister occupied seemed like a gloriously vast expanse of wide-open countryside from her spot on the wall just above the fetid banana peel in Charlotte's compost bin. Her sister wouldn't compost anything here, but would deliver this to the community garden where she volunteered. The stench of rotted banana skin and cherry pits made Mercy's mandibles water. It all looked so lovely through her compound eyes, like a stained-glass window or the inside of the world's most complicated kaleidoscope, one with a thousand facets.

Of course, it was too late to observe Charlotte and her lover in person. They had both already left for the morning, but even though they were not present, there were many clues left behind. She could spy.

Of those items left behind, the most incriminating was in the garbage can, which sat less than a foot away from the compost bin in the kitchen. It wasn't very well hidden. Her sister had tossed it aside carelessly, and used only a scrap of junk mail to partially cover it where it sat.

It was a used prophylactic.

If the purpose of the Rite of Binding was procreation, then why was her sister using birth control? This seemed to be evidence of her deception, of the lack of sincerity in her intentions. Their father certainly would be displeased. Something had to be done about this.

She had to tell her father immediately.

SECOND INTERMISSION

"Things seem to be going well," Eros said, popping up quite suddenly behind Somnus. Somnus had all of his monitors turned on where just anyone could see them. He waved his hand and turned them around, embarrassed, like a husband whose wife walked in while he was browsing porn on the Internet. In fact, they merely showed the families a very limited number of his thousand sons.

"Charlotte and Flynn do seem to love each other," Somnus admitted.

"That never stops humans from mucking it all up," Eros warned. "And the girl, she's only half human. Sometimes I think she's not sure if she wants to kiss him or dissect him with a steak knife. I mean, I understand why you selected her. With any of her sisters, there wouldn't really be an 'if', you know?"

"What about Mercy?" Somnus asked.

"Mercy doesn't care about him," Eros cautioned. "She cares about that girl, Happiness… the one who calls herself Charlotte. They relate as sisters more than they know. Mercy is jealous of her little sister, who is the apple of her father's eye. Charlotte is jealous of her big sister, who is immortal and larger than life. Mercy isn't self-aware enough to understand why she wants Charlotte to have children so desperately. She wants there to be something left to remind her of her mortal sister once Charlotte's dead and gone. These girls need a therapist."

"Very funny," Somnus grunted. "Well, her father is very impressed with Charlotte's comic. It inflates his already enormous ego."

"Oh that reminds me," Eros announced. "Have you seen her latest episode?" He waved his hand over the cave wall and bought up one of the monitors Somnus had hidden. On it was displayed Charlotte's webpage.

"That's me!" Somnus shrieked. "I'm in it! I'm in my granddaughter's comic!"

"Right," Eros said. "So we're square, right? I don't owe you anything anymore?"

"Yes," Somnus said happily. "This is so much more than I ever expected. I don't think you owed me this much. I think now, I owe you. You have been very kind. Thank you, old friend."

Act III: Reconciliation

Affection

Little girls were given storybooks full of fairytales with brave knights on powerful stallions as white and pure as fluffy clouds who came to sweep them away from all of their problems. Good little girls like Cinderella were properly rewarded for all of their obedience and elbow grease by being swept off their feet and promised a lifetime with their one true love.

Flynn wanted to be rescued. It just wasn't fair.

He sat across the table from Charlotte at the coffee shop. It was one of those tall, round tables with the barstool height chairs that left your legs to dangle a foot or two away from the floor. Flynn was leaning over with his elbows on the table, kicking his feet in the air, staring at Charlotte like he was a boy with a schoolyard crush experiencing his first erection.

He was watching the way she drank her iced latte and noticing how much lipstick she left on the lid of her cup. The color was a thick, matte plum that set off the lighter mauve dye in her hair. The purple smudges she left on the white coffee lid looked like bruises. Hers was a plump little sexy mouth, round and fleshy like a plum. He remembered that mouth being all over him, kissing him, biting him, bruising him, tasting him and leaving her mark on him just as surely as she left it on the rim of her coffee cup.

When they were together, everything felt solid and real. He was counting on her to keep him anchored to the spot, like he was a balloon tied to her wrist. Without something to cling to, life threatened to release him, to leave him floating off into the ether, rising high into the clouds one moment and then deflated soon after when the helium ran out. Tumbling from the sky and dropping useless and depleted onto the sea.

A story flitted through his mind, and he remembered the Little Mermaid, not the cheerful singing version in Disney's animated musical, but the tragic figure in the original Hans Christian Andersen story. She loved a man who could never return her love. She suffered and suffered but ended up as nothing but sea foam. He often feared that would be his fate.

But today, he felt infinitely more fortunate. He wasn't invisible to Charlotte. She saw him.

This was his beautiful Charlotte in the flesh. This was not the flawless Charlotte of dreams. He decided that he would try to take note of all of the differences between the real girl and the dream girl, so that if he ever got lost, he would have a roadmap back to reality.

She had the most amazing eyes. Hiding under smoky untrimmed eyebrows, and rimmed with long dark lashes. Her irises were some color on a spectrum between ruby red and amber. He'd never seen human eyes like that before.

He remembered she claimed to be only partially human. He tried not to think about that. It made him feel like the fabric of the world was being pulled out from under his fingers.

Her olive skin was covered in various little spots and bumps in darker browns or harrowing reds that were currently covered in pancake make-up. He remembered her naked face in the bathroom mirror this morning, when she was leaning over the medicine cabinet handing him an extra toothbrush out of her five-pack from the dollar store.

He remembered touching her face, and marveling at all of these tiny anomalies. He said they were cute and she got angry, maybe not so much mad as just a little irritated with him. He meant that they made her seem human, and he was very invested in seeing her as human, but of course, that's not what he'd said.

Now that they were out of the hospital, she always wore her jewelry. It wasn't shiny or jeweled the way it was in the dream, but rather flat, and steel. The jewelry embedded into her face was arranged asymmetrically. She had three snakebites keeping close quarters on the left side of her mouth, and a ring in her eyebrow on the same side. She wore a nose ring on the opposite side, a little stud that was shaped like a tiny tarantula.

Disaffection

After they finished their morning caffeine intake ritual, Charlotte took Flynn down to Telegraph, where all of the clothes stores, head shops, record stores, tattoo parlors and piercing salons could be found. They held hands in the clumsy, conspicuous manner of uncertain new lovers. He held her hand as though she might disappear if he let it go. She held his as though she was concerned that left unattended, he might absentmindedly wander out into traffic.

She worried about him, with his willful blindness and his longing for self-sacrifice. She wanted to see him informed, and enlightened. She wanted him to know enough to make his own choices, rather than have her, or worse still, her father making them for him. But accepting the way things were caused Flynn a great deal of heartache, and Charlotte was constantly forced to dance around the subject. She began to lose patience, and by the time they got to the jewelry store, they were bickering.

"Why didn't your holes close when you had your jewelry out in the hospital?" he asked her.

"What do you want me to say? I've had all of those piercings for a long time and that's why they won't close?" she asked. "You already know I'm not human, why are we playing games?"

"What would you do if you were me?" he pled with her. "I've been told all of my adult life that there is something wrong with my mind, and I can't entirely trust what I see. If I'm crazy, and I've been assured that I am, then can't you see why I find certain things you're saying to me difficult to accept?"

"But you've seen them with your own eyes," she reminded him.

"I can't trust what I see," he repeated.

Charlotte stopped trying to explain things to him, and gave his hand a squeeze instead. Clearly, he just couldn't deal with certain things right now. He was human, and they really hadn't been together very long. She decided to stop pushing him to accept the fact that she wasn't human for now. She could afford to stick with familiar things and stay within his comfort zone for a while, to see if that made him feel any better.

She quickly changed the subject by pointing out the different styles of jewelry in the display case.

"Look at these ones," she said, tapping on the glass. "They have little eight balls on the beads."

Flynn grabbed her around the waist and whispered in her ear, "Are you going to insert them for me? Hmmm?"

"Sure," she teased. "Just pull your shirt up and we can do it right here."

"Well in that case, yes. Those ones are perfect," he said. "How about those other ones with the skulls? Do you prefer them? Just tell me what you like."

And just like that, the spat was over.

Sorrow and Whimsy

"Whoa, get over it, Mercy," Sympathy said, rolling her eyes. "You're totally obsessed with Happiness. You should get over it."

"She's concerned with the pursuit of Happiness," Whimsy declared. He gave Sorrow a meaningful look. "I mean, who isn't? We've all been there before, am I right?"

"You suck," Mercy told all three of them.

They were all at the big shindig Brash was throwing in anticipation of his future successes, now that he would be taking the human world by storm. The soiree was at his palace, with everyone in theme-appropriate costumes. Sympathy couldn't figure out how to work tentacles into the whole Greco-Roman thing, but she was working that Gorgon thing with a head full of serpents. Her long serpentine tail dragged out behind her like a bridal train.

Sorrow was her companion. He was her date for the party, and they were often seen together since he ended his little fling with Happiness. Sorrow and Happiness were very poorly matched, and often in conflict, but there was no such friction between Sorrow and Sympathy. They were now, and had always been perfectly suited to one another. Sure, sometimes Sorrow went without Sympathy. He had his brief flirtations with Happiness, Wrath and Lust but they never lasted. Sorrow and Sympathy were meant for each other.

He showed up to the party in the expected black wings, and a face with minimal features. His eyes were enormous black pits of despair, his skin bore an unnatural pallor, and his nose was miniscule, overwhelmed entirely by those eyes and the jagged tear he called a mouth. It all gave him a rather alien, or insect-like appearance. His chest was torn open, exposing the ribcage. It looked like a bomb went off under the skin, leaving nothing but ragged tatters.

He gave Mercy his best sardonic smile. "You should really get out and have some fun, you know? Sympathy and I have been visiting this fan of those Hellraiser films lately. They're kind of dated, I know, but this guy! Let me tell you, he is *totally* into those movies, in the most enticing ways. Do you have any idea how much rending of flesh from bone is involved in his dreams?"

"I've inflicted my fair share of nightmares," Mercy complained. "You're not educating me here. I already know how to go out and get a meal."

Mercy had presented her father with evidence of Charlotte's betrayal, and he'd snubbed her, accusing her of spending too much time among the humans and beginning to experience envy. Envy snickered and said she'd know damned well if Mercy was experiencing her, she'd surely remember that, and in fact she wanted to invite Mercy to drop by and experience her any time she liked.

Everyone had laughed, everyone except Mercy.

"Charlotte's got something up her sleeve," Mercy warned. "All of you are just too frivolous to notice it. I just hope father comes to his senses before it's too late."

THE RITE OF UNDOING

The daylight was nearing an end now, and the grass felt cool against Flynn's skin. Charlotte had taken him down to People's Park off Telegraph. Food Not Bombs, a local soup kitchen was serving free vegetarian plates there. Charlotte and Flynn each had a paper bowl of lentil soup and a slice of wheat bread. They were hanging out with a friend of Charlotte's who called herself Sunshine. She was a resident of a local board and care home, a middle aged one-time vagabond in a tie-dyed Grateful Dead t-shirt with a head full of dirty-blonde dreadlocks and a gap-toothed smile. She was a fellow veteran of the mental health system, and they easily laughed as they discussed their various stays at places with names like Langley Porter, St. Helena's, John Muir and John George.

People's Park was always crowded. Mostly homeless and marginally housed people spent their days there. The marginally housed included formerly homeless individuals who had government-provided single resident occupancy hotel rooms with shared bathrooms, and mentally ill individuals who lived in dorm-like boarding care facilities where they had very little privacy.

Whether they slept in the park or just visited it to avoid the heavy weight of loneliness they experienced in the efficient little cubicles social services provided to them as homes, all of these people enjoyed being in the park with the roofless sky above them. They loved the camaraderie and acceptance they found here among friends. Even those who did live indoors were of limited income. Sunshine was no exception.

"Yeah the last time I was admitted at John George, I spent the first night sitting in an easy chair eating graham crackers and drinking juice boxes while they waited to check me into a room," Sunshine complained.

"Why do you think I had my nervous breakdown in Concord?" Charlotte said, laughing.

Both of the women had been hospitalized often enough to know that some psychiatric hospitals were more pleasant to stay in than others. Some were understaffed, underfunded, or located in areas where there was a large population of homeless individuals. About a third of the homeless had psychiatric issues that contributed to their ending up on the streets.

The stress often exacerbated things so that people like Sunshine ended up in and out of the mental hospitals until they were stabilized in some kind of longer-term treatment program. Homelessness had at one time made it harder for Sunshine to stay on her medication. It added to her stress by exposing her to threats such as assault, rape and domestic violence, common problems faced by homeless women. Often, she was too discombobulated to figure out where she was, much less where a better psych ward might be. Nowadays Sunshine was relatively stable, but the park remained the core of her social life.

Charlotte called Sunshine over because she needed a magic believer to assist her with the ritual. Sunshine was a longtime friend of the Metaxas family and knew about the somnali. She needed someone to stand in for Tamara.

"So this won't take too long," Charlotte had told her. "I just need a third person."

That was an hour ago. Since then, they'd been hanging out, eating and sharing a 40 ouncer. Now they were losing daylight so she figured they needed to get the show on the road.

"Okay, take your shirt off," she told Flynn.

He was a little uncomfortable about being shirtless in public, but he would hardly be the only bare-chested man in the park, and anyhow, he was a guy. Not like it was illegal. The beer, now that was illegal. He shrugged, pulled his shirt off, and handed it to Charlotte.

She laid it on the ground behind him and said, "Okay, now lay down on it."

"Fine," he said, dropping down on one elbow. "So I know you already explained this, right? But you say we have to mimic everything we did in the dreams, but what about that orange stuff you had me drink? I don't remember doing that."

"Remember when we were out at the club, and I gave you the rest of my beer?" she asked.

"Yeah," he said, suspicion creeping into his voice. "Why? What was in it?"

"Just a little blood, nothing to worry about," she said. He shook his head, and finished lowering himself to the ground.

"Okay, Sunshine... so, hold his hand," Charlotte said,

"You want me to hold your boyfriend's hand?" Sunshine asked nervously. She wasn't interested in Charlotte's boyfriend. He wasn't her type, and he looked like a little boy to her, even with his shirt off. She just knew that some women got jealous and would give you a black eye for less.

"Yea," Charlotte said. "In the dream, another girl was holding his hand, so I need you to hold his hand now for the undoing ritual."

"Which is for?" Sunshine asked.

"It's so that the somnali can't use those dreams to have power over either of us," Charlotte reiterated. "It's like a protection spell, in a way. Okay?"

"Sure," Sunshine said, taking another sip of her Four Loco. "Kill swill?" she asked, handing it to Charlie.

"No girl, that's all you," Charlotte said with a wink.

Sunshine drained the can, crumpled it, and tossed it a brown paper grocery bag that was already partially filled with cans and bottles for the recycling center. Recycling all her friends' empties was sort of a hobby of Sunshine's. She used the extra money to buy art supplies.

She sat down next to Flynn, took one of his hands in hers, and patted it.

"I'm sure it won't hurt or anything," Sunshine told him.

"No, it won't." Flynn agreed. It wouldn't bother him if it did hurt, but there was no reason it should. He was more concerned about being looked at. Either way, it would be over in about two minutes.

"Omigod, look at those? They're just adorable. Where did you get the jewelry?" Sunshine asked, noticing the little skulls in the piercing rings. "I need to get some like that." Charlotte and Flynn gave each other a funny look. Neither of them wanted to speculate about where Sunshine might have piercings.

"Just hurry up and get this over with so I can put my shirt back on," Flynn told Charlotte. He blinked uneasily and trickle of sweat ran down his temple.

"He's shy," Charlotte told Sunshine. She was sitting on the ground beside him with her legs unselfconsciously sprawled out beneath her. She leaned over him and quickly removed one of the little pieces of plastic by pressing against one side of his nipple with her thumb. As soon as it popped out, she swiftly inserted the jewelry and snapped the little skull-shaped ball into place so it wouldn't fall out.

Flynn was looking up at her, squinting into the sunlight. He shaded his eyes with his free hand. He felt the delicious pressure of her pressing and tugging as she repeated the procedure on this other nipple. He smiled off into the distance, daydreaming about Karl's grimy beard. He was determined not to get an erection here in the park, with Sunshine holding his hand.

"There you go, all finished," Charlotte told the other two.

"Thank God," Flynn said, sitting up and putting his shirt on. Sunshine relinquished his hand with no protest at all.

"What happened with the girl in the dream?" Charlotte asked him suddenly.

"Oh, Tamara," Flynn answered. He had forgotten that he'd never admitted these dreams could be real. "She was my first girlfriend. We broke up after I went away to college and started having emotional problems. The doctors say they're mental problems but to me it seems like something is wrong with my emotions, not my mind."

"My first boyfriend broke up with me when I got sick, too," Sunshine said sympathetically. "But he wasn't my last boyfriend. You know what I'm saying? Life goes on, and you have Charlotte now."

Flynn nodded. "That's right. I do."

"Do you still speak with her?" Charlotte asked casually. "How is she doing?"

"She's doing great," Flynn replied. "I haven't seen her in years, but Danny still speaks to her. She still lives in Daly City. She's married now, and Danny tells me that they are going to have a kid. She invited Danny's sister to her baby shower. Now if that doesn't beat all."

"So she would probably give us her blessing?" Charlotte inquired.

"I guess," Flynn said nervously. "I mean there's no reason why she shouldn't, she's happy. Why should she care about what I'm doing?"

"Well that's good," Charlotte said. "According to the Rites of Binding, our union could be challenged if I failed to get Tamara's blessing. So if I wanted to meet her, could Danny hook it up?"

"For fuck's sake, Charlotte. Why? I haven't seen Tamara in five years," Flynn growled.

"Because you gave her your virtue," Charlotte explained.

"My virtue? You can't be serious." Flynn stared incredulously.

"It does sound a little provincial," Sunshine interjected. "I always thought you were sex-positive, Charlotte. Why should it matter who he lost his virginity to?"

"I don't write these rituals, I just perform them," Charlotte said huffily.

"Do you have to get the blessing of every chick I ever fucked in my life?" Flynn said irritably.

"No, of course not," Charlotte responded. "Just the first one."

"I'll think about it," Flynn said.

"That's fine," Charlotte nodded. No matter what else just happened Flynn was no longer contesting her claim that the dreams were real and that she was really in them. That meant that he might be able to accept the existence of the somnali and if he could, there was a much better chance that they could fight off her dad and her sisters.

Her sister.... Shit! She realized that she was going to have to tell Flynn that Mercy was her sister sometime soon. She'd been meaning to get around to it, but now so much time had passed. She needed to find a way to tell him.

"So, did it hurt?" Sunshine asked, changing the subject.

"No," Flynn said. "She just changed the jewelry, of course it didn't hurt."

He reached down and picked up another beer. Popping the tab, he slugged it down. If this conversation went on much longer, he was definitely going to need a few more of them. He thought, "Here it comes. In one, two, three..."

"I mean did it hurt when you got them?" Sunshine asked.

"Yes, it hurt a lot," he said stoically. Charlotte winked at him.

WORRIES

His fun little outing with Charlotte was over, and now Flynn was on a BART train to the 80 Bus back home with his head leaning against the window. He tried to ignore the cacophony of problem-related thoughts his restless mind was crapping out like stream of consciousness diarrhea.

First he thought he could get the extra $190 that his landlord wanted by getting a payday loan at the check-cashing place. Then, he remembered that he needed a job or some kind of steady income to get one. Next, he started asking himself whether or not the check-cashing place would figure it out if he just brought in his last two paychecks. He worried that might be fraud. What if he went to jail? But he needed the $190. He worried that he could end up homeless if he didn't at least try to get it. Wasn't it worth it?

A random concern entered his mind about dinner. He'd been in the hospital for two weeks, and he wasn't sure what food was canned and what was fresh. Was his refrigerator filled with rotting vegetables and mold? Would it stink when he got home? He really needed to clean the refrigerator. He couldn't remember whether or not he had any Ramen left and it was frustrating. He thought he might have a can of beans.

He would have stayed at Charlotte's again, but he didn't want to give her the impression that he was too needy. He cared about her, and he didn't want to mess things up. Since Tamara left him five years ago he'd dated a handful of women but nothing ever went anywhere. He met a few girls in college, even hooked up a couple times. Most of them were there to study and didn't necessarily want to get involved. One girl told him that she thought it would distract her from her educational goals. He wasn't sure if it could be called a "relationship" since it only lasted two weeks. She told him he was too clingy and he needed to lose her number.

He was already having mental and emotional problems by then. They complicated everything. He was having a hard time keeping his head together and staying in school, and trying to navigate potential relationships was just one more layer of added pressure. Then there was the medication issue. The side effects were interfering with both his libido and his ability to maintain an erection. He had been barely old enough to buy a beer at the time. Those problems made him feel like a prematurely old man.

Things never got any better. Instead, they abruptly grew worse. Just two years after he'd broken up with Tamara, he'd dropped out of school and wound up on the streets. It had taken him another sixteen months to get back on his feet again. He had only been stably housed and intermittently employed for only a year when the nightmares started. With all of those problems, he hadn't had much of a love life. There had been a half a dozen dalliances of one kind or another, all of them too brief to be considered relationships.

But now, maybe he had a girlfriend. Just the thought of it made his head swim.

What if he couldn't keep his apartment? What if he couldn't get another job again? Should he sell his Xbox? It was too old to pawn. Should he pawn his computer? He remembered just how bad things had gotten. He was panicking about all of the things that could possibly go wrong.

Flynn stepped off the BART train at El Cerrito Del Norte and made his way to the escalator that went down to the stop for the Solano Transit 80 bus to Vallejo. He spotted a man on an escalator headed in the opposite direction up to the platform. He was the spitting image of Howard Lowe, the man who had injured himself in the hospital.

Suddenly the memory of Howard standing there, clawing at his face, neck untouched below the fresh wounds on his cheeks and the raw, seeping mass of his shredded torso came to the surface of his mind, and Flynn felt nauseous. He instantly regretted his choice to put on a brave face and go home. He did not want to be alone right now.

He didn't have to be. Charlotte wasn't the only person he knew. He pulled out his cell phone, looking for a lifeline. Just before he started scrolling through his list of numbers, the phone rang. Flynn stared at it stupidly for a moment, as if the thing had somehow read his mind.

Then he realized it was Danny calling. Of course! He must be back from Sacramento now.

Flynn quickly answered the phone.

Fluids

Charlotte wrinkled her nose.

"Ugh!" she said aloud to no one. "The things we do for love."

Was it love? She wasn't sure. What was love, really? She felt a complicated mixture of affection and lust that would be better described as infatuation, but she supposed it might become love. That was what she hoped for, anyway. In the eyes of her father's kind she'd already made a commitment to this young man. She might still be hedging her bets, but she needed to prepare for the possibility that she would see this courtship through to its intended conclusion. If that happened Flynn would be the father of her children. That was now a probability more than a mere possibility.

She had been studying the text called the Rites of Undoing, looking for solutions to any issues that might arise in future dealings involving Flynn and the inhuman members of her clan. One of the rites was the physical world companion to the Feast of Tears. It was an important one, since the Feast couldn't safely be repeated in the flesh.

While Flynn was sleeping, she'd carefully collected and refrigerated the ingredients. She used a sewing needle to remove the flesh she'd excised from his body from beneath the ends of her fingernails. She'd collected it when she'd buried her claws into his cute little behind mid-coitus. Charlotte smiled at the memory as she dropped the skin onto a pat of butter carefully arranged on the top of a clean tea saucer in the refrigerator.

Beside the saucer was a matching teacup with a quarter cup of fresh milk in it. She'd used an eyedropper to add miniscule amounts of his bodily fluids to the milk, as the rite required. The blood and the semen were easy to collect. She hadn't had the heart to make him cry. She'd known about his frequent nightmares for some time now. She'd waited until he had a bad dream and carefully collected his tears before he awakened.

There were other things in the butter, a tiny bit of hair, and a sliver of fingernail.

She shook her head as she dumped everything into the bowl with the sugar cookie batter. She realized that she probably wouldn't be able to taste any of these bodily fluids, but the idea was strange and a bit less than appetizing. She put it out of her mind and rolled the cookie dough out and used the gingerbread man cookie cutter to shape it.

It was a perfect, tiny little cookie man. She took the scraps and used them to decorate the cookie with tiny eyes, a little smile. She couldn't waste any part of the cookie. She had to eat everything. Finally, it was ready. She put it in the oven.

Mmmmmm… it smelled yummy.

She finished eating the cookie just before her mom called. It was delicious.

"Hey, how did the conference go?" she asked Maribelle.

"Great," her mom answered. "That kid Danny picked up some information on a few companies that are hiring for your… for Flynn. Did you have fun together?"

"Yes, we did." Charlotte said. "And it's okay to use the b word. I guess he is my boyfriend." She swallowed nervously, the sweet taste of her cookie-man still lingering on her tongue. She decided that she did love Flynn. She loved the way he was tender and affectionate. She also loved the way he was hers.

Time

Outside of the mental hospital, time seemed to pass by more quickly. The old adage went "time flies when you're having fun." There must have been more to it than that. It wasn't all fun. A lot of it was duty and completing the tasks necessary for comfortable day-to-day living. Flynn cleaned out his refrigerator throwing away a container of watery stinking sour cream, a few moldy tomatoes and a plate of leftovers that had turned into a high school science experiment. He made the phone calls and excursions to the Unemployment necessary for maintaining an income, searching for a job, and paying the rent. He kept seeing Dr. Lester.

He spent the rest of the weekend hanging out in sports bars playing pool or watching the game with Danny, who complained about the lack of decent nightclubs attended by hot, young women in Fairfield and Vallejo. Vallejo didn't have dance clubs, only bars and karaoke lounges filled with middle-aged people, old cowboys and couples. The few available women were vastly outnumbered and hotly pursued by the men. They consisted of well-fed country girls and middle-aged alcoholic barflies. None of them were really to Danny's liking.

He bragged about San Jose's superior nightlife, and invited Flynn to come visit him.

The next weekend, Flynn's anxiety over not having enough money to buy gas or a BART ticket to go down and visit with Charlotte was short-lived. It was alleviated when she suggested she come up to see him for the weekend instead. They held hands and went walking around the boardwalk at the Marina. They spent time hanging out playing the only two player games he actually owned, the entire classic Mortal Kombat series. They spent many hours in bed trying to perfect the art of pleasing each other.

Flynn had nightmares he didn't talk about. Charlotte resisted the urge to visit him in his dreams uninvited and chase away the daemons. She comforted him by running her hand along his spine and kissing his neck instead. He was solid and warm and heartbreakingly human. She was besieged by an overwhelming need to protect him. Increasingly, she was certain that this was love.

Hannah and Shelby showed up one Friday night and the four of them went out to karaoke over by the ferry building. Flynn attended Lorena's church in Richmond a total of three times. Mike and Nancy added Flynn on Facebook, and Twitter. Nancy also added him on Pinterest where she kept a massive array of cat-related pins of various kinds. He also followed Mike on Instagram. Mike regularly updated a comical series of photobomb selfies that were obviously staged so that various hot looking women in the background appeared to be sitting with him. There was the girl on the beach two towel-lengths over and another who was sitting behind him in the bleachers at a 49ers game. Mike was really trying to master the art of using perspective in photography in order to perpetuate a clearly fictionalized version of himself as Mike the Chick Magnet.

The three of them never actually saw each other or did anything together. They were all too broke and lived too far away from one another, and no one was all that motivated to make anything happen. Mike repeatedly messaged Flynn about how things were going with him and his hot girlfriend, and sometimes asked if Charlotte had a friend or a sister. Flynn didn't know about Charlotte's sisters and if he did, he wouldn't have wanted to hook Mike up with any of them. That was how hours passed into days, and days passed into weeks, and weeks into months until three months passed had passed by rather uneventfully.

But things couldn't stay uneventful or pleasant forever, at least not for Charlotte or Flynn. Although Flynn didn't know it, and even Charlotte was not aware of the full extent of it, they were at the nexus of a great battle over the doorway between the world of flesh and the world of dreams. If they didn't make certain choices on their own, someone or something else was likely to force their hands.

Cohabitation

In late May, spring semester came to a close. Charlotte was only taking one class during summer session and it didn't start for six weeks, so she found herself with plenty of free time. Suddenly the couple found themselves spending every night together. First, Charlotte came up to Vallejo and spent two weeks with Flynn.

After that, when she said she needed to go down and start registering for fall classes, Flynn casually suggested that he had been thinking of looking for work in Berkeley and Oakland, since there really were no graphic design positions available in Vallejo and he hadn't found anything in nearby cities like Fairfield and Napa. There seemed to be some jobs closer to where she lived. He asked her if he could he come stay with her for a week and check them out.

Things went on like that for about a month before they started talking about moving in together. Flynn was having trouble keeping up with his rent, and having money left over for travel to job-hunt or = visit Charlotte. He couldn't afford gas money anyway, so he sold his Chevy about a month after he got out of the hospital in order to come up with the back rent he owed his landlord. He only got $700 for it and that didn't last long. He didn't mention any of this to Charlotte, but it certainly weighed on his mind during these deliberations.

Charlotte was more concerned with keeping an eye on Flynn when he was sleeping. She hadn't been in his dreams in months. She noticed over the past three weeks that he had nightmares every night. She needed to know what was going on with him, and she had to keep him safe. She couldn't do that if she couldn't keep him close.

The desire to watch over him was irresistible. Of course Charlotte wasn't aware that Somnus and Cupid had her under their spells, compelling her to love and protect Flynn. It wouldn't have mattered if she had known anymore, because she'd already grown to love him of her own accord. It gave her tremendous pleasure to know that they would be sharing one roof and one bed. Their love was fated but that didn't guarantee it would come to any positive end.

And so it was that five and a half months after they had started dating, six months counting the two weeks when he was in the hospital, Flynn gave up his apartment and moved in with his girlfriend and entrusted himself completely into her care. It was a matter of trust. He trusted her not to be fickle or careless, and he trusted her not to toss him out into the street the next time they had an argument. He trusted her, perhaps unwisely, because she kept so many secrets from him.

He trusted her, and he loved her, too.

For a time, they were happy.

NIGHTMARE

Flynn was having the same nightmare he'd been having for five months now. He was back in the hospital, sitting in the television room. No one else was there, and he began running through the hallways, calling out familiar names, hoping to find someone, anyone who could tell him why he was back and what was going on.

He tried to get out, but all of the doors were locked. He was trapped.

Unable to escape or find anyone to help him, he gave up and walked back to the room he was staying in, hoping to find some kind of clue there. That's when this dream veered off from the others.

That's when he noticed that there was someone laying in one of the beds.

The figure was covered in a white, blood-spattered sheet. When it sat upright, the sheet dropped and revealed the shredded visage of his former roommate Howard Lowe. Howard had scratched off half of his own face and dislocated one of his own eyes, which was dangling by some meaty cords from its socket. Long gouges covered his painfully infected chest. A raised, discolored welt five inches long bisected his turgid abdomen. It was covered in a moist scab oozing green and yellow pus. Only the skin on his neck was strangely untouched, leaving his vocal cords and the quality of his voice crystal clear and eerily intact.

"Lucky boy," Howard hissed. "Flynn is such a lucky boy, so very special."

Flynn gulped. "Howard I... I thought they took you away. They said you went to a specialist to get emergency treatment and reconstructive surgery. What are you doing here? Are you... did you die?"

"I wish I had died," Howard complained. "If I'd managed to kill myself, I wouldn't be trapped in this vegetative state being tortured by Mercy. Remember her?"

"I don't know what you're talking about," Flynn deflected.

"Well you should," Howard said accusingly. "You've been fucking her sister. Did Charlotte happen to mention that she was closely related to the demon who tricked me into tearing off half my face?"

The wound on Howard's chest was beginning to bubble over. A glob of thick, baby-shit colored mucous-like gel spilled out of a wound on his belly and began oozing down over the ravages of what might have once been a belly button. Flynn felt a little queasy.

"I think she'd tell me," Flynn defended.

"Would she, now?" Howard mocked him. "Would she tell her delicate little hot house tomato? Oh no, no. She has to protect you from her sister, reality, and any bad feelings that might bruise your little ego, doesn't she? You were chosen, and she was chosen to protect you."

"Why do you think that?" Flynn asked. "I was chosen for what?"

"A little bird told me," Howard said with a shrug. "The fate of the somnali lies with you. You were chosen to live, or to die. Perhaps you were chosen to be the one simple little sacrifice that will allow the eradication of the most vile and vicious line of the somnali. Perhaps you were chosen to open the doorway between their reality and ours, and let them finally enter and infect the world of the flesh as they have longed to do for millennia."

"I don't think so," Flynn argued. "What happens to me can't be that important."

"And then, she'd be human," Howard continued. "Your Charlotte would be entirely human and her shithead father and all of her unnatural siblings would be wiped out of existence forever. Don't you think it would be worth it? Don't you want to offer yourself to her? Don't you want to die for her?"

"I like living, thank you," Flynn responded.

"Well, so did I, back when I had a face," Howard said snippily. "The fates haven't decided yet, whether you live or die. If it were up to me, you would die."

"Fuck you," Flynn said.

"One of these days Charlotte is going to ask to kill you, but she'll say it's just a game, in a dream." Howard said tauntingly. "She'll tell you that you'll wake up and be fine in the morning. But sometimes things that happen in dreams also happen in the flesh. Maybe there is a way to make sure you aren't okay. But why wait? Perhaps I should kill you now."

Howard stood and walked across the room. Flynn turned to run, but he couldn't move. He was frozen to the spot. He stood there helpless as Howard put both hands around his neck and began to strangle him. He felt heat and pressure in his chest as his lungs filled with carbon dioxide.

Impatient with the slow progress of asphyxiation, Howard leaned in and bit off Flynn's nose. Flynn tried to scream, but no sound came out. He felt something wet pour down his cheeks and he realized that he was crying. The tears mingled with blood coursing down from the hole in the middle of his face. He could taste the fluids as they passed over into his contorted, silently screaming mouth.

A Talk

Charlotte shook him. Flynn was crying in his sleep again.

"Wake up, sweetie, you're having a bad dream," she said, rocking him back and forth trying to rouse him. She finally woke him, but he didn't stop crying. She held him for some time, sobbing and shaking on the bed.

After about ten minutes, he stopped crying and sat up.

"Mercy... she's your sister?" he accused.

"Yes, she is." Charlotte admitted. "I kept meaning to tell you, but..."

"What else are you not telling me?" he asked, instinctively moving away from her.

"Many things," she admitted. "I wanted to talk to you, but every time I bring up anything supernatural, you just kind of shut down. I didn't know how to talk about it without upsetting you."

He sighed. "That's no excuse. You need to tell me things, even if they upset me. You can't keep hiding things from me."

"So let's talk," she suggested.

"Fine," Flynn mumbled. His body language suggested he was anything but fine with what she was saying. He grabbed one of the covers from the bed and drew it up around his body protectively, stood up and walked over to an easy chair and bundled himself up in it. He pulled his knees to his chest and huddled into a fortified little ball under the blanket. Charlotte didn't move to stop him.

They didn't own a couch, but Flynn was too angry with her to sleep in the same bed as her. It was too late for him to go back to his old apartment. That was gone. He was determined to sleep in this chair.

"My intentions were good, I want you to know that," Charlotte protested. "I was trying to save your life."

"Why?" Flynn asked. "Did you know that Mercy came to one of my roommates and tormented him in his sleep, making him hallucinate that there were bugs under his skin? His name was Howard. Sometime after you checked out, he clawed the skin off his face and chest trying to get at the imaginary bugs. He attacked a nurse in front of me. He... I heard that he gouged own eye out and pulled it from the socket. That happened two days before I got out of the hospital. Did you know about that?"

"No," Charlotte said calmly. "No, you never told me that."

"I..." he paused for a moment, "never told you? I'm very angry now, and maybe that is why it seems like you're accusing me of something. It sounds like you are trying to say that this is somehow my fault. I would have to say that's more than a little hypocritical. You have clearly neglected to tell me many, many things. Please tell me I'm reading this the wrong way. I am pissed off, don't get me wrong, but I'm also very hurt to find out you've been keeping things from me."

"I'm sorry if it seemed like I was accusing you of something," Charlotte said carefully. "I don't speak with my sister, I haven't in years. If you are asking if she told me what she did to Howard, or if anyone else on that side of the family told me, then no. I rarely see my father, and the others don't speak with me."

"I'm asking again, why?" Flynn repeated. "Why would you choose to protect me, and not Howard?"

"It's complicated," she protested. "I couldn't just... protect everyone. I was lucky that I was able to protect you. It wasn't easy, you know. It wasn't then and it won't be simple moving forward."

"So, why?" he repeated. "Howard said you were chosen to protect me, like it's your divine destiny.

"I'm not aware of that," Charlotte said, shaking her head. "If so, that would explain a lot, I suppose. In my father's world, things work that way. Cupid hits you with an arrow and bang, you're infatuated and you feel like you need to be with someone. It was how I felt with you, anyway. I wanted you, and I didn't know why. Does anyone know why? Not a day goes by where someone doesn't feel this way about someone. Love is very common. It's not all that interesting."

"I do find your love interesting," Flynn said gently. "For me, love has been rare. But I need you to be honest with me, because this argument isn't about love. It's about trust. I need to know what you did to protect me, what kind of bargain did you make?"

"I took you as my consort. I told you that already. But what it really means is that…" she hesitated. She knew Flynn was furious, but she leaned forward and took his hand anyway. "I've promised to have children with you, human children. That's a very complicated process when someone like me is involved."

Resting his chin on his knees and staring at the floor, Flynn absorbed this. Charlotte gave him all the time he needed to process what she'd just told him. After some time, he told what had upset him. "I dreamed about Howard," he said gloomily. "I've been having nightmares about him every night. Tonight he tried to kill me. He said I had to die."

"I won't allow anyone to harm you," Charlotte said decisively.

"He says you're going to kill me," Flynn countered. "As a part of a ritual, is that right?"

"Only symbolically," Charlotte said with a shrug. "In a dream, it's part of a ceremony. You have to give a life to get a life."

"What does that mean?" Flynn asked.

"It's the only way I can get pregnant," Charlotte said. "And if I don't get pregnant, I will lose any claim I may have to protect you from… my sister, or whatever."

"Howard said that if you do get pregnant, you're going to unleash these creatures onto the earth," Flynn growled.

"Really?" Charlotte was genuinely surprised. "I've never heard of that before. Are you sure? I mean… my mother has had me performing rituals to prevent that kind of thing, but I thought she was just being paranoid."

"Apparently not," Flynn said. "Listen, I have a lot to think about, and if you don't mind, I'm going to sleep on this chair for a while."

"That's fine," Charlotte said. She was relieved that he wasn't grabbing his things and running out of her apartment, trying desperately to get as far away from her as possible.

"I'm not, you know, trying to break up with you or anything," he said nervously. "I just need some space. This is a lot for me to deal with."

"I understand," she said tenderly. "It would be a lot for anyone to deal with." She gathered her courage and walked over to the chair. She put her arms around him and held him tight. She was relieved when he returned her embrace. She didn't want to, but she let go and walked back to her bed. She sat down and asked casually, "Do you want to watch TV or something?"

"Yeah," he said. "I think so. Let's just watch TV."

"Okay," she said. "Uhm, I have some other blankets. Do you want another blanket? It might get cold on that chair."

"Sure, that would be nice," he said. He gave her a curious look. Apparently, Howard was right about a lot of things. He was right about Charlotte treating him like someone fragile. His nerves were shot, and he didn't feel like complaining about it. Sometimes he liked being babied. What she was doing wasn't bad but it *was* interesting. She spread the blanket out over him and kissed him on the cheek.

"Do you still have enough covers for yourself?" he asked.

"Oh yes, I'll be fine," she answered.

Very shortly thereafter, Flynn found himself becoming extremely drowsy. He could barely keep his eyes open. It occurred to him that this probably was not natural.

"What did you do to me, Charlotte?" he asked.

"I'm sorry," she said uneasily. "I wasn't thinking. When I kissed you, I changed your body chemistry so you would fall asleep. I was worried. I don't want you to have any more nightmares."

"Did you do it on purpose?" he asked.

"It is instinctive," she answered. "If you hug someone because you want to comfort them, it's a gesture of affection. It isn't meant to manipulate. It's natural. For me it is, anyway."

"Oh. That's alright, then," he said drowsily. "You didn't mean any harm." Moments later, he was peacefully snoring."

The apartment was tiny, and Charlotte didn't want to wake him. She picked up her cell phone and locked herself in the bathroom so he wouldn't overhear her when she called her mother.

Unheeded Advice

"What he said, what he dreamed, it was weird," Charlotte told Maribelle. "I'm not sure what's going on, mom. But he's in way over his head, and so am I."

"Maybe I should talk to him," Maribelle suggested.

"Whatever for?" Charlotte asked.

"Because I understand some of what he's dealing with in a way you probably don't," Maribelle insisted. "You don't know what it's like to be a consort. I mean sure, you're not as callous as your father, but you're not human. I know that you care about this boy but you're not giving him enough information to make informed decisions about his own fate. That's not cool. It sucks."

"Are you trying to say that I'm emasculating him?" Charlotte snipped.

"Perhaps you are," Maribelle said irritably. "But that's not what I'm talking about right now. Let's leave gender out of it for a moment here. In the language of the old religion of your grandfather, you're a demigod. You are mortal, but you possess strengths and abilities that no mortal has."

"So?" Charlotte asked.

"Don't pretend not to understand what it means to be human. I'm not accusing you of emasculating him. I'm saying you're dehumanizing him. You keep him in the dark not knowing what he's caught up in. You keep him locked away like Cupid's Psyche, and we all know how that turned out."

"They got married, right?" Charlotte yawned into the phone.

"Seriously?" her mother countered. "Not until after she decided he was a monster, tried to kill him, and was captured and tortured by his ill-tempered, jealous relatives. Are you seeing any similarities here? Perhaps?"

"Yeah, okay fine," Charlotte sighed. "I get your point."

"I don't think you do," Maribelle informed her. "You know what? I'm not doing this over the phone." her mom insisted. "I have something to give you. I'm coming over."

"Can it wait until tomorrow?" Charlotte asked. "Flynn has a job interview the morning."

"Fine. See you in the morning, before I go to work," Maribelle said, hanging up the phone.

Second Thoughts

Charlotte sat in a chair watching Flynn sleep. She thought about what her mother said. Maybe her mom had a point. She did keep a lot of secrets from him. Things that concerned his life and his future, things he deserved, and needed to know.

She also had a peculiar relationship with his defenselessness. It excited her. Maybe she liked rescuing him. Wasn't that what attracted her to him in the first place? If he hadn't been being abused by Mercy, would she have even noticed him? If a man treated a woman that way, Charlotte would have verbally assaulted him with the text of several heavy feminist tomes indicting him for fetishizing victimization. But didn't she find Flynn's vulnerability enticing?

Did that make her a hypocrite? Wasn't that what she was doing to Flynn?

Maybe she was so busy trying to save him over and over again that she wouldn't allow him to be anything other than the poor, distressed soul she was repeatedly rescuing from dragons. She remembered once, when she was a girl, she thought to herself that Superman's rescuing of Lois Lane seemed somewhat disingenuous considering it was his relationship with her that was constantly putting her in jeopardy.

Wasn't she placing Flynn in danger just by being with him?

Maybe she would try to be a better girlfriend. Not now though. It could wait until morning.

BREAKFAST

An extremely awkward conversation took place in the kitchenette over coffee and pastries. There was no wall dividing the kitchenette from the living and/or bedroom. There were, in fact, only two rooms: a bathroom, and a living-bed-kitchen room. If they had moved into Flynn's apartment, they'd have had a bathroom, a bedroom, a living room, and a tiny, bathroom-sized kitchen. Charlotte's place was kind of small for a couple, especially a couple that was fighting.

Flynn was lounging against the kitchen counter eating a bear claw when Charlotte approached him with this question:

"Do you think I'm objectifying you?"

Flynn leaned back a little and smirked, failing miserably at hiding his incredulity.

"I'm serious," Charlotte said. "Do you think I'm just using you as a sex object?"

"I *like* it when you use me as a sex object," Flynn said. "The first time you took me home, I thought you were going to dump me because I kind of couldn't fuck. Well, not for longer than what, six minutes?"

"Seven minutes," Charlotte joked.

"Right," Flynn said carefully. "So I like it that you want me. I love it, really. Even the thought that you might secretly want to eat me alive, I've got to be honest, kind of turns me on. There is nothing you do to my body that I don't really enjoy. I'm upset with you because I think you're treating me like I'm an idiot."

"You think that I think you're stupid?" she asked.

"Stupid, maybe, or a child," he explained. "It's the way you refuse to treat me as an equal outside of the bedroom that I have trouble with. I don't keep any secrets from you. I trust you completely. But you keep betraying that trust. I want you to stop lying to me."

"I uh…" Charlotte began. But she didn't have to answer she was saved by the bell. Her mother called from downstairs needing to be buzzed in on the intercom system. She rang her in.

"Oh I forgot, Mom wants to give me something," Charlotte said breathlessly. "So, yeah, you look great. Knock 'em dead at your job interview."

Flynn shook his head and laughed. "See? You're doing it right now. You think that you can hustle me out the door and talk to your mom about whatever without me finding out. *Whatever* probably being me, and don't lie about it... am I right?"

"You are right," Charlotte admitted. "She told me I had no idea how disempowering it can be to be the consort of some demigod." She defensively blurted it out in a single angry stream of potentially shocking words intended to grind the conversation to a halt.

"Mmmm hmm," Flynn said, taking a seat on the same chair he'd slept on. "Talk to me, not at me."

Charlotte ran to the door and let her mom in.

"I can see you two are fighting," Maribelle said, taking a seat at their tiny tea table.

"Your daughter has just now announced she's a demigod," Flynn observed.

"Technically she is." Maribelle said drolly. "She is a Greco-Roman demigod. No, she's not one of those really famous ones like Heracles, Perseus or Jason. I blame myself. Her dad isn't very well known. I have to be honest here. I mistook him for Morpheus. I mean, all of those winged Oneiroi kind of look alike, right? Big black wings, nice upper body, really gorgeous... chicks used to dig the wings. Very impressive, but many of the sons of Somnus have them, and he has a thousand sons. Nine-hundred and ninety-nine of them *aren't* Morpheus, including Charlotte's father, Brash."

Flynn blinked a few times. "Okay, so you're saying that she's the granddaughter of Somnus and the niece of Morpheus?"

Maribelle looked surprised. "You know who they are?"

"He's a gamer, mom," Charlotte said sarcastically. "He has about six of those games. Morpheus and Thanatos are both in them. Also, he's functionally literate."

Flynn gave Charlotte a serious look. "I have also read your comic, you know, Somnalia? I've been reading it since we started dating. What kind of shit boyfriend would I have to be not to? Somnus is the twin brother of Thanatos," he rattled off. "The somnali are the grandchildren of Somnus."

"Right," Maribelle said. "Of course you do. So, you've got a job interview, right?"

"Yea," Flynn said, "But I don't have to leave for an hour."

"Okay, fine." Maribelle said.

"Go ahead, Mom. In front of him," Charlotte said, tilting her head towards Flynn to indicate who *he* was, as if it wasn't patently obvious. Flynn grinned at Maribelle amiably first, then gave Charlotte a feigned look of shock and surprise.

"Really? Then it's okay for me to speak about your father's family freely in front of this mere mortal now?" Maribelle winked at Flynn conspiratorially. "Fine, then. Here, I've bought something for you… for you both, I suppose." She plopped the pine green tote bag she'd carried in to the room with her down on the little table. Flynn walked over and took a look inside.

"What is it?" Charlotte asked.

"They are books; Homer's *Iliad*, Ovid's *Metamorphoses*, and Apuleius' *The Golden Ass*." Flynn said. "Wow. Thank you, Mrs. Metaxas."

"Oh, Metamorphoses and the Iliad are a little family history," Charlotte said with a smirk. "And *The Golden Ass*… you want me to read the story of Eros and Psyche?"

"It's a *love story*," Maribelle said meaningfully.

"Thanks, I'll read them," Flynn said. He loved mythology and he also loved to read. The idea that it could have anything to do with Charlotte just made it all the more interesting.

"I have to go," Maribelle said. She stood up to leave, and was about to turn to go when she gave Flynn a hug on impulse. "It's going to be okay," she told him. "It just takes time."

He nodded. "Okay. Thank you Mrs. Metaxas."

"You can call me Maribelle," she said with a nod and a smile. Then on impulse, she reached over and gave the young man a hug. "I really have to get going," she said. She gave Charlotte a hug as well, and left.

INTERVIEW

Job-hunting in Alameda County had been far more promising than the three and a half fruitless months he spent searching in Solano County. He'd been in Berkeley three weeks and had had at least one interview every day he'd been out here, in Berkeley, Oakland, or surrounding areas. Today he had an interview for a $20 per hour, thirty hour per week position at a t-shirt design company.

He'd done his research beforehand. The company offered one line of surf-and-skate-centric designs, and another of urban inspired themes marketed under two separate brand names. They were local and moderately successful. His job wouldn't involve creating t-shirt designs, however. After years of outside subcontracting, they had decided they were finally big enough to justify hiring a permanent staff member to be responsible for both their print and online catalog.

"The print catalogs go out to various retailers who carry our product," Tim Brockman, the head of human resources had explained during a phone interview. "Your resume caught our eye because you have a great deal of experience with printed media."

"Yes," Flynn said confidently. "I recently relocated from Solano County where most of my work has been in print media, working for local magazines and newspapers. In addition to layout and design work, I've been involved in preparing color separations for the printer."

"That's great," Mr. Brockman said. "It's increasingly a digital world, but many of our clients are small storefronts in beachfront towns, family-run businesses that are always going to have young, tech-savvy buyers. We need someone capable of managing both our online and print catalogs."

He was nervous as hell, but Flynn passed the phone interview. Now he was on the BART train headed to MacArthur station, where he would catch a shuttle bus to Emeryville. He was anxious, and distracted by thoughts regarding his complicated personal life, but he was also excited. The company offered excellent medical benefits to all employees who worked twenty or more hours per week. A thirty-hour a week job was within the range of hours Dr. Lester recommended he work – the high end of it because she said twenty to thirty, but still. Twenty dollars an hour was a high enough wage that he could afford to work less than forty hours.

This would be a perfect fit. He really hoped he would get the job.

He felt kind of weird and spaced out. He didn't like arguing with Charlotte, but he felt he had to stand up for himself. Not having his own apartment made him feel unsafe disagreeing with her. He was glad she wasn't tossing him out in the street, but it felt risky. Working would make him feel more secure. He would be in a better position to contribute to their household. That way maybe they could afford to get a bigger place eventually. But right now, it seemed premature to think about that. He didn't have a job, and he wasn't getting along with Charlotte as well as he would have liked to, either.

Getting off of the BART train, he found he had a ten-minute wait for the shuttle bus. While he was waiting he decided to read the copy of Apuleius' *The Golden Ass,* the one that Maribelle had given to Charlotte. He still remembered how happy it made him when she said it was for them both. He remembered Charlotte's mother embracing him as if he were someone she might be proud to have as a son-in-law someday. Maybe he could give her a reason to be proud. Maybe he could be more than some nearly homeless bum her daughter picked up in the psych ward. He was still reading it when he got on the shuttle and was so caught up in the stories that he almost missed his bus stop.

THREE DAYS LATER

Maybe it was because he got the job, and that made him feel better about his ability to contribute to the relationship and about life in general. Maybe it was because he'd been noticing the parallels between his romance with Charlotte and the story of Eros and Psyche that her mother rather deliberately pointed out to them. It could have been because Eros himself was watching over them, and remembered all the terrible fights with Psyche during their courtship. Humans could be so temperamental. Maybe Flynn needed a push.

Whatever the reason, three days after they argued Flynn no longer wanted to sleep in a chair. He wanted Charlotte in his arms, in his bed, and once again, in his dreams.

So he walked over and sat on the edge of the bed, and asked her.

"Do you think it would be alright if I joined you?"

"Of course," she said with a shrug. "I never kicked you out of bed." She didn't look exactly thrilled, though. She was pouting a bit. She didn't bother to move over.

Flynn started taking his shoes off.

"Are you sure you want to lay down with me?" Charlotte asked him. "Aren't you convinced I'm some kind of a monster?"

"In this book Psyche thought Eros was a monster, but that's because she was in the dark," Flynn said, screwing his face up a little. "When she got a good look at him, she decided he was the most beautiful thing she'd ever seen. Too bad she hurt him. But it wasn't entirely her fault, if you ask me. After all, he kept her in the dark for too long."

"Oh very clever," Charlotte said snippily. "Really, Flynn, just quit it." She moved over a little bit to let him into bed. She was still angry, though. She sat up in bed with her arms crossed over her chest.

Flynn took his shirt off.

"Oh don't even bother," she said. She glared at him. "I guess you think you can just take all your clothes off and I'm going to forget all about everything and it will be just like we never argued."

"Of course not," he said, taking his pants off. "But I wanted to ask you something."

"Oh really," she said, turning her back towards him. "And what is that?"

"Well, your father in his natural form has these beautiful black wings," Flynn began. "I wanted to know, do you have wings? I mean in the dream world, you know, in your natural form?"

She rolled over and looked at him, shaking her head a little bit. "You can't be serious. I was born on Earth. I wasn't born there. This is my natural form."

"But you could have wings," he asked, prodding a little. "I mean if you wanted to."

"I could look anyway I wanted to over there," she explained. She finally started to get an idea of where this might be heading. "Why, what did you have in mind?"

"Well in this book," he said very slowly, "Psyche's family gave her to this monster. They offered her, like a gift. They thought it was a monster, at least. I think it was a punishment for the arrogance of these humans. And they left her on a hill and they exposed her. And I've been thinking about what it would be like to be naked and exposed and waiting to be punished."

"Oh…" she said. "Oh, okay then." She blushed, something that almost never happened. "It's been a long time since I took you to the Demos Oneiroi. If you want me to, I will."

"I do," he said. "I want you in every way a person can possibly be wanted. I don't think I can breathe if you won't have me. Please say you will."

Charlotte smiled. "Are you begging me?"

"I am," he said. "Please."

MAKE-UP SEX

Charlotte rolled over and yawned.

"I'm really tired," she said. "I think you should be on top." She raised her arms up over her head and said, "Take my shirt off, I don't have enough energy."

Flynn didn't say anything. He sat up in bed and straddled her with one leg on either side of her hips, and reached down to pull off her Emily the Strange nightshirt. He slowly rolled it up, revealing her belly, soft and slightly rounded. She wore a navel ring with a little skull in it, some sort of matching piercings couple thing that was probably nauseatingly adorable to people not actually a part of said couple.

He rolled her shirt up over her breasts, which rested against her ribcage in obedience to the laws of gravity. He ran his hand over the gentle curve of her left breast and sought her nipple. It was already stiffening before he began to massage it between his thumb and index finger. It was as thick around as his pinky, and the same reddish brown as the spattering of freckles on her shoulders.

He finished pulling her shirt off, and tossed it to the ground. When he kissed and suckled at her breast, she moaned and threw her arms around his neck and drew him closer to her, adjusting her body slightly to give him better access. He was amazed at how sensitive her skin was.

His nipples were never erect unless someone was biting them, something that made him instantly tremble in paroxysm of unadulterated delight. He knew her body well enough to understand that he had to be much gentler with her than he would ever want her to with him. It pleased him to know that he could excite her. It thrilled him to know that she was demanding this from him.

He could feel her hips buck up against him, began to anticipate sliding deep inside her. He consciously set the thought aside, and used every mechanism he had in his limited repertoire to pace himself. It wasn't easy because he was desperately excited by not just the sex, but reconciliation. He felt a sense of complete and utter belonging. He was hers, and he belonged to her. He wanted to please her.

"I think you'll need to take off my underwear," she whispered, running her fingers through his hair. She put her hands on his shoulders and gently pushed down. He trailed kisses down her belly, and ran his finger between her skin and the elastic waistband of her plain black bikini panties. He slid down the bed a little further so he could look at her newly revealed flesh as he pulled them down.

She kept the dark hair over her pubis short-shorn. It was soft and thick like a velveteen rabbit. He ran his hand over her crotch, and suddenly had to stop himself from losing control.

"You are so wet," he murmured. He wasn't just talking dirty. He was having a moment, wondering how he could excite her this much.

"Thinking about all of the ways you will please me," she said slowly and deliberately, "and about all of the things I can and *will* do to you is really turning me on."

"What will you do to me?" he asked.

"I'm going to need to have an orgasm before I can reveal that mystery to you," she told him. "Just keep it up, you'll find out soon enough. Don't talk. Fuck me."

So he did. He fucked her like nothing existed except for their two bodies and whatever sensations they might provoke in one another, and for a wonderful moment there was nothing, nothing at all that could touch this.

And then she came, and she put her hand on his him and whispered in his ear, "Good. Now you will feel what I feel."

What he felt was like a wave that threatened to crest several times without doing so, and next, came crashing down repeatedly until his body was trembling and his eyes were rolling back in his head and everything was so sensitive that if his skin were touched it would probably be uncomfortable. Then he collapsed on top of her in a pool of sweat and felt as though it would be nearly impossible to move.

After he stopped panting and feeling as though his skin was made up of raw, sensitive nerve endings, Flynn rolled off her and said, "Whoa! What the fuck was that?"

"Congratulations," she said. "Now you know what multiple orgasms feel like. Are you tired?"

"I'm fucking exhausted," he admitted.

"Good," she said with a devious smile. "Go to sleep."

He rolled over onto his stomach and passed out.

Charlotte patted him on the back. "Sweet dreams."

OFFERED

Flynn was having second thoughts about wishes granted. Perhaps the somnali were tricksters, like the djinn in the *Wishmaster* films, who only granted wishes in twisted ways resembling W. W. Jacobs' story *The Monkey's Paw*. These kinds of wishes only resulted in further tormenting for the wish maker, and Flynn struck by a tinge of guilty excitement because he knew he might enjoy such torments.

He was also afraid, for once again he found himself in the hands of Mercy.

"It's good to see you again," the daemon said salaciously. She was in her favored red headed form, this time with jet-black wings that arose from her shoulder blades, extending four feet out in either direction, like those of a Valkyrie. She was in the process of binding him in chains to a large boulder.

"It would be more fun if you would struggle," she suggested. He was standing against the giant rock, both of his ankles and one of his wrists already shackled to it with heavy chains. She was roughly securing his remaining hand when he first became aware of where he was and who was with him.

"You look good strapped down," she teased. "I remember once, when I young, my father told me about the punishment of Prometheus. Did you know Zeus punished him for giving fire to mankind?"

"I think every school boy knows that, "Flynn answered. "What am I doing here, with you?"

"I've been given the honor of formally presenting you to my sister," Mercy explained. "You will be offered to her as a gift, bound and naked. It is what you both wanted, isn't it?"

"This isn't quite what I had in mind," Flynn said.

"As I was saying before you so rudely interrupted me," Mercy continued, "a big bird tore out his liver every day. And it kept growing back – the liver, not the bird. The bird represented Zeus. So he was strapped to this rock, for all eternity, suffering, and being devoured by a god. Wouldn't you like that?"

"Uhm, no," Flynn said, shaking his head. Where was Charlotte? He was growing increasingly agitated. "I don't have any desire to do that, and certainly not with you. I'm not yours, am I?"

"Not anymore. Nonetheless," Mercy purred. "You were mine once, and in accordance with our somnali customs our father has asked me to formally give you over to Happiness. My father said, 'before he can experience Happiness tonight, me must be left to my Mercy,' and so here you are, left to his Mercy."

He was covered in a long, black robe with red trim along the cuffs and edges. Mercy untied the robe and exposed his bare legs and torso to the elements. The robe fell loosely around his arms and back now. They were high up on a cliff and a cold wind made his skin break out in gooseflesh. Suddenly he remembered that in none of his previous dreams had Mercy seen him entirely naked.

She pulled a sharp, curved knife from her belt and began to cut through the remaining threads that held the robe in place. The severed cloth fell uselessly to the ground. Mercy laughed, and held the blade against his throat.

"How I would love to cut you with this," she said. "I would make small wounds, slowly inflicted in various places all over the playground that is your flesh. Then I would stand back and admire my work, watching as your wounds weep all over your fragile body. I would slowly gauge the rate at which your life force was leaking from the useless husk that contains it. I could spend days watching you slowly die. It would delight me."

Flynn remembered the nightmare he had where Howard Lowe warned that if Flynn died, Mercy and all of her siblings would die with him. He remembered Howard suggesting that Flynn's sacrifice would be a fair exchange for ridding the world of monsters like Mercy. He found himself wondering if Howard was right. He wasn't a hero. He wanted to live. But maybe he could accept this fate.

She slid the knife down his throat, over his chest, and down to his navel where she pressed gently with its sharp end.

"One little slip of my blade could end your life," she observed. "How terrible it must be for you, to be mortal. Even if you lived to one hundred years, your life would be brief. It will inevitably end in that tragic event you call death."

Mercy looked him up and down. She wore a vaguely military tunic that was belted at the waist. After a moment she stepped back, lowering the blade and sheathing it in a loop in her leather belt.

"It is not my role to end your life," she said finally. "I was asked to leave you out here, exposed to the elements, so that you and my sister can play your precious little love games. It seems like an awful lot of fuss over one mediocre stud horse, but my sister is a mortal. Perhaps her standards are low. I have lots of other prey. I'm happy to leave you here as a gift."

"What do you mean other prey?" Flynn demanded. "Are you talking about the terrible things you did to that poor sap, Howard Lowe?"

"Would you have preferred to take his place, to be my victim?" Mercy asked. "Would your inevitable mortal death feel less futile if you could exchange yourself for the life of another?"

Flynn looked down and said nothing.

"When Charlotte protected you, she knew I would find someone else to ruin. I caused Howard Lowe's self-destruction because exerting power in the mortal realm grants increases my power over your mortal world and here, in the Demos Oneiroi. The public nature of his decline was the stuff legends are made of. We are empowered by such tales. Even now, my sister has promised to tell stories of me in exchange for the gift of your life. Even if I hadn't relinquished you, though, I would have eventually finished with you and gone on to the next, so you would not have saved Howard, only declined along with him."

Flynn quickly realized that Mercy was unaware of Howard's prophecy.

"You know, I was about to leave, then I realized that the weather here is very temperate," she observed, thoughtfully tapping her chin with her forefinger. "You're supposed to be exposed to the elements. This will never do."

She made an expansive gesture with her arms held high above her head, and then quickly dropped them down, bringing down a torrent of rain. The icy water came down hard and fast and pelted his skin. Water poured down his face and his hair was soaking wet, plastered against his skin. His teeth began to chatter.

"That's really not enough," Mercy said. She waved her hands again and in an instant, the rain became snow. Flynn was beginning to shake, and the sudden temperature change sparked the onset of a headache.

"You are absolutely scrumptious looking spread out on the feasting stone," she cooed sensually. "I wish I could stay and devour you personally, but I've got things to do and people to maim."

Satisfied, Mercy left him naked and trembling, bound to the stone.

TAKEN

He waited for an hour, but Charlotte did not come. The snow stopped eventually, but the air was frigid, and he began growing weak and ill. By the time someone arrived to whisk him away, he was so feeble and sickly that he couldn't hold his head up and could barely open his eyes. When he tried to see who was there, all he could make out was a fuzzy silhouette. A mysterious shadow began to unshackle him with long, slender fingers that warmed him where they brushed against his frozen skin.

He wasn't sure if it was Charlotte. The shadow lifted him from the stone and wrapped him in something soft and warm. Flynn felt feverish and thought himself a fool for having ever subjected himself to this. Clearly, he hadn't thought things through. He hadn't considered how dangerous this was, or how uncomfortable he would be when he agreed to this little game with Charlotte. He certainly hadn't anticipated Mercy's involvement. Once he was swaddled in furs, he barely cared who had come for him.

"Thank you," he whispered. He was slipping in and out of consciousness.

The thing threw him over one shoulder and hauled him off into its dark and cavernous lair. The creature laid him down in a pile of furs and blankets, and crawled into the little nest beside him. It pushed back the covers and slid in beside him. Flynn believed it had to be Charlotte, but it was nerve-wracking for him not knowing for sure who, or what, the entity was. Despite his misgivings, when the creature sought him out in the darkness, he accepted its hungry touches and warm embrace. He felt sick, and the heat of its body was comforting, healing. Still, he had to know.

"Is it you, Charlotte?" he asked. "I'm so sorry. I was such a fool to ask for this. We don't need to play this game. I just... I wish we were home again, in the safety of our bed, where things aren't so strange and upsetting."

"Of course it is me," the shadowy figure whispered to him. She stroked his cheek with her fingers and kissed him in the darkness. "Who else would it be? But you're not supposed to know it's me, now are you?"

She found the wings frankly rather burdensome. It was impossible to lay on her back very comfortably with them. She rolled Flynn onto his back and climbed on top of him, her head on his shoulder, whispering in his ear.

"I will have to eat you, you know," she stated. She kissed and bit his fingers teasingly. "It is a part of the ceremonial rituals that are required, but it won't happen until after I get my father's approval for our union. After that, he'll reach into the depths of your mind and discover what kinds of creatures might be best suited for the task of devouring your flesh."

She took his hands in hers and pressed them down into the rabbit fur blanket beneath them. She started biting his neck and his ears. Flynn struggled a bit beneath her, legs flailing until she rested her weight down on them.

"I love it when you are writhing underneath me," she purred in his ear. "Would you like me to stop?"

"No," he begged. His breath was heavy, labored. "Please don't stop."

"Perhaps I should be gentler?" she asked.

"Harder," he gasped. "You should be much rougher with me."

"You have been bad," she whispered. "You should be punished for displaying such ingratitude as to complain after I've gone through the trouble of fulfilling your silly fantasies. After you denied me sex and refused to perform your duties as my consort for three entire days."

She bit his ears, neck and shoulders, pausing occasionally to rhapsodize about the pleasures they would both experience if he would only agree to allow her to violently consume his flesh. She rolled him over on to his belly. He moaned and squirmed, but otherwise eagerly submitted to her as she delivered a series of bites and nibbles to his ass and the backs of his calves.

"Perhaps you have fantasized about a ravenous werewolf sinking her fangs into your plump, juicy little behind," she said. "You try to escape, but as you run away, you stumble and fall. Her mouth waters in anticipation as she sinks her teeth into layers of flesh and muscle, her hunger fulfilled when she tastes the raw, warm meat. Have you ever had a delicious, rare piece of still-bloody rump roast? She is starving, and you taste so good she can't stop until she has finished her meal."

Flynn didn't use any words, but spoke in a simple vocabulary of whimpers, moans, and heavy breathing. He offered no resistance when she used her hands to push and shove him in various directions to reveal new skin to nip at. He listened to her words and fantasized about the greater pressure that would be required to rend flesh from bone.

"Do you like zombies?" she asked. Without waiting for him to answer she said, "Perhaps you would prefer to be eaten by a zombie. Her unquenchable desire to taste your flesh will be slowed by her dull, omnivorous teeth. They won't slide through her meal as easily as the knife-sharp teeth of her carnivorous brethren, so she will have to pull. How hard do you think she will have to tug and bite before your skin tears open, delivering to her the delicious font of your hot, gushing blood?"

She took his nipple in her mouth and bit down on it, securing the metal ring behind her teeth so that it wouldn't slip as she stretched the sensitive flesh. She increased the pressure she exerted every time he squealed. His face flushed with excitement as he thought about what she was doing to him and what she only threatened to do.

Next, she slid down between his thighs and started licking and sucking his scrotum and pretending as though she might bite it. Every time she acted like she was going to use her teeth on him, he grasped the fur in his hands and balled them into fists while his lower back and thighs tensed with anticipation.

"You want me to, don't you?" she teased. She nipped him gently and he began to tremble all over. She stopped at once, because although she loved driving him crazy in that way, she needed to consummate her relationship with him in the dream realm just as she had in the physical world. She knew he couldn't withstand much more provocation without having an orgasm.

"Don't you dare," she hissed. "You're not allowed to cum right now." She climbed on top of him, straddling him before he could ejaculate, and then she just sat there on top of him without moving. Flynn knew this game, and he didn't move either. He just concentrated on not instantly blowing a wad inside her.

"Wow," he said. "No condom."

"It's a dream, we don't need a prophylactic," she reminded him, keeping the conversation light and easy until he could regain some self-control.

"I'm good now," he said, putting one of his hands on each of her hips.

If she wanted him to be on top, she'd let him know. Since she wasn't putting him there, he accepted his position below her with pleasure. He was very submissive by nature and he trusted Charlotte with his body in a way he'd never trusted anyone else. She studied his body language as though it were of the greatest importance to her to acquire some fluency in it. He followed her cues and his body moved in the directions her hands and thighs suggested. He synchronized the rhythm of his body to hers, his hips moving when hers did, inhaling and exhaling when she did. He let his flesh be an extension of her intentions, her motions, and her will.

Charlotte threw off the blankets and unfurled her wings in the darkness. The air stirred in response to their gentle fluttering, and Flynn couldn't resist the urge to let his hands wander up her back and touch them. He wished they weren't in the dark, so he could see the muscles he felt moving beneath his grasping hands and outstretched arms.

"Sit up," she ordered. Flynn obeyed, shifting his body so that was seated, not quite upright, by leaning against his elbow. He crossed his legs under her ass so that he could sit up straight without falling over onto his back. Now that she was on his lap, facing him, with his arms wrapped around her back, it was much easier for him to touch her wings. The feathers brushed lazily against his arms, tickling him. Feeling them brush against his skin was glorious.

Charlotte enjoyed him thoroughly. He was wildly responsive, signaling his arousal with myriad changes in his body movement and temperature, his hot excited flesh against her, shaking and screaming. He was very vocal and extremely demonstrative. She didn't have any difficulty determining what he did or did not enjoy.

Her cruelty wasn't boundless like Mercy, Sympathy, and her other eight sisters who were much older and wouldn't give Charlotte the time of day. She did share some of her siblings' sadistic nature. Flynn enjoyed her sexual sadism, and it gave her great pleasure to know that he wanted it. His consent meant a lot to her. He was her willing victim and it made her all wet just thinking about it.

She bit and kissed his ears, neck and chest while they were fucking, not hard enough to draw blood, but with enough force and pressure to leave a string of hickeys he would have had to cover up to go to work if this had not been a dream.

When she came, he responded like someone had flipped a switch and came immediately after. It wasn't surprising, since he'd been using every bit of restraint he had not to. By having an orgasm, she essentially gave him permission to do likewise.

Afterward, they fell asleep in Flynn's dream and awakened in the apartment they shared in Berkeley.

FOOD

Fucking in both worlds left Flynn feeling drained. He was glad it was a Saturday morning and he didn't start work until Monday. Neither of them had enough energy to cook anything for breakfast, so they sat at their little tea table drinking microwave coffee and eating bowls of generic cold cereal.

Flynn was looking at Charlotte over his bowl of Sugar Coated Fun Flakes when he broached the subject.

"So, Charlotte," he asked, "can you explain to me about the whole cannibalism thing?" He was pretty kinky, but actually being eaten alive was a little out of his comfort zone, no matter how much it turned him on when she alluded to it while biting him. Being bitten was delicious. Dying was just plain scary, even temporary pretend dream dying.

"When a woman gives birth, labor is extremely painful, isn't it?" she said with a shrug. "People keep at it because it is necessary for the continuation of the species. In fact, no amount of suffering you endure will spare me the pain of childbirth if I get pregnant. My father did something terrible when I was conceived. This is far less unpleasant."

"What did he do?" Flynn asked.

"He caused every other pregnant woman in the neighborhood to miscarry," Charlotte said.

"Oh my God, that's horrible!" Flynn gasped.

"It really was," Charlotte acknowledged, shaking her head. "My mother didn't find out until much later. Anyway, I'm afraid to let things coast, because my father or my sisters might take things into their own hands. It could get very ugly."

Flynn looked a little green around the gills. "How can you just say things like that? Just like that, like it's nothing? This is so not normal."

"If you don't want me to eat your flesh, we can talk, figure out something else," Charlotte said with a shrug. "I'm not pushing it on you."

"I didn't exactly say no, I just said I had some questions," Flynn said testily. "I mean… it's a bit much. And now you're insinuating that if I don't, your relatives are going to start slaughtering fetuses, for fuck's sake! Don't you think it is normal for me to have questions?"

"Sure," Charlotte said. "I'm sorry you're stuck in the middle of all this."

Flynn was pacing around their tiny kitchenette, looking agitated.

"So why are you in such a big hurry to get pregnant?" he asked. "We've only been together six months. You won't even be twenty-three until next month. You have plenty of fertile years left."

"I kind of agreed to." she said, shrugging. "I begged for your life which was incredibly impulsive on my part." Charlotte paused for a moment, sipping her coffee and collecting her thoughts. Was it really impulsive? If what Howard Lowe told Flynn in the dream was true, then their love was fated by the gods. Maybe it was inevitable, and she was destined to love him.

"That was part of the agreement," she continued. "My father doesn't have any other earthly children, and as you can see, continuing the line is extremely complicated. It's something he really wants, that he can't have without my cooperation. That gave me a lot of leverage."

"Okay," he said. "So that's what Mercy was telling me in the dream. That's the only reason they haven't killed me, it seems. Is that right?"

"Yes," Charlotte agreed. "That's exactly right. I keep stalling them, but they aren't going to wait forever."

"I think I'm starting to get a headache," Flynn said.

"Understandably so," Charlotte said in a matter of fact way. "I've been dealing with this bullshit all my life, you're just having a lot of crap dropped on you at once. I'm sorry."

"Yeah…" he said. "So, do you want to go out and get a drink tonight or something? I'm not going to be able to wrap my head around all of this right now."

"Sure," she said. "That reminds me, check your voicemail. Hannah and Shelby called. They're down from the North Bay for some kind of conference in San Francisco, not work, fan girl stuff. Anyway they asked about getting together and hanging out, probably here in Berkeley. Maybe you should give them a call, hook it up. Oh…Shelby said they bumped into some dude named Mike down there at the convention. She said you and Hannah know him from the hospital. According to Shelby, he's kind of a douche but Hannah thought you might want to see him, too."

"Oh yea, dudebro Mike from the hospital." Flynn nodded. "Yeah, unless he has a fake ID I don't think we'll be hitting any clubs with him anytime soon. But we could meet them all in the city."

FRIENDS

Shelby and Hannah were recently engaged and proud homeowners who owned a three-bedroom, two-bathroom home in the intimate North Bay community of Suisun City. Like much of the North Bay, Suisun remained affordable to the working class. It was one of the few places in the Bay Area where people like Shelby and Hannah could afford to achieve the American dream of homeownership. Thanks to changes in the California State Law, they were also able to fulfill another dream, that of wedlock.

Proposition 8, banning same-sex marriage, was shot the California State Supreme Court. Afterward Shelby told everyone that she was too young to marry. Hannah, who was two years younger at twenty-two, had no such qualms. Shelby finally said "yes" to Hannah's proposal of marriage, although she qualified it by saying that she believed in long engagements. Truthfully, Shelby did not believe in marriage and was dragging her feet.

Shelby was stably employed as a postal carrier. Despite all the clamoring about email and the decline in the use of the old-fashioned snail mail service, she felt secure in her job, and her future, and enjoyed her benefits. Hannah joined the Navy immediately after high school, and met Shelby soon after coming home from her tour of duty.

Hannah's status as a military veteran helped them get a low cost loan to purchase the home. However, her income was lower than Shelby's. She worked in a hip, artsy independent bookstore in Napa and made the twenty-mile trip to work on her motorcycle. They rented an extra room to a student named Cory, who attended college in nearby Fairfield.

They all met at a coffee shop in the Castro, one of those places with crepes, breakfasts that featured home fries and thirty different kinds of coffee. Hannah came bearing gifts for Charlotte.

"Got something for ya!" she bubbled, handing Charlotte a comic book. "Whaddya think?"

Charlotte turned it over in her hand. It was a black and white, forty-page compilation of the first year of her comic series *Somnalia* with a color cover. It was quite beautiful.

"I love it!" she said, stunned to see her work in print. "How did you do this?"

"Well, my boss, you know Ms. Lewis, right? Anyway, she noticed that there's a ton of local writers having a hard time getting published, and artists like you who've been putting their stuff online but might be ready for the next step, and she wants to help you guys out," Hannah explained. "So, couple of weeks ago, she ponied up and had a small printing press installed in the back room of the shop. She put me in charge of getting the word out and signing folks up. Pretty cool, huh?"

"So now, and this is totally up to you," Hannah continued, "but I was thinking how cool it would be if you had a table at Alternative Press Expo! I think you could have more than just an online audience for *Somnalia*."

"It's great!" Charlotte said enthusiastically. "Deets, Hannah! I need to know who to meet with to work out a contract."

"I'm totally authorized to negotiate a contract with you," Hannah said, pulling some additional paperwork out of her briefcase. "We don't have any graphic novels or comic books, this was my idea. My boss put me in charge of the division. It's pretty cool, right?"

Father would be so proud, thought Charlotte.

She wasn't the world's most strategic thinker, but she did do a little mental calculation as to the likelihood that this maneuver, if successful, would help place Hannah under her father's protection. Brash was a prominent feature in the *Somalia* comics, which were all about Somnus and his grandchildren, but tended to focus on Charlotte's branch of the family. The muscular, handsome, and perpetually shirtless Brash was a fan favorite. If the comic's audience became broader, so would his reputation. He'd be able to seduce women and boys based upon his own reputation, instead of by pretending to be Morpheus.

Protecting Hannah and Shelby could be important, especially if all hell broke loose. Considering her sister's tendencies and appetites, and what Flynn had told her that morning about Howard's dream visit, she felt this seemed quite likely. If Mercy started to systematically lash out against people close to her and Flynn things could get very bad.

Unfortunately, that kid Mike had shown up. If they could just ditch him, the four of them could discuss the somnali threat openly. Flynn was trapped, listening to the teenager as Mike made salacious comments about which chicks were hot and speculated endlessly about which babes were checking him out. They were in the Castro, San Francisco's gayest neighborhood. Most of the women in the cafe were not even into dudes, much less a pudgy, pimply little twerp like Mike.

But now, something else had caught Mike's attention... the comic book.

"Hey, let me see that," Mike asked, reaching over Flynn towards the comic book Charlotte was holding. She immediately handed it over.

"This is some gorgeous artwork," Mike said appreciatively, poring over the pages and blessing the rest of the table with a well-warranted break from his endless stream of juvenile, sexist chatter. Charlotte thought this was great, and wondered why she didn't she think of it sooner. There was no reason they couldn't discuss the somnali in the context of the comic book, and if Mike was familiar with it, so much the better.

"I was thinking that we could go ahead and print a limited run of the first six years of the series," Hannah said casually. "After that, we can publish at a rate of one per year, since each comic represents a year's worth of strips from your website. I'm also thinking that we could release the first six years combined as a graphic novel. It would come in at about three hundred pages once we complete the front and back materials, and the interviews. You're cool with interviews, right?"

Charlotte leaned back a little and smiled. "Uh, yes... I am very cool with interviews."

"The kid who stays with us, that college student, Cory..." Shelby cut in, "he's really good with audio/visual production. He makes them for his little rapper friends. Hannah thinks that he can make some little promo shots for your comic. What do you think about that?"

"Yea, there could be this whole marketing blitz," Hannah said.

"Hannah is a huge fan of your work," Shelby explained. "She was chatting people up about it at the convention today, and she's not the only one. You have a lot of support, especially locally. We would really love to see you out there, networking."

"They think you guys are just holing up in your apartment all day screwing," Mike crudely contributed. "I mean not that I blame you, Flynn... she's hot, but no one ever sees you and we never do anything together, and you know people need a social life, right? You can't forget your bros."

"If you say bros before hos," Shelby warned, "I'm going to smack the taste out of your mouth."

"I've been job hunting," Flynn said defensively, his cheeks burning as last night's festivities returned unbidden to his mind. "I mean, I just got a job at Marco's Tees. You know, the place that sells all of those t-shirts to the surf shops up in Santa Cruz and ah... yea... I have a job now. I'm not, it's not like that."

"Actually, it is like that," Charlotte said pointedly, looking Mike directly in the eye. "We pretty much just can't stop screwing each other. When you went to the bathroom earlier, we took off and went to that special room in the back where couples go to hump when the single people aren't looking. It's way in the back, and of course, you wouldn't know about it. Yea. It's like a smoking section, but for smoking hot sex. And Hannah and Shelby, it's the same way with them. Hot sex, twenty-four/seven… must suck to be you."

Hannah laughed. "Don't fuck with him like that, Charlie."

"Fuck you, Charlotte," Mike said good-naturedly.

Club

Mike's continued presence limited their nightclub choices to one of a handful of all-ages clubs in San Francisco or the East Bay, most of which were punk or goth clubs. The punk clubs featured live music and the goth clubs, mostly DJs. Charlotte picked out a club she had frequented between the ages of eighteen and twenty. It was one Hannah and Shelby were both familiar with as well.

Mike and Flynn weren't club kids, and only Flynn was even familiar with the music. Mike had long, greasy blond hair with conspicuous split ends. Flynn's hair was naturally black and he had worn the same raggedy asymmetrical bowl cut since seventh grade, when kids used to tease him about its resemblance to Pokémon trainer Ash Ketchum.

The ladies fretting over the guy's fashion sense lead to all five of them hanging out in Hannah and Shelby's hotel room, where Hannah was instructing Mike on the proper use of shampoo while Charlotte tried to spike Flynn's hair with liberal applications of Shelby's hair product.

"We've got to do something about their wardrobe," Shelby said, shaking her head. Mike wore beige Bermudas shorts, a faded blue Cookie Monster tee, and hippie man-sandals. Flynn wore his battered Converse All-Stars, baggy blue jean shorts and a Call of Duty t-shirt.

"It's not so bad," Hannah said with a shrug. "I mean except the shorts. Oh and whatever the hell that is Mike has on his feet. Yikes! Those are terrible. I think my grandma has those."

"Man's foot was not meant to be caged in sweat inducing, mass-produced corporate rubber and plastic," Mike preached. "My shoes are made of organic leather and hemp. I can't believe you. You're like the fashion police, total conformists."

Flynn laughed. "Yeah, I agree with what Mike just said."

"What's up with your feet, dude?" Hannah continued. "Do you like, have painful bunions?"

"Let me take your shirt off," Charlotte told Flynn. "I'm afraid I'm going to drop hair gel on it and mess it up."

"At least his shirt is black," Hannah observed. "And the Cookie Monster is cool, but khaki board shorts? If Mike is going to wear those with those shoes maybe we should go to a Berkeley lesbian bar."

"Very funny," Shelby said.

Flynn let Charlotte pull his shirt up over his head, and then immediately wrapped his arms around his chest self-consciously. Charlotte responded by gently taking both of his hands in hers and setting them down on his knees.

"This is San Francisco," Hannah said. "No one cares about your body modifications, Flynn. You're in a room with another dude and a couple of lesbians. No one is trying to check out your goodies."

Shelby chuckled under her breath. Unlike Hannah, she was aware of the dynamic at play between Charlotte and Flynn. He wasn't doing anything particularly immodest, but he was body shy enough to feel embarrassed, and Charlotte enjoyed pushing him a little outside of his comfort zone.

"Here!" Shelby said, snatching a fishnet t-shirt out her suitcase. "Maybe you should get him to wear this," She tossed it to Charlotte.

"Good idea," Charlotte said. She was going to see a bunch of her old friends, and she wanted to show off her shiny new boyfriend. She thought he was hot and she wanted everyone else to think so too.

"How can you just let her dress you up like a Ken doll?" Mike asked.

"It's okay. She's my girlfriend." Flynn said, shrugging. "She's allowed to." He enjoyed having Charlotte fuss over him and groom him. There was something natural about it, like chimpanzees picking bugs out of their loved ones' fur.

"You should get off his back," Shelby said. "You know, they live together. He just sold his artistic skills to the highest bidder so he can earn a living making t-shirt catalogs while his girl finishes college and makes comic books. That's old school manly shit. Don't you think? He is taking care of the little woman, just like I do." Shelby winked at Hannah.

"So I've been thinking about the comic," Hannah said, deliberately changing the subject. "Your new storyline, it's tripping me out. So why is Harpy's father so anxious for her to get pregnant? Is this like, some kind of Rosemary's Baby shit?"

"Nah," Charlotte countered. "That demon baby storyline is as old as hell, no pun intended. A lot of times, I just have to go where the characters take me when I'm weaving these tales, but I'm pretty sure we're not going to go there."

"Then where is it headed?" Hannah asked.

"Spoiler alert!" Mike said, putting his hands over his ears.

"I was just going to go get some smokes from the shop down stairs," Shelby suggested. "If you don't want to overhear, why don't you come downstairs with me?"

"Nah, that's okay," Mike said. "I think I want to eavesdrop."

Shelby shrugged, and left.

"I think we're going with old school nepotism as a motivation here," Charlotte said. "You know... Okay so this is a little back-story. Brash has a huge inferiority complex. I'm sure he'd hate to hear me say that, right, but it's true. Gods like Zeus and Poseidon were major players, spreading their seed all over the earth, creating demigods who got shit done and went down in history.

Some of the other gods like Ares and Hades had half human children, but Zeus and Poseidon were total pimps. Brash was jealous, and wanted to be just like them. He wanted to make a whole army of human babies, and he went out to seduce human women. Unfortunately, he picked the wrong woman. The woman he tried to knock up was one of Zeus' many, many mistresses. Crossing Zeus was a bad idea.

If the other gods weren't kind of afraid of Brash's grandmother, Nyx, he might have been wiped out outright or sent to some kind of horrifying eternal punishment in Hades. As it was, Zeus decided to punish him by seriously mucking up his ability to procreate. See, Zeus can just show up in a shower of gold flakes or something, and seduce a human. Brash has to spill human blood to procreate. It's a curse. That is why human women are very reluctant to get it on with him."

"Harsh!" Mike chirped. "Zeus is totally cock-blocking him."

"Not just him," Charlotte continued. "The curse affected all of his children, his twin brother Rash, who was indicted as a co-conspirator, and all of his children as well. Rash's line eventually died out but the nature of the curse made Brash and his children an increasingly bloodthirsty and filled with a lust for influence over mankind and the material world. But it has been prophesized that a human grandchild of Brash will break the curse, allowing him to return to his former, womanizing ways with impunity."

"Awesome!" Mike squealed. The other three people turned and looked at him simultaneously. It was a little too obvious that he was heavily identifying with Brash by now, envisioning fulfilling his mission to populate the world with thousands of little Mikes.

"Oh. So that's why Brash is so determined to see her have this grandchild," Flynn said, as if he was talking about a television soap opera and not something that directly involved himself.

"I am so glad someone is as excited about the comic book as I am," Hannah said to Mike. "You know, I have some Somnalia t-shirts, if you want one. I mean, I had a couple made for promotional purposes, for our street team."

"I could be on your street team," Mike said eagerly. "I go to a lot of conventions. I can work at your booth, if you want." He was calculating the odds that volunteering at Somnali would eventually place him into direct contact with females. Knowing *the* Charlotte Metaxas might give him some indie cred. He decided that Flynn's old lady was pretty cool.

Shelby came back in just then with a cardboard tray full of paper coffee cups in one hand and a paper bag hanging over her wrist. She sat the coffee on an end table and threw the bag down on the bed.

"I got you guys some pants," she said. "And Mike, I got you some shoes."

Mike shook his head.

"You can wear them with the t-shirt," Hannah said immediately. "So you can represent Somnalia, you know, now that you're on the street team."

"Not even going to ask," Shelby said, picking up her chai latte. She walked over to the bed and rifled through the bag for a minute. She pulled out a baggy pair of black bondage pants with an array of straps and zippers. She went back in and fished out a pair of worn, old combat boots.

"Here, put these on," Shelby told Mike, handing him the boots.

Mike gave her a hostile look. "Really? Why would I do that?"

"Because those kind of pants look good on chubby boys and you might want to get laid sometime in your lifetime," Shelby said sharply. "We are about to go to a nightclub that has heterosexual women in it. You might want to dress accordingly."

"Whatever," Mike said, picking up the boots and the pants and heading towards the bathroom. "I shouldn't have to change what I wear to talk to women. Women shouldn't be so shallow. They shouldn't care what I wear. That's objectifying me." He was practically shouting by the time he slammed the door behind him.

"Nice vocabulary," Hannah chuckled.

"I'm just trying to help that kid," Shelby said grumpily. "What's up with him and that attitude?" She flipped the bag over and dumped out a pair of plaid peg-legged bondage pants. They were much tighter than the first pair.

"Here, Flynn," she said. "They match your shoes."

He nodded. "Thank you, Shelby. Where did you get these?"

"I went to that second hand store down the street," she said. "I noticed it when I was getting my smokes. They have a lot of cool shit in there. You can totally tell you're in San Francisco."

"That twerp has cooler pants and shoes that Flynn does now," Hannah bitched. "So unfair."

"He needs them more," Shelby observed. "Maybe if they fit perfectly and he can manage to keep his hands to himself and his pie hole shut, a girl will allow him to dance somewhere in her immediate vicinity without mace becoming involved."

Charlotte sighed. "Why would you want to inflict that on the straight women of the world?" She had finished fucking with Flynn's hair and was fixing her eyeliner in the dressing table mirror. Flynn was still on the bed, carefully trying to squeeze into the fishnet shirt without messing up his hair.

"He's still young," Hannah said. "He might not remain a dipshit indefinitely."

"I'm not touching this conversation with a ten foot pole," Flynn said, finally getting his shirt on properly. He grabbed the pants and sat them on his lap, waiting for his turn in the bathroom.

Mike finally emerged from the bathroom and promptly sat on the bed.

"Don't you dare say anything," he said.

Flynn ran into the bathroom to change and hide out, avoiding the conversation.

"But you need a trim," Shelby told Mike. "You have so many split ends."

"No," Mike said. "Get off me, woman."

Going Out

Walking into the club, Flynn clung to Charlotte's hand and stared around the room like a kid on his first trip to an amusement park. He was intimidated and full of wonder, and happy to be surrounded by friends. It was good to have friends, any friends at all, really. It was especially good to have ones just as strange as he was, ones unrepentantly unashamed of being considered damaged, or crazy, or broken. Every single person he came to the club with knew about his mental illness, and not a single one of them really cared. He felt a sense of belonging.

Shelby, Charlotte and Hannah kept running into old friends and making introductions. Charlotte and Hannah were the same age, went to the same Berkeley high school, and knew many of the same people, some of whom had not seen Hannah since she left to serve overseas in Afghanistan. The protracted war in Iraq so overshadowed everything else that many Americans forgot we even had troops in Afghanistan. Charlotte and Flynn both had mental health issues that tended to have an onset at adolescence, while Mike was an adoptee who had a series of early childhood diagnoses that were exasperated by his birthmother's drug and alcohol abuse during pregnancy. Hannah, on the other hand, was considered to be mentally healthy before she came back from the war.

"Hey Gypsy," Hannah called out to a girl with Predator-film like dreadlocks intertwined with multicolored yarn. The girl had some kind of cybergoth Neko outfit, with cat ears sitting behind radiation symbol goggles, knee-high fuzzy boots, a tail, and day glow fishnet stockings under black booty shorts and a matching bikini top.

"I don't go by that anymore," the girl said. "You can call me Rose. That's my name."

"Oh, I know." Charlotte said. "Rose Byrne. We went to high school together."

Rose snapped her fingers together. "Oh right! Charlie and Hannah, wow. It's been a long time. How are you guys doing? Wow. Gee, I can't believe you are still together."

Hannah laughed. "We aren't together. We were never together. Charlotte's straight."

Rose scratched her head. "Uhm, okay, if you say so." Hannah and Charlie were inseparable in their sophomore year of high school, and since Hannah came out that year, a lot of people assumed things. Charlotte wasn't dating anyone human, so no one saw her with anyone. The truth is that the girls had been best friends since the seventh grade, and neither one of them had any intention of not being best friends. Hannah had a crush on Charlie, but it wasn't the central feature of their friendship.

"So what's up with your name?" Charlotte asked bluntly.

"Uhm," Rose explained self-consciously, "I met this girl in college, and she said she was Roma and that gypsy was some kind of racial slur, and I shouldn't call myself that."

"Well, she's right, it is." Hannah confirmed. Hannah was of Russian Jewish heritage and knew a lot about the history of the Roma alongside the Jews in the concentration camps.

"I was named after that movie, Gypsy 83," Rose said defensively.

"Yea, I remember," Charlotte said. "I loved that movie. We saw it together at your house when we were like ten." Charlotte and Rose went to the same grade school, but they didn't meet Hannah until they started junior high in the seventh grade. Hannah went to a public elementary school, while Charlie and Rose attended an artsy charter school. Rose was a second-generation goth chick, and they watched that movie with her mom.

Just then, Shelby and Mike, the only smokers in the group, returned from their cigarette break. The smoke breaks were a great opportunity for Michael to hone his social skills while interacting with a select club into which admission could be gained with a lighter and a roll of stinky dried plant matter burning in a paper cylinder.

"Stevie Nicks is really cool," Shelby said with a wink, sneaking up behind Hannah and putting her arms around her waist. She kissed her on the side of the neck. It was a most modest but decidedly possessive maneuver. Just in case this half-naked cat lady got the wrong idea about her girl.

"Hi, I'm Michelle, Hannah's fiancée," she announced to Rose, conspicuously laying her hand over Hannah's shoulder in such a way as to prominently display her diamond chip encrusted silver engagement ring. "I am very pleased to meet you."

Shelby's legal name was Michelle Baptista. Shelby was a nickname she picked up when she was in the same junior high school class with two other girls named Michelle. They were dubbed Michele H., Michele L., and Michelle B. Shelby got tired of being called Michelle B. and shortened her moniker to Shelby. No one called her Michelle except co-workers and bill collectors.

"Oh," Hannah blushed. "I'm so sorry baby. I didn't see you standing there. Rose, this is my better half, Shelby. Shelby, this is Rose, she went to high school with me and Charlie."

"Nice to meet you, Shelly," Rose said awkwardly.

"Shelby," Hannah corrected. "It's short for Michelle B. Well, anyway…"

173

"Is that Charlotte's boyfriend?" Rose said, gesturing at Mike, who was, after all, wearing a Somnalia t-shirt. "I remember the comic… wow, is that still going on?" Rose babbled.

"Oh hell no, that is not my boyfriend," Charlotte protested.

"I'm totally single, babe," Mike said with his usual charm. "Let me know if you're available, because I didn't come here to go home alone tonight."

"Oh my God…" Hannah muttered under her breath.

Just then, Flynn showed up with a mixed drink called a screwdriver in one hand and two bottled domestic beers in the other. He handed the mixed drink to Charlotte, and gave Hannah one of the beers.

"Oh Shelby," he said, surprised to see her back so soon. "I didn't get you anything... here, you want my beer?"

Shelby pursed her lips. "Pabst Blue Ribbon? Nah, no thanks bruh, I'll pass."

Hannah hooked a thumb towards Flynn. "Now, that's Charlotte's sex slave."

"Shhh…" Charlotte said. "We don't discuss that in public."

"No, we don't." Flynn said, leaning his head against Charlotte's. "I assure you our relationship is very chaste and pure. What is this s-e-x that you speak of?"

"And if we were having sex, it wouldn't be dirty or nasty," Charlotte said. "It would be beautiful. It would always be tender lovemaking that only occurred on a bed of freshly plucked rose petals while bluebirds sang sweetly in the background."

"Right," Rose said, nodding at first Hannah, then Charlotte. "I see you two haven't changed much. Charlie is still sarcastic as ever. Well, very nice to meet you Shelby and... I'm sorry, I didn't catch your name?"

"Flynn," he said, extending his hand. Rose didn't take it.

"I think she means me," Mike suggested. "My name is Michael Shaw, but you can call me Mike. I mean a hottie like you can call me anything you want to."

"Okay," Rose said prissily. "I've got to go now. I need to pee." She abruptly departed before Mike could breathe on her any further, or she had to endure more of Hannah and Charlotte's blatant attempts to show off their precious little arm candy.

As they watched her mincing walk away from them and towards her usual crowd, Charlotte caught a glimpse of Rose in profile, looking as though someone had dropped a smallish turd in her absinthe.

"Do you think she's dying over there?" Charlotte asked Hannah.

"Oh yea," Hannah answered. "She's so verklempt she had to rush off to the little girl's room to hyperventilate in private."

"I'm surprised Mike didn't offer to go watch her pee," Shelby admitted.

"Fuck that bitch," Mike said. "Did you see that fox in the black wedding dress? She was totally checking me out."

"She's gay," Shelby countered.

"No she's not," Mike protested. "Did you see when we left? She was totally looking at my ass."

"She was totally looking at *my* ass," Shelby disagreed.

"I'm going to go find her," Mike said.

Shelby laughed. "You have fun with that."

Sleepover

Mike didn't pick up any hot chicks. He did make some friends, though. A guy who lived in San Mateo offered to give him a ride home so that he wouldn't have to wait around for the BART train to start running in the morning, in exchange for five dollars for gas and a couple of cigarettes.

Hannah and Shelby invited Charlotte and Flynn to crash on the floor in their hotel room and get dragged along to day two of the comic book convention Sunday. They stripped the rough coverlet from the top layer of the hotel supply bedding and tossed it in the corner by the closet with one of the pillows.

It was a bit chilly on the floor. Flynn returned Shelby's fishnet shirt, which went directly to the dirty clothes bag, and put on his t-shirt and a hooded sweatshirt. Charlotte borrowed a pair of Shelby's sweatpants. It felt safe and warm, bundled in street clothes in a corner on the floor. Flynn felt good. He felt human.

The last time he crashed on the floor of someone's hotel room with a girl was with Tamara back in high school. There was something extremely comforting about the smell of fabric softener and Shelby's Winston cigarettes. There was something reassuring about the weight of Charlotte's head on his chest, the pressure of her arms around him, and the innocence of sharing a pillow.

Shelby and Hannah climbed into bed with the confidence only newlyweds seemed to know. They weren't yet married, but they were headed in that direction, and they didn't have that crusty old carelessness that can settle on longtime lovers. They were still convinced that their love was a secret only the two of them were capable of knowing. Their kisses under covers were silent, stealthy, and ripe with the knowledge that they lived together. A night without sex was no big deal because they could always make up for it later. They were, after all, practically married. They had all of the access to one another as any married couple, but none of the complacency. And soon, they would have that recognition on paper that sanctified their relationship in the eyes of both of their families and the law.

If they weren't from the Bay Area, maybe their families would have been less accepting.

Charlotte and Flynn weren't at the same place. The first four months of their relationship they were essentially just dating. Neither of them saw other people, but they lead separate lives and only saw each other on the weekends. For the past two months, they had been living together, but since Flynn was job-hunting the whole time, they hadn't done very much socializing.

Being taken around and introduced to Charlotte's old friends made Flynn feel like things were serious. They were a couple and this was real. He was just beginning to overcome his insecurities, the feeling that she would probably dump him at any moment over any one of a number of personal flaws.

He was mentally ill, and up until two days ago, unemployed. He no longer had a car. He was on a plethora of psych meds and sometimes they interfered with his ability to perform sexually. The kind of sexual activity that gave him a raging boner regardless was socially unacceptable. He was insecure, and could be a little needy. She could have dumped him over any and all of that, but she didn't. She liked him, the way he was. Loved him, he guessed.

Soon, all four of them were asleep. The humans among them had dreams that were peaceful and uneventful. Charlotte was not so fortunate.

Family Meeting

Earlier that night, Mike told Charlotte and Hannah how hot Mercy was in the comics. The women exchanged a look and explained to him that in reality, he would not want to run into Mercy in his worst nightmares. His repeated invocation of Mercy's name seemed to have an undesired side effect, sort of like those horror films where the teenagers repeat the name of Bloody Mary in a mirror.

Mercy wasn't hurting Mike, exactly. She was hanging around his dreams having creepy conversations about the joys of erotic asphyxiation. If Mercy hadn't been fucking with Mike's head she wouldn't have been called on the carpet by her father.

Charlotte found herself standing in front of her father in his palace, but not in the ordinary place. She was seated at an enormous slate dining table, carved out of the stone like everything else. Father and Sympathy were there, along with two brothers, Fuss and Irate and eight sisters Charlotte she never bothered to mention in her comic books. Her sisters were Irksome, Aloof, Morbid, Callous, Cranky, Colicky, Sweetums, and Coy.

Mercy and Sympathy were the two youngest, although they were hundreds of years older than Charlotte. They were Charlie's childhood babysitters, escorts in the world of dreams, which made her closer to those two than any of her other siblings.

"Heeeeyyyyy Happy-Charlie-girl," Sympathy sang, waving her tentacles around. "Where's your consort?"

"He's resting," Charlotte said casually, smiling a little because Sympathy acknowledged her relationship with Flynn. It was a big deal.

"Where is Mercy?" Sweetums asked.

Brash snapped his fingers and everyone jumped back a little as Mercy and her current prey appeared buck naked in the middle of the table. Mercy was fucking Mike and had a belt looped around his neck.

Charlotte put her hands over her eyes. "Yuck! I do not want to watch Mike on Mercy porn."

"Don't hate," Mike said. "What the hell are you doing in my dream anyway? Hey! Get out!"

Brash snapped his fingers and sent Mike away to whatever his regularly scheduled wet dream might have been – Charlotte didn't want to guess, and she wasn't asking.

"Don't dick around with Charlie's consort or her friends," Brash said, shaking his head.

"Her friends are off limits, since when?" Mercy said angrily.

"Since my oracle predicted that my influence in the mortal realm would be determined by the success or failure of their comic book," Brash said peevishly. As if to underscore the point, he waved his arm and had his oracle appear. The oracle was a creepy, eight-foot tall bald fellow with deathly mottled skin whose eyes were sewn shut with thick, black thread. His wings had been severed, but the stumps continued to tick back and forth as though the motion had a purpose. He never spoke to anyone except Brash, and then only when directly addressed.

"And what is the prediction about the consort?" Brash asked his monstrous oracle.

"If he dies unnaturally, so will you all," said the oracle.

"Oh please," Mercy said. "Does he mean that if that boy is hit by a drunk driver, we all die?"

"Oracle?" Brash asked.

"If he dies of unnatural causes, then everyone at this table will be able to enter the mortal realm, as Mercy wishes." said the oracle.

"How can that be?" Sympathy asked, perplexed "Those two things don't seem to go together."

"These oracles are kind of tricky," Mercy said. "We can't be sure what he means."

"Flynn said that the man he dreamed about told him that if he died, I would become human," Charlotte said. "Like fully human, not half. But your oracle says I will die."

"Oracle?" Brash asked. "Can you clarify?"

"Whether or not the boy dies, she will die," he said, pointing at Charlotte. "She is already going to die. If the boy dies before his time, then you and your other children will also die."

Coy was the smartest among them, and she put it together first. "All things in the mortal realm must die, because death is what makes them mortal. If they did not die, they would be immortal. Are you trying to say that if he dies unnaturally, we will all be mortal?"

"Well?" Brash asked. "Answer, oracle."

"Yes," the oracle said, frowning slightly at being forced not to speak in riddles.

"Fine," Mercy said. "I'll leave him alone. I will leave the friends who work on her comic alone." Mercy began quietly calculating the number of friends Charlie might have who weren't off limits.

"You play at a dangerous game," Irate warned Mercy. "You think you can pick off other people they know, I see it in your eyes, and I hear it in your voice. The problem with your plan is that the boy already threatened to take his own life in order to protect that Howard fellow."

"No," Mercy protested. "He offered to allow me to take his life. See? Much different."

"Nonetheless," Brash agreed, "Your brother is right. If the boy becomes convinced that the only way to protect his friends is to offer his own life, he might be willing to sacrifice himself just so he can take you with him. Lay off."

"Fine," Mercy said angrily. She really couldn't help herself. Mercy was a serial killer. If she had been forced to become mortal, she would just go around wiping people out like any human psychopath does, hunting until someday she was caught. It didn't matter what she promised her father… she knew in her heart of hearts, she would continue to lash out against these ridiculous restrictions. She would just have to be more careful.

These four friends of Charlotte's, perhaps, were useful, but Mercy was convinced that at least some of them were replaceable. How hard could it be to find some schmuck to wear a t-shirt? What about this Shelby, was she really necessary? It was the Hannah woman who was brokering the deal. And what about after the deal was done, wouldn't she be expendable afterwards?

There was no sense in explaining all of that to her father. And Charlotte's consort, well, Mercy decided that he had more of a will to live than her father and siblings seemed to think. She didn't think he would off himself just because a few acquaintances of his dropped dead.

As soon as she had a chance, she'd start testing that theory.

For now, she decided the only thing she needed to focus on was mastering the art of lying.

"Yes, father," she said. "Of course."

GIRLFRIENDS

Years of working at the postal service made Shelby an early riser. Even on weekends, her idea of sleeping in was staying in bed until 8:00 in the morning. As a result, she was already up at seven in the morning, making hotel coffee in the tiny two cup serving pot provided in the bathroom. She managed to finish making the coffee, drink both cups, shower, get dressed, pick up and put on some more coffee for Shelby before anyone else got up.

Her job required a decent amount of walking, and when she wasn't at work, Shelby liked to hit the gym. She was the most physically fit person in the room, with long legs and well muscled calves and thighs. At five foot nine, she stood a good eight inches over her tiny girlfriend. Hannah was short and skinny, a bookish looking punk chick who wore combat boots and glasses.

Hannah rolled out of bed around nine, groggy and needing to pee as she always did first thing in the morning. She was a tiny person, weighing in at about ninety pounds. She dressed like Darla off of that old MTV cartoon, only with a mohawk. Like Flynn, she picked a fashion some time in middle school and never really changed it. She dressed like a mid 90s/mid 2000s feminist stereotype and she didn't care. She was a pretty girl, though. She was a delicate thing, slender, boyish, what they used to call gamine. It didn't take her long to get dressed.

They rolled out of the hotel room at about 9:30 A.M leaving Charlotte and Flynn passed out on the floor. They were going to go out and get some breakfast, eat somewhere decent and maybe bring a doggie bag back for their unconscious guests.

    Hannah and Shelby were happy to be in San Francisco. Everyone pretty much knew they were a couple in Suisun, but they didn't feel like they could just walk around the streets holding hands and kissing like youngsters there. It wasn't just the fact that some people were still shocked by same-sex unions. Small and affordable cities in the North Bay, East Bay and Peninsula were the Bay Area's equivalent of the suburbs. They were places were people who were starting families with children could afford to live. Demographically, San Francisco had half as many children as other major metropolitan areas did on average, and part of that was because of the lack of space and high cost of real estate.

    Anywhere else, walking around holding hands and French kissing in public was something teenagers did. In cities where people had kids anyone old enough to be the parents of aforementioned children kissing in public was considered by said children to be "gross." Twenty-two year old Hannah couldn't pick up a pack of cigs for Shelby without being carded, but twenty-five year old Shelby looked more mature and resembled many of the local moms dragging their kids off to preschool or kindergarten. As a postal service worker, she was a fixture of relative respectability in the community with some kind of reputation to uphold.

    There was an anonymity they enjoyed in San Francisco. They did not have to worry about what their neighbors thought or if they would run into anyone Shelby knew from work. They were staying, in a motel on Market Street about equidistant between the Castro, a gay neighborhood, and South of Market, a hub of local nightlife. No one South of Market or in the Castro cared if they exchanged sloppy kisses on the corner while waiting for a traffic light to change.

    They were a cute couple, but incongruous – not what people expected a couple to be. Hannah was an old school feminist and she resented the heteronormative expectations being foisted onto same-sex relationships. Why should one of them have to be butch and the other femme? Neither of them claimed, or wanted to be male.

    Shelby was a statuesque Portuguese woman. She wore her black hair long, and was a fan of contemporary make-up and jewelry. Today she was in black skinny jeans and a red and white racer back tank top with a skull and crossbones logo on the chest. Last night at the club she had been rocking a blue and green plaid pleated miniskirt and knee high boots with five-inch stripper heels.

She was six feet tall in three-inch heels, and in the five-inch heels or platforms she loomed over women and men alike at six foot-two. She loved that Glamazon look. Shelby was athletic and shapely. Unless you were big enough for the World Wrestling Federation, there was a good chance she could kick your ass. She wouldn't, though, because it would not be ladylike.

Shelby, like Charlotte, was modern and fashion conscious. Shelby knew how to ease in and out of styles from all kinds of different sets. She saw dressing up as some kind of theater.

Hannah had colored yarn braided into her Mohawk this morning, and looked kind of like Tank Girl. She was wearing the same skirt Shelby wore the night before, but on her, instead of being a micro mini, it fell to mid-thigh. She wore it with knee-high black stockings, combat boots, and a black version of the pirate tee Shelby wore.

She was hugging Shelby's waist and enjoying the sunshine.
Life was perfect and they wanted for nothing.

Morning

Charlotte was slightly round and pear-shaped, like a woman in a Botticelli painting. She was taller and thicker than Hannah, and so her friend's baggy sweatpants were snug and Capri-length on her. When she woke up in the morning, Hannah and Shelby were out and about. Flynn was snoring like a freight train with his arm and half of his shoulder weighing down on her back. Charlie rolled out from under him.

She was used to his snoring. She'd been sleeping with it every night for the past two months. They were as far away from the bed as they could get, so hopefully the noise hadn't disturbed Hannah and her girlfriend last night.

Charlotte left Flynn lying there and clambered off to the shower. She had a lot on her mind.

She was a bit annoyed when he popped up moments later and followed her into the bathroom.

"We aren't at home," she said irritably. "Go back in the other room and watch television or something. Hannah and Shelby could be back any minute now. They don't want us in here together contaminating their bathroom."

"Uhm… okay, fine, "Flynn said with a shrug. He had no idea why Charlie was in such a bad mood. He sat on the edge of the bed, and turned on the television. He was pleasantly surprised to find something about Greek mythology on the History Channel.

Sitting on the bed reminded him of last night, when Charlotte was fixing his hair. Soon his mind was wandering to the nightclub, where Charlie shoved him against the wall and made out with him in some dark corner. He remembered how she said she didn't want to leave any marks above the neck that might embarrass him at work before she started putting hickeys on his chest. He remembered telling her how much he wanted her to break the skin and make him bleed. He remembered wondering if there was any saliva on Shelby's fishnet shirt when he quietly placed it in the bag of dirty clothes.

Now he was touching the tender spot on his side just above the hip, wondering how Charlotte could possibly be serious about her sudden interest in propriety. He shrugged. It wasn't their hotel room. She was probably right.

Charlie wasn't really all that concerned about potential immodesty. She just wanted to be alone. Her father's words weighed upon her heavily. It bothered her that the fates or anyone would place Flynn in such a pivotal role. Brash was only ruthless, his children were brutal.

How many enemies did her siblings have? How many people would want to see all of them dead? Some of those who might seek vengeance were more powerful than the wounded mortal who appeared in Flynn's dream. Some of them were immortal. Would any of them hesitate to break Flynn's neck if they thought it would destroy the despised children of Brash? Charlotte didn't think so. Anyway you sliced it Flynn's life would always be in danger now, right until the day he died.

Third Intermission

Thanatos curled his lip. "So much potential for death," he purred, looking down into the murky waters of the underground river his twin used as a scrying glass. "If your grandchildren live, they will continue to carve a path into the physical universe through flesh and bone."

"And if they do not," Somnus added, "how rare a thing it is for an immortal to become mortal? How rare is it for one to experience death, to have a life that can be cut short by the whims of fate?"

"How delightful," his brother sighed.

It was just then that Brash barged into the room.

"Father," he said humbly. "Surely, there is something you can do to help get me out of this mess."

"I tried," Somnus assured him. "You know how it is. I'm unable to directly intervene. I could, but I won't. We all know what happened to old Prometheus for interfering in the affairs of men. It's not my place. Your children are being punished for their cruelty, and since that cruelty has manifested as a result of the curse you bought down on their heads, you are likewise implicated. But I was able to appoint your granddaughter to protect him."

"Charlotte," Brash said. He didn't ask. It wasn't a question. Who else could it be?

"She's under the spell of Cupid's arrow," Thanatos laughed. "We have here the makings of an epic tragedy, don't you think? Even his beloved has considered how much better life would be for mortal kind if she just suffocated him with a pillow in bed, the humanity!"

Somnus shook his head and rolled his eyes. "And he'd probably let her, too."

"Oh, my beautiful Charlotte," Thanatos said, mocking Flynn. "Kill me now, here in our premarital bed. But tie me up first, so that I won't accidentally bruise your lovely thigh kicking and struggling as you snuff out my life."

Somnus laughed.

"That is not funny," Brash squawked. "You have to do something about it!"

"I can't," Somnus complained. "My mother has a very strange sense of humor. She probably picked him out because she knows what he is like. He is so sweet and easy going, so passive and compliant, such a little lamb. It would be all too easy to take him out back and slaughter him."

"Is he a eunuch?" Thanatos jested. "He doesn't seem to have any balls."

"Despite all of this, he did beg for his life," Somnus added. "It caught my mother's attention when he asked to live. Something in him wants to survive, so there is hope."

"I don't see how that little girl Charlotte can protect him," Thanatos observed.

"She might surprise you," Brash said. "She has always surprised me."

"Perhaps," Thanatos said. "We will see. Mother gave them some time, to get to know each other, so that Charlotte would even want to protect that boy. Mother won't protect those two much longer. Things will become more difficult soon. Their trials are about to begin in earnest."

Act IV: Trials

A Change of Plans

It was difficult for Mercy, keeping her cool, pretending to be a kind and decent human being. She wasn't kind, or decent, and she definitely wasn't a human being. This time she decided to take a different approach in her attempts to unravel Michael Shaw's mind and usurp Charlotte's hold over him. In order to accomplish the deed, she adopted a different kind of form altogether.

But it was cool. She liked going around in drag.

She… or rather he was sitting on the low concrete wall surrounding a 7-11 parking lot with his new best friend, Mike. They were drinking 40 ouncers and girl watching. Mercy was a little surprised by the content of his dreams, not the girl part, but the beer part. She would have never pegged him as the kind of fellow to have public intoxication in his list of unfulfilled fantasies.

"Yeah, look at those bitches," the male Mercy said, slapping Mike on the shoulder. "Just shaking their asses all full of themselves like they think they're hot shit, you know?"

"Yeah, fuck em bro," Mike said. "Watch this." Michael took a big swig of Old English and spewed it out all over a college girl in a tank top and yoga pants. The girl screamed, and Mike bellowed out a riotous laugh, like this was the funniest shit ever invented by mankind.

"Have a drink, ho!" he yelled after her as she ran off.

"You let her off easy, man," Mercy said, slapping his knee and laughing. "She just got a little free beer shower, I'm sure she's had nastier fluids on her chest than that, if you know what I mean."

"I know," Mike laughed. "Look at those pants all pulled up her ass, you know it, right?"

"Riiiiggght," Mercy said. "But fuck these bitches, I got magic, you know, like a super power. Watch this."

Mercy waited until a girl with high heels came walking by, and then with a snap of the fingers, made her heel break off. The girl went tumbling to the ground, where she scraped her knee and broke her glasses.

"Holy shit!" Mike screamed. "That was kind of mean, but whoa… have skills, bro."

"Mean?" Mercy argued. "No, she deserved it."

She wondered how hard it would be to convince Mike to escalate if she perpetually indulged his revenge fantasies. She wondered how long it would take for him to snap. She wasn't absolutely sure that Mike was the kind of guy who would go on a killing spree, and just in case he wasn't, she was hedging her bets. There were a few of Michael's more hardcore buddies who might kill for her if pushed and prodded in the right way. Mercy also infected the dreams of other resentful men who were completely uninvolved with Mike here.

If programmed the right way… instant bloodbath, good old-fashioned stuff like what her father used to inspire back in his heyday.

She wasn't planning riding on her father's coat tails. She'd have a legacy of her own.

CONVENTION

Flynn was down at the convention hall clasping the hand of his almost famous girlfriend, unaware of the fact that his submissive behavior was apparently so blatant that it had become the butt of jokes being bandied about by the old gods.

Of course, Somnus and Thanatos weren't entirely correct in their assessment. Charlotte didn't want to kill Flynn, and Flynn didn't want to die. But the list of things that he would consent to if she asked him to was a pretty extensive one, and the number of things she'd enjoy subjecting him to was equally long.

Today, the only thing Charlotte asked him to do was to model Hannah's *Somnalia* t-shirt while they hit up the booths and checked to see what everyone else was into, because for whatever reason, Mike called up this morning to decline.

Hannah was smart. It was a good strategy.

They were about three booths in when the first fellow cartoonist recognized the artwork.

"Hey, I love *Somnalia*!" the girl said. "That's a really cool t-shirt, where did you get that?"

"I made it," Hannah said, grinning broadly. "I work for a printing company and bookstore out of Napa. We love to work with independent artists and our rates are very affordable." She slipped her the card.

"Is *Somnalia* one of your clients?" the young lady asked. "I've been following it since I was in high school, but they say Charlotte Metaxas is a shut-in, she has agoraphobia or something? Anyway, no one has ever seen her, or met her, that's what I heard."

"Actually, we went to high school together," Hannah said.

"She's my girlfriend," Flynn said. "She's really cool, you should meet her."

"Then why are you holding hands with that girl?" the chick at the booth asked, pointing at Charlotte.

"Oh," Charlotte said, extending her hand. "I'm Charlotte Metaxas, nice to meet you."

"No fucking way!" the girl chortled. "My name is Stephanie Chun. I, wow, sorry about all that stuff I said about you,"

"No need to be sorry," Charlotte said with a shrug. "I put it on my website. It sounded a lot more mysterious than 'Charlotte is a student at UC Berkeley who spends her spare time in the psych ward. So, yeah, I'm thinking of putting it in print. Hannah there tells me that might involve going outside and meeting humans, so here I am."

It pretty much went on that way for the next five hours, with Charlotte making new friends and contacts and Hannah blatantly peddling her wares. It was hard, slightly embarrassing work, but it was also fun. Charlotte and Flynn didn't get out that much, but Hannah and Shelby were very outgoing socially. It was really fun, and exciting to think that it might go somewhere.

The day ended with promises to spend more time hanging out and to continue this business venture and all of the usual things. Usual things were good. There was a sense of normalcy to everything that let all of them forget about otherworldly threats and night terrors.

Confessions

Charlotte and Flynn had left their car at home and returned to their little apartment on the BART train. They got home relatively early, around seven at night. Both of them wanted Flynn to be well rested for his job interview in the morning, and neither had any thought of staying up late.

It was the first time they'd been alone together in two days.

The apartment was small, and after two days with no air conditioning or open windows it was hot and muggy in the house. Flynn went to the bathroom and while he was going he decided to go head and drop his pants to the floor and kick them all the way off. It was much too hot to wear pants. By the time he made it out of the bathroom, he was in his underwear.

Charlotte got out of her pants, and managed to slip her bra out from under her t-shirt without taking it off and hook it on the back of a chair. By the time he got to the living room, she was in a t-shirt and underwear, turning on the air conditioner.

"It's hot," she complained. She took her t-shirt off and tossed it on the chair with her bra.

Flynn shoved all of the blankets into a pile in one corner at the foot of the bed and then clambered up on top of the fitted sheet, sweat beading up on his neck and forehead, waiting for the air conditioning. Charlotte climbed on the bed next to him, plopped down on her back and grabbed the remote control.

"Hey," he said softly, "We fall asleep with the television every night, right? And the TV isn't going anywhere. I was thinking maybe we could just sit and talk for a while."

"Sure, okay," Charlotte said, setting the remote down on the end table. She swiveled over on to her side, leaning against one of her hips and holding herself up on her elbow so she could look at and listen to him. "What do you want to talk about?"

Flynn eased down on the bed until he was at eye level with her before speaking. "I just wanted to let you know that, yes, I do have fantasies about being eaten," he said shyly.

"Oh, okay." Charlotte said calmly. "Would you like to tell me about them?"

"Well, you know, we, as humans… well, I, at least, am human. We're on the top of the food chain and we kill animals and we consume their flesh," he began. "Even the plants we eat to live are alive. It's like we are taking their life force and absorbing it to give us life, to give us energy."

"Sure," Charlotte said, nodding. "You're talking about circle of life and all that noise."

"Right," he said. "When we die, in the natural order of things, plants and animals consume us and we become a part of the ecosystem again. Only we often don't, because our bodies are preserved in boxes with chemicals to prevent us from becoming one with nature."

"You sound very philosophical about all this," Charlotte observed. Flynn swallowed nervously. Clearly, this wasn't easy for him to talk about. She said, "I'm sorry. I didn't mean to interrupt you."

He hesitated. "Look, this is not easy for me to say. I mean, Mercy, she's your sister, right?"

Charlotte nodded. "It's okay. I know what she did to you."

"For her," he said, "to her, it was like I was a steak, or a salad, you know? I was something lower on the food chain, but she knew about my fantasies, and she tried to use them against me."

Charlotte furrowed her brow. "Was she trying to get you to agree? I mean to consent. There is a lot of power in a willing sacrifice."

"Yes," he said nervously. "She wanted me to offer her my life, but I don't want to die. I'm afraid of dying."

"So am I," Charlotte said. "I don't blame you. I mean I guess you're right, I'm not entirely human, but I am just as mortal as you are." She took his hand in hers and gave it a squeeze.

"But when you asked me if I would let you eat me," he said, "I couldn't stop thinking about it. I mean what it would be like to feed myself to you. I thought about how it would be if I could nourish you with my flesh, but not just my body, all of me. I thought about offering myself, and how it would feel to have you devour me until there was nothing left of me, until I was nothing. You see what I'm saying?"

"Listen to me," she said seriously, "we are mortal and soon enough, we will both return to dust. Fifty years, or even a hundred, they are nothing. Compared to the likes of Mercy, our lives are pitifully short. But I love you, Flynn. You're my lover, and I want you in my life, in my arms, and in my bed, not racing through my digestive tract."

"You love me?" he said, amazed. "I mean I know you do. But you've never actually said it before. I mean when I say I love you, you just say 'me too.'"

"I love you very much," she said. "Dying in a dream isn't the same as dying in real life, Flynn. I don't know what it means to die out of this world, although my father swears I'll have an afterlife. He says that dream world is part of the underworld, where dead mortals go. He says that since I'm his child, I will end up there, not in any other part of Tartarus, and the same goes for my mother, as his consort, and I suppose for you, if he is to be believed. I just haven't seen any evidence. To me, it seems like a tale he told to comfort me as a child. I don't know what comes after death, and I'm in no hurry to see it or have you see it, either. But I've died in a dream before, and really, you just become a disembodied spirit. When you wake up, everything resets, and the next time you dream, it's like it never happened. There is no continuity of that sort in dreams. Time there doesn't work the same way it works here, there. But it might be upsetting for you anyway."

"I see," Flynn said. The air conditioning was starting to affect him and the cooling sweat on his skin left him shivering. He reached down and pulled the blankets up over him. They were still holding hands. When the blankets came up over them, they instinctively huddled closer to one another, to keep all body parts under the blanket and to enjoy the extra body heat.

"Besides," Charlotte warned him, "the Feast of Tears is a fertility ritual. You'd wake up horny as fuck and we'd have sex and I absolutely would get pregnant, so unless you want to become a father nine months from now, we probably shouldn't do that."

Flynn laughed. "Yeah, we should probably, I don't know, live somewhere with more than two rooms before considering procreation. I guess we can wait, then. But someday, if you want to, I just want you know that I'm willing."

"Thank you," Charlotte said. "That means a lot to me."

"Let me ask you something else," Flynn went on. "I want you to be honest with me. The prediction – the one Howard Lowe made – do you know if it is true?"

"It is true," Charlotte said, frowning. "Don't do anything stupid, Flynn."

"Thanks for not lying to me," he said with a shrug. "I thought you'd try to hide that from me. I noticed you've been acting tense lately, well, I wondered if that was why."

"Yes," she said. "Yes it is. My father told me. So any number of persons and things would like to see you dead now, and I'm very sorry for that."

"Howard said it would be worth it," Flynn reminded her. "He said that my sacrifice would keep hundreds, even thousands of humans safe. He also told me you'd be unharmed."

"Are you fucking stupid?" Charlotte snapped. "I have human emotions just like you do. I love you but you think that if you run off and play the slaughtered innocent I'm somehow going to remain unscathed? I would think that the death of my boyfriend, my consort, which is a little bit more than just a boyfriend; and my siblings and father, as loathsome as they might be, would be extremely traumatic for me. I'm not sure I would recover from it. Are you?"

"Of course not," he said, lacing his arms tightly around her waist. "If your siblings do enough harm, though… I think we do have to consider it."

"I don't want to think about that right now," Charlotte said. "It's too upsetting. I just want to go to bed. Can we go to bed?"

"I do have work in the morning," Flynn admitted.

Neither of them said anything for a long time. They were both trying to go to bed, but unable to do so, and each was afraid to stir and disturb the other.

About thirty minutes went by before Charlotte squeaked, "I can't sleep."

"I can't either," Flynn said. "I'm afraid, Charlie. I don't want to die."

"I know," Charlotte said. "I don't want you to die, either." She was crying, but she didn't want him to see her tears. She buried her damp face in the covers and quietly patted him on the hip. She thought about trying to help him get to sleep, that was the least she could do. Maybe it was the most she could do. There was so much she could not do, and she felt so helpless.

"But we both know I might have to," Flynn said stoically. "I might have to die."

"Just try not to think about it," she said tensely.

Charlotte kissed and caressed him until he became too drowsy to keep his eyes open. She kept touching him until he was unconscious and all of the worries of the waking world were far beyond him.

And then she wept openly. She was devastated by the thought of losing him.

WORK

Considering that he was on the supernatural world's most wanted list, Flynn was in surprisingly good spirits. He had a job, his girlfriend said she loved him, and she let him drive her car to work. There was no sense in moping. No one had said he needed to die, so he might as well live.

He thought of himself as a kind of boring person, not at all exceptional, at any rate. He was a talented artist, but not the most talented. He was alright. He was never what you'd call special before, but now he was very special, just in a tremendously fucked up way.

He was a bargaining chip. Charlotte's great-grandmother was leveraging his life against the cooperation of her father and her nasty little siblings, or so Charlotte said. Charlotte's dad was raising hell with his children, demanding that they cool it off before they were all wiped out. Charlotte was his knight in shining armor. She was going to save him.

Whether things turned out well or badly for him, his life was definitely a fairytale, possibly one of those the Brothers Grimm were known for where things sometimes went horribly wrong, but still, a fairytale. He was going to live and die in a fairytale. His mind was blown.

That made it a lot easier to cope with trudging off to his boring ass job.

Mom

Charlotte only had one summer class, computer animation, three hours a day, three days a week. After it was over, she went over to her mother's house to catch her up on the latest goings on with Brash, Flynn, and the world of the somnali.

"Well I think you might be overreacting," Maribelle Metaxas told her daughter. "Flynn's not exactly suicidal. He only said that he was willing to make a heroic sacrifice for the good of all mankind if it became absolutely necessary. Our job is to make sure it never comes to that."

"But Mom…" Charlotte began.

"No, no 'but Mom,'" Maribelle shushed her. "We can mourn him when and if he dies. This is not the time to mourn. This is the time to fight."

"I just worry that it's my fault," Charlotte said. "You know, I did ask him if he would endure the Feast of Tears and…"

"Naturally, you would have to, wouldn't you?" Maribelle asked. "Did he refuse?"

"No, he said that he would. He said that he dreamed about me completely consuming him, until there was nothing left. It kind of frightened me," Charlotte said.

Maribelle shook her head. "I think you're taking that the wrong way."

"And how should I take it?" Charlotte asked.

"Huh," Maribelle coughed a little. "Let me make us some tea, my dear."

Charlotte pushed the chair back a bit and blinked. "Tea? Really, Mom?" She didn't get an answer, because Maribelle had already risen from her chair and hustled off to the kitchen. Unwilling to let it rest, she got up and followed her mother into the kitchen.

"What's wrong, Mom?" she asked.

"This is a lot more uncomfortable than I thought it would be," her mother sighed. "After talking to you about periods and puberty and boys and birth control and everything, you would think it would be old hat, right? Talking birds and the bees with your adult child? But it's not."

"Oh," Charlotte said uneasily. "Alright then, just spit it out."

"Do you think that your father and I could have conceived you if I didn't have anything, let us say, in common with Flynn?" her mother asked.

"Oh. Ooooh, okay, I think I see what you're saying," Charlie said. She whistled. "Okay, so you're saying that for some humans this is normal behavior?"

"You're twenty-three years old," Maribelle said. "Do I really need to start handing you copies of BDSM primers? I mean, everyone's read Fifty Shades of Grey by now, haven't they?"

"Twenty-two," Charlotte corrected. "My birthday is in four days."

"Okay damned near twenty-three," Maribelle ranted. "Old enough to know, you and I both know you didn't actually accidentally happen upon this young man. This was arranged. Your father and probably your siblings, at least Sympathy and Mercy, would have chosen him for you and done everything possible to offer him to you because he is the way he is."

"Okay," Charlotte shrugged. "And?"

"And to him," Maribelle said, "to offer himself to you in an act of such total devotion as what the Feast of Tears requires would be an incredibly sensual experience. It's not the same as dying. It's a sex game."

"But there would be a child," Charlotte countered.

"One who would never need to know how perverted its parents are," Maribelle argued. "At least not until it becomes a mouthy adult old enough to drive, vote and drink in a bar."

"Yeah, I guess I didn't know about you," Charlotte said with a shrug.

"I refused to endure the Feast of Tears for your father," Maribelle said, "although I might have felt differently if I knew that he would commit infanticide and murder and destroy the lives of so many others if I didn't comply."

"Yeah, there is that," Charlotte said, washing out teacups as her mother nervously waited for the pot to boil.

"But just because he is…" Maribelle paused, struggling for the words.

"Extremely submissive and masochistic," Charlotte offered.

"Yes," Maribelle agreed, "more so than I ever was, apparently. Even though he is, that doesn't mean that he views laying his life down to end the somnali threat in the same way. That's really not sexy. He's just trying to be the hero."

"Oh," Charlotte nodded. "I get it. A heroic act of self-sacrifice, just like in one of the video games he likes to play or movies he likes to watch. "

Maribelle made a Vulcan hand gesture and did her best Spock in the Wrath of Khan imitation. "The needs of the many outweigh the needs of the few, or the one."

"Yeah, you're right," Charlotte admitted. "He's a big old dorkmeister, and he totally does think that way. But it's not that easy for me. He's my one."

Maribelle nodded. "That's right, he is your one. So we can't let it go down like that. Do you still have the book? The Rites of Undoing?"

"Yeah, I do." Charlotte said.

"I need to see it," Maribelle said. "We need to see if there is a way to unbind his fate from the fates of your father and your siblings."

Charlotte nodded.

"He won't like that, though," Maribelle warned. "Right now he has the power to stop them all by falling on his own sword. That probably makes him feel like a superhero. You'd be taking that power away from him."

"Why does shit have to be so complicated?" Charlotte complained. The tea was finally ready, and Maribelle poured it into the by now far too well scrubbed teacups. They took them and retired once again to the dining room.

"So what are you doing for your birthday?" Maribelle asked.

"Karaoke," Charlotte said. "What do you think? Jack's or Lou's?"

"I think I should hire a KJ and we should have it here," Maribelle announced. A KJ was a karaoke jockey. "I only have one child, after all. We can invite all of your friends, and his friends, and I'll have it catered and there will be an abundance of alcohol. And I will invite some of my witchy little friends who can help figure out certain aspects of this situation."

"And we have to invite Hannah and Shelby," Charlotte trilled. "Hannah asked me to be her maid of honor, did I tell you? They're getting married in the fall."

"That's beautiful," Maribelle said. "And Shelby is okay with your being their maid of honor?"

"Oh no, not the maid," Charlotte corrected, "A maid, Hannah's maid of honor. Shelby has her own maid of honor, one of her coworkers, a nice woman named Gloria Simms or Janes or something that ends in s."

"But no best man," Maribelle surmised.

"Well neither one of them has a brother," Charlotte said by way of non-explanation.

THE BRIDES TO BE

Hannah was laying belly-down on the cream-colored couch in the living room kicking her feet up in the air. She was reading a bridal magazine when Shelby came home from work. Shelby dropped down to her knees so they were face to face and planted a wet one on Hannah's mouth, but Hannah didn't even let go of the magazine long enough to put her arms around her.

"Put down the damned magazine," Shelby said, shaking her head. "Don't look at the women in there. Look at this woman, right here. See? Your future wife is home."

"Why so cranky? Hannah asked.

"I don't get why you're so obsessed with this wedding," Shelby said grouchily. "I never thought of you as the traditionalist type."

"It won't be traditional," Hannah protested. "I mean I'll be wearing white combat boots."

"But you'll be wearing white," Shelby signed. "Like somehow, someone is a virgin. I mean the whole institution of marriage was originally designed to subjugate women so we could become breeding machines. Best men were thugs who kept the bride from escaping her fate."

"But we don't have a best man," Hannah pointed out. "We have two maids of honor, right? No patriarchy here." She didn't understand why Shelby had to be such a pill about the whole thing. Hannah had been dreaming about her wedding day since she was a well-read eight year old pouring over a ratty copy of Jane Eyre.

"We could just go to the courthouse as far as I am concerned," Shelby said. "I am just doing this because it's what you want. I don't need a big ceremony to validate our love. It's all you ever talk about anymore."

"It's not all," Hannah said, folding the magazine up. "Hey, guess what! I got a raise today."

"Oh wow I'm so happy for you, baby," Shelby said. She gave her a big hug, and tried to get over her premarital jitters and sullenness. Shelby's parents were divorced, and her mother was divorced twice. Her impression of marriage was jaded and unfavorable. She thought that married people took one another for granted, and she interpreted Hannah's paying more attention to the magazine than to her as a sign that the taking for granted had already begun.

"So do you want to go out and celebrate?" Hannah asked. "Or we could celebrate here at home."

"We can go out later if you want," Shelby offered. "My feet are killing me."

Hannah was rubbing Shelby's feet when their roommate came out of his room fifteen minutes later. His name was Cory Landers, and he was in college studying multimedia arts including animation and audio/visual production locally. Cory was twenty, tall and lanky with deep-set hazel eyes and muddy brown hair.

He'd been having some really strange dreams lately.

"Yo," he said, almost tripping over Hannah, "excuse me."

"Huh?" Hannah said, with a shrug. She was hardly in is way. She didn't move, but let him walk around her. Cory slammed his door on the way out.

"What's up with him?" Shelby asked. "Is he on the rag?"

"Hell if I know," Hannah said with a shrug.

She decided Cory must have been getting bent out of shape over their innocent public display of affection because a girl named Linda from school had recently dumped him. Dumped probably wasn't the word for it, since they'd only been on two dates, but Cory really wasn't taking it well at all.

"So this raise," Shelby said with a smirk, "is it enough money so that we won't have to rent that room out to some snotty little shit like Cory next semester?"

"Oh hell yeah," Hannah said. "We can finally afford to live without that noise.

PARTIES

Charlotte picked up the phone on the second ring. It was Hannah. She was expecting the call.

"What's up, girl?" Charlotte spoke into the phone. "How is your bride to be?"

"Grouchy, but luckily she's kind of hot when she's mad," Hannah said. She wore a smirk Charlotte could almost hear over the phone. It was almost like old times, in high school, only now they were grown, and both of them were getting laid.

"Shelby looks hot all the time," Charlotte said appreciatively. Shelby was one of the prettiest women she knew, and not in that unapproachable princess way. She was hot in that built like a dancer, you can see the muscles move when her body hits the floor, J-Lo and Beyonce kind of way.

"It's a good thing you're straight," Hannah joked, "Taking about my woman like that."

"Ah right," Charlotte laughed. "So, how did things go with your boss today?"

"Great," Hannah said. It was hard for her not to start jumping up and down and screaming into the phone. She said – for the third time today, and with reasonable decorum, "I got a raise. Can you believe it? I mean sure, it's to go with the new job title she gave me two weeks ago, but I guess I bought in enough contracts for her to feel like my division will bring in money."

"That's fucking awesome," Charlotte said. Her voice betrayed all of the worry she tried to hide.

"What's wrong?" Hannah asked, picking up on it immediately. "You don't sound like things are fucking awesome at all."

"Boy problems," Charlotte lamented.

"I'm surprised," Hannah said. "You guys looked really happy this weekend, you know, when you were on the bed making his hair look like Sid Vicious."

Charlotte laughed. "That was kind of old school, wasn't it?"

"It matched the plaid bondage pants," Hannah teased. "You should have put him in suspenders. That would have completed his wardrobe's time travel to 1983."

"He looked cute," Charlotte protested.

"He's a cute boy," Hannah said. "He could be in one of those boy bands."

"Oh fuck you," Charlotte said.

"So how is your melting man?" Hannah asked.

Charlotte smiled at the song reference. Rose Byrne's mother, Jeannie, was a huge Siouxsie and the Banshees fan. Charlie became obsessed with the song *Melt* and memorized all the lyrics. It was one summer before Rose started going by the name Gypsy and ditching Charlotte out to go hang out with sophisticated upperclassmen. After she met Hannah, Hannah broke down the lyrics for her and explained all of the ways in which they probably referred to sadomasochism.

"He's at work," Charlotte said gently. "But I think he's in a great deal of trouble, you know, because of my family."

"Oh them," Hannah groaned. "I'm surprised you have any friends. After that shit your dad and your sister pulled in the psych ward, I'll admit even I was a bit put off."

"They aren't after him," Charlotte explained. "He's in trouble but so are they. He's basically cursed. If anyone kills him, they'll wipe out my whole family somehow. Well, my dad's side at any rate. From Dad on down, they'll all fall. They have a lot of enemies, so I fear for Flynn's life."

"Fuck," Hannah said. "Yeah most of your sisters just give people nightmares, but your dad and your brothers and Sympathy and Mercy are all off the hook. There is a long list of people would love to see them dead, and probably wouldn't care too much about collateral damage."

"Yeah," Charlotte said, "and apparently Flynn is one of them. He basically said that if they can't be controlled, maybe his life wouldn't be too high a price to pay to stop them."

"Shit," Hannah said. "I'm so sorry. No wonder you're upset. That's terrible."

"It is," Charlotte admitted. "But my mom said she will try to get some of her friends to help figure out how to keep him safe."

"The soccer mom coven," Hannah teased. "Real Housewives of Berkeley."

"Yeah, you know Jeannie Byrne will be there," Charlotte said. "And Lorena Young, she was giving me lots of grief for hitting on Flynn in the hospital."

"I bet," Hannah said. "Lorena's freaking hilarious, though."

"Yeah she is," Charlotte said. "So mom invited them all over for my birthday party. It is Saturday, at mom's house. I was hoping you and Shelby could make it."

"Definitely," Hannah said. "I wouldn't miss it."

"Oh my dad loves what you've done with the comic," Charlotte chimed in at the last minute. "Really loves it. Told my whole family you're under like, special Olympian protection or some shit."

"Your dad doesn't live in Olympus," Hannah said. "He lives in the underworld. That's in the opposite direction. Still, no wonder my dreams have all been so pleasant lately. I gladly accept his generous offer of protection."

Charlotte laughed.

"Speaking of your father," Hannah continued, "he can't be too happy to have a bit of human kryptonite walking around. I mean, if anything bad happens to Flynn, something bad happens to Brash, that's like… I think what you'd call an Achilles Heel."

"Very funny," Charlotte said. "No, he doesn't like it. He told Mercy to stop torturing Flynn's associates because he's afraid it will make him want to snuff himself. Apparently Flynn already threatened to die over that whole Howard Lowe thing. Mercy was asked to stand down, and she's furious."

"So she'll start trying to mindfuck people Flynn doesn't know to death," Hannah predicted.

"Right," Charlotte said. "This cannot end well."

Ex-Soccer Moms

"I'm afraid the boy is right," Lorena Young said with a frown. "The Sisterhood of the Undoing are entrusted with the knowledge of the somnali and we know a limited number of rituals and spells we can use to keep them under control. What we cannot do is destroy them. They are immortal. Flynn's condition gives us a tremendous amount of leverage over them."

"And it's not good as leverage if we are only bluffing," Jeannie Byrne said. "The cold war was only able to occur because people knew that someone had once been willing to use the atom bomb. That was the basis of the standoff, the feat that the other side would use the weapon of mass destruction."

"Uh, nah," Maribelle said. "He's Charlotte's consort, that doesn't exactly make him my son-in-law, but close enough. He's not a weapon of mass destruction; he's my daughter's boyfriend."

"But he's willing to make the sacrifice," Lorena said. "I like him, he's a nice kid. I really hope it never comes down to that. But we can't just deactivate his curse. We need to keep him as a back-up plan."

"I am sorry." Jeannie said. "I have to agree."

Charlotte's friend Sunshine Green was sitting in the corner, sipping her herbal tea and self-consciously twisting one of her dreadlocks around her finger. She was a bit intimidated by Maribelle's more affluent friends. Jeannie and Lorena weren't nearly as well heeled as Maribelle herself, but Jeannie was a schoolteacher and Lorena was a retired bus driver.

They were both respectable and had husbands with decent jobs. Jeannie's house was smaller than Maribelle's and located at a much lower elevation in Berkeley, nowhere near any hills, and in a poorer area near University and San Pablo populated by 99 Cent Stores and 7-11s. Lorena had a little house on the suburban outskirts of Concord. But they both had homes. Sunny lived in a board and care home. Still, she had opinions. Her daddy always said opinions are like assholes, everybody's got one. That included her.

Sunshine confronted Lorena and Jeannie. "You say this like it's nothing. May I remind you that you're talking about human sacrifice? Surely, you can't be willing to condone such a thing."

"It's his choice," Jeannie protested. "Look, all we are saying is that we should leave him that option. No one is suggesting that we drag him out to an altar in the forest and slit his throat."

"Oh no," Maribelle said angrily. "Are you suggesting that we allow him to kill himself, so that my daughter can come home from school one day to find him with his wrists slit bobbing in the bathtub? Or maybe she can gently hold his hand while he overdoses on psych meds? I mean whatever, as long as you don't have to get your hands dirty."

"Now no one is saying that," Lorena said. "I just said that we shouldn't go behind his back and sever his connection to the somnali. We all know he wants to play the hero. Your daughter treats him like he's a child, but he's not, Maribelle. He's a man, trying to be strong the only way he knows how. Don't you think you should at least ask him first?"

Maribelle shook her head. "Great. So now you're saying we shouldn't try to save his life because that might be emasculating? You're shitting me, right?"

"Enough," said Gertrude Singer, who had been quietly enduring the younger women's bickering up until now. Gertrude was an eighty-three year old woman who became friendly with Maribelle's mother, Sandra Metaxas in the years after she was widowed. The ladies were around sixty when they met. Sandra and Gertrude were from a different generation, and were unwilling to comment as to whether their relationship was more than a friendship, but Maribelle long suspected that this was her mother's girlfriend. Sandra was gone six years now, but Gertrude still wouldn't talk about it. Gertrude had known Maribelle since she was in her late twenties and with Sandra gone; it was left to her to bestow wisdom upon her alleged ex-lover's long-grown daughter.

"You miss the point entirely," Gertrude said, tapping the book of the Rites of Undoing with the obscenely long nail on her wizened index finger. "Instead of worrying about him, you need to worry about them. The somnali aren't meant to come into this world, they are meant to stay in dreams. Why and how are they gaining influence in this world? What can be done to stop it?"

"If they're all dead, that will put a stop to it," Lorena said.

"Will it?" Gertrude asked. "Didn't the prophecy say that if he dies, the somnali would become mortal? And then how is that good? Sure, they can die in this world, but how much more harm could someone like Mercy do in the flesh? I think it would be unwise to set her and her kind loose in the material world."

"Oh," Lorena said. "Yeah, now that you mention it, well there is that."

Consolation

When Flynn came home from work, he walked up behind Charlotte and put his arms around her. She was startled.

"I didn't see you there," she said.

"I'm so sorry," Flynn said, holding her tighter. "I heard you crying last night. I don't ever want to make you cry."

"I thought you were asleep," she told him. She turned around and hugged him in return.

"I can hear you, even when I'm asleep," he said. Her body tensed against his and he feared the words he said were going to make her start crying again. He wished that he could soothe her with the slightest gesture, the way she often comforted him. He wished that his hands were endowed with that kind of magic, but he could only offer her his human touch.

It was the best he could do. He was only a man.

"You were asleep when I left for work, and I didn't want to wake you up," he told her. "But I have been thinking about it all day. You told me you love me, and I didn't tell you that I love you so much. I don't know how I could live without you. I'm sorry that I asked you to try to live without me, and I hope you didn't take it the wrong way. I don't want to leave you, Charlie."

"It's not about that," Charlie protested. "Dying isn't the same thing as leaving."

He stood there and said nothing, but felt the weight of her body against his, the smell of her cheap coconut hair conditioner, and the warmth of her breath against his chest through his t-shirt. Moments like this one were perfect, those brief intermissions without words, or explanations. She pressed the side of her face against his chest and he knew she was listening to his heartbeat. It was an old ritual by now, a regular exchange of affection between two lovers.

But sometimes it was necessary to speak.

"It is about that," he said finally. "Death is a separation. Our loved ones leave us when they die. We hope and pray that we will be reunited with them. Most of us don't know for sure. All of us feel their loss, even those of us who believe."

"Right," Charlotte said. "And I don't believe."

"No," Flynn said. "You don't. I realize that. From your point of view, I said that I would wander off into the eternal darkness and leave you here alone. I didn't think about how that would make you feel."

Standing there in the room where they lived so much of their lives, Flynn was overcome by a sense of overwhelming insignificance. They were just little people, living small lives, in their tiny apartment. She pushed his shirt up because she loved the feeling of his skin against her skin. He bent down to kiss her because her mouth was a tempting secret only he was allowed to know. Flynn realized that he and Charlotte mattered to each other in that way lovers do to one another. None of these things mattered to anyone else in the world, though.

Other people had their own lovers, their own children, their own parents and jobs and problems to worry about. He didn't think his life was more important than anyone else's, but he acknowledged that to Charlotte, it probably was. He didn't understand before, but she loved him like he loved her.

"Did you think that if you died," Charlotte asked, "we'd be together again someday, in some kind of afterlife? Maybe we could become stars, or plants, I think that type of thing happened a lot in the myths of my grandparents."

"I had hoped," Flynn admitted. "I hoped, somehow, we'd stay together."

"Yeah, I don't think so," Charlotte said. "I think you'd just be a corpse."

She let go of him and walked over to the bed, which was the closest thing they had to a couch in their studio apartment. She unceremoniously plopped her ass on the edge of it. She didn't want him distracting her with his gentle caresses or the promise of his yielding flesh.

"So you're not into necrophilia?" Flynn joked.

"Dude, you are so not funny," Charlotte replied, but she smiled in spite of herself.

"People die every day, Charlie," he said, sitting beside her. "We are mortal. Most of us die of diseases or by accident, but sometimes soldiers go off to war. Sometimes people have dangerous jobs that put their lives at risk. Sometimes people risk their lives to protect the ones they love."

"But you're not talking about that," Charlotte challenged. "You're thinking about being a human sacrifice."

"Yeah, when you put it that way, it sounds kind of barbaric, doesn't it?" he asked.

"It is," she said without hesitation.

"I just wanted to tell you that I don't want to," he said seriously. "I don't want to die. I don't want to leave you. I just want to wake up next to you every day between now and when we die in our sleep at some ridiculously ancient age."

CORY

Cory was wigging out. Instead of going to school this morning, he drove out to Linda's house and circled the block a couple of times, casing the place, looking to see if she was still home and if her parents were off at work yet. He knew her class schedule, and her first class didn't start until 1:00 P.M. so he had a four-hour window between when her parents left and when she might leave.

He had his art supply kit with him, which included a box cutter and several mounted razors he used for his prop and set design classes. The girl in his dreams had shown him so many things, such wondrous things he might do with these cutting instruments.

Sitting in his yellow Camry a block away from Linda's house, Cory used one of the box cutters to slice into the flesh on the back of his hand. He needed to make sure it was sharp enough. The box cutter blades came as a scored strip of metal, and the one at end could be broken off to reveal fresher, sharper steel below it.

It wasn't sharp enough, so he fished out an art knife, which had pointed blades you screwed into the tip, and tried it. Finally, he tried a second type of box cutter, the kind that had a straight razor screwed into the tip of it. He felt the sting as it sliced through the flesh and left a thin ribbon of red across the back of his hand. He laughed as he watched it spread.

Mercy explained to him how it would be possible to inflict a series of these wounds for days, weeks, or months, without actually inflicting enough damage to cause the kind of blood loss that would result in death. She described the burning sensations caused by the rubbing alcohol he would use to cleanse the wounds to avoid the premature introduction of infection. She explained all of these things in glowing, lurid detail.

Four hours wasn't enough time to do that kind of work. He was going to have to kidnap her.

SURVIVOR

Howard was getting out of the hospital today, in a manner of speaking. A team of doctors and a social worker would still closely monitor him but he was at last deemed sufficiently stable to transfer him to a boarding care home.

As chance would have it, the boarding care home he was released to was the same one Mary "Sunshine" Green lived in, but she wouldn't recognize him. She wasn't in the hospital during his major meltdown.

The extent of his injuries had been rather exaggerated during the urban legend like spread of the story of the incident. In reality, Howard managed to detach his own retina and had to have emergency surgery and wear a not very jaunty metal and cotton gauze eye patch afterward. He required two additional surgeries and the period of time he wore an eye patch was long enough for the rumors to get started. Most of the people thought he was now a one eyed man.

In reality, Howard lost some visual acuity and now had to wear corrective lenses. He would also be at an increased risk for developing cataracts. It was painful, upsetting, and dangerous, but it was not as bad as everyone said it was, and certainly not as bad as the spirit pretending to be Howard in Flynn's nightmares presented it as being.

There was a lattice network of thin scars on Howard's face, chest, and arms that made it look like he'd been attacked by a pack of wild housecats. Howard kept his fingernails very short and spent a good amount of time filing them into dullness since the traumatic incident.

Mercy still occasionally visited him in his dreams, much to his displeasure, although she had other, more cooperative targets to spend the majority of her time with. Fortunately, Mercy had no real motive for sending a possessed Howard off to strangle Flynn. Mercy no longer had any desire to see Flynn dead, so Howard was safe from her.

Whatever was co-opting his image in nightmares was a different story. That guy might decide come around and take Howard for a spin someday.

Examination

Sympathy and Mercy both had their alien costumes on. One of their favorite tag-team dream scenarios was the classic alien abduction. They had the inside of their UFO set up with a big metal examination table in the center and all kinds of strange instruments for poking and prodding their human victims.

Generally, Mercy would beam a victim in at some random point in his or her dream and start in with the fun. They might go through five or six victims in a night that way.

"So what's on the agenda tonight?" Sympathy said. "Anal probes?" She was in her space squid get-up and didn't really need anything metal to probe people with, but she liked variety in her examinations.

"Follow up with a little dissection?" Mercy added.

"That'll be fun," Sympathy agreed. "Well, you want to start with one of mine?"

"No, my treat, I've got a surprise for you tonight," Mercy said. She snapped her fingers and a bound and gagged unusually buxom blonde with bunny ears and a tail appeared on the table. She was wearing a very scant bikini.

"Oh, I didn't know you liked girls," Sympathy cooed.

"Technically, this is a balding, paunchy middle aged guy named Joe Martin from Austin, Texas," Mercy said. "This is what his Second Life avatar looks like. He has a lot of dreams where he's her, so you know… I know you like girls sometimes. Her name is Joie."

"Close enough, then," Sympathy said. "No wonder her boobs defy gravity Hi Joie." She winked at the bunny babe. Joie didn't say anything back. First of all, she was gagged. Second of all, everything Symp and Mercy said sounded like a series of weird alien clicking noises.

Mercy cackled, and reached for one of the laser cutting devices. Clearly, the flimsy pink bathing garments would have to be removed before Sympathy could penetrate all of the requisite orifices. She tried to snatch off the bunny ears, but they wouldn't come off. Joie tried to kick and scream. Due to the metal restraints built into the exam table, she was reduced to writhing and making muffled squealing noises.

"Can you ungag her?" Sympathy requested. "It's much better when I can hear the screaming."

"Why of course!" Mercy said most affably. She cut the gag loose and Joie let out a series of high-pitched shrieks that would make any b-movie horror scream queen proud.

"Well you sure scream like a girl," Symp cheered. "That's it, holler for mama. I like to fill up all of the holes, even those tiny ones on the front and sides of your head." She lifted a fat, arm-sized tentacle and shoved it roughly down Joie's screaming pie hole. Two tiny tendrils squirmed on either side of it and made their way up her nostrils, and two more slid eagerly towards her waiting ears.

Mercy was standing at the top of the table, watching the agitated twitch of the bunny ears. They were absolutely fascinating.

"Can I pick it up by its ears?" Mercy asked. "Can I please, can I, can I?"

"Sure, why not?" Sympathy said agreeably. Mercy wrapped one of her tentacles tight around the quivering ears and hoisted the struggling figure high up in the air. She forgot to unstrap her from the table, so the entire metal examination apparatus rose up with her.

"Oh, isn't that funny?" Sympathy giggled. She began freeing Joie from the table. Her typical modus operandi was to fill every available orifice until the dreamer began to split open. The table was blocking access to several important holes, and it had to be done away with.

"I think the ears are starting to give way," Mercy said pragmatically.

Sympathy decided to take some of the pressure off of Joie's ears by sending some vine-like tendrils wandering up her thighs, where they began to slowly penetrate her ass. The tentacles were throbbing, pulsating with the liquid somnali used to drug their less complaint victims. As the chemical changes took place in her body, Joie found she was unable to resist the urge to repeatedly impale herself on Sympathy's many members.

"That's it, baby. You're a sexy little bunny, aren't you? You know Sympy's got the big one. You like that, don't you?" Sympathy cooed to the flailing human. Joie couldn't understand a damned thing Symp was saying, but that didn't stop her from spreading her legs wide to invite the insertion of the final and largest of the tentacle appendages.

Joie was having an orgasm and gushing like a hot little airlifted geyser. Sympathy was pleased with this result. She liked them to be nice and gooey before she went in for her messy grand finale. She pressed every tentacle in deeper and further until the human flesh began to tear at the seams.

The bunny girl's sounds of pleasure turned into screams of pain.

"Too bad everything will be back to normal when she wakes up," Sympathy sighed. "I want to tear up real human flesh in their fleshy human world, you know?"

"Yeah, I know," Mercy sympathized. "Maybe you should join me for some of my extracurricular activities. I'm finding it's a lot easier to get these humans to hurt each other than to hurt themselves."

Mercy wrapped her squiggly limps tighter around Joie's ears and throat in order to keep her from falling as she buckled and squirmed under the increasing pressure Sympathy placed on her innards.

"What about that curse?" Sympathy asked. "I thought that Charlotte's boyfriend could go jump off a bridge and take us all out. What if he finds out and gets upset or something?"

Mercy shrugged, and accidentally dropped one of Joie's ears while making the gesture.

"How the hell is he going to find out?" Mercy said. "Humans snap and kill each other on a daily basis. You should read a human newspaper sometime."

Sympathy had removed the tentacle from Joie's throat just then, to allow for fuller enjoyment of her terrified shrieking.

"You should bring him over here sometime." Sympathy said. "We can play with him."

"I don't think so," Mercy complained. "That's a big no-no. Charlotte's getting ready to take him out back and do the deed."

Right then, one of Joie's ears – the one Mercy was still holding - tore off at the base, leaving nothing but a gaping wet hole surrounded by blood-clotted white hair. Mercy turned to face the captive and began chomping down on the ear in front of her.

She wished that she could get into it, but frankly, she was a little bored. She kept thinking about how much fun she had torturing someone who actually liked pain. Maybe Flynn wasn't consenting any more than poor Joie here was, but Mercy truly got a kick out of all of his repressed masochism and sexual embarrassment.

She was a little bit jealous of Charlotte. That was weird. She wasn't supposed to have emotions. Perhaps she was evolving. How disgusting that would be?

That thought went through her mind just before she got to work on one of Joie's watermelon-sized physics-resistant breasts with a series of rapidly grinding shark-like teeth. Mercy liked the taste of fresh human meat. It tasted like pork, not chicken, but everyone knew bacon was delicious. She tore away a strip of flesh from across the top of Joie's massive mammary like a strip of raw bacon. It was delectable.

She would have kept eating if Joie didn't explode right at that moment.

"Ewwww," Mercy complained. "Damn it, Sympathy... that's fucking disgusting."

Sympathy wasn't paying any attention. She was busy vacuuming Joie's steaming hot intestines up off the table with a hose-like extension that ran from her mouth. She always was a messy eater.

Mercy decided that she would go spy on Flynn. If she kept her hands to herself, maybe Charlotte wouldn't fink her off to daddy.

PRACTICE

They were in their apartment and Mercy was not yet watching. The party wasn't until Saturday, but Charlotte's birthday was today. Flynn wanted to make it special.

Charlotte and Flynn were playing the little game they always played before they did anything in the dream world. It was a game called "practice." They were playfully discussing what would happen in the dream and drawing their lines. It was a fun way to determine what they did or did not wish to try.

They were practicing for the Feast of Tears.

Flynn was playing a game with his hands.

"Am I to be bound?" he asked Charlotte. He played with a thick swath of lace on the table, something he'd stolen from her sewing kit. It was four inches wide and would have been used for trimming a dress. A thick band of lace would have been rolled off the spool and sewn over the bottom of the dress over the hem.

"Lace?" she asked. She was taking it easy, taking her time with him. This was a really big deal, and she wanted to make sure there was enough wiggle room for him to slow things down or change his mind if he needed to.

"Like in the song you like so much," he teased. He was conspicuously toying with the spool of lace so that she could see it. He wanted her to take the bait.

"It's very festive," she said. He slid the spool over to her.

"Why do you like to play things out in the flesh?" he asked. "In the dream realms the possibilities are almost limitless. So why simulate everything here?"

"For one thing I want you to know what you're getting into." Charlotte said. "For another thing, what we have here is definitely finite. Time moves in one direction here. We can't roll it back, the way we can there. Do you know that according to my father, that dream world is where we will spend our afterlives? I mean if he is to be believed."

"So you feel it's like a kind of death?" Flynn asked.

"In a sense… I suppose I do," Charlotte admitted. "There is no real privacy there. It's not really real, like this."

"Do you think that if we did die, we'd go there?" he asked.

"Who knows?" Charlie shrugged. "I have never seen any spirit of any human offspring of my father's in the dream realm, ever. If we really go there, where are they? And if you die, my father and his whole line die off, so there wouldn't even be a place to go to. I mean there is no place except his palace which is an extension of him, so I think that's all forfeited."

"Depressing," he said. "So I'll do my best not to die."

"Are you sure you want to do this?" Charlotte asked.

"You're the one who is going to be having my baby," Flynn shrugged. "Shouldn't I be asking you that? I mean it's a super big deal."

"It's going to hurt," she warned.

"I enjoy it when you hurt me," he taunted her. "You'll show me what to expect, you always do. I trust you. Take me in hand and bend me to your will. I can take it."

"Fine," she said, picking up the lace. A shiny object fell out of the bottom of the spool and on to the table. Charlotte picked it up and held it in her hand. It was a very modest diamond engagement ring.

"Are you asking me to marry you?" she asked. She was astonished.

"Charlotte Metaxas, will you be my wife?" he asked.

"Aren't you supposed to be down on one knee?" she asked. He responded by immediately dropping down to one knee.

"How did you afford this?" she asked, looking at the setting. The diamond was a little speck, but it was obvious what it was. The band was old-fashioned, extremely ornate, and blended strands of gold and silver."

"I got it at a pawn shop," he admitted. "I hope you don't mind."

"I will," she said tenderly. "Of course I will."

"Good," he said, handing her the roll of lace again. "Now take me with your hands and bind me to that bed, and prepare me. Show me where your teeth will penetrate my skin, and how I will feel when you tear into my flesh. Tell me what it will be like for you when you taste me. I want you to devour every part of me."

Charlotte took the lace and winked at him. "You're a freak, you know that, right?"

FEAST OF TEARS

There really was no privacy in the Demos Oneiroi. There was no room that was impenetrable. There wasn't a place into which one of the daemon that dwelled there couldn't peer. For this reason, Mercy, who had the desire to watch, was easily able to conceal her presence during the Feast of Tears.

Although they played at and practiced it in the world of the flesh, the actual performance of the ritual was far from predictable. Certain choices could be agreed upon while both were in their right states of mind. One of these was whether or not Charlotte would give chase. Once the transformation came over her, she would be overcome with a ravening hunger for his flesh, and would lose hold of all reason in pursuit of it.

Flynn could have been hunted, but he chose not to. He asked her to restrain him. For him, there was something highly erotic in the very act of offering himself to her. He appeared before her, naked and on his knees. He held the bindings out to her. They were thick bracelets of leather that would hold him still but not interfere with the enjoyment of her meal. It was very likely that in her berserker blood frenzy, she would try to eat whatever he was restrained with, so metal was out of the question.

From the bands extended leather thongs, which were easily threaded through the holes in a series of wooden spikes buried deep in the ground. He was spread eagle, bound by his ankles and wrists. The wood and leather was not so secure as to entirely prevent the possibility of escape, but it would hold him in place long enough for them to begin.

Charlotte uncurled his fingers and kissed the palms of his hands.

"I just want you to know," she said, "you look absolutely delicious."

"Am I appetizing?" he asked.

"Very," she said. "So, I know we already went over this, but once I start, I will be unable to stop."

"I know," he said. "You will lose all human restraint and become a feeding animal. You won't come to your senses until you drink my tears, which won't happen until sometime after you've brutalized me, and left me broken and weeping on the ground. You're going to eat me alive."

She nodded. "That pretty much covers it."

The way it worked was that she would probe the deepest recesses of his mind and come up with whatever creature he most fantasized about being eaten by. As it turned out, he was a great fan of both versions of Cat People, and almost wanted to share the fate of that cat lady who died and was devoured by her horde of starving felines.

She was in the form of a great, sleek leopard when he extended his fingers towards her. She circled him twice, before seating herself around his head. He could feel her tail flicking against his cheek. Flynn's body tensed with anticipation. She grabbed his hand in both of her paws. He could feel the sharp claws slide into his flesh.

When he turned to look, he could see his blood springing forth from half a dozen tiny wounds. Charlotte licked it with her rough tongue, bristles scratching the sensitive skin on his palms and between his fingers. She climbed up on top of him and began licking his face. Her coarse tongue tickled and stung the soft tissues of his vulnerable mouth. He whimpered when she began kneading her pads into his chest.

Her long, curved nails cut through the skin and dug into his pectoral muscles. Flynn bit his lower lip to stifle a scream. It was a part of the game they agreed on beforehand, he would stay composed as long as possible. This hurt, but he knew that the worst of his suffering was still to come. He felt her hot breath on his cheeks.

She was playing with him. It was natural for her, in human form, and certainly within the repertoire of normal feline behavior where food was concerned. The cat was taking over, and there was less and less Charlotte left.

Mercy sat on a cliff just above them, giggling in delight, although neither of them registered it because she was in the form of a blackbird. Her laughter came out as little bird chirps and whistles, and blended with other natural sounds in the woods Charlotte and Flynn had dreamed up to play out this little scenario. Mercy was amused by Charlotte's last, fleeting attempts to comfort Flynn with her beastly tongue.

The woman Charlotte hadn't yet been entirely usurped, so she was trying to express hormones and other chemicals in her saliva to give Flynn a more pleasurable experience. The gesture was sad and sweet and entirely futile. In a moment, the beast took over, and her little sister securely latched her powerful jaws onto the long, golden fingers on Flynn's left hand and snapped off all four of them with a single bite.

He was still stoically resisting the urge to scream when she sunk her teeth into his tender breast and ripped out a chunk of flesh the size of a fist. She was staring at him with big, bold eyes that were in their entirety, the same deep scarlet-flecked amber as her human irises.

She was slowly chewing the delicious, raw meat. She wanted to let him know how much she was enjoying herself, and how satisfying she found the taste of his flesh. Flynn's earlier arousal began to give way to terror as he realized she had barely gotten started on her mission to systematically rend his flesh from his bones.

As she devoured his breast meat, the leopard bit into something cold and hard that she did not like. She spit at him and he closed his eyes and winced as his nipple ring hit the side of his face. When he opened his eyes and looked down he saw bit of silver glinting on his cheek. The leopard lowered her head and licked the bleeding hole in his chest. Flynn accepted the heat and sharp prickles of pain that accompanied her tasting his ruined flesh.

He tried to hold very still for her, but it became impossible when she harvested his mouth-watering flank. She crouched down, paws on either side of his belly, tearing away at the tender flesh between his hips and ribcage. She bit a huge chunk out of his side, and carried away by her voracious hunger, greedily tore into his belly.

Flynn was screaming now. His arms and legs flailed helplessly against the grass and dirt. He felt hot liquid gushing down his thigh. As the earthy smell assailed his senses, he came to realize that he'd literally pissed himself in fear.

Charlotte's lovely paws were as tawny as the sand she spilled his blood on. Her spots were as fetching as the autumn leaves that fell to the ground near his severed fingers. Those beautiful paws were absolutely soaked in his blood, and Flynn was beginning to grow lightheaded due to the blood loss.

Flynn was beyond any conscious desire to comply or submit, and was now thrashing against the ground, trying to free himself and get away from her. He managed to pull his uninjured hand free by wrenching the wooden stake out of the ground. It was still connected to his wrist with a leather thong. When she came at him again, he couldn't resist his instinct for self-preservation. He began to strike her on top of her sleek feline head with the wooden spike that dangled from his hand. She turned around and snapped the offending appendage off at the wrist.

"Fuck! Fucking fuck you Charlotte, this fucking hurts!" he screamed. The leopard responded by raising its face up to his own, and looking him directly in the eye before sinking its teeth into his lower lip. He could feel it tear his mouth open.

That is when he began to sob.

He was screaming and crying when the big cat broke his jaw trying to get at his tongue. She tore it out and swallowed it, and his wailing ceased. There was nothing left but the salty water that rose up in the corners of his eyes and flowed lazily down the contours of his cheeks.

The beast began licking away the tears. The moment she tasted his tears, he left his body, and all of the pain that had been inflicted on it was instantly at an end.

He drifted away from his body as a formless mist, and at first he was confused. As his form solidified, his consciousness began to return. He was a gray shadow, sitting alone on the grass some two feet away from his half-eaten body. Charlotte was still consuming his flesh. He just wasn't in it anymore.

"Shit. I'm dead!" he cried out.

Mercy flew down from her perch and settled on the ground beside him, forming a somewhat darker shadow. She wanted to get a better look at the show.

"Yeah, you are dead," she said. "Want some popcorn?"

Flynn shook his head. He recognized her. "What are you doing here?"

"Kind of a voyeur," she shrugged. "Nobody's perfect, right? Whoa… your girlfriend is totally gobbling your goodies right now."

His eyes opened wide. Sure enough, the leopard was down between his legs, worrying his dick and balls like a dog would a chew toy. He decided he was glad he was watching from this angle, instead of stuck inside his rapidly disappearing carcass. One of his arms – the one that wielded the spike like a mace – had been completely devoured.

Mercy materialized a bowl of popcorn and sat it down between them. She started popping it in her mouth, but Flynn declined. He didn't have much of an appetite, but he was fascinated by what was happening. He couldn't stop watching the progressive decimation of his flesh.

"Charlotte really enjoys you," she said. "Now, I didn't think she would do it. I mean she loves you. That's got to complicate the whole tearing into the flesh of your lover thing, don't you think?"

"Probably," Flynn shrugged. "What's it to you?"

"I would have dissected you like a frog a long time ago," Mercy remarked. "She kept saying she needed your permission first, and I was like, what a crock of shit. I didn't think you would ever agree. Also, I thought even if you did, she would be unable to endure putting you through it."

"It was kind of fun, until I started pissing my pants and screaming," Flynn said.

"When you wake up," Mercy explained, "you'll be overcome by a terrible sense of your mortality and what it means to die. You'll relive your death and the fear of death and nothingness will become overwhelming. You will weep – probably in Charlotte's arms, because you two are into that shit. Once your tears subside, you will be caught in the throes of deep need and desire. It will be an extremely amplified version of the ordinary human desire for procreation, really. You will have this irresistible urge to fuck her brains out and fill her womb with little Flynns because that will be the only thing that can ease your terrible fear of death."

"Wow," Flynn mocked, "that is romantic."

"And that is how demisomnali are made," Mercy said, eating popcorn. "Or at least one of the ways, some are even more complicated. Ah, look! How wonderful is the circle of life."

Flynn looked up in time to watch Charlotte sucking the eyeballs out of his mostly fleshless head. It looked like she was holding a package of raw hamburger with two eyeballs in it. It was all incredibly surreal. He began to wonder how much pressure it would take for her to cave in his skull, so she could eat his brains. His body no longer seemed like a part of him. He was separated from it, and it was only meat to feed Charlotte.

He was a little disappointed when he realized that as a big cat, Charlotte would be incapable of eating all of him. He watched as she carefully licked and sucked as much meat as she could off of his bones. The bones would have to be left behind.

He walked up to her where she lay on her belly, licking his blood from her paws, and he tried to stroke her fur, but his hand went right through her. He was suddenly overwhelmed by a feeling of disconnection from her in this form or any other, from all living things.

This feeling of being torn asunder, ripped from the fabric of the living, was more excruciating than any of the wounds Charlotte inflicted on his ruined body. He wished that he had a body that could ache, that he could still feel the searing pain of broken bone.

Anything was better than this nothingness.

That was when he woke up, in tears, clutching desperately to Charlotte's warmth. They were alive, gloriously among the living. He buried his face between her breasts and wrapped his arms around her back. He didn't ever want to leave this safe place in her arms, in her bed. His mouth latched onto her nipple and he pressed his fingers into the small of her back. In an instant, his comfort seeking transformed into a primal hunger, and he could not rest until he was deep inside her.

PUPPETMASTERS

Mercy's need to destroy human life was primal, a basic instinct. She was like a kid who burned ants with a magnifying glass only those ants were humans. If she could have entered the dreams of cats and dogs, she probably would have killed them, as well. She was a psychopath.

Psychopathy wasn't an automatic consequence of being somnali. Mercy, Sympathy, Fuss, Irate, Irksome, Aloof, Morbid, Callous, Cranky, Colicky, Sweetums, and Coy all had different personalities. Mercy, Sympathy, Fuss and Irate were all very sadistic, a trait that many of Brash's children seemed to have, Happiness included.

Brash was a psychopath, but he wasn't nearly as sadistic as some of his children were. He had no real need to torture his human sacrifices. In his mind, they were inferior creatures that could be dispensed with on a whim if it gave him any kind of advantage, but he had no problem disposing of them in a humane, painless way.

His callous disregard for human life, and his lack of any particular attachment to sadism made it difficult for him to comprehend why Charlotte would chose to torture her consort when she could just go out and cause some miscarriages, but who was he to judge?

Mercy and Symp were partners in crime, and they could not go a day without tormenting someone either in dreams or, if they were able to, in the flesh. Fuss and Irate had a similar desire to influence the lives of the living, and these were the chief reasons for the concern the other gods bothered Nyx with before she summoned Somnus and Thanatos and gave her edict.

Irksome, Aloof, Cranky, Colicky, Sweetums, and Coy were satisfied to bring on nightmares, as they were designed to do. These nightmares were possibly some kind of lesson or illustration for mortals, they really did not know. The point was these six were innocent of the charges leveled at their siblings.

Morbid and Callous were far less sexually sadistic than the other four, but not any less interested in influencing the world of men. Indeed, both were guiltier than any others of casting their spirit and emotional cruelty on mankind, creating generations more morbid and callous than the ones before them. Callous was particularly proud of her work with white-collar criminals, who stole from the elderly and the poor.

Morbid bragged about her increasing influence in psychiatry and pharmaceuticals, and was very proud of her role in her father's recent co-opting of Gary and Nancy's drug-addled bodies. Institutionalization was on the rise and possession was easier than ever.

Mercy had her own following. Some of them were known as the Angels of Death, but there were other types of Mercy killers. She was the one who convinced the psychotic couple in San Diego that simple depression was a good enough reason for assisted suicide, or perhaps just sadness, or a really bad ingrown toenail. Why would anyone have to suffer when they could be released into the sweet mercy of death?

Sympathy was cloying and sweet, like heavy lavender incense that could cause an asthma attack. She came along with Mercy to coddle and convince Cory that he was in the right. He had been wronged, and deserved Sympathy. All of the self-pitying monsters that plotted and enacted revenge killings wanted Sympathy. Mercy gave Cory Sympathy, so he could give Linda hell.

They were the puppet masters, stirring up feelings of violence and vengeance in mankind. They wound up men and women and sent them out into the world like targeted, heat-seeking missiles to tear up all living things in their paths.

For Mercy, it was inevitable.

She knew that her father had threatened consequences, but she couldn't help herself.

She needed to kill.

LAIR

Cory didn't come home the day of Charlotte's birthday party. If he had, then he might have learned that his landlords were planning on being out of town that weekend. He might have decided that two days might be long enough to complete his grisly task. He could have turned Hannah and Shelby's home into a murder scene.

He didn't come home, though, so he never found out they were out of town.

Instead, he rented a storage locker in an isolated location.

The main issue with the storage locker was that it wasn't supposed to be occupied. Cory used a thick layer of moving blankets to block out any exterior light that came into the unit. It was his hope that by doing so, he could prevent light from escaping at night. He didn't come home the night before the abduction, because he was busy down at the storage facility, flickering lights on and closing and opening doors to see whether or not he'd successfully concealed his lair.

There was nothing to keep people out of the storage facility except for a tall fence with barbed wire at the top. A card key was used to enter and leave the unit during the daylight hours. Just before 9:00 P.M the management would check to see if anyone else was on the lot, with both a physical check and a card sweep.

Cory decided that the easiest way to break in was not to scale the fence at all. He could stroll right in during the daytime, go and swipe the card to leave, and just stay inside while the gate closed. As long as he waited until the woman who worked in the office was using the bathroom, there would be no one to check and see if he'd actually left.

The tricky part would be hiding the car. If he drove it in, how could he get out of driving it back out? Finally, the solution occurred to him: he would rent a larger unit, one large enough to drive the car into. Cory made the arrangements, and then spent a second night-light proofing the new unit. Yet again, Cory stayed away from home.

By then, Hannah was starting to worry, so she called his cell phone. She wasn't sure why she was worried, exactly: he was a jackass. But he told her that he was going to visit his parents for the weekend and wouldn't be home until Tuesday. That was the end of that conversation.

Friday night, Shelby and Hannah hopped on the Yamaha and headed down to Berkeley. Meanwhile, Cory Landers was chloroforming Linda Myers at the bus stop down the street from her parent's suburban home. He stuffed her unconscious body into the trunk of his mustard colored Camry and drove down to his storage locker.

PASSENGER

She gazed into the bathroom mirror through the damaged eyes of Howard Lowe. He wore sharp new glasses that made him look more like a nutty professor and less like a just plain nut. The glasses didn't perfectly correct the damage Mercy inflicted on this poor man's eye, and one of them was now permanently bleary.

Nyx felt everything Howard felt, and she knew just how deeply his fear of cataracts and eventual blindness ran. Howard was always afraid of spending too much time baking under the sun. Both of his parents developed cataracts, and his lighter-skinned mother also developed skin cancer. Nyx didn't know if Mercy intentionally damaged the man in such a way as to capitalize on his deepest fears, but she suspected that to be the case.

She shook his head. She hated possessing humans, but she didn't intend to spend much time behind the driver's wheel right now. She mostly needed to be a passenger. She was trying to hitch a ride to Charlotte Metaxas' birthday shindig.

Mary "Sunshine" Green had been flirting with Howard ever since he landed here in the transitional booby hatch, but he was way too distressed to notice it. He still had scratch marks on his face and even more hidden by his now perpetually long-sleeved shirts. Sunny didn't notice any of that, she just picked up on the fact that he was tall, and chocolate, and had dreadlocks falling all of the way down to his waist. She had been mincing around like they were both fifteen, not fifty.

In fact, Howard reminded her of a boy she liked when she was fifteen. In reality, that boy, Rodney Miller, was now a fat, balding man with a wife, two kids, and grandbaby. He was a deacon at his father's church, an outreach ministry in Oakland and would take over some day. Sunny went there for food pantry more than once. One of those times Rodney actually handed her a bag directly and she didn't even recognize him.

Such was the fate of youthful crushes, but Howard made her feel like she was fifteen again.

Howard himself had never been terribly interested in relationships. He was one of those people who could be perfectly happy being single. The few women he'd become involved with had one thing in common: they had all been pushy and hotly pursued him.

Sunny and Howard would probably never be an item, but she could make him feel better about the scars on his face, and he could make her feel like a teenager going to prom. Nyx was just going to push it a little. Sunny was too old fashioned to ask a man on a date, and Howard was too aloof to ask a woman.

Nyx finished washing Howard's face and brushing his teeth, and then rambled on out to the common room to ask Sunny Green for an invite to the party.

Oh Brother

Mercy ran into more difficulty than she anticipated in trying to convert Michael Shaw to her way of thinking. Despite his ranting and raving, it turned out that Mike didn't actually hate women. He had been hanging around a bunch of other guys who hated women, including his older brother, Elroy Shaw.

Mercy and Sympathy had been spending a lot of time in Roy's dreams, sympathizing with his terrible luck with women. Roy spent less and less time commiserating with other miserable single guys and more and more time plotting revenge.

Truthfully, Roy had a lot in common with Mercy and Sympathy. His need for punitive behavior over the smallest of slights, real or imaginary, stemmed from his lack of compassion for others. Not just women, but all people existed to please and cater to his needs. If his needs were going unfulfilled, someone needed to pay. Fuck that, everyone needed to pay.

Roy began stockpiling guns.

By the time Charlotte invited Mike to her birthday party, his brother had collected a small arsenal.

Tamara

Tamara was surprised that Danny invited her to accompany him to Charlotte's party. Danny and Tamara were dear old friends, but she was married now. She almost never went anywhere without her husband. In fact, since she had the baby, she almost never went anywhere at all.

Like Flynn, Tamara was of mixed Polynesian origin, but while both of them were mixed or what was jokingly called Heinz 57 or Poi Dog, Tamara was pure Pacific Islander. She was Samoan, Hawaiian, Tongan and Pilipino. Flynn's mother was Hawaiian and Portuguese, and his dad was Chinese and God only knew what else. Flynn and Tamara grew up in a peninsula community with a lot of expats from the State of Hawaii. Danny also grew up there. Although he was not a Pacific Islander, Mexican-Americans represented one of the largest ethnic groups in California and could be found just about anywhere.

Flynn hadn't been back to see any of his old friends since his mom moved out of state. Even Tamara's husband, Kimo, went to the same high school. He was a chubby kid who had been crushing on Tammy for years and was probably over the top when she dumped Flynn. By then he'd dumped the baby fat and had a decent job and a car. After they got married, he started to put the weight back on, but it didn't really bother Tamara. When she was pregnant everyone made jokes about sympathetic pregnancies but Tammy dumped the post baby weight more readily than Kimo did.

"I can get Kimo to watch Leilani," Tamara said, referring to her husband and her toddler. "I just don't get why you would want me to come to Flynn's girlfriend's birthday party."

"Well, fiancée," Danny corrected. "They're engaged now. She wants to meet you, Tamara. You're the only other girlfriend he's ever had, you know? It's normal for her to want to know about where he grew up and who he grew up with."

"Do you think she's jealous of me or something?" Tamara asked. "I mean it was years ago. It's long over."

"Maybe, but I think she just wants Flynn to have closure of some sort," Danny said. "You and him were friends. You were friends for a long time before you dated. The only reason you and I are still friends, I'd guess, is because you dated him, not me. But we all came up together."

"Yeah, that's true." Tamara admitted. "I feel kind of shitty about it, but I couldn't really deal with his mental issues, either. I guess that even if we weren't dating, if we were just friends – I would have had a hard time being there for him like you were."

"I wasn't always there," Danny said. "I mean, the truth is, a lot of the past bunch of years for Flynn, they were really bad. His mom left the state, and he doesn't really have anyone out here. It's like, they're going to announce their engagement at her birthday, but other than me, he really has like, no friends. You know what? Bring Kimo and Leilani with you, if you want. It's just like… we're the only family he's got."

"Okay," Tamara finally conceded. "I'll bring Kimo, and I think his parents can baby sit Leilani. She's a little too young for karaoke."

Danny laughed. "I know it will mean a lot to Flynn. To both of them."

"I guess I'd better practice those Adele songs," Tamara said. Then she hung up the phone.

SIDE EFFECTS

Charlotte had asked Danny to invite Tamara and her husband, and she was relieved it was done. All of these little rituals took on an additional significance to her now that she felt threatened by the idea that Flynn's life was constantly in danger. She wanted to be able to claim in him the afterlife, if there was any. She had to cross all her T's and dot all her I's, just to be safe.

Now that she was pregnant, she was in the position to demand that her father officially acknowledge the union between herself and Flynn. She wasn't sure how valuable that would be later on; if Flynn did die and Brash became mortal and powerless. She decided that there was a possibility that if her father recognized the union, his parents and grandparents, who were much more powerful, would as well.

But that meant that she would have to present her consort to Brash in person.

"I'm exhausted," Flynn complained. "How can you be sure you're pregnant, anyway?"

"Take my word for it," Charlotte said. "I'm sure I'm pregnant. I'm not human. I know these things."

"Did I tell you I saw Mercy?" Flynn asked for the third time.

"Yes, yes I know you saw Mercy," Charlotte snapped. The idea that her sister would sit there and watch her mauling her boyfriend to death really got on her nerves. Flynn, on the other hand, seemed to be over whatever horror he experienced as he was being eaten. He kept asking Charlie to roar and give him play bites.

He was experiencing the male equivalent of being in heat, she supposed. That was probably why he was exhausted. He wanted to do nothing except fuck every non-working, waking hour. He was wearing her out. He was all wound up and could barely sleep. She needed him to sleep.

"Let me make you sleep," Charlotte asked.

"I don't want to sleep right now," Flynn insisted, rubbing her ass. He was super horny and it was getting on her nerves. She supposed it wasn't his fault. It was a side effect of the ritual. Still, she was going to have to do something about it.

"I guess I'll just go for a walk, then," she told him.

Flynn pouted. "Are you sure you don't want to stay here with me?"

"You're under a spell that makes you sexually insatiable," she said. "No. I don't want to fuck anymore. My cunt hurts. I don't really even understand how you can think about sex. Don't you hurt?"

"My whole body aches." Flynn admitted. "I am starting to get some kind of rash, too. It's like chaffing."

"Right, that's what I am saying," she sighed. "You're under a spell, and if you don't let me undo it, you're probably going want to keep fucking, even if your dick starts to bleed."

"Yeah okay, fine," he said. "Do your thing." He was hoping that she would touch him or kiss him, which was what she usually did to calm him down. Instead, she got some horrible concoction out of the refrigerator and handed it to him.

"Drink it," she commanded. He took the shot glass and consumed whatever the musty yellowish substance in it was. He made a face.

"Ew," he said. "That was nasty. What was in it?"

"Sorry, it wasn't very fresh. Those were my bodily fluids," she confessed.

"Yeah okay," he shrugged. "Not like I haven't tasted most of those before. Why do all of your rituals have to be so…"

"Earthy?" she suggested.

"Right," he said. Then he started yawning. "Wow, I am tired."

"Go to sleep," she said. "I'll be right behind you."

INTRODUCTIONS

Flynn was a little bit stunned when he appeared in Brash's throne room.

"Wait! Where am I now?" he asked. "Where is Charlotte?"

Looking around the high-ceilinged, cavernous room, it appeared to be naturally formed out of solid lava rock. Brash gestured for him to kneel, and Flynn lowered himself to the ground. He looked dazed and confused.

"No, lower, boy." Brash said gently. "Prostrate yourself on the ground, flat on your face until my daughter comes to fetch you."

Flynn did as he was told.

That was when Charlotte arrived.

"Father, what do you think you're doing?" she demanded.

Brash laughed. "He's so subservient. It really is quite marvelous."

Charlotte took Flynn's hand in hers and lifted him up off the floor. He was dressed in a simple, beige loincloth. She sighed. It was a Roman manual labor slave garment.

"Why is he wearing that?" she asked her father irritably.

"Good question. Why is he?" her father said salaciously. He waved his hand and Flynn's tiny garment fell to the floor. Flynn immediately clasped his hands over his crotch.

"That's not funny, Dad," Charlotte chided. "You and Mercy both have serious boundary issues. He's my boyfriend. Surely you can find someone I'm not fucking to drool over. What the hell is wrong with you people?"

Brash rolled his eyes. "Fine, cover him," he said. "Oracle! Send out some of my toys, I'm bored." A half dozen naked men and women entered the room and began to pose like statues on either side of his throne. Brash nodded his approval, and threw a black silk cloth to his daughter. Charlotte tied it around Flynn's waist with a bit knot at the hip.

"Thank you," Flynn said. He was really embarrassed.

"It is done, father," Charlotte insisted. "We have completed all of the required rites, and I am with child. I ask that you acknowledge Flynn Keahi as my consort and my future husband."

"Is that right?" Brash chortled. "Then why, this is cause for celebration." His statue people were grouping and regrouping into various distracting and occasionally vulgar poses. One of the women was apparently, some kind of contortionist, and currently had bent over backwards, inserted her head between her legs, and was making suggestive gestures with her tongue. One of the male contortionists pretzeled himself into a similar self-fellating pose.

Flynn began to nervously giggle.

"Come closer, my dear," Brash gestured towards his daughter. "Show me that ring."

Charlotte shook her head, but she walked right up to him and stuck her hand out in front of his face. Brash took her hand in his and began inspecting the ring. Moments later, he pulled out a jeweler's loop and took a closer look at it.

"Well, it's not very big." Brash said. "I guess it will just have to do, right? I mean as long as it gets the job done. So let's celebrate! Bring in the food and drink. Let's just eat everything in sight"

He waved at the nude servants and all six of them scurried out of the room and returned shoving a long, low table along the floor. Moments later they returned to pile it high with various fresh fruits, a roasted pig, and three jugs of alcohol.

"Then do you acknowledge it?" Charlotte said firmly.

"Yes yes, by all of the stars I acknowledge you and your consort, who has presented himself so tastefully," Brash said. She finally realized her dad was trying to drop sarcastic comments about her recent consumption of her lover. Flynn either didn't notice, or wasn't biting.

"Come here, sweetie." She gestured for Flynn to come stand beside her. "Shake my father's hand." Flynn came over and did as instructed.

"I ah... I'm very pleased to meet you, sir," Flynn said, shaking the man's hand. Brash had a very youthful appearance, and in fact looked about the same age as Charlotte. It was very confusing.

"When you are married," Brash asked, "will you become Charlotte Keahi?"

"I think so," Charlotte said. "That way I'll have the same last name as our child."

"You mortals are so strange," Brash said. "I only have one name. Why complicate things?"

"Would you like us to break bread with you?" Charlotte calmly inquired. There was a formal significance to eating together.

"Yes, yes," her father said. "Let's sit and eat. Do you need chairs, or can we sit on the floor?"

"We are humble," Charlotte answered. "We can sit on the floor." She took Flynn by the hand and they walked over to the table. She sat on the floor, and he nervously sat down beside her. Flynn began filling his mouth with grapes in order to avoid being called upon to speak. They were absolutely delicious.

Brash noticed. He turned to Flynn. "Why are you so quiet, young man?"

"I'm afraid to say the wrong thing," he admitted.

"Do you remember when I visited you in the hospital?" Brash asked. "I was wearing the man, the Gary person."

"I do," Flynn said. "It was very strange and unnatural, the way he moved and spoke."

"I do have concern for my daughter's well-being," Brash said carefully.

"I would never do anything to hurt Charlotte," Flynn promised.

"But if you died," Brash said, "you wouldn't just hurt me and my other children, you would also hurt Charlotte. Do you understand?"

"Yes, sir, I understand," Flynn said anxiously. Brash wanted him to promise not to allow himself to die for any reason, but that wasn't a promise Flynn was willing to make. He resumed eating.

"We should go now, father," Charlotte said, sensing the tension.

"Yes, of course," Brash said. "Visit again soon. Happy birthday! Congratulations on the baby and your marriage. You two have a nice weekend."

Charlotte whisked them away home before any further awkward conversation could ensue.

PARTY

Maribelle's friends were the first to arrive. Nancy Allen showed up early with her niece, Tess, who was now twenty and hoping to make some friends closer to her age. Lorena Young showed up next, with her husband Jeffrey and their sixteen year-old twins, Alma and Elba. Jeannie Byrne, a single parent, showed up with her scandalously young boyfriend Ross, while her daughter Rosie arrived separately and much later.

Hannah Cohen and Shelby Baptista were the first of Charlotte's friends to arrive. They were happy and quickly became tipsy, insisting that the entire party call them by their new Hollywood couple name, Hanby.

"I can just see it now," Shelby said pretentiously. "It will be in all of the local social columns in Suisun. Hanby wins the inhumanitarian award for their immaculate housekeeping. Hanby adopts underprivileged Burmese cats from the local SPCA."

They found Charlotte and Flynn sitting at a table out in the backyard, downwind of the smoking section. Charlotte was sipping a club soda while Flynn inhaled margaritas.

"Oh okay... you guys are definitely off," Shelby said. "He almost never drinks that much and she almost never doesn't drink like a fish."

"Uh huh," Hannah said. "Look at her finger." Hannah took Charlotte's hand and held it up so that Shelby could see the ring. Shelby pulled up a seat next to Charlotte and took a closer look at her engagement ring.

"Is that? It's so tiny, is that like, a diamond fetus?" Shelby asked.

"Yes," Flynn slurred. "It will grow into an adult diamond in time."

He was halfway collapsed against the side of the white patio chair he was drunkenly slumping down into. They were sitting at a round metal lattice patio table set with a red and white umbrella erected at the center of it. Maribelle had four of those in her backyard, and a small, landscaped stream flowed down the middle of it, with two seating arrangements on either side. There were also several pretty ornamental fruit trees, some of which bore tiny peaches and oranges, and a large palm tree.

Flynn took another sip of the blue margarita, which was supposed to be part of some tropical theme or the other Maribelle had going on.

"Slow up on the drinking," Charlotte warned. "Your ex-girlfriend is coming to the party. Do you want to puke on her? Nobody likes blue spew."

Shelby cracked up. Hannah looked at Charlotte. Then she looked at Flynn. Then she looked back at Charlotte again. She took a seat on the opposite side of Charlotte from Shelby.

"Uhm, boss… are you pregnant?" Hannah asked Charlotte.

Charlotte nodded. "I am pregnant." She pointed at Flynn. "He did this to me. And now, he needs coffee. Either that, or a med check."

"I'm cool," Flynn said. "I'm alright with the fact that there will be a shotgun at our wedding." He dropped his head down on the table.

"Getting pregnant first and married later is a long standing tradition in the heterosexual community," Shelby quipped. She patted Flynn on the back. "Congratulations, son, you're not firing blanks."

"Someone please get him a coffee," Charlotte pled.

"Sure," Hannah said. She looked at Shelby. "You want anything, baby?"

"I want these bitches to start calling us Hanby!" she said boisterously, slamming her hand down on the table by Flynn's head. Flynn bolted upright and immediately burst into drunken laughter. "Hanby… yeah I get it, like Kimye and Brangelina." Then he kept laughing for way too long.

Meanwhile, in the living room, Sunshine Green arrived on the arm of Howard Lowe wearing a pretty blue sundress and sandals with a smile as bright as her name. Unaware of his secret passenger, Howard stood proud and honored to have been asked to escort this gentle lady to the party. He had no recollection of having asked her, so in his mind, the invitation was her idea.

By the time Mike and Roy Shaw showed up, the karaoke was already getting started. Flynn even invited Richard Zhang and Cindy Lowenstein from the accounting department at his last job. They were huge karaoke fanatics, and Flynn didn't have a lot of friends he could brag to about his impending entry into marriage and fatherhood.

Speaking of which, well aware of the fact that a formal announcement for a wedding wasn't usually associated with a previously existing pregnancy, Maribelle and Charlotte Metaxas decided to just get the word out by letting the rumor mill fly.

"At least he's doing the right thing," Lorena said sympathetically when Maribelle told her in the kitchen, over hot-spiced apple cider and rum.

"Well, I saw that cute little ring he gave her," Maribelle told Jeannie. "At first, I was wondering why they didn't wait until he could afford something more appropriate, but then I noticed Charlotte has morning sickness."

"Oh my," Jeannie said, thoroughly scandalized. Maribelle tried not to laugh at the shocked looks on the faces of the women who were suggesting not a fortnight ago that her son in law be sacrificed.

"At least he's doing right by her," Jeannie said, giving Maribelle that same commiserating look. "How do you feel about being a grandma? I mean you aren't even fifty yet."

"I'll be fifty before the baby is born," Maribelle said stoically. "You know, I didn't think I was going to be able to have kids. Charlotte was something of a surprise. I'm glad I'm going to be a grandmother, a very young, glamorous one, of course." She winked at Jeannie.

Hannah came into the kitchen just then, looking for the coffee.

"Why is Flynn so upset?" she asked Maribelle. "I know it's not about the baby. What's going on?"

"In a way, it is about the baby," Maribelle told her. "He called his mother to invite her to the wedding, and she asked if the girl was pregnant. He admitted she was, and his mother had a lot of unkind things to say about how he was genetically defective. She said he inherited the crazy from his father. She also accused him of picking his future wife up in a psych ward, and let's face it, he did."

"Oh wow," Hannah frowned. "That's so mean."

Lorena interrupted suddenly. "That is so unfair. That young man would lay his life down to protect Charlotte and that baby, and we all know that. I don't care what his mother says. We all know he's a hero."

Hannah saluted Lorena. "Yes, ma'am, well, everybody in this kitchen knows." She grabbed the hot coffee and went back out on the porch to rescue her devastated friend.

On the way out back, she ran into Howard and Sunshine. She almost dropped the coffee giving Howard a bear hug.

"Oh man, I am so glad to see you," she said emotionally. "We heard so many terrible things about you, Howie. I'm really glad you're okay."

"I had to have three surgeries on my eye," he told her. "Got these." He gestured to his glasses. "They aren't perfect, but they help a lot. Man oh man, I thank the Lord it wasn't worse."

"Hi, my name is Sunny," Sunshine said, sticking her hand out possessively. Shelby laughed.

"Whoa, no worries lady," Hannah laughed. "My name is Hannah. I'm totally a lesbian, so I'm definitely not hitting on your man."

"Oh, this is my date," Howard said very formally. "Sunny, I am sorry. I rarely have the pleasure of attending a social function with a lovely woman such as yourself, and please forgive me if I have offended you in any way."

"Oh no, of course not," Sunny said sweetly.

Howard really didn't want to hurt Sunny's feelings, but he had been celibate for most of the past ten years. Maybe he had low testosterone or one of those other conditions that can strike fifty some year old men. Maybe it was that he never really was the biggest skirt chaser on the planet to begin with. Howard wasn't exactly asexual. He was just a man who was comfortable in his own skin, and in his own company. He spent a lot of time happy, alone, reading or people watching. Sex was very low on his list of priorities.

Relationships were usually kind of high maintenance, but if this woman was that interested in him, he could try and see how it went. At least she liked the outdoors, so they had something in common. They went hiking yesterday and that was nice. As long as she didn't want to have sex all the time. He honestly didn't know how some people could stand it. It was so boring and repetitive after a while.

Sunny and Howard followed Hannah out back. She set the coffee down in front of Flynn, and pulled up chairs for Sunshine and Howard.

"Sunny and Howie?" Charlotte asked, incredulous. "Wow. You make a cute couple, though. Never saw that one coming. How you been?"

Sunshine primped and preened like a pigeon on $1 popcorn day at the racetrack. "Why, thank you," she said. "I'm not sure why you never imagined it, but I agree, we are a cute couple, don't you think so, Howard, dear?"

"This is our second date," Howard said irritably. "I think it's a little premature to use the c word, don't you?"

"Fine," Sunny said, pouting and feeling somewhat rejected. "We're just dating. How is your... date? Charlotte? He looks a little green around the gills."

"I think it's safe to say they're well past dating," Shelby told her. "He got her pregnant."

Howard patted Flynn on the back. "Good going, old roomy! You remember me?"

Flynn sat up and blinked a few times to make sure he wasn't imagining things. "Howard? Howard! Oh I am so glad to see you." He almost knocked over his coffee reaching over the table to try to hug the man.

"You just sit back and drink your coffee, youngster," Howard said with a laugh, patting Flynn on the back. "I thought you might be worried about me. I saw you in the room when that terrible thing happened, and I am so sorry that you had to see that."

"I'm sorry that happened to you," Flynn said. "I felt like it was my fault. You were my roommate, and I should have done something to stop it."

"That really wasn't your fault," he said. He slapped Flynn on the shoulder the way men do when they want to show affection but are too macho to hug. The turn of the conversation brought it all rushing back upon Flynn, and he realized something was unexpected about Howard's appearance. Then it hit him. He had two eyes. "Your eye, Howard! I would've sworn you'd lost it," he blurted out disbelievingly.

"What? Oh! No, only detached the retina, thank God. Couple of surgeries and I'm almost good as new. My vision's a little blurry in that eye now, but that's what these glasses are for."

Then Nyx took over for a moment. She leaned over and lifted Flynn's chin with her finger and looked him in the eyes. "You can't take the burden of the entire world on your shoulders, young one," she and Howard said in unison. She was vibing with Howard right now, and it was easy. Nothing she wanted to say to them was in conflict with what he would say. They worked together concert. Their thoughts and actions were synchronized.

"Bless you, son," they told Flynn. "Bless you and your woman, and that beautiful child you will be having with her."

Flynn smiled at Howard's strangely maternal but comforting words and demeanor. He thought it was weird, but he was very drunk and everything seemed weird. He decided it must be some kind of hippie or Rastafarian thing. "Bless you, too, man. One Love."

Nyx did what she came to do. She blessed the couple and the fruit of their union. Now it was time to go. Howard found himself once again alone in his body. He never even realized he had a visitor, because Nyx was so discrete.

Flynn sat up straight and started in on the cup of coffee in front of him. It was Charlotte's birthday, and he needed to pull himself together. He realized that the terrible dream he had with Howard in it was somewhat distorted. Someone tried to play on his guilt. Now, he wasn't sure what to believe.

He pulled his shit together and accompanied Charlotte to the living room just in time to spot Daniel, Tamara, and Kimo coming through the door. Kimo was much taller and somewhat thinner than the last time he saw him, although by no means thin. He was broad shouldered and husky, like a retired quarterback whose muscle was going a bit back to fat. He was also taller than Danny or Flynn now – he used to be a couple of inches shorter. Flynn guessed Kimo must be six foot four. The last time he saw him he was only sixteen years old.

Kimo was two years younger than Tamara and had a crush on her since before he got his first pubic hair. Flynn supposed that for Kimo, marrying Tamara must have been the fulfillment of all of his youthful dreams. He looked so proud and happy right now.

"Flynn," Kimo said excitedly, barreling through the door and patting him on the back. "Look at the baby!" Kimo pulled out his smart phone and shoved it in Flynn's face. There was a picture of a pudgy brown toddler in a pink dress with a bow on her head. She was grinning broadly and displaying what appeared to be her only two teeth. It was adorable.

"Yeah, Danny told me," Flynn said. "Leilani, right? She's beautiful."

"Just like her mother," Kimo said. "I'm the luckiest man in the world."

"I'm really happy for both of you," Flynn said. "I want you to meet my girlf.. I mean my fiancée, Charlotte."

Charlotte stepped up and extended her hand. Kimo ignored it and gave her a big hug.

"Hey, brah," he told Flynn, "She's not bad looking, but you know she can't hold a candle to my Tamara."

"Stop that," Tamara said, coming up behind Kimo and giving him a dirty look. "This is not a competition. We are married and you don't need to be up in here acting jealous of him. Everyone knows we're together. Chill your jets."

She gave Flynn a hug, and then turned and gave one to Charlotte. "You're looking well, Flynn. Charlotte, it's very nice to meet you. Thank you so much for inviting us to your lovely home."

"It's my mom's lovely home," Charlotte admitted. "We live much more modestly."

"She's a starving artist," Danny said, coming up behind them. "Hey, I hope you don't mind, but I let your mom set me up on a date with one of her friend's kids, Rosie something or the other?"

"Oh not at all," Charlotte said. She was happy to be off the hook. "They're in the kitchen," She lead the entire gang past the karaoke and the big screen television in to the kitchen, where Nancy was busy introducing Tess, her niece, to a Michael Shaw who was on his absolute best behavior.

Rose was in the corner, looking as gorgeous as ever. Danny and Rose shook hands and soon after, wandered off to speak more privately.

"I don't know about you," Tamara said, tapping Charlotte on the shoulder, "but I'm nervous as hell right now."

"Right?" Charlotte said. "Me too, and I can't even get drunk to take the edge off because I have a bun in the oven."

"You know?" Tamara patted herself on the belly. "Me too."

"Does Kimo know?" Charlotte asked.

"Not yet," Tamara admitted. "I was planning on telling him tonight, in a room full of drunken party goers, in song, using a karaoke machine. Care to join me?"

"Oh yeah, that would be fun," Charlotte admitted. She went out back with Tamara to write up a list of karaoke songs about pregnancy. *All that she wants is another baby. She's having my baby. Papa, Don't Preach. Baby, baby.* There were tons of songs about pregnancy or with baby in the name. This was going to be a blast.

And it was.

And Tamara did give Charlotte and Flynn her blessing.

But they didn't need it; because that was the last happy night they would spend together on earth.

THE LAST INTERMISSION

Thanatos kicked back in the ratty brown easy chair watching Monty Python's *The Meaning of Life* on Betamax. He never could understand why the format never blew up. It was clearly superior to VHS. The vagaries of human consumerism and the overall poor decision making ability of mankind was a mystery to him.

He was watching his favorite part, the one about death. He loved it when people thought about him. Comedy was fantastic, but he also loved Julian Richings' portray on *Supernatural*. But enough of all that... mother was coming over.

"I know what you're up to," Nyx said, taking a seat beside him in a much cleaner black leather easy chair. "You haven't fooled me, son."

"Whatever do you mean, mother?" Thanatos asked, shutting off the video player with his remote. With a flick of the switch, he changed the image on the screen to footage from a mall security camera on Earth.

"You know what I mean," Nyx said sharply. "I mean this madness you have been stirring up with your nephew and his children. It was you, visiting Flynn's dreams in the guise of Howard Lowe. I know all about that. Don't you realize that if Flynn dies, all of their lives are all forfeit?"

"People fear death too much, mother," Thanatos countered. "They don't understand it. They don't understand me. Nothing so terrible will happen to Brash and his children. They will be cast out of the underworld, sent to live out their brief and wretched lives with the humans. Is that really so terrible?"

"That boy, and the girl, they did nothing to deserve this," Nyx complained.

"No mortal ever does," Thanatos said. "They are born, and they die. It is their lot in life. But all of the great romances end in death, *Romeo and Juliet*, *Braveheart*, *Titanic*. Where would Shakespeare have been without me? Or George R.R. Martin, for that matter."

"Whatever," Nyx said angrily.

"Don't you want to see what happens?" Thanatos asked.

"Yes, I want to see what happens," Nyx said. "Play it in reverse."

"Play it what?" Thanatos asked.

"In reverse," Nyx said. "Play the death scenes in reverse order."

"Ah Okay," Thanatos agreed. He clicked on the remote for his mother. "I know you want to see how it ends for the young lovers."

"But their story may not be over yet," his mother protested.

"I mean their story on earth," Thanatos said gently.

Act V: Death

Lethe

Charlotte and Maribelle Metaxas sat on the edge of the river Lethe. Charlotte clung to her mother's neck, sobbing into the shoulder of her black business coat. She was inconsolable.

"Why, Mom? Why?" Charlotte cried. "I don't understand."

Maribelle held her daughter tightly and stroked her messy purple hair. "I know you don't understand, sweetheart, but you need to calm yourself if you can. You have to be the one to make these decisions. Flynn doesn't have a choice anymore, but you still do."

Flynn was on his back on a wooden raft, still tethered to the shore. He was wrapped in warm blankets that wouldn't do him good for much longer, because he was dying. His breath grew increasingly shallow. He couldn't speak, but he could hear Charlotte. She was crying. He wanted to comfort her, but he couldn't move. He was growing so cold.

"Go to him, Charlotte," Maribelle said firmly. "He doesn't have long now. You have to decide. You have to decide for all three of you. You can send him ahead of you, if you believe."

Charlotte stood up and walked over to him. It was hard to see what she was doing. She was crying so hard her eyes were beginning to swell shut. She took Flynn's hands in her own and crossed them over his chest. She smiled when she realized he was wearing the same Final Fantasy t-shirt he had on the day they met. She kissed the insides of his hands, and then she took off her ring. She cupped both of his hands together around the ring, and then she bound them together in lace.

When she was done, she pulled the blankets back over his hands so that he was covered to the neck. She kissed him on the forehead. Then she pressed her thumb against his neck to feel his fading pulse. She couldn't let him go while there was still life in him. She stayed until he went into the deep sleep from which he would not awaken.

"If I send him," Charlotte told her mother, "they will never find his body. We will never be able to find out who poisoned him. But if I don't send him, I can't even pretend to hope that I'll ever see him again."

"It's up to you," Maribelle told her. "I can't guarantee you'll see him again. These are all old legends and myths."

According to the legends, if he drank from the water of the Lethe, he'd lose his memory and be reincarnated with no memory of Charlotte. She kissed his still-warm lips, and waited. When she was certain he was dead, and all of the heat was out of his body, she pulled a piece of gray duct tape from the spool in her hand and put it over his mouth.

She stood over him and said the words.

"I am Charlotte Metaxas, daughter of Brash, granddaughter of Somnus. You, Flynn Keahi, are my consort. I send you ahead of me to wait at the side of my grandfather, Somnus, until I am able to join you and claim you as my own. I send you with this ring, which you gave to me when you promised yourself to me in marriage. Keep it with you until the day I rejoin you."

She kissed him on the forehead and pulled the blanket the rest of the way up over his head. Finally, she cut the rope that held the raft in place, and watched him float gently down the river.

THREE DAYS EARLIER

The night of the party, things were already starting to fall apart. They just didn't know it yet. Cory Landers was in his storage unit slicing into the flesh of his non-girlfriend Linda Myers. She was a nice girl from school who made the fatal mistake of dating him twice.

Cory, afterwards, felt that he had the right to expect Linda to become his girlfriend. Linda had been very careful to go dutch both times, and to duck his kiss at her parent's doorway, but that did nothing to change his unreasonable expectations.

Maybe he would have let it go, if Mercy and Sympathy weren't in his head, busy explaining in excruciating detail how long it would take for someone to bleed to death from hundreds of shallow, superficial cuts.

But it wasn't just Cory… it was Cory and a dozen people like him, all acting on their revenge fantasies in real life. Cory was a budding serial killer. Linda was the first of what would become many girls. Others, like Elroy Shaw, were more interested in taking out as many as possible in a single fell swoop before committing SWAT team suicide.

Unlike Cory and Elroy, most of the killers Brash's somnali unleashed upon the world were completely unrelated to Charlotte or Flynn. Perhaps none of them would have been, if Thanatos hadn't been secret cheerleader to his two rebellious nieces, Mercy and Sympathy, encouraging them to shit where they ate.

He was hopeful that they would go too far, attract negative attention, and give him the gift of a lifetime: the mortal death of thirteen immortals. Neither of the girls was bright enough to suspect, but Sympathy was by far the duller of the two. She was far easier to secretly manipulate. She was the one he talked into selecting Elroy Shaw as a target.

For every Cory or Elroy, there were dozens of Joe Martins, poor schmucks the girls' tag-team tormented until they were suicidal, much as they had attempted to do with both Howard and Flynn. Not all of the attacks were successful to the point of death, but they had patience and plenty of time on their hands.

Soon, there was a ripple effect.

The ripple effect took hold on the second day, when the news broke.

Two Days Earlier

Michael Shaw was on a date with Nancy's daughter Tess when his brother Elroy decided to shoot up the local mall. Rather than experience any kind of vicarious pleasure where young Mike was concerned, Roy became particularly enraged by the idea that his younger brother could find a date when he could not.

He posted some hateful rants to his blog about how, in the older days, a younger son wasn't even allowed to court until the older son, the heir was already married off. How dare his brother skip the natural order of things? He had joined together with the women and all of these lesser men who were conspiring to keep Roy from his fair share. They had to be stopped.

The enraged thirty-year old followed his nineteen year-old brother down to the food court. He unleashed fire, killing Mike, Tess, and seven others.

The news of Elroy's mass murder at the mall would hit the news around two o'clock.

By the time the late night news hit the television, Daryl Fowler, the night security had noticed the strange light visible from the crack in Cory Landers' storage locker door. Suspecting a homeless person of sleeping within, the guard, as per policy, checked the exterior lock. Finding the lock hanging open, Fowler slid up the pleated metal sliding door, and caught Landers in the act of slicing the girl open.

Seeing he was caught, Cory used the box cutter to slice open the girl's jugular vein, hoping to ensure her death occurred before the police could arrive. He spun around immediately afterward, and ran at Fowler with the box cutter. Fowler shot Landers in the center of his forehead, and he slumped dead on the ground.

Uninjured, Fowler called the cops and the ambulance.

Landers had been pronounced dead on arrival. The unfortunate Linda Myers died on the operating table that very night. By the time the morning news aired, both the murder and Landers' connection to Shelby and Hannah were being broadcast. The press was parked outside of their Suisun home, sticking microphones in their faces.

Between the news about Mike's brother's killing spree and Shelby and Hannah's murderous roommate, Charlotte and Flynn absolutely were not sleeping. They passed out in Maribelle's guest room after the party, and Flynn was just waking up with a terrible hangover about the time news of Mike's death appeared on Charlotte's Facebook feed.

They were Facebook friends, and while Mike's parents and cousins weren't posting any details, soon the news reports began to filter in. It was like they were being lobbed with a spray of bullets, just one thing after another. First, they found out about Mike. Next, they learned that his brother was the killer. After that, Nancy Allen called, in tears, to let Maribelle know that her niece, Tess Allen was out on a date with Mike Shaw when the shooting occurred. She didn't know if she was alive or dead.

Charlotte and Flynn were too upset to go home, and no one in Maribelle's house could sleep that night.

Tomorrow would be no better.

ONE DAY EARLIER

Flynn was sitting in Maribelle Metaxas' kitchen drinking a cup of coffee when she decided to kill him. It wasn't his fault, really. He was a very sweet boy, and she knew it would break Charlotte's heart, but it had to be done.

She'd just gotten off the phone with Nancy, who learned that Tess was among the dead, and that Mike's brother Elroy was the killer. She hadn't even finished the call before the television news started to broadcast the story about Cory Landers and the girl he slaughtered in a storage locker. Maribelle knew that these killings were caused by the somnali. They practically reeked of Mercy and Sympathy.

Flynn's life had value, but was it really more important than the life of Mike, or Tess? What if that security guard hadn't caught Cory, would Shelby and Hannah have been next? Was his life worth more than theirs, or a stranger's?

As long as he lived, everyone close to him was in danger, including her daughter, and his unborn child. As a keeper of the Rites of Undoing, it was really her duty to undo the evil caused by the somnali. How could she let sentimentality cloud her judgment?

She was sorry, but he had to go.

She'd made her mind up, but since he was still living now, the least she could do was to be kind. She began plotting the best ways to put him out of his misery, the ones that would be least likely to cause him unnecessary suffering. She sat across the table from him and looked him in the eye.

"I'm so sorry about your friend," she said. "He seemed like a nice kid."

"So did Tess," Flynn mumbled. He looked terrible. He'd been crying all night, and Charlotte was too heartsick herself to do anything about it. There were big, dark circles under his bloodshot eyes.

"It's so unfair," Maribelle said. "They were so young."

"I feel like it's my fault," Flynn said. "I feel like somehow, I could have stopped this. I mean if I believe the prophecy, then I could have."

"You shouldn't have to make a decision like that," Maribelle said, patting his hand.

"Charlotte begged me not to," he said.

"She shouldn't have to make a decision like that," Maribelle said. "Neither one of you should have to. You're very innocent, Flynn."

He was a sweet kid, really. It was a shame. But she had to do what must be done.

He was merely a pawn in the games of some petty gods from a dead religion in a big, ugly power struggle. None of it was his fault, but as long as he lived, the somnali would have access to this world. Worse of all, as long as Brash roamed free, he would have influence over Flynn and Charlotte's child. There was the baby to think of now.

It broke her heart, but Lorena and Jeannie were right. He had to die. Almost as if he could read her mind, Flynn answered her, told her how much he was suffering. He must realize that equally innocent people were dying because he lived.

"This is tearing me up inside," he admitted. "I don't know how much longer I'm going to be able to live with this. Maribelle, can you take me to the hospital? I'm falling apart."

She could end his pain.

"Maybe I'll take you two out to the county tomorrow," Maribelle said. "It will be nice and peaceful. You can both relax, and get some rest. You need it. How about we see how you feel afterwards? Does that sound okay?"

"That sounds good," he said. "Do you have any pain killers? I have a terrible headache."

"Yes, I do," she said, smiling.

She didn't poison Flynn that day. She couldn't handle the idea of forcing her daughter to wake up next to a dead body.

THAT DAY

Maribelle felt a little sick to the stomach when she handed Flynn his coffee that morning. By the time they piled into the car, the poison that would eventually stop his breathing was already taking affect. He grew drowsy, and began to lose consciousness. Eventually, his lungs would cease to function. She made sure there would be no pain.

The river Lethe wasn't supposed to exist, but of course, Maribelle knew where it did. She knew where one of its thousands of entrances was. She'd seen it, before Charlotte was born, when Brash came to her. She thought about all of the terrible things that Brash did in her name. Those things that he said he was doing for her. She was glad that soon, he would die, like every other man.

It was too bad that now, she was a murderer, just like him.

Her innocent victim sat in the back seat with his head on her daughter's lap, and Maribelle wanted desperately to arrive at their campsite before either Charlotte or Flynn discovered what was happening to him.

By the time they got out of the car, he was having trouble keeping his eyes open.

Neither one of them had been able to sleep for days. It was peaceful by the riverside. They piled out of the vehicle, and rolled out their blankets and sleeping bags. Charlotte and Flynn lay down on a blanket in the sunshine, and held each other. Neither one of them knew he was dying in her arms.

Charlotte noticed something was wrong for the first time when she got up to go to the bathroom. Flynn's husky voice was barely audible.

"Baby, I can't move," he whispered. He was on his back on a checkered blanket. It was the type picnickers ate on. He had been asleep until he felt Charlotte stir beside him, but now he was wide-awake. He was dressed in a t-shirt and jeans, but the wind against his bare arms was frigid.

"What's wrong?" Charlotte asked, immediately returning to his side.

"I can't move my arms or my legs," he told her. "Is it cold? I'm freezing."

"No, it's not cold," she said. It was a warm summer day, just a little breezy. Birds were singing in the trees, and the river rolled lazily by, murmuring gently. She rested the back of her hand against his forehead to see if he was hot, but he didn't have any fever.

"Do you think you can get me some blankets?" he asked. "I'm so cold."

"Sure, I can," she said anxiously. "I'll be right back." She got up and ran out to the parking lot, looking for Maribelle. She couldn't find her mother, or the car, and was alarmed. They needed to take Flynn to the hospital.

Unable to find her, she ducked into the bathroom, took a pee, and began attempting to call her on the cell phone. There wasn't any signal. Where was her mother?

Charlotte returned to Flynn with a pile of blankets from the supplies her mother left behind. There was also a cooler, and a bag with a tent, which had yet to be erected, a raft, and some fishing poles.

She piled the blankets around Flynn and propped his head up on a rolled up sleeping bag.

"There, do you feel any better?" she asked.

"I'm more comfortable," he said. "I don't think I'm getting better, though. I'm getting weaker."

"Let me walk around and see if I can get a cell signal," Charlotte said, standing again.

"Please, don't," he begged. "I think I'm dying, and I don't want to be alone."

"I don't think you're dying," she said. She was clutching his hand in her own, but when he tried to return her squeeze, his grasp was so weak she couldn't tell if she was just imagining it. The color was running out of his cheeks. She kissed him.

He gently returned her kiss, but he couldn't lift his head up or turn it by now. He could feel her fingers stroking his cheek. He was glad she was touching him. If he couldn't stay, he wanted the last thing he knew on this earth to be her touch.

He could barely speak anymore. "I was poisoned," he said.

"Did you do this?" she asked. He tried to shake his head, but he couldn't move or speak any more. He suddenly regretted not choosing his last words more wisely. Perhaps he should have told her that he loved her instead.

Charlotte balled her hands into fists and cried tears of frustration. He could feel them falling hot against his nose, his eyelids. He could see her face contorted with grief. He decided that no one looked beautiful when they were crying. Still, she was perfect. She looked just like the woman he loved. She looked like a woman who loved him and whose heart was breaking. He wanted to stay with her.

She lay down beside him. She caressed him the way she always did when she was putting him to sleep. He could feel her fingers stroking his belly under the blanket, and her gentle kisses on his cheeks. Even now, her touch comforted him. He was saddened to think this time would be the last. He wouldn't wake up again. His face was hot and wet. He realized for the first time that some of the tears on his skin were his own.

By the time Maribelle came back from the store, it was apparent that something was desperately wrong. It was far too late to save him. She was glad for that. They would be saved the long, harrowing and ultimately hopeless ride back to civilization and Maribelle herself could evade discovery.

"Someone poisoned him," Charlotte said, still sitting on the ground with her hand against his cheek. "I don't think he did this to himself, he said someone else did it."

"Are you sure it wasn't suicide?" Maribelle asked. She knew it wasn't, but she had to deflect guilt from herself.

"Someone sacrificed him," Charlotte said defiantly. "We both know it, why pretend?"

Maribelle said nothing. She had a plan.

If she could convince her mentally unstable daughter that this was the Lethe, and if she could talk her into sending her lover's lifeless body drifting away, she might evade detection. There would be no body for the police to test for poisons or other evidence. She began to weave her fanciful tale around Charlotte's head as her only child wept in despair.

The truth was Maribelle had no idea if this would ease Flynn's transition into the afterworld. She had no idea if it would help them reunite in some possible future. All she knew was that it would be the end of the somnali.

She hoped that the ritual gave her grieving daughter some comfort.

GRIEF

Maribelle Metaxas told the police that Flynn disappeared out in the woods. She said they had no idea where he was. She told them she was concerned because he had expressed suicidal thoughts. She explained about the tragic death of his friend Michael, and how much it weighed on him. If the body popped up, she wanted to make sure they thought it was suicide.

It was two weeks before they found Flynn's body.

Lorena, Jeannie, Sunny, Shelby and Hannah all suspected that he was dead before the body was found. Charlotte never told them what happened. She was too shaken up to even consider the possibility that her mother had poisoned him, and although Lorena suspected Maribelle of engineering Flynn's death, she didn't have the heart to tell Charlotte.

A long time would go by before anything would be normal again for any of them. For most of them, it never would.

Linda Allen and Maribelle Metaxas started a support organization for the victims of shootings like the one that took Tess and Michael's lives. Michael's parents were older people in their forties when their unexpected youngest child was born. They changed their names and did he best they could to stay out of the limelight after the tragedy.

Shelby and Hannah would not remain under scrutiny by the press and police due to Cory's murderous actions for long. The shock of what happened under their roof, to their friend Michael, and to Flynn cast a shadow of gloom over their wedding plans. They wouldn't marry for another two years. By the time they married, Charlotte and Flynn's daughter was over a year old. Her name was Faelyn Keahi.

Although Charlotte suffered from post partum depression and a lingering devastation over the loss of Flynn, she loved Faelyn. Still, she had a sad look in her eye that never really seemed to go away. Life was a chore for Charlotte, who spent most of her free time sleeping, searching for her lost lover in dreams. She never found him there, no matter how long she sought, but she thought about him constantly. She imagined what it would be like if she could hold him and touch him again. She knew these were just fantasies, but they were easier to face than her loss.

Charlotte was human now. Memories of the somnali began to fade. There were no somnali anymore, and wherever her fathers and siblings ended up when they were reincarnated as humans, she would never see them again, and they would never see each other, at least not in this lifetime. They were scattered all over the earth just to keep them apart.

Charlotte was extremely depressed. She rejected suggestions her mother and concerned friends made about finding someone new. She couldn't imagine taking another lover, but she often imagined taking her life. She didn't. She had a child to care for, Faelyn was beautiful and perfect, just like her father. Seeing her daughter was the only thing that gave Charlotte the will to live.

When Faelyn wasn't looking, Charlotte often cried. She was broken.

Maribelle became a bit harder, and a bit more efficient. She had to be a good grandmother to Faelyn, who no longer had a father. Charlotte couldn't do it alone. Some days she was little more than an empty shell.

When Maribelle looked at her granddaughter, she often saw Flynn. She had the same caramel complexion, the same crooked smile, and the same untamable black hair as her father. She had amber eyes, just like her Charlotte, but Faelyn's eyes were bright and lively. Her mother's eyes were haunted and lost.

Maribelle knew that part of Charlotte's grief was because she secretly suspected her of Flynn's murder. How could she not suspect? No one else was anywhere near them when he died. The burden of the great secret she kept for her mother was crushing Charlotte's soul.

But there was nothing that Maribelle could do about it.

Maribelle had had no idea that her daughter loved that boy so much. All she did was talk about Flynn, draw pictures of him, and daydream, as if she could somehow will him back into existence. Her heart was broken, and she wasn't recovering. The world was full of sad, lonely people barely hanging on. Charlotte was now one of them.

The only thing Maribelle could do for her daughter was to try to get her to spend time with the people who loved her. She encouraged Charlotte to be in the world as much as she could bear. She told her she needed to stop daydreaming and spend some time with Faelyn.

Charlotte couldn't stand living in the apartment anymore. Hannah and Shelby rented her Cory's old room. Not long after they married, the couple adopted a three year-old boy named Kyle. They raised their child alongside Faelyn and tried to help Charlotte recover.

In time, she began to remember what it was like to live again. She remembered how much she loved the taste of peaches. She picked up her daughter and even though she was in a daze much of the time, Charlotte felt the weight of her. She noticed her growing. She recognized the passage of time.

She set aside her constant dreaming so that she could touch and know things, the way only the living can know. To be alive was to be truly awake. Sometimes being awake was painful. Sometimes, it was more comforting to fall back asleep. Charlotte did live. She was alive, and she was awake. She could touch and know things many things, but she never seemed to be able to accept the fact that she couldn't touch Flynn or know him anymore.

REST

Nyx was visiting Thanatos when Flynn arrived. Charlotte had sent Flynn to Somnus, but Somnus wasn't at home when Flynn arrived. Somnus lived next door to Thanatos, so Nyx went over to her other son's house to fetch the boy out of the water. When she fished him out of the Lethe, his clothes were thoroughly soaked, and he was shaking with the cold.

Nyx threw a blanket around him. It was jet black and covered in stars. They weren't painted on, but they twinkled and shone and planets encircled them in their orbits. The minute it touched him, his clothes and his hair were dry. He wrapped it tightly around himself, and nodded to her.

"Thank you," he said. "You saved me."

"Hello, Flynn Keahi," she said. "It was the least I could do. Charlotte asked my son to do it, but he's not home right now. My name is Nyx. Somnus should be home soon. Welcome."

"Yes, I know who you are," he said. "I read a lot. You're Charlotte's great grandmother. Were you at her birthday party?"

Nyx looked at him curiously. "Yes, I was. I blessed your union and your child at the same time as your friend Howard did. I'm surprised you recognized me."

"I didn't until now," he admitted. He looked around for a seat. The furniture was shale and stone and even more intimidating than the furnishings in Brash's castle. What if he had accidentally sat on someone's throne? Afraid he would offend someone by sitting the wrong chair, he sat on the floor instead. He felt very safe wrapped in his blanket of stars.

"Why am I here?" he asked Nyx.

"Charlotte sent you to wait for her, child," she explained. "You can't wait here, though. I've come to fetch you."

"Can you untie me, please?" he asked. Sitting on the floor, he held out his hands to her. They were still bound in lace. Nyx quietly unfurled the ribbon and plucked the ring out of his hand. She pulled out a braid of her long, black hair. She slipped it through Charlotte's ring, tied it in the back, and then slipped it over Flynn's head. She folded the lace and handed it back to him.

"There you are," Nyx said. "I can untie your hands, but that won't change the fact that you are Charlotte's consort, bound by her, imprisoned in the Demos Oneiroi, better known to humans as The Land of Dreams, until she returns."

"That's fine," Flynn said. "I enjoy being bound by Charlotte."

Nyx laughed. "Yes, I know that. Everyone knows that. You two are legendary."

"How long will I wait?" he asked. Everything was very foreign, but for some reason, he was not afraid. He was Charlotte's and she would come for him.

"Another fifty or sixty years," Nyx said, smiling. "It probably seems like forever to one as young as you, but it is not very long. She inherited her father's kingdom, but I don't think you'll want to stay in his castle. You can stay in the forest, where she liked to take you when you were here together. The Lethe runs through it, and it has better memories."

Flynn laughed. "That is the place where she ate me. We have a cave there, somewhere, I think."

She snapped her fingers, and they were standing there in the forest.

"You're giving up a lot for her," Nyx remarked. "And it wasn't your choice. But I suppose you love her, and it's worth it to you."

"Can I visit her?" he asked.

"I'm afraid not," Nyx explained. "I wish someone had explained to Charlotte how these things work, because she keeps looking of for you. She's very upset. She can't see you until she dies unless her powers are somehow restored, or through divine intervention. Now in the old days, she would have seen the star and known it meant you had safely arrived. It's like a telegram. Unfortunately, she probably has no idea about that. Would you like to see your daughter?"

"I have a girl?" Flynn asked. Nyx waved her hand over the water, and it began to ripple. When the surface calmed, they could see six year-old Faelyn at school, writing her name across the top of her schoolwork.

"She has not been born yet," Nyx said casually. "But she will be, and this is how far I can see into her future now."

"Oh man, why did her mother name her that?" Flynn groaned.

"She's named after you," Nyx told him.

"I don't even like my name," he shrugged. "Oh well, I'm dead. I guess the living can't read our minds. Cute kid, though. She looks like my mom."

"She looks like you," Nyx said.

"Hey, does Charlotte know I'm waiting for her?" Flynn asked.

"Maybe," Nyx said. "Her mom had her send you off to get rid of the evidence, but I think Charlotte believes. She daydreams about you all day long. She won't even look at another guy. Why would she, when she has you? You're a hero."

"I am really sorry I left her there alone," Flynn said. "How can you say I'm a hero? All I did was die. Maribelle is the one who actually killed me. Did it work? Are the somnali gone? If so, isn't she the hero?"

"You are the one who allowed it," Nyx shrugged. "You can both pretend that she took the choice out of your hands, but we're not idiots here. We know otherwise. You and Maribelle knew that your child would never be free of Brash and the somnali unless they were banished and removed from power.

Maribelle tried other means, but ultimately, your death was the only way to make it happen. She made a choice but you are the one who made that sacrifice. You suspected what she was up to. You could have left. You could have refused the coffee. You might have told Charlotte.

You chose not to because you cared more about protecting your child and your loved ones than you did your own life, you are just too modest to admit it. Your sacrifice wasn't for nothing. The somnali were reincarnated as human. They have no power. They are off growing old and dying like all other mortals. I am just sorry that you can't be there to see your child grow up and have a family of her own."

"Thank you for letting me know that my daughter is safe," Flynn said.

"Yes. So you're a hero, it's a thankless job. Well I can't stay and chat, night sky, firmament and all that. I've got an important job to do. You go find that cave you and Charlotte stayed in when she was doing her little Eros imitation and set up house or something. I have to go."

"Is that all?" Flynn asked.

"Yes, that's all," she said. "You humans amaze me. So what did you expect? Charlotte sent you down her as her consort with some incantation about how you're to prepare a place for her. Seriously, that's all you can do. How you do that is up to you. You'll have a long time. Maybe you can chop down some trees, build a mansion."

"Well, thank you," he said. He started to wave goodbye, but she was gone before he could finish raising his hand.

He walked over to the edge of the water and touched the surface, hoping he could find Charlotte and see what she was doing. Without someone there to do it for him, he couldn't.

Suddenly he realized that Charlotte was right. He did leave her. He passed out of her world and into this one, and now they were separated. They would spend sixty, maybe eighty years apart until whenever Charlotte's natural lifespan ended. Flynn was twenty-six years old. It sounded like forever. In all of that time, Charlotte would have no idea he was here, waiting for her.

"I am so sorry, Charlotte," he said aloud. "You tried to warn me, but I didn't listen. I am so sorry. How will you ever forgive me?"

He was surprised when he looked up and saw a figure standing before him, nearly as shadowy and mysterious as Nyx. He was a tall man and excessively winged. Large, purple wings extend from his back and smaller ones at the sides of his head. He nodded at Flynn.

"Hi, I'm Somnus," he said. "I'm Charlotte's grandfather. You will have to forgive my mother. She means well, but I honestly don't think she understands how humans work. Fifty odd years is a very long time for a mortal."

"Oh, hi there, how are you?" Flynn said nervously.

"I suppose it's my fault you're here," Somnus said. "I'm the one who had Cupid hit Charlotte with that arrow. I guess she couldn't stand being without you, so she trapped you here. I know you love her, but I can't have you wandering around here crying for your lover for the next fifty years."

"I don't regret it," Flynn said. "I love her very much. I thank you for bringing us together."

"My mother also had something to do with that," Somnus said. "Of course, she was just trying to get the somnali in line. Now she has them on a hamster wheel of reincarnation until they develop some kind of empathy. They will eventually be allowed to return. For some of them I think it will take a very long time. Come walk with me."

Flynn was still sitting on the ground. He stood up and wrapped his blanket around him like a cloak, and followed Somnus. They walked alongside the river, which babbled and murmured its seductive lullaby.

"That is the Lethe," Somnus said, pointing at the river. "You floated all the way down here from Solano County on a raft. I'm not surprised you didn't wake up. If you listen to the Lethe long enough, it will lull you to sleep."

"It's beautiful here," Flynn said. They were in a forest, surrounded by tall eucalyptus trees. Scrubby flowers of many colors grew wild and ensnarled themselves around rocks and fallen branches Poppies were everywhere. The honeyed aroma of morning glory, milkweed and marigolds attracted a variety of butterflies. A monarch landed on the back of his hand.

"Charlotte used to bring me here," Flynn said. "But I never noticed how wonderful it is before. I guess that all I noticed was her.

"Yours was an epic love story," Somnus said. "We don't get many of those these days. My wife, Pasithea, speaks of nothing else."

Flynn blushed.

They kept walking, until they came upon a cave. Flynn was surprised when Somnus handed him a torch. He didn't remember him having any such thing before. It seemed to appear from nowhere.

"Go in," he gestured towards Flynn. "The last time you were in that cave it was dark, but I think you will recognize it. It is one of the places you lay down with your love. Go take a look around."

Flynn did recognize the pile of furs Charlotte warmed him in after she plucked his cold, wet body from the stone. He was surprised to see that there was a fireplace, one that remained unlit during his previous visit, no doubt in order to keep the room in darkness. He took the torch and lit it now.

"Thanatos believes he is the master of storytelling," Somnus complained. "He has his Cleopatra and Marc Anthony, and all of his heartbreaking tales of tragic love that always end in death. He wove a lot of that into your story. He thinks my stories aren't as good as his are. He said they are fairytales, filled with sweet lies, to console the wide-eyed children. Well, I think otherwise. There are a few love stories I can think of that involve sleep and enchanted forests. I am Somnus and I am Sleep, and I think this forest qualifies as enchanted, don't you?"

Flynn smiled. "If you say it is, I think so."

Somnus nodded. "I do say so. I think you should settle into your bed of furs, and cover yourself under a blanket of stars. I think you should sleep the sound sleep of the dreamless until the day you're awakened into a dream that lasts forever by your lover's kiss."

Charlotte was divided now, no longer demisomnali, but a human on earth who would become somnali on the day she died. She would return to her father's kingdom. She would claim it as her own, just as she would claim her power. She would take her consort to her side and make him her husband. Until that day, her power and her kingdom had to be hidden from any interlopers.

Somnus placed them in the safest place he could find. He left them in Flynn's care. He hid them deep within Charlotte's lover's body, where they wouldn't be released until she was able to take him in her arms and fulfill their promises to each other.

Flynn's eyes grew heavy, and he consigned his aching body to the warmth of the deep, soft furs. A folded square of lace was clutched between his fingers. Charlotte's ring was worn around his neck. Somnus covered him in the blanket of Night, and he fell into a deep, sound sleep.

For the first time in a long time, Flynn dreamed of nothing.

Somnus looked down upon him and smiled. He knew that when the time came, this one would give Charlotte the power that was rightfully hers. Flynn would never withhold what was rightfully hers.

Flynn always given her everything he had to give.

The End

Glossary of Terms for Happiness and Other Diseases

People

Nyx /niks/: Goddess of the Night, mother of Somnus and Thanatos

Thanatos /than-uh-tos, -tohs/: God of Death, twin brother of Somnus.

Somnus /som-nuh s/: God of Sleep, twin brother of Thanatos. Also known as Hypnos.

Morpheus /mawr-fee-uh s, -fyoos/: One of the Oneiroi, God of Dreams, and brother of Brash.

Phobetor /foe-bah-tohr/: One of the Oneiroi, God of Nightmares, and brother of Brash.

Phantasos /fan-tuh-sos/: One of the Oneiroi, God of Surreal Dreams, and brother of Brash.

Pasithea /puh-sith-ee-uh/: Wife/consort of Somnus, mother of Brash.

Brash /brash/: One of the Oneiroi, son of Somnus and Pasithea, God of Erotic Nightmares, cursed by Zeus.

Maribelle Metaxas /mə'tæksəs/: Human mother of Happiness, Consort of Brash, and Priestess of the Undoing.

Happiness /ˈha-pē-nəs/: The somnali name of demisomnali Charlotte Metaxas.

Flynn Keahi /kay-ah-hee/: Human consort of Happiness.

Mercy /mur-see/: Somnali daughter of Brash.

Sympathy /sim-puh-thee/: Somnali daughter of Brash.

Zeus /zoos/: King of the Gods.

Eros /eer-os, er-os/: God of Love. Also known as Cupid.

GROUPS

Oneiroi /own-nuh-roy/: Sons of Somnus, personified aspects of sleep.
Somnali /somn·älē/: Grandchildren of Somnus.
Cursed Somnali /kur-sid, kurst/ /somn·älē/: Children of Brash.
Sisterhood of Undoing /sis-ter-hoo d/ /uhv, ov/ /uhn-doo-ing/: Coven of "soccer mom" mages in opposition to Brash.

PLACES

Demos Oneiroi /dahy-mos/ /own-nuh-roy/: Domain of sleep gods.
Lethe /lee-thee/: River that runs through Deimos Oneiroi.

RITES

Rites of Binding: Bind a human consort to a sleep god or demigod.
Sacrifice of the Innocents: Blood sacrifice to allow cursed Brash or somnali to procreate.
Feast of Tears: A lesser blood ritual to allow a cursed demisomnali to procreate.
Rites of Undoing: Rituals to reduce somnali influence over bound consorts and their offspring.

Appended Illustrations

Original Cover Art – The cover art is by Sumiko Saulson. This was the original iteration, drawn in pencil and colored with acrylic paints.

Other Variations – Charlotte's clothing was changed in Photoshop, and Flynn's clothing was removed.

Other Variations – Flynn with a towel on (added in Photoshop).

Cover Art Joke Cartoon – This artwork was used in advertising.

Family Matter Joke Cartoon – This was used in advertising.

Hands Joke Cartoon – This was a response to fan input on the cover art on Facebook.

Flynn and Charlotte out dancing.

Flynn carrying Charlotte to bed.

Made in the USA
San Bernardino, CA
17 July 2015